# DOCHERTY

## William McIlvanney

*with an introduction by the author*

**Hodder & Stoughton**
LONDON  SYDNEY  AUCKLAND  TORONTO

## Acknowledgments

The publishers would like to thank the following for permission to reproduce material in this volume:

Carcanet Press Ltd for 'King Billy' from *Poems of Thirty Years* by Edwin Morgan; *City Limits* for Nick Kimberley's review of *Docherty* and *The Big Man* from *City Limits*, 30 August, 1985; John Farquharson Ltd for the extracts from 'Growing up in the West' in Karl Miller (ed.) *Memoirs of a Modern Scotland* (1970), © William McIlvanney; Harper Collins Publishers Ltd for the extract from *A Century of the Scottish People* by T. C. Smout (1985); Hodder and Stoughton Ltd for the extract from *The Big Man* by William McIlvanney and *Walking Wounded* by William McIlvanney; Octopus Publishing Group Plc for 'Initiation V' from *The Longships in Harbour* by William McIlvanney; the estate of the late Sonia Brownell Orwell and Secker and Warburg for the extract from *Collected Essays, Journalism and Letters* by George Orwell (1968); Oxford University Press for the extract from *Annals of the Parish* by John Galt, World's Classics edition edited by James Kinsley (1986); Pergamon Press for the extracts from *Ten Modern Scottish Novels* by Isobel Murray and Bob Tait (1984); Polygon for the extracts from *Scotland – The Case for Optimism* by Jim Sillars (1986); Trevor Royle for the extract from an interview with William McIlvanney in *Scotland on Sunday*, 1 January, 1989; Scottish and Universal Newspapers Ltd for the map of Kilmarnock and the extracts from *The History of Kilmarnock* by A. McKay (1909); Unwin Hyman Ltd for the extract from *A History of the Scottish Miners* by R. Page-Arnot (1955).

Every effort has been made to trace and acknowledge ownership of copyright. The publishers will be glad to make suitable arrangements with any copyright holders whom it has not been possible to contact.

ISBN 0 340 49983 4

First published in this edition 1991
First published in Great Britain by George Allen & Unwin in 1975
Copyright © William McIlvanney 1975
Introduction copyright © 1991 by William McIlvanney
Notes copyright © 1991 by Alan MacGillivray

Photoset in Linotron Sabon by
Rowland Phototypesetting Ltd, Bury St Edmunds, Suffolk
Printed in Great Britain for Hodder and Stoughton Educational, a division of Hodder and Stoughton Ltd, Mill Road, Dunton Green, Sevenoaks, Kent by Clays Ltd, St Ives plc.

# CONTENTS

*Introduction by William McIlvanney*              v

Docherty                                          1

*Notes by Alan MacGillivray*                    281
  Introduction                          281
  The Local and Historical Background   282
  Religious Division in the West of
    Scotland                   292
  Language as a Social Issue in the West of
    Scotland                   296
  Scottish Working-class Life and Attitudes   297
  Democratic Socialism and the Celebration
    of the Common Man          305
  William McIlvanney as a Writer        308
  Critical Comment on *Docherty*        314
  Bibliography                          317

# INTRODUCTION

In any street an epic, any room
Strange stories never told, testaments dumb.
The richness overwhelms. A chance remark
Can touch new land, unload another ark.
Transactions of small change will sometimes yield
Coins of a minting you have never held.

Break any casual stone and find strange veins.
The colours blind. The anecdotes will range
Through wild geographies of spirit, form
Plain men with unknown flowers in their arms.
In each face new horizons, any day
An archaeology more rich than Troy.

I remember as a boy being alone in the living-room of our council house in Kilmarnock. I would be maybe eleven years old. I was lying in front of the coal fire with my head resting on an armchair. It was, I think, late on a winter afternoon. The window had gone black and I hadn't put the light on, enjoying the small cave of brightness and heat the fire had hewn from the dark. Perhaps I was a far traveller resting by his camp-fire. Perhaps I was a knight keeping vigil for the dawn when wondrous deeds would be done. For I could be many people at that time, as I still can.

Maybe controlled fantasy is everybody's natural habitat and it's just that some of us lose the vulnerability to admit it, even to ourselves. We hardly go shopping without blessing the bread with half-formed thoughts of what else we might be doing, without some vague sense of who might be eating it with us. Ghosts of the past, ghosts of the future haunt our daily lives.

I remember that ghost of me at my hearth of small, butterfly dreams but I don't know how I came to be alone at that time in that place. In our house, with six not unnoticeable presences, it wasn't an easy trick to be alone, even without counting the cavalcade of aunties and uncles and cousins and friends who seemed to be constantly passing through. I wonder if I had come home from school to find the house empty. But that seems improbable. My mother was a ferocious carer who had an almost mystical capacity to conjure solid worries out of air that to the rest of us looked untroubled and clear. Maybe somebody else was supposed to be with me and had gone out briefly.

I don't know. I am simply aware of myself there. The moment sits separate and vivid in my memory, without explanation, like a rootless flower. Whoever I was being, traveller or knight, I must have been tired. For I fell asleep.

The awakening was strange. I think I must have been aware of the noise of people entering the house, one of those slow fuses of sound that sputteringly traverses the unconscious until it ignites into waking. My consciousness and the room came into the light together. My eyes were bruised with brightness. What I saw seems in retrospect to have had the shiningness of newly minted coins, all stamped unmistakably as genuine, pure metal, the undepreciable currency of my life.

What I saw in fact was pretty banal. My father had his hand on the light switch he had just pressed. My mother was beside him. They were both laughing at what must have been my startled eyes and my wonderment at being where I was. Around them was a room made instantly out of the dark. It was a very ordinary room. But it was wonderful. How strange the biscuit barrel was where my mother kept the rent money. How unimaginable was the image of Robert Burns with the mouse, painted on glass by my uncle. How incorrigibly itself the battered sideboard became. The room was full of amazing objects. They might as well have come from Pompeii.

And at the centre of them were two marvellously familiar strangers. I saw them not just as my mother and father. I knew suddenly how dark my father was, how physical his presence. His laughter filled the room, coming from a place that was his alone. My mother looked strangely young, coming in fresh-faced from the cold and darkness, her irises swallowing her pupils as she laughed in the shocking brightness. I felt an inordinate love for them. I suppose what I experienced then was the transformation of the ordinary into something powerfully mysterious.

The compulsion to write is fed from many tubers, most of them blessedly untracable. For if we could find the roots and subject them to rational analysis, who is to say we could make them grow again? Creativity occurs in the heart as well as the head. It is passionate intelligence. It demands for its appreciation the mind, of course, but that mind must come dressed in body and suffused with feeling. Mere intellect comes to fiction like a day-tripper, capable of appreciating the scenery but not of emotionally sharing the life that fills it. When emotion and intelligence fuse in appreciation, they recreate the work in a way that is almost as mysterious as the source of the work itself.

But, if it is impossible to trace any work effectively to all its origins, I'm around me was a fascination with language. Given my background, I was of the experiential paradigms from which *Docherty* (and perhaps everything I've written) grew. It was a moment which has had many relatives in my experience. When I consider them, I realise that they have several features in common. In those shared features can be glimpsed the genealogy of the compulsion from which *Docherty* was born.

One of them is a belief in the grandeur of the everyday, the conviction that for experience to be significant it needn't be masked in exoticism or buskined with social status. The ordinary is just the unique in hiding. As it says in *Docherty*, 'messiahs are born in stables'. That being so, as a boy I kept finding Bethlehem round every corner. So many things amazed me.

There were the stories surrounding me, for a start. *Docherty*, I should think, began its gestation in the mouths of the people all around me. Our house was an incredible talking-shop. As the youngest of four, I seem to have grown up with an intense conversation going on endlessly about me as my natural habitat. By one of those casually important accidents of childhood, the two youngest of us had to sleep in a fold-down bed in the living-room. Lack of space has its advantages. This meant that from a fairly early age, I could be involved, however marginally, in debates, often going to sleep with the sound of disputation as a lullaby.

As time passed, I didn't want to sleep at all until the issues had been resolved. I remember when I was fifteen and attending Kilmarnock Academy, there was an earnest man in his late twenties who had decided that my life would be enriched if I joined the YMCA. He pursued my conversion quite assiduously. One night he came to the door about eleven o'clock and expressed some shock that what he called 'a three-language student' wasn't in bed yet. The slight prissiness of his attitude and my dismay at it were expressive of the cultural distance between us. He was a social missionary who knew what was good for me. I was a native who believed that my life had more going for it than the missionary's. Who wanted to go to sleep when new ideas and unimagined facts were going off all round the room like fireworks? Leaving him, I went back to the fray. I didn't join the YMCA.

To this continuing seminar on life and the strange nature of it came many visiting speakers. Our house often felt to me like a throughway for talk. Relatives and friends were always dropping in. They brought news of local doings, bizarre attitudes, memorable remarks made under pressure, anecdotes of wild behaviour. Most of it was delivered and received with a calmness that astonished me. I vaguely sensed early on the richness they were casually living among, rather as if a traveller should come upon the Incas using pure gold as kitchen utensils. The substance that would be *Docherty* was beginning to glint for me in fragments of talk and caught glimpses of living.

But writing is not experience. It is what you make of your experience. The processes involved in the making are many. They include observation and perceptiveness and the skill of honesty towards both feeling and thought and the developed ability to comprehend your experience fresh for yourself, the earned right to recreate it justly into what it means to you. The unifying factor in all these processes is, of course, words—their seductiveness, their treachery, their capacity for freezing the flux.

Cognate to my awareness of the rich and largely uncommemorated life convinced that that moment in the living-room at St Maurs Crescent is one lucky to be in a house where books were part of the practical furniture, not there as ornaments but to be read and talked about. My mother was the source of the activity. My sister and my two brothers had established reading as a family tradition by the time I was old enough to join in. Only my father, someone—it has always seemed to me—educated spectacularly below his abilities, was never to be comfortable with books. His presence on the edges of our immersion in reading became, I think, in some way formative for me. I wanted him somehow to be included in the words.

The scene in the film *Viva Zapata!* where Marlon Brando hesitantly and vulnerably acknowledges that he can't read, and asks his bride to teach him has always had a special and moving resonance for me—like seeing a variant of your personal life made public and enlarged into the fictive. For, soon after they were married, my mother spent a long time improving my father's literacy. My awareness of the partially stifled intelligence in him convinced me that users of words should use them in the service not just of those who have them but of those who don't. When writing, I decided, you should be including not just those who will listen but those who can't. Otherwise, literature becomes the complacent activity of a cultural clique. This cliquey-ness is perhaps inevitable to some extent but it should never be self-satisfied. It should find forms that give expression to the absent. This principle of mine was of particular relevance to the writing of *Docherty*, which is in part an attempt to articulate in the context of a book on behalf of those who may be inarticulate in a literary way. Hence the central paradox of the book: it is written for people, most of whom will never read it.

Love of reading led naturally, it seemed at the time, to efforts at writing. If books were not the most sought after domestic adjunct in our housing scheme (depraved orgies of poetry-reading behind closed curtains), the desire actually to write the poetry could have been construed as proof of mental aberration. But this was my next move, one I effected without being ostracised by my peers because, perhaps, I was also very good at football. Having successfully undergone my masculine rites of passage in the West of Scotland, I could indulge in a little limp-wristed scribbling.

Here, again, the family situation helped. No one—least of all my father (despite being uninterested in books)—ever questioned the validity of the time I spent arranging words on pieces of paper. I took such tolerance for granted. It was only much later I realised how different it might have been for a working-class boy with ambitions to write. A woman writer-friend told me some years ago of a man she knew who came from a background similar to my own. He was bedevilled by a longing to write plays, much to the embarrassment of his relatives. On one occasion an older brother beat him up severely in an attempt to bring him to his senses and get him to stop inflicting shame upon the family. Such an attitude had been unimaginable to me in my boyhood. If I had met opposition, though, I think I would have withstood it, for, besides reading, there was another strong family tradition, this time from my father's side: 'You never shite on anybody else and nobody shites on you.'

I first wrote what I called a poem when I was fourteen. It was a Sunday, I remember, one of those Scottish ones that feel as if you've wandered into the antechamber to a featureless eternity. All external life is monochrome and any colour will have to be self-mixed in the head. I wrote a poem. It came with amazing ease. I stared at it in wonder. Can such things be?

Like a person who has found a piece of some extra-terrestrial substance in the living-room (which is where I was writing), I had to check it out against someone. I took it to my brother Neilly, eight years older, and—the choice wasn't accidental—enormously charitable to my slightly feverish imaginings. He read it over very carefully. I waited to find out what it was that I had done. He looked up slowly. 'You,' he said, shaking his head, 'didn't write that?' I was tremendously elated. My subsequent realisation that his response could be taken two ways (the second being 'God, I hope you didn't write that') didn't trouble me for long, because I knew which way he had meant it. I sometimes think all my books should carry the epigraph: 'Neilly's to blame'. It was all the encouragement I needed.

My uncertain vision of the lives around me and my hesitant attempts to express myself in writing were on course to converge at some point. But the course was parabolic rather than direct. This is, I would imagine, the experience of most people who are trying to write. What you want to express and the verbal skills you are seeking with which to express it will wander in mutually exclusive terrain for a long time and it is only when they meet at some unexpected border that you will witness them mysteriously merge into the one entity and you will discover that the voice you are speaking with is yours and no one else's.

That is certainly how it was with me. My early efforts at writing had scant connection with the pressing reality of the experience about me. That first poem demonstrates this. I can still remember it word for word but, feeling charitable, I shall restrict myself to paraphrase and minimal quotation. It is a poem ostensibly written by a man who is simultaneously committing suicide with a knife, presumably making sure that the blood doesn't obliterate his words. He has, it seems, killed his friend and his guilt ('I have sinned 'gainst God and man') makes him rather hard on himself. I suspect the shadow of a woman somewhere in the poem, too. The poem ends on the knife-thrust: 'I drive the blade my body through and all is calm within me.'

The archaisms and the inversions and the alien subject matter are what strike me in retrospect. The borrowed forms echo the borrowed content. Suggested adultery, murder and suicide weren't exactly the staple diet of a fourteen year old in Kilmarnock in the 1950s. But they were testing things to write about. In a way, the initial separation from myself of what I was writing about was essential. If you wish to engage as effectively as you can in a contest, you don't just walk into it. You train. You develop yourself in imitation conflict with yourself before you take the real risks. And writing *is* a conflict, an endless lover's quarrel with the word. Some readers may miss this because what they are reading will be the terms of the truce.

This dichotomy between what I was actually writing and what I wanted to write persisted for a long time. There were lapses, of course, times when —instead of wandering like a tourist into some established writer's sanctum and listening to my mimic echo—I would stumble unexpectedly into my own and find myself, awestruck, writing not towards what other people had written but directly out of where my compulsion lay.

But mainly I spent my time being an ancient Greek or Shakespeare or

William Saroyan or Ernest Hemingway (despite the dearth of big-game hunting in Ayrshire). I continued trying to write poetry and short stories. I don't know how long my experience and my writing might have continued living apart and flirting with each other, but circumstances arranged a shotgun wedding between them. When I was eighteen and in my first month at university, my father died of lung cancer. The impact of that terrible event was indescribable and I was compelled to try to describe it. My love of words had come upon a personal reality it must try to confront.

But the effect on my attempts to write was hardly immediate. Creativity works by indirections. At university I read countless writers and no doubt ventriloquised many of their voices. But at the same time I kept returning to struggling with my own necessity, which was to make an understanding of my father's death.

I worked on it over several years, winning found fragments of meaning from the pain. The result was to be a long poem called 'Initiation', not published until fifteen years after the event which it described. Four years before that, *Remedy is None*—a novel to which the experience is also central —had been published.

The poetry and the novel and a second novel, *A Gift from Nessus*, had —besides simply being written for themselves—brought me nearer to an understanding of my boyhood experience and heightened the confidence I needed to attempt the finding of a form to express it. Other things had helped to prepare me as well.

One was my reaction to being the first of any branch of my family to go to university. After the initial awe, I became progressively unimpressed. Later, I would give to Laidlaw, in the book that carried his name, some of my feelings: 'I took acres of fertile ignorance to university. And they proceeded to pour preconceptions all over it like forty tons of cement.' With some very honourable exceptions, I couldn't accept the mechanistic shallowness of much that was on offer.

I remember one moment that haunts me still. Between the second year and the third year, we had to submit an essay to the English Language Department on some aspect of Anglo-Saxon. On my first day in Junior Honours, I nervously entered the lecture room, wondering what was ahead of me. It didn't take long to find out. A lecturer I had never seen came in and dumped his leather case beside the lectern. When he opened his mouth, he was, it transpired, a very bluff Yorkshireman.

'Mucklevaynee,' he said. 'Where is 'e?'

For a country boy in Academe, still occasionally wondering when he would be found out, it was a tense moment. I raised a palsied hand.

'Stand oop,' he said.

I unravelled myself slowly among thirty or so students. The lecturer stared at me as if he was viewing his first Martian.

'You lad,' he said. 'Use words ah can oonderstand. Siddown.'

I sat down into a disillusionment that had two more years to grow. Part of my discontent was to crystallise into an anger at the absence of the life I came from in what was called literature.

Also, when I was in my early twenties, I had written a long blank verse play about working-class life—a kind of *Hamlet* in jeans. This was a bizarre enterprise called *Actions in Generic Tense*, a title not calculated perhaps to have them queuing round the block. But that misguided endeavour was very important for me. It made me try to express the resonance and importance of the lives around me in words that made no concessions to their assumed lowliness. That, too, brought *Docherty* nearer.

The third novel I started to write was called *Tribute to the Minotaur*. I had written over twenty thousand words when I stopped, never to return to it. The reason wasn't so much a revulsion away from that book as an overwhelming compulsion towards another.

I wanted to write a book that would create a kind of literary genealogy for the people I came from, the people whose memorials were parish registers. Since their history was largely silence, I would be constructing a communal fabric of myth. That didn't bother me since I had long looked on history itself as being a form of decadent mythology. I wanted the sort of feeling I had experienced in the living-room at St Maurs Crescent, an almost mystical conviction, to be given flesh.

I began to write *Docherty*.

When Perseus wanted to confront the Gorgon, he had a problem. He knew that if he looked on her directly, he would be turned to stone. But, borrowing a burnished shield from Athene, he was able to approach Medusa through her reflection, survive her lethal stare and claim her head. He came off whole. The Gorgon can be seen as the incomprehensible nature of experience. You cannot capture experience raw. Try that and your endeavour becomes lifeless. Experience is too multiform. You can only reflect it, in more or less coherent fragments. You need a shield between you and the annihilating variousness of experience. The shield is art.

Every writer of originality makes his or her own shield. Some shields are more elaborately original than others. And you will find people who regard themselves as connoisseurs of shields making whole careers out of praising the designs along the edges, the unimaginable patterns chased out on the metal. I think they miss the point. These are dilettantes of experience who think that such shields were made just to be hung on walls and reflect nothing but themselves.

To realise the serious but not solemn purpose of creativity, you only have to consider its origins. When the people huddled in the Lascaux caves made their pictures on the rock, it may have been a kind of play, but they knew it was a game with mortal consequences. They were trying to magic the animals they depicted into meat to sustain them. Catch the image, catch the creature. Understand the beast or die.

Our need to understand the beast in its ultimate form—the nature of experience—continues. 'We have art,' Nietzsche says, 'in order not to die of the truth.' While I can see what he means, I think I would prefer to say that we have art in order to die of the truth. Mortality is incurable. The most that we can ask of our lives is that when we die, it is not—as it was for Joseph K —'Like a dog', but that the awareness with which we meet death will transform its emptiness into a meaning of our own, that it will not negate our living merely but be obliged to fulfil our living in some way against its will, by the cunning and the art of our approach. To comprehend our life justly is to overcome our death because we will make its meaninglessness just the backdrop to our meaning. We will write a meaning on the void.

That is why for me the shield of artistic technique is so important. It is one of the means by which we determine the justness with which we approach our dying, the validity of the terms by which we live. That is why I think that many of the criteria currently in vogue for judging the efficacy of the shield are frivolous and irrelevant. Mere novelty is often confused with originality. The more wilful and arbitrarily different the shape and pattern of the shield, the more likely it is to offer a distorted reflection. And the reflection is all. The criteria that matter most will be the accuracy, the justice, the intensity and the comprehensiveness (how far the pieces justly imply the whole) of the reflection of experience that is given.

Each new book is to some extent a newly structured shield. If the experience it is hoped to reflect is working-class experience, Perseus has another problem. He had better make the shield himself. There is no sustained tradition of such craftsmanship.

In the writing of *Docherty*, I was aware of this loneliness. I had precursors, of course, from Langland's 'field full of folk' to Robert Tressell and the work of Zola and Lawrence and Sillitoe. But, though they helped, they didn't answer my purposes. One reason for this is, I think, that people writing about working-class experience have tended to approach from a predetermined angle, perhaps because they have never known it as a given reality that surrounds them from birth (and therefore their reason for coming to it in the first place has an ideological bias), or because, having been born there and left it, they are rationalising the nature of their departure.

Zola, for example, writes in his work notes: 'The bourgeoisie betrays its revolutionary past in order to safeguard its capitalistic privilege and remain a governing class. Having conquered power, it does not want to pass it on to the people . . . I must express the important, decisive idea, that the bourgeoisie has played its part, that it has gone over to the reaction to preserve its power and riches, and that all hope for the forces of tomorrow lies with the people.'

I have no quarrel with this as a political analysis of Zola's time as I understand that time to have been, but it seems to me a patricianly simplistic way to view a vast and complex area of human experience. It is yet another example of how those who see themselves as part of a revolutionary agenda have always been eager to patronise working-class people out of their present into a future they did not ask for, rather like the bestowing of a knighthood by a king in exile, the status to become effective come the millennium. Given that tourism may be noble, this is noble tourism. But I think I understand and believe in the nature of working-class experience too much to endorse this attitude.

D. H. Lawrence, on the other hand, was part of this experience and escaped. His version of the experience is largely a justification of his getting away from it. His literary career can be seen as offering some parallels with David Livingstone's life as a missionary. I find the irony of Livingstone heading for darkest Africa, while apparently not noticing the squalor of the darkest Blantyre that he was leaving behind, is echoed in the way D. H. Lawrence abandons the significance of his earlier life to explore the wilder and more abstract shores of visionary theory.

*Sons and Lovers* is, for me, mainly a libel on the nature of working-class experience. It is the vision of a man in flight and that is inevitably a distorting perspective, since it will reflect the significance of going rather than the significance of staying. It shows positive moments in that way of life, it is true, for Lawrence was a writer who tried to practise a kind of desperate honesty, but I believe it offers a vision so essentially negative that it could only seem just to those who have never known that way of life or are glad not to know it any longer. Being, like so much that has been written about working-class life, a kind of gospel according to Judas, it is a testament of some value, but of a limited value in trying to obtain a just sense of the nature of working-class experience, its richness and its dynamism.

In trying to arrive at the vision of working-class experience I was hoping to reflect, therefore, I had to begin by knowing what I couldn't use, by discarding what would distort the image I felt to be true. It would not be the familiar story of the boy of abilities and sensitivity winning his way out of an underclass into a more enriching form of life, for this is to presuppose the comparative shallowness of the life he is leaving—an assumption with which, having experienced the old life left and the new life found, I have never been able to agree. There is a simple reason for the consistency with which this erroneous assumption has been maintained: it is that to judge working-class culture, once you have left it, by the standards of the established literary culture you have entered is to judge it by terms which were created to deny it. You have no option but to impoverish your own past. The rules are made to work that way.

For one of the keys to working-class life is precisely that it lives along the edge where thought and feeling keep fusing in experience and are not formally 'culturised' into separate entities. Both live in dynamic interrelation, as I believe they should. In my sense of it, working-class life is rich in an intelligence that re-earns itself constantly on the pulses of life and doesn't abstract itself into mere intellectuality, which is then able to pursue ideas for their own sake, regardless of how they may fail to relate to the realities of experience. Therefore, I believe that to judge the passion of working-class life by the clinical procedures of middle-class culture is like assembling the data of an autopsy and calling it a life story.

It was for that reason that I was determined that *Docherty* wouldn't be an escape story with the escapee patronisingly looking back on the lives of those who were still inmates. The vision would be from within, frontal not tangential. In this connection, Conn's instinctive refusal to seek an alternative life to the one he has is central to the book.

Also, the book would not be conceived through the lens of an ideology, would not be angled and selected to support a specific political stance. I believe this would have been wrong on two counts. First, I think that good writing is a report from some kind of front line of experience. You find out what is happening, you don't pre-decide it.

If you want to understand the nature of experience, you had better let it tell you. To go simply looking for the data that will support your thesis is the ultimate insult to experience and she won't forgive you. Your complacent perceptions will be cuckolded by reality. Secondly, working-class experience is especially recalcitrant to the intellectualism of an ideology, as many frustrated revolutionaries in their visionary cabals have found to their despair. Its reality keeps proliferating spontaneously, overgrowing the conceptual borders the theorists would set for it. Lenin understood this problem and, being, like all good revolutionaries, capable of theorising to the point of denying his own humanity, he came to the conclusion that theory should subordinate spontaneity. But it can't. Theory may stifle spontaneity for a long time but it cannot control it permanently. If it could, humanity would be over.

So, I knew what I wasn't after. That's important. It means you can discard the reflective devices that seem to offer distortions. But what I *was* trying to reflect accurately about the nature of working-class experience? A poem I had written some years before, called 'Eugenesis', gave me one of the clues.

> On the first day They eradicated war.
> Nations were neutralized. In desert places
> The cumbered void rusted with defused bombs,
> The gutted chambers. In random heaps
> The rockets lay, like molar monuments
> To brontosauri sentenced to extinction.
>
> On the second day They fed the starving.
> The capsules gave immunity from hunger.
> Faces filled. The smiles were uniform.
> The computers had found a formula for plenty.
>
> The third day ended work. With summer
> Processed to a permanence, the sun-
> Machine in operation, every day
> Would be as long as They desired it.
> Season-chambers were erected. The nostalgic
> Could take a holiday to autumn if they wished.
> The computers thought of everything.
>
> On the fourth day death was dead.
> Synthetic hearts, machine-tooled brains,
> Eyes and limbs were all expendable.
> Immortality came wrapped in polythene.
> Every face was God's you saw upon the street.
>
> By the fifth day crime was cured.
> Mind-mechanics, They located every hatred,
> Extracted it, and amputated angers.
> Each idea was sterilized before its issue.
> The computers fixed a safety-mark for thinking.
>
> The sixth day saw heaven's inauguration.
> Benignity pills were issued. Kindness meetings
> Were held on every corner. They declared
> Love as the prerogative of all.
> That day became the longest there had been.
> But as long as there was light the people smiled.

On the seventh day, while They were resting,
A small man with red hair had disappeared.
A museum missed a tent. Neither was found.
He left an immortal wife, the changeless years
Of endless happiness, and a strange note
In ancient script, just four historic letters.
The Autotongue translated: 'Irrational Anger'.
The Medic Machine advised: 'Rejection Symptoms.
Source Unknown. Primordial and Contagious'.

It was too late. The word ran like a rash
On walls and daubed on doorways. Cities emptied.
In panic They neglected Their machines.
The sunset was unauthorised. Its beauty
Triggered the light-oriented metal cocks
That crew until their mechanisms burst.
Fires twinkled in the new night, shaping mattocks.
On the dark hills an unheavenly sound was heard.
The Historometer intoned into the silence:
'Ancient Barbaric Custom Known as Laughter'.
Seizing up, the computer began to cry.

The small man with red hair would help me construct my shield.

In the process of constructing the shield that is your book, you will catch reflected fragments of the creature you are after. Such moments can be encouraging. They convince you that the beast you seek is out there all right. What its exact configuration will be you still don't know, but you are already catching pieces of it. For the writing of a book is the process of discovering what it is about. The thing you are trying to ambush is constantly ambushing you. You keep glimpsing it among the foliage and its observed nature keeps surprising you. You realise that in getting so close to it you must have been doing something right and you try to remember what it was. In this way, you gradually learn the habits of the beast you want to trap, the manner of approach that won't disturb it, the lures it will respond to. Such devices may be very simple, even banal, but, handled with skill and tension, they may bring you an expression of life not quite seen before. (This in no way means, of course, that commentators will appreciate its rarity, for critics tend to be like the tourists at the end of 'The Old Man and the Sea': seeing mainly the bones, they find it hard to tell a shark from a marlin. Show most critics a unicorn and they will see a deformed horse. They're also quite good at thinking deformed horses are unicorns.)

Working on *Docherty*, I learned and forgot and relearned the habits of my quarry, what presumptions frightened it off, what methods encouraged it to come nearer. That methodology is now a thing of the past: it belongs to the book that made it. For a while, I lived with it almost daily. But when it has fulfilled itself, it is over and you must move on.

A new book is a new risk or it is nothing. As Rilke says, you begin again.

Any past achievement is mainly valuable in providing the terms of the bet you can hazard on the future. You first renew your wonder. Then you relearn the techniques to express it.

A writer's greatest gift is a continuing capacity to try to achieve more. After completing the vastness of *Moby Dick*, Herman Melville could write to Nathaniel Hawthorne: 'As long as we have more to do, we have done nothing. So, now, let us add Moby Dick to our blessing, and step from that. Leviathan is not the biggest fish;—I have heard of Krakens.'

But, if I can't recreate the endless tensions and shifts of perception and the number of occasions I was knocked off my horse to discover that Damascus had never been my destination in the first place, I can remember some small awarenesses of the time that helped me towards the making of *Docherty*. They're just small pieces of scoria that hardly suggest the reality of the eruption, but maybe they're better than nothing.

I knew I was after a book that would make no concessions on the truth I believed I saw to anybody, not to the people I was writing about, not to the people most likely to read it, not to the intellectual 'supporters' of the people I was writing about—not to anybody. This made for an appropriate loneliness, which for me is where creativity begins.

It meant that, while I was writing partly on behalf of people many of whom didn't read much, the prose would in no way make obeisance to that fact. It would express my vision to the limits of my own articulacy, not pretend to imitate theirs. The most basic premise on which I was writing was that their lives were full of an immanent significance which, not being made explicit in literary form, was often regarded as not existing at all. The only way to demonstrate its existence was to express it as fully as I could.

This in turn meant the risk of alienating some readers by expressing the unspoken experience of characters to a level beyond their own achieved articulacy. But such a risk was central to the endeavour. Without it, there would be no book. Writing for me involves isolating the area where you must take your own risks, not the risks already taken by others. To me, this risk was inescapable. Besides, I did have precedents. It was just that it had not been deemed appropriate to apply them to working-class life. What prince of Denmark or Roman general or Scottish king ever spoke like Shakespeare? Elizabethan blank verse brings poetry often from the mouths of ruffians— high-class ruffians, maybe, but ruffians. What kind of snobbery would allow a convention of heightened articulacy to them but not to a narrative of working-class experience? And where did that rough seaman, Ishmael, get all his allusions if not from Melville?

This, of course, was an offence not just to those whose effete snobbery would disenfranchise the ferocious energy of working-class experience from entry into the salons of culture. It was an offence also to those self-appointed guardians of the significance of working-class experience, those weekend intellectuals, who—like ideological social workers—patronise a reality dynamic beyond their own capacity for living by dressing it up in second-hand ideas. I wanted to create working-class people who were so fiercely themselves, whose collateral was not in houses or career or erudition or in the future, but was what they walked about in, who were so strongly present that they could walk into any room in any time in any place and forbid condescension.

As I wrote, I knew that *Docherty* would be a seriously subversive book (whether anyone happened to notice the fact or not). I sensed the hard place it was trying to go towards. Today, I'm not sure how many have followed it there. A Paris graffito once said, 'When a finger points at the moon, the fool looks at the finger.' It's maybe just your average authorial paranoia, but I suspect a fair amount of critical finger-watching in relation to my books (though not from lay readers).

*Docherty* can be said to be the story of a working-class mining family in the West of Scotland in the first quarter of the twentieth century. That's what it is, all right. But that's not what it's about. That's what the shield is made of, but what it was built to reflect is something much bigger. Whether it successfully does so or not is another matter.

For a start, it has for long seemed to me that the essentials of working-class experience form a kind of esperanto. By this I mean that working-class people in any given country are liable to have more in common with the working classes of another country than with, say, the middle classes of their own place. I remember reading Steinbeck's *The Grapes of Wrath* as a teenager and being amazed, in my naivety, at how Scottish the Okies were (even down to some of the terms they used, like 'redd' for 'clear up'). I suppose what I really meant was how Okie working-class Scots were. I remember the numerous frissons of recognition I felt in reading about Hardy's yokels, often relating to how similar their sense of community was to the one I had been taught—their ability to appreciate the communal as a means not of strangling the eccentric and the individual, but of letting it flourish in mutual tolerance. I remember the joy of discovering Albert Camus' essay, 'Summer in Algiers', and realising that he was talking about my own people, with great insight and compassion. Such generously shared perceptions from other places and times were like finding out that what you had thought was a dialect was, in fact, a language and one spoken in many parts of the world. It gave me the confidence to believe that, while I was writing out of my own experience, I was also writing towards the experience of countless others. The accent might be Scottish. But the message, whether they wanted it or not, was for everybody.

What that message was only emerged for me slowly in the writing. All the shifts and adjustments and failed endeavours and altered structures were moving towards the catching of a central image. Often I wasn't sure myself what that image was. It was only when the book was finished that I thought I knew. (The way in which the book was finished, incidentally, illustrates the kind of creative dementia I was working in. I had already written some thirty-odd thousand words past the point where the book now ends. My editor was becoming slightly despondent of ever seeing an end to it and he was beginning to suggest that we might have to sell the book through a building society, when I realised suddenly and surprisingly that the book was over. I had been going on with the writing of a novel that was finished.)

By the time I had finished the book, I thought I at last knew what it was about. Like any novel, it has its confusing variety of pointing fingers (novels being a process first of discovering understanding out of experience and only then of inventing experience out of understanding), but, if you can see beyond them, it seems to me, they are all pointing generally towards the same core of significance. The shield may be made up of many facets but they combine for me in offering the same coherent central reflection, which is the subject of the book. *Docherty* is essentially an attempt to democratise traditional culture, to give working-class life the vote in the literature of heroism.

The obsession that fuelled me in the writing of it did not have its antecedents, as some commentators have suggested, in George Douglas Brown's *The House with the Green Shutters* or Lewis Grassic Gibbon's *Scots Quair*. This seems to me about as perceptive as listening to the common accent of two voices and concluding that the content of what is being said must be essentially the same. I have read and enjoyed these books, but knew, even as I read them, that my obsessions were elsewhere. Of course, since these books all grow out of Scotland, some similarities will be found. There may be heard in the corner-standers of Graithnock, for example, an echo of the 'bodies' of Barbie. But it appears a pretty thin echo, not yielding any very fruitful comparison. To see any great kinship between the books on this kind of basis seems to me cultural myopia. After all, the device was hardly discovered in Ayrshire. The Greeks, too, had their choruses.

And the Greeks had more effect in determining what I was after than any previous Scottish novels. The three areas of my reading which have had the greatest impact on me are Greek myth, Greek tragedy and Elizabethan drama. The nature of heroism lies at the centre of them all. But it has always been a heroism based on an implied premise: social status. It has been a commonly enough remarked-on element. But it was A. C. Bradley in *Shakespearean Tragedy* who first emphasised it for me. It was one of many illuminatingly simple observations I found in him. (He has often been mocked subsequently for his intellectual naivety in treating Shakespeare's characters as if they were real—'How many children had Lady Macbeth?'—but I find his intelligent innocence a truer approach to the nature of literature than much of the etiolated intellectualisation that came after him.) That required social status of the hero or heroine troubled me. From Gilgamesh onwards, it was there. But while it was established as a historical fact, it did not seem to me a philosophically necessary ingredient of heroism. It blocked my path towards what I wanted to write, like a Gordian knot I had to unravel to get where I was going.

To do that, I had to come to my own understanding of the nature of heroism. I had to break it down from its achieved and assumed forms into its elements and see if it was possible to reconstitute it successfully without the dimension of social status. This meant, first of all, purifying the idea of heroism of some of the debased modern accretions it has acquired.

Heroism in its origins is a way of living, the definitive actions of a life. It is a story, not a gesture. So the contemporary tabloid debasement of heroism as a single act of courage will not serve. This is not to say that heroism will not be found in lives reported in the tabloids, just that it won't be expressible in such terms.

Nor does calling the main character in a book or play the 'hero' or the 'heroine' clarify things. They need exhibit none of the characteristics of heroism and yet assume its name. This is to abuse a word to the point of making it meaningless.

In trying to crystallise my own perception of heroism, in trying to arrive at my meaning of the word, I tried to relate its derivation to its contemporary usage. The ancient hero occurs in myth and myth was a precipitate of past experience. It was an endeavour to illuminate in human terms the darkness of the past. The ancient hero comes bringing with him the religious mists from which he emerged. He begins as superhuman, god-descended and sometimes god-becoming.

Much of the mythology that tends to define the modern idea of a hero, it seemed to me, is born of our fears, ignorance and half-knowledge, not of the past so much as of the future. It is prospective, not retrospective. It is born less out of the darkness of the past than out of the darkness of the future. Made credulous by the technological advances of the past, we look forward in trepidation to those that can only be imagined and to their effects.

In such an atmosphere of the comparative loss of the importance of self, it is perhaps not too surprising that a modern cult hero, like James Bond and many of his cinematic descendants, should move among pointless and spectacular carnage in which human life spins, aimless as an orange in a fruit machine. We are offered as hero a robot stylisation of the individual virtues, man evolving to the demands of his environment, surviving by adapting himself into an imitation of the machines around him, stripped to a few standard reflexes that emerge when circumstances push the appropriate button: self-protection, gastronomy, copulation. His bible is an unarmed combat manual. His sacrament is not love but sex. His only comprehension of the 'good life' is a gourmet's. This is the hero as less than human.

Between these two impossibilities, ancient origin and current distortion, superhuman and less than human—neither of which we should try to be—I was looking for the possible hero. I thought I found him between the two. The key for me lay in the realisation that the greatest thing we can be is definitively human. The hero celebrates humanity above all dogmas, codes, ideas. He becomes remorselessly and undeniably himself, against all profferred chances to imitate mere social mores and evade his own identity. (Hence, the importance of events, of happenings, those things that take us beyond thoughts or ideas and make us occur in fact. Heroic narrative is the record of humanity learning to be itself.) In this way, true heroism does not lie in eccentricity but in concentricity. It is individuality in essence. And those who are most individual are most other people. Individuality is the confirmation of other people's nature through your own. A hero is someone who is more ourselves than we are because, by rejecting the compromises of our nature that we accept, he shows us our potential to be more than we pretend to be. He is our unacknowledged self.

From this central dynamic of liberating us into our own humanity emanate all his virtues. Like Prometheus, he steals the secrets of the gods to enrich our living here and now. Like Antony after Actium, deciding on 'one more gaudy night,' he says, 'Go out as you choose, not how they tell you to go. Your life is not just what they tell you it is. It is also what you say it is.' Because, like Oedipus, he demands fully to know, he says to us in the meridian moment before his fall, 'Know, too, who you are. You are falling anyway—loud or quiet.'

But what he demands is also to be known, not just to know. One source of the effeteness of much modern literature, I believe, comes from the fragmentation of the hero's quest. The down-market modern hero seeks to be, without knowing. He will function effectively without having to know, insight and wisdom reduced to cunning and competence. The up-market modern hero will often seek to know without the responsibility of being his knowledge (which Oedipus had to endure)—literature as some kind of abstract science that need never be applied. One is soulless experience, the other experienceless soul.

The complete hero encompasses both dimensions. He will know as far as he can in his understanding, which is at least variable and at most won't take him far. Hercules was no sage and Gilgamesh no philosopher. But they were heroes. For who will judge a hero by his intelligence alone? His intelligence, in its variable limitations, only matters in how honestly and uncompromisingly it leads him into the further knowledge of how to be, most fully and most justly. Beyond the failure of his understanding, the hero must endure Keats's knowledge of the pulses, Kafka's physical inscription of 'In the Penal Settlement'.

The hero liberates us into the possibilities of our own nature because he enacts the subjective victory over objective circumstance, and in so doing can teach us that we may do the same. Having a vision beyond his given horizons and the courage to live by the vision, he defeats those imposed horizons. His achievement is the transformation of experience through spirit. That is why his ultimate challenge is death, the final experienceable border of human nature.

He will die, of course. But in meeting death he will transform its significance. He will fill its emptiness with his own humanity. His spirit will survive his dying, a part of us that diminishes death.

In *The Epic of Gilgamesh*, Gilgamesh, ruler of Uruk in Babylonia, loses his great friend, Enkidu. Faced for the first time with death not as concept but as experience, Gilgamesh wishes to find how to live forever. From Utnapishtim, a variant of Noah, he learns of a rejuvenating plant at the bottom of the sea. Acquiring the plant, he is on his way home when he decides to bathe in a pool. The plant is left on the bank and is eaten by a snake, thus explaining how snakes can slough their skin and renew themselves. Gilgamesh's search has failed. Immortality reverts to nature beyond man. But there remains the stature of the quest, a quality of spirit endlessly renewable to match the endlessness of death.

Having worked out my definition of heroism, I believed that I could see how the social position of the hero was irrelevant. That quality of engagement with living could be practised daily anywhere. It seemed to me, for example, that many of the disadvantaged and the handicapped, creating to the point of death lives defiantly fuller than their circumstances offered, were living, in the most stringent terms, heroically. I had often thought that subsumed in *The Odyssey* was a *Eumaeid*, the story of Eumaeus, the swineherd who never leaves Ithaca during the twenty years of travel of Odysseus.

Heroism was, of course, in this sense a literary convention. But what I was suggesting to myself was that some of the trappings of that convention were unnecessary, that the convention could be purged of anachronistic elements and made to work again. The hero need not be socially important or exceptional in terms of his experience. These appeared to be historical dead-weight, carried over from outmoded social structures, descriptive not so much of the essential nature of the hero as of the disguises he had to wear to meet the social assumptions of the time. Indeed, these factors seemed to me ways of diminishing the liberating power of the image of the hero. His social importance could be seen as relating to his fall and a warning to most of society not to try and emulate him. If that's what happens when you put your head above the parapet, keep yours down. If his experience is seen as exceptional, his kinship with us is blurred. He becomes a scapegoat, leaving us to practise our repetitive compromises undisturbed.

I wanted to divest heroism of its incidental historical robes and put it on the street. It wouldn't be the impressiveness of the experience that made people heroic but the impressiveness of how they confronted it. I would try to express heroism through working-class life. If my belief was that heroism could be found anywhere, not just in arched chambers and among dissolving dynasties, I would locate it in the most unlikely place. I brought it into the family. In time, I thought it settled in quite well.

The material of *Docherty* is largely my own experience of family life, enlarged by what was going on around us. But the Dochertys are not my family. I start from the premise that you cannot render actuality in prose, only an impression of reality. No living person ever appeared in a novel. People are too various, too shifting, too much. To write is to create, more or less, well or badly. The most neutral reportage is a fictive form. Just to select —and the very act of perception is a process of selection—is to create your own reality out of the actuality.

Also, I deliberately moved the raw material of my experience back in time. In setting the novel in a time before I was born, I was obliged to pass it through the transforming agent of research, oral and written. The experience became not an end but a means. It was as if it belonged to other people and I had to recreate their circumstances and responses. The material became malleable and I could try to shape its various parts into a whole that would reflect a true image.

What I thought that image essentially was, I have suggested. But what is reflected remains outside the thing that reflects it. So, while *Docherty* was made to be about the nature of experience anywhere, its reflective surfaces belong to a certain time and a certain place. Precisely because you are claiming to demonstrate, as I was, that a heroic ability to engage life can be found anywhere, you cannot then import alien materials to prove your case. To do that is to undercut your own contention. *Docherty* remains imaginatively rooted in the West of Scotland in the first quarter of the twentieth century, in its speech, its ethos, its conditions of living. The code, as it were, in which its wider significance is expressed, is very specific and needs patience if it is to be cracked.

This causes a couple of problems. The first is that a lot of people won't bother to read it at all. (I remember my agent showing me letters from American publishers, praising the novel and saying they wouldn't consider publishing it, since it wouldn't be accessible to an audience there.) The second is that sometimes those who do read it, it seems to me, breach the terms of the contract that is necessary between reader and writer. They demand a late twentieth century sensibility from early twentieth century lives.

For example, the social and political objections feminists might bring to the superimposed nature of Jenny Docherty's experience are understandable. But in lamenting the lost potential, it would be wrong to undervalue the achievement. That would be a slander on her heroism. Given the terms she inhabits, she is just as heroic as Tam Docherty. It is just that, there and then, the terms for her were different. Heroism, I was suggesting, lies in the quality of the subjective response to the objective conditions.

But then any idea of working-class heroism as a philosophically serious concept, out with its usefulness as a source of simplistic slogans for political purposes, is bound to offend social reformers. It is an uncomfortable attribute for them to accommodate because it represents a form of human fulfilment here and now, in defiance of the circumstances. And if circumstances cease to be all, the question of social programming ceases to be all-important. The need for reform is not denied—how could it be, given the social conditions we live among?—but it is seen to be part of something much bigger and more complex. Zealots never like that. They might have to rethink their priorities.

That is why I have suggested that *Docherty* is a subversive book. It is subversive not just of traditional cultural attitudes but of many contemporary cultural attitudes as well. The idea of heroism as something belonging to now offends traditionalists because it diminishes the importance of the past and it offends reforming revolutionaries because it diminishes the importance of the future.

What *Docherty* is essentially offering as the definitive characteristic of both working-class life and of heroism is rebelliousness. That lies at the centre of what it is reflecting, the primal feature of the beast. That is why we are what we are. That is both what we die of and what defies our death. That is why heaven and Utopia are places on our mental map at which we can never arrive, because we would have to deny our nature to get there. We must improve the shared conditions in which we live, of course, but the essential purpose of that will be in order to inhabit more fully the necessary and unalterable terms of our existence. Take away the avoidable injustices of some lives that we may humanly share in the unavoidable injustice that is all our lives.

This rebelliousness is all that finally survives in *Docherty*. If you take away the terms in which I tried to identify it, if you transform completely the working-class conditions where I thought I saw it, it will still be there. I believe the small man with red hair will be here as long as we are. I'm glad. As long as he's around, our humanity may be saved. That is why *Docherty* is primarily a celebration of rebellion and a negation of revolution.

Rebellion is the discovery of a possible future through an argument between the present and the past. Revolution is the invention of the certain future through a denial of the past, or at least a definitive reading of the past, by the present. Rebellion is fitful, questioning, potentially all-inclusive. The rebel is potentially the saviour of the man he rebels against, by reminding him of the just limits of his own nature. Revolution is systematic, dogmatic, inevitably exclusive. The revolutionary is predeterminately the destroyer of the man he revolts against.

A rebellion denies categories, a revolution invents them. Rebellion is made by individuals, revolution is made by committees. The loneliness of a rebel establishes kinship. The kinship of revolutionaries creates loneliness. One proclaims individuals, one denies them. Whoever proclaims individuality establishes a fraternity with our own. Whoever denies individuality through a cause leaves us alone with ours.

Revolution is a bourgeois and essentially reactionary phenomenon because it deifies the establishment, the *principle* of the establishment. It is petrified rebellion. The revolutionary is the sophist and pharisee of our time. Sophistry is speaking from the mouth, pharisaism is living in the mind. That is why revolutions become messianic and murderous.

But rebellion is pragmatic and salvationary. It moves forward constantly in doubt. It tries to confront the simplifications and lies of ideology and dogma with experience, the reality of our living. It renews our sense of our own humanity. To be true to our own experience, to its multiplicity and its incompatibility with received preconceptions as to its nature, is to rebel towards a more just way of living.

That's why *Docherty* ends as it does, not neatly resolved. The thirty thousand words I had written beyond where it ends were, I came to realise, a form of obedience to an aesthetic that wasn't the book's. The ending had to hang like an unfinished phrase in the air, to be continued by other lives. The novel is about the generosity of the individual dream being broken against the inadequacy of circumstances. That story doesn't end.

'There is no epiphany as yet in his prose,' one critic has said of *Docherty*. I would have thought there was. But if it is there, it's the epiphany of constant rebellion. The book was made to be that way. If it had a patron saint, he would be Spartacus, the slave who led a rebellion to the gates of Rome, which was there for the taking, then turned away and went back to Sicily, where his rebellion had started, and died—seeking to engage the opposing general, Crassus, in combat, refusing either to be crowned with what his enemies called success or to yield:

> What news is there of Spartacus?
> The slaves of time don't need to ask.
> They simply go where he has been
> And do not ask, 'What did he see?'
> Rome is before them still today:
>
> Still chosen hills, the in heat town
> That says no and undoes the gown,
> The gates that open wide like thighs,
> The defences that are coquetry.
>
> He turned away. And so they must
> Who in the honest heart of action
> Find victory a cheap seduction.
> Where is he now? When will he come?
> He can't who is already here.

His long descendants don't know where
But in their daily lives they find
The small, hard legacy he left,
A nub of truth, eyes lie-bereft,
A dreadful justice of the mind
That will not palter with success
And knows power lies and force, if just,
Seeks judgement on itself at last
That it may still have honour.

He is the timbre of the voice
That, trapped in time, makes human choice:
I will not be victorious
And I refuse to say 'defeat'—

Which is, of course, the best of us,
Who *are* the news of Spartacus.

# Prologue: 1903

The year came and receded like any other, leaving its flotsam of the grotesque, the memorable, the trivial. On the first day the Coronation Durbar at Delhi saw King Edward established by proxy as Emperor of India. In the same month 5,000 people died in a hurricane in the Society Islands and 51 inmates were burned to death in Colney Hatch lunatic asylum. In July Pope Leo XIII died at ninety-three. In November the King and Queen of Italy visited England. Rock Sand was the horse, running up to his fetlocks in prize-money: 2,000 Guineas, Derby, St Leger. In Serbia King Alexander and Queen Draga were murdered, Peter Karageorgevitch became King, and dark conspirators regrouped around the throne, like actors obsessed with their roles although the theatre is on fire. In London Buffalo Bill Cody's Wild West Show made genocide a circus. In Kitty Hawk, North Carolina, two brothers put a heavier than air machine into flight for fifty-nine seconds. In High Street, Graithnock, Miss Gilfillan had insomnia.

She called it 'my complaint', not unaffectionately. It grew as the year waned, so that by December her eyes seemed lidless. Most nights she nursed her loneliness at her window, holding aside the lace curtain to stare at the tenements across from her, to judge the lives that lay in them, to think that she would die here. The thought was pain and comfort. She would die among strangers, hard faces and rough voices, hands that hadn't much use for cutlery, drunken songs of Ireland's suffering in Scottish accents, swear-words in the street, children grubbing out their childhoods in the gutters. But her death would be a lifelong affront to her family, an anger in her father's grave. So each night she would perfect her disillusion, her regret was a whetstone for her family's, and High Street was the hell they would inherit.

Late at night on 26th December one circumstance accidentally gave a special poignancy to her self-pity. Across the cobbled street two upstairs windows were still lit. Behind one window, Mrs Docherty was near her time. This would be her fourth. She would be lucky if it was her last. Here, where hunger and hopelessness should have sterilised most marriages, people seemed to breed with an almost vengeful recklessness. It appeared to her that the sins of the fathers *were* the sons.

Behind the other window, Mr Docherty would be sitting in the Thompson's single-end, banished to that uselessness which was a man's place at such times, sheepish with guilt, or perhaps just indifferent with usage. Some of the folklore of High Street concerned the martyrdom of women: wife-beatings, wages drunk on the journey between the pit-head and the house, a child born into a room where its father lay stupified with beer.

With Mr Docherty, she felt, it would be different. She knew him only as someone to pass the time of day with, as it was with everybody here. She preferred to form no friendships. Pity, contempt, or sheer incomprehension, were the distances between her and everyone around her, so that she knew them by their more dramatic actions. Her vision of their lives was as stylised and unsubtle as an opera, and even then was distorted by those tears for herself that endlessly blurred her thinking, as though something had irreparably damaged a duct.

Her impression of Mr Docherty was not of one man but of several. It was as if among all the stock roles to which she assigned the people of the street, wife-beater, drunkard, cadger, or just one of the anonymous chorus of the will-less poor, he had so far settled for none, played more than one part. She knew him coming home from the pit, small even among his mates, one of a secret brotherhood of black savages, somebody hawking a gob of coaldust onto the cobbles. Cleaned up, dressed in a bulky jacket and white silk scarf, a bonnet on his black hair, he looked almost frail, his face frighteningly colourless, as if pale from a permanent anger. Yet shirtsleeved in summer, his torso belied the rest of him. The shoulders were heroic, every movement made a swell of muscle on the forearms. Below the waist he fell away again to frailty, the wide trousers not concealing a suggestion that the legs were slightly bowed.

She had watched him in the good days of summer, when chairs were brought outside the entry doors on to the street, playing with his children. At such times his involvement with them was total. But what impressed her most was the reflection of him that other people gave. The men who stood with him at the corner obviously liked him. Yet she had often sensed in passing them a slight distance between him and anybody else. It was a strange, uncertain feeling, as if wherever he stood he established a territory. She half suspected it might mean nothing more than that he was physically formidable. In High Street the most respected measurement of a man tended to be round the chest. But her own observations kept crystallising into a word, one she admitted grudgingly: it was 'independence'.

She felt it was a ridiculous word in this place. For what claim could anyone who lived here have to independence? They were all slaves to something, the pit, the factory, the families that grew up immuring the parents' lives, the drink that, seeming to promise escape, was the most ruthlessly confining of all. Whatever hireling they served, owed its authority to a common master: money, the power of which came from the lack of it. Poverty was what had brought herself to this room. It defined the area of their lives like a fence. Still, in that area Mr Docherty moved as if he were there by choice, like someone unaware of the shackles he wore and who hadn't noticed that he was bleeding.

Like an illustration of her thoughts, he came out of the entry at a run, still pulling on his jacket, and became the diminishing sound of his boots along the street. It was a bad sign. Earlier, she had seen Mrs Ritchie go in. A midwife should have been enough. Doctors were trouble. Poor Mrs Docherty. She was a nice woman. They called her a 'dacent wumman', which was High Street's VC. Given the crushing terms of their lives, decency was an act of heroism. Now she lay in that room, trying to coax a reluctant child out of her body. The reluctance was understandable.

Out of the thought of what that child was being urged to come out and meet poured her own frustrations, and she felt all the injustice of her life afresh. She remembered her father, the benign stability of his presence, the crisp, hygienic order of their lives. The solemn family outings. Miss Mannering's School for Young Ladies. Every memory of that time, no matter how fragmentary or trivial, from her father's moustaches to the flowers she had sewn on a sampler, was held in a halo of warmth and security. Everything else, dating from and including the death of her mother, was in partial darkness, merely another imperfectly glimpsed particle of a chaos from which she was still in flight. Even the cause of her mother's death was to this day obscure to her—she only knew it was a disease which had spread its contagion through all their lives. Much later she had understood that the coffin in the darkened parlour contained the corpse of a world as well as a woman. Her father became someone else, the house developed the atmosphere of a seedy hotel where strangers met for meals. When the bakery business folded, her father's heart ran down as if it had been a holding company. He left her what money he had. Her two brothers (which was how her thoughts referred to them, disowning intimacy) wanted nothing to do with an unmarried sister. She had moved from Glasgow to Graithnock and then, as her capacity for pretence diminished with her capital, circumstances had brought her to High Street.

One solitary memory, the persistence of which suggested that it might not be as fortuitous as it seemed, stayed with her as a clue to the chaos that had overrun the serenity and order of her early life. It had happened in childhood: a family breakfast, herself, her mother, father and two brothers. The room, above her father's bakery, was brightly warm, although a November drizzle retarded the daylight outside. The table was heavy with food. They were talking and the boys were laughing a lot when she noticed her father glance at his watch. He sent a question downstairs to the bakehouse. The answer that came back pursed his lips.

Ten minutes later there was a knock at the door and a boy of fourteen or so was pushed into the room. He pressed against the door, as if he was trying to stand behind himself. The old jacket he wore was a man's, the cuffs turned up to show the lining, the pockets bumping the knees of his frayed trousers. His boots were a mockery, ridiculously big and curling up at the toes and misshapen by other people's feet. His scalp showed in white streaks through the hair where the rain had battered it. Hurry seemed to have sharpened every bone of his face to a cutting edge, and had left him hiccoughing for breath. In the warmth of the room he steamed slightly, the smell of him mixing unpleasantly with the fresh cooking odours of the food. The boys giggled.

'Ah'm sorry, sur. Ah'm awfu' sorry. Whit it . . .'

Her father's raised hand stopped him. They all waited while her father chewed his mouthful of food.

'So you are late again.'

The boys were quiet now. The moment had acquired a terrible solemnity.

'Ah'm awfu' sorry, sur. It's ma wee brither. He's that no' weel. An' ma mither . . .'

'Excuses aren't reasons.' Her father was sadly shaking his head. 'This makes three times in less than a fortnight. I've warned you twice before. When you're late, my deliveries are delayed. When my deliveries are delayed, my customers complain. Then they take their custom somewhere else. And my business suffers. You'll have to learn responsibility to other people. Until you do, I can't afford to employ you. You're dismissed.'

Why had that small scene stayed with her? All it had meant to her at the time was the authority of her father – and the kindness of her mother, who had prevailed against her father's better judgement to let the boy have a full week's wages, which came to a shilling, she remembered. Yet compulsively that morning came back to her from time to time, tormentingly, as if that one skinny boy had been the cause of everything that had happened afterwards, as if his unhealthy presence had infected their lives like a microbe. Dimly she sensed herself being nearer to the solution of the enigmatic equation that morning had presented to her: the boy's misdemeanour plus her father's punishment was somehow equal to the disintegration that had taken place in their lives afterwards, was somehow a formula for the kind of chaos she had learned to live in, but not with. And that was as far as rationalisation took her—a vague feeling, not one that she tried to examine, but one that she preferred to smother.

Faced with it, as she was now, her method was always the same. She took a dose of nostalgia, like a drug. In the special atmosphere of this room, she could indulge in a sort of retrospective trance like a religious ecstasy. There were certain passages of her life that she went over again and again, her personal beatitudes. Tonight she thought of the long walled garden at the back of their house, re-creating it flower by flower. It was as something of hallucinatory inconsequence that she was aware of Mr Docherty returning along the dark street with the doctor. The gas-lamp identified them for a moment, and then the close-mouth swallowed them.

Mr Docherty led the doctor up the dark stairway, knocked gently at the door of his house and let the doctor in. Then he himself crossed to Buff Thompson's and went in without knocking, in case he would waken his sons. Mick and Angus had been moved through to Buff's to sleep in the set-in bed nearer the door. Buff, on the chair by the fire, stirred and opened his eyes. Aggie Thompson must have gone back through to help Mrs Ritchie.

'It's yerself, Tam,' Buff said, sat up, coughed quietly, and put a spittle on the fire to fry. 'He's here, then?'

'That's him in noo.' Tam Docherty hung his jacket over a chair and sat down on the stool. 'Hoo's Jenny been?'

'The same, jist much the same. Aggie went through a wee while past.'

They sat watching the fire as if it were a lantern show. The wind was plaintive. One of the boys wrestled briefly with a dream. Water boiled in the kettle Aggie had put on the hotplate. Tam reached across and laid it on the hearth.

'It'll be fine, Tam,' Buff said quietly. 'Don't fash yerself. If it's like the world, that's everything.'

'Aye. As long as it's no' too like.'

Their silence was listening.

In the room across the lobby, the scene that met Dr Allan was like a tableau of all that High Street meant to him. Though the address might have been different, he had come into this room more often than he remembered, to find the same place, the same women, the same secret ceremony happening timelessly in an aura of urgency. It was as if everything else was just an interruption.

The gas-mantle putted like a sick man's heart. Dimmed to a bead of light, it made the room mysterious as a chapel. The polished furniture, enriched by darkness, entombed fragments of the firelight that moved like tapers in a tunnel. The brasses glowed like ikons. Even in this half-light the cleanliness of the room proclaimed itself. Jenny Docherty had scrubbed her house against the birth as if the child might die of a speck of dust. Beside the fire, where the moleskins lay ready for the morning, Aggie Thompson was standing, watching the water boiling, saying to herself, 'Goad bliss ye, dochter. Ye'll be a' richt, noo. Goad bliss you this nicht,' with the monotony of a Gregorian chant. Mrs Ritchie was leaning over the set-in bed, which was as shadowed as a cave, and was translating Aggie's sentiments into practical advice. Over the bedclothes an old sheet had been laid for Jenny to lie on, and under her thighs newspapers had been spread. Her gown was rumpled above her waist. Legs and belly, wearing a skin of sweat, were an anonymous heave of flesh, a primeval argument of pain against muscles.

'Turn up the light,' Dr Allan said.

'Oh, dochter. Thank Goad ye're here.'

'I'll want to wash my hands,' he said pointedly, hoping to soothe Aggie Thompson's nerves with work. 'How long since the waters broke?'

'A good 'oor past, dochter,' Mrs Ritchie said, 'An she's had a show o' bluid. Ah hope ye don't mind comin' oot. But ye couldny put a wink between 'er pains. An it's still no' showin'. An' knowin' the times she's had afore.'

'I wouldn't miss it.' His jacket was off. He was rolling up his sleeves. 'Would I, Jenny? Have these sterilised, Mrs Ritchie.' She took the forceps. 'We didn't do so badly with the other three now, did we?' Her mouth was forming 'No, dochter' when a pain rubbed out the words. He felt her gently, watching. Surprisingly, in the moments of quiescence, she didn't look much more than her thirty, but when the pains came they were centuries passing across her face. Each would leave its residue. In High Street primes were not enjoyed for long.

'Yes I think so. Not long now.' Washing his hands in the basin, he kept talking, more for Aggie Thompson's sake than for Jenny's, who was beyond the use of words as a palliative.

'You must have a terrible comfortable womb in there, Jenny. Your wee ones are never anxious to come out. They need some coaxing. Towel. Thanks.'

In the street outside somebody had started singing. Aggie tutted in shock: 'Is that no' terrible.'

'I have heard better,' Dr Allan said, taking out the pad of chloroform. 'Well, that's enough pain you've been through for triplets, Jenny.'

His hand was a sudden coolness on her forehead. The bottom half of her face came against something soft that seemed to erase her jawline. She fought against a darkness that swooped and then billowed above her and left her falling. Out of emptiness looped one long sound like a rope at which her mind clutched till it snapped: a phrase of song.

'Josey Mackay,' Buff pronounced after a few attentive seconds, as if identifying the call of one of the rarer birds. 'He's late oan the road the nicht.'

The song diminished into garbled mutterings that suggested Josey was in loud and incoherent conference with himself. It wasn't long before he had perfected a public statement, delivered through a megaphone of drunkenness: 'Yese don't know whit it wis like. Yese haven't lived. The lot o' yese. Ah saved yer bacon. Me an' the likes o' me. Mafeking. Ah wis there. For King an' Country. At Mafeking. Queen an' Country.'

'Christ, no' again,' Buff sighed. 'It's weel named the Bore War, eh?'

'The Boer War!' Josey said defiantly. And then more obscurely, 'Honour the sojer. Wounded in the service of his country.'

'Josey's only wound's a self-inflicted wan. He's dyin' o' drouth. An' it's like tae injure a few innocent bystanders. Such as his wife an' weans. There canny be mony gills o' his gratuity left.'

'Sleep soundly in yer beds this nicht,' Josey urged with unintentional irony. 'Thanks tae the sojer laddies. Asleep in foreign soil.'

The Last Post came through Josey's clenched hand. When it was over, they waited for further bulletins. But the silence was restored as abruptly as it had been broken.

'Ah doobt they've goat 'im,' Buff said at last. 'We'll bury 'im in the mornin'.'

Outside, Josey had ceremonially unbuttoned himself and was urinating against the wall below Buff's window. With a soldier's instinct his eyes scouted the winter street. He was conscious of a face somewhere. Cautiously, he didn't look back round but reconnoitred the street again in his mind, trying to locate whose face he had seen. Having decided who it was, he made his plan. Wheeling abruptly, he bellowed, 'Present—arms!' and presented something else. Then he shambled on up the street, buttoning his trousers.

Miss Gilfillan's hand jumped away from the window. The lace curtain fell between her and the street, an armour as ineffectual as her gentility. Her heart protested delicately. She almost wept with shame and anger. She withdrew still further, feeling her privacy under siege, when she saw a dark shape at the Thompson's window.

'Ah canny see 'im,' Buff said. 'He must be away.'

He crossed and sat back down at the fire.

'Away tae yer bed, Buff,' Tam said. 'Ye'll be needin' yer rest.'

'Naw, naw,' Buff said. 'Ah'd like tae see the wean.'

Twenty-past eleven. The minute-hand seemed struggling through treacle. The fire, having forged itself to a block of embers, made the area around it molten with heat, and they sat steeping in warmth. They spoke little. Yet their silence was a traffic, more real than words. They had known each other for a long time and both were miners. Their friendship was fed from numberless tubers, small, invisible, forgotten, favours like help with shifting furniture, talk in the gloaming at the corner, laughters shared. Intensifying these was that sense of communal identity miners had, as if they were a separate species. When Buff coughed, it wasn't just an accidental sound disturbing the quiet of the room. It was part of a way of life, a harshness bred in the pits and growing like a tumour in his breathing. He was at sixty much of what Tam, in his early thirties, would become. And as Buff was Tam's future, so Tam was his past. The mere presence of one enlarged the other, so that now just by sitting here they were a dialogue, a way of ordering the uncertainty of this night into sense.

At ten to twelve a sound came. It was a tear in the stillness of the night, high, cold and forlorn, seeming to pass on through the house as if it would unravel the silence of the town itself. Through the hole it made there bled a steady crying. Looking at each other across the sound, their eyes enlarged into laughter.

'Somebody's arrived,' Buff said.

Tam was on his way to the door when Buff stopped him.

'Hing oan noo, Tam.' Buff was on his feet himself. 'There's things tae be done yet. They'll send fur ye when ye're wanted.'

The next few minutes had no purpose in themselves but only as an ante-room. Tam walked up and down in them, rounding the stool, crossing to the window, and coming back again, making the room a landscape of his impatience. Every time he passed Buff he would nod and smile at him inanely, or wink, or say 'Eh!' as if Buff were several acquaintances and each had to be acknowledged, however absently. A couple of times he punched his right hand into the palm of his left and said, 'Come oan, then,' in a tone of brisk challenge. Once he stopped dead, muttering, 'It must be a' richt,' confidentially to the floorboards, and then went on with measured steps, as if pacing out the exact dimensions of his happiness.

'It's no' short o' lungs, onywey,' Buff said. 'Is it no' hellish, though. Ye go through a' that bother tae get born. An' the first thing they gi'e ye is a skelp on the erse.'

The remark opened a valve on the tension of the whole evening, and they started to laugh. Tam's worry ran out in a kind of controlled hysteria. 'Aye,' he said. 'Aye.' They nodded and smiled. The moment was a conspiracy, a compact sealed – two men agreeing that the fear of each hadn't been noticed by the other.

The door opened and Aggie came through.

'A' richt, then?' Tam had already started to go past her.

'Wait, wait. Fur Goad's sake, man.' She was flushed with the excitement of the sanctum. For a few seconds her experience worked an alchemy on her, made her incongruously almost girlish, a sixty-year-old coquette. 'Whit dae ye think she's been daein'? Passin' wind? Give 'er time. She's no' ready for ye yet.'

'Are things a' richt?' He knew from her face they were, but he felt a superstitious need for the humility of such a question, as if presumption would be punished.

'Everythin's fine, Tam. Jist fine.' Her reassurance became licence for more teasing. 'Nae thanks tae you. If ye saw whit your pleasure costs that lassie. We had an awfu' time bringin' that wee yin intae the world.'

He couldn't feel chastised. Everything that touched him was transmuted into pleasure, even his impatience.

'Whit is it?' he asked.

'It's a lassie. Naw. Ah mean it's a boay'. Her excitement had left her honestly confused.

'Hell, wumman!' Buff said. 'You're a handy messenger. If it's no black, it'll be white. Clear as mud.'

'Shut up, you.' The child was everybody's excuse for having a holiday from habit. 'Whit would you ken aboot it? When you rolled ower an' went tae sleep that wis your joab done, as far as you were concerned.' It was a bitterness fermented over years and only served up now when occasion made it palatable. 'Naw, Tam, that's richt, son. It's a boay.'

'It'll be an auld man before Ah get tae see it.'

A tap at the door refuted him. It was Mrs Ritchie. Going through they formed a little jostling cavalcade behind her, Buff being the tail of it. As soon as he entered the room, Tam took it over. His pride was the master of ceremonies. He flicked his right hand at his wife in a private tic-tac of affection and smiled at her. Freshly washed, her face was a gentle bloat of weariness on which her smile floated, fragile as a flower. Her eyes were already palling with sleep. Tam lifted the child in its sheet and, checking by the way that Aggie's second thought was right, held him up in his hands to inventory his perfection. He had hair, black, a rebellion of separate strands, going in all directions. One temple was badged with dried blood. His face made a fist at the world. The twined remnant of umbilicus projected vulnerably. Hands, feet and prick. He had come equipped for the job.

The room was discreetly tidy. The debris of birth had all been spirited away. Dr Allan stood with his back to the fire, genteely jacketed again, insulating himself against the walk back home.

'Thanks, dochter,' Tam said. 'Aggie, there's a drap whusky in the press there. Fur the dochter.'

'No, thank you. I'll be getting back round. And we'd best all get away and let the lassie sleep. She's a far distance to come back from.'

'We'll no' be long. But ye'll hiv some. It's Hogmanay the nicht, as faur as Ah'm concerned.' Knowing that Tam Docherty didn't keep drink in the house, Dr Allan decided not to offend against the special provision he had made. 'An' wan fur Buff as weel.'

'Whit's he done tae deserve a whusky?' Aggie had found the whisky and two glasses Tam had laid ready.

'Ah've suffered you fur foarty year,' Buff said.

'Well.' The doctor raised his glass of whisky. 'Here's to . . . whoever he is. Have you got a name?'

Tam hoisted the baby round to face them: 'Cornelius Docherty to the company.'

The name seemed to drown him, like regal robes on a midget. The doctor sipped.

'That's a terrible size of a name for such a wee fellow.'

'He'll grow tae fit it. Don't you worry.'

'Whit aboot yerself, Tam?' Aggie asked. 'Ye could likely dae wi' a drap.'

'Naw. Thanks, Aggie. But Ah'm drunk enough already, withoot drink.'

'Ah'd oaffer ye mine, Tam,' Buff said, looking disconsolately at what wasn't so much a finger as a fingernail of liquor, 'if Ah could fin' it.'

The doctor took another sip, and spoke meditatively, as if whisky were philosophy: 'What are you going to make this one, then? A Hindu? You've got two religions in the house already.'

'He's a' Ah' wid want tae make 'im as he is. A perfect wee human bein'. Whit mair could ye want? Except fur him tae get bigger. Be mair o' the same.'

'He'll certainly have to get bigger. Before he's ready for the pits.'

'He'll never be ready fur the pits. No' this wan. He'll howk wi' his heid. Fur ideas.' He winked at the baby. 'Eh, Conn? Ah'm pittin his name doon fur Prime Minister. First thing in the moarnin'.'

Their laughter ebbed to a still contentment. Mrs Ritchie sat smiling in self-satisfaction by the fire. Buff took his whisky a meniscus at a time. Aggie had put temptation back into the press. Jenny was adrift in drowsiness, her body flotsam abandoned to her weariness. One white hand was being held in Tam Docherty's, while in his other arm he still cradled his son. Dr Allan leaned into the cushion of heat behind him. His professionalism being disarmed by tiredness, he saw the scene as a fortress of people built protectively and perhaps hopelessly round a child. He remembered how at the birth he had put the child to the bottom of the bed, a parcel of useless flesh, while he concerned himself with the mother. It was Mrs Ritchie who had skelped him into life. She would talk about that and it would swell in the telling, would become a story of a life stolen from the jaws of death. The child came trailing legends, became in the act of being born more than himself. For Tam Docherty he had existed before himself, had been a name, an idea, just waiting for flesh. He saw a tacit but deeply held sense of triumph in which all these people shared. No matter what their lives did to them, this was what they salvaged, this unsmirched new beginning. Conn lay, hubbed in their middle, raw as a fresh wound, and seemed suddenly to Dr Allan impossibly burdened with the weight of all their lives. As the doctor lifted the glass again to his mouth, it was a private toast. With it there went a solemn wish for the kind of fulfilment to this beginning that they dreamt of. It was wished for all the more intensely because he could not for a second begin to believe in it.

Across the street Miss Gilfillan's figure glimmered tall and pale as a candle in her window. Around her, High Street, its tenement windows gutted by shadows, closes gaping like abandoned burrows, seemed as dead as Pompeii, a desolation where people were frozen into the sordid postures of their grovelling lives. In her mind there echoed still among them the sound of the child's cry from the lighted window. It came to her not as a birth but as a wail against dying. The ooze of hopelessness had already claimed it. None of them here had any chance. Watching a cliff of cloud slowly erode in the wind, she felt herself dwindle to a small helplessness, her heart contracting to a pebble. The comfort of the past dispersed like a vapour, leaving her shivering in a void inhabited by what people called 'progress'. She sensed it only as a malign presence, like a legendary monster, fabulous with the future, devouring the past, a self-begetting sequence of deformities. As this year died, what successor, more hideous than itself, would it be spawning?

*BOOK I*

# CHAPTER ONE

'This'll be a guid clear nicht fur the poachin',' Tam said. 'Are ye up the road the nicht, Dougie?'

'Naw. It's temptin', mind ye.'

'Up by Silverwood wid be the thing. Whaur Barney saw the ghost. Ye mind?'

'That wis a nicht.'

It was a Saturday evening in summer. Tam and Jenny Docherty were out at the entry-door and had been joined by Dougie McMillan and his wife, Mag. The women sat in the two chairs Tam had brought out. Conn, still too young to have the wider tether of Mick and Angus and Kathleen, who were over in the park, was playing quietly at their feet, already wise enough to forestall bedtime by being unobtrusive.

'We're aboot due fur the "Store Races" again,' Jenny was saying.

'Aye.' Mag shook her head.

It was a term coined by the corner-wags for the beginning of the Co-operative Stores quarter. Jenny lamented the chance it would give certain people to exploit what she called 'their fella bein's'. The method was simple enough, though not without its risks.

Since the dividend was good, usually above two bob in the pound, some members made a habit of allowing non-members to buy goods in their name, with the proviso that the dividend from the purchase came back to them. Since such an order was on tick and didn't have to be paid till the end of the quarter, the non-members could enjoy a brief Utopian sense of luxury without cost.

'The day of reckoning,' Mag pronounced.

'Aye, an' the cost isny jist in money,' Jenny said.

Living next door to the grocery, Jenny had seen the effects often enough: families 'racing' to the shop at the start of the quarter, descending like locusts on the counters, to take away provisions in clothes-baskets, hand-carts, bogeys. The crunch came at the end of the quarter. Furtive visits were paid to people like Suzie Temple in New Street. She was fabled to have wealth (though she lived in a house where strips of margarine box were nailed across the frames of old chairs). The eyes of certain women took on a desperate, preoccupied look. 'Store Fever' it was called.

'They say Suzie Temple's no' keepin' too grand,' Mag said.

'Christ, yon wis some nicht.' Dougie had been re-creating it in his memory. 'Ye mind Ah wis sittin' oan the bankin' at the side o' the road. Stringin' the rabbits. Ah had them roon ma neck.'

'Barney had been et the dancin', had 'e no'?'

'Aye. Nae moon tae speak o'. Ah gets up an' says, "Barney. Whit time wid it be?"'

Tam was starting to smile.

'He stoapped deid. A' he could see wis the white o' the scuts. Swingin' in the daurkness. An' he's away.'

'Oot o' trap wan. Through hedges an' fields. They tell me you coulda stertit a ferm wi' the muck that came aff his troosers.'

'Wi' his ain brand o' manure thrown in, nae doot.'

They had coaxed themselves to laughter, Tam leaning on the wall for support.

'Your time has come,' Tam said. 'That's whit he said the ghost said tae 'im.'

Along High Street other families had brought out chairs and were chatting in the mellow sunshine. A well-to-do family—husband, wife and two daughters—were strolling towards where Tam and the others stood. That was a common enough occurrence. Quite a few families from better districts made such a walk a Saturday evening event in summer. It could be very interesting.

On this occasion the man was pointing things out to his wife as they went past. A phrase of his talk drifted towards them—'people actually living there'. The girls looked mostly at the ground, blinkered with apprehension. The man's hand patted Conn's head lightly as he passed. Looking up, Conn felt his father's hand fit tightly, like a helmet, over his head.

And his father's voice cleft the calmness of his play like a lightning-flash.

'Why don't ye bring fuckin' cookies wi' ye? An' then ye could throw them tae us!'

Conn's mother hissed, 'Tam!'

Immediately Conn had a feeling he would forget but would experience again. It was a completely familiar and secure happening transformed instantly into something foreign and frightening. He saw and heard but couldn't understand.

The man stopped without looking round.

'Aye, sur,' Tam Docherty was saying very quietly. 'Come oan back, then.'

'Please, Tam. Please,' Jenny was whispering.

The woman's linked arm took her husband on. Jenny's face was flushed.

'Is somethin' wrang, Tam?' Dougie asked and felt himself contract in the look Tam Docherty gave him.

'Ye mean tae say ye hivny noticed? Whaur the hell dae you leeve, Dougie?'

Some of the dust of that brief, explosive moment settled on Conn for good.

# CHAPTER TWO

Igh Street was the capital of Conn's childhood and boyhood. The rest of Graithnock was just the provinces. High Street, both as a terrain and as a population, was special. Everyone whom circumstances had herded into its hundred-or-so yards had failed in the same way. It was a penal colony for those who had committed poverty, a vice which was usually hereditary.

High Street and its continuations of Soulis Street and Fore Street made a straight line to the Cross at the centre of town. Together, they had at one time been the main street of the town, a residential district for the rich. But when this predominance was taken over by the roughly parallel line of Portland Street and King Street, the older area, like a tract of land gone marshy, had been abandoned to the poor. Among the less impressive flora and fauna that were now to be found in it, there remained the occasional ghostly reminder of a more grandiose past, like a monument among weeds. One of these was the name people gave to one of the buildings in the Foregate, as Fore Street was more commonly called. The building was known as Millerton Close and was said to have been the town house of Lord Millerton, who had a large estate near Graithnock. During Conn's early years Millerton Close contained at various times in its musty recesses an alcoholic, a family with rickets, and a consumptive mother of six.

In that harsh climate people developed certain characteristics common to them all. Where so little was owned, sharing became a precautionary reflex. The only security they could have was one another. Most things were borrowable, from a copper for the gas to a black suit for funerals.

Wives looked in on one another without ceremony. The men gathered compulsively each night at the street corner, became variously a pitch-and-toss school, a subdued male-voice choir, a parliament without powers. Especially in summer, they would stand long, till the sky had raged and gloomed to ash above their heads. The children, when not at school, were seldom in the house during the day, but could be found indiscriminately deployed among backcourts and doorways and corners of the nearby park, as if they were communal property. The authority of the nearest adult was understood to apply to them all. Conn learned early that when any adult asked him to go an errand, his parents' authority was backing the request, even in the case of old Mrs Molloy (secretly called 'chibby heid' by the boys because of the strange lumps that covered her scalp), who invariably encouraged his compliance with the words: 'Heh, you wi' the big heid an' nothin' in it.'

Underpinning the apparent anarchy of their social lives and establishing an order was a code of conduct complex enough to baffle the most perceptive outsider yet tacitly understood by even the youngest citizens of High Street from the time that they started to think. One of its first principles was tolerance. Being in a context where circumstances blew up the ordinary trials of life into terrible hazards and seemed to have them arranged with the unexpectedness and ingenuity of a commando assault course for living, people learned to accept the crack-ups it led to. Behind every other trivial occurrence lay a stress-point upon which poverty or despair or a crushing sense of inferiority had played for years. Consequently, frustrations tended to explode in most of them from time to time.

Sometimes men would disintegrate spectacularly, beating a wife unconscious one pellucid summer evening or going on the batter with cheap whisky for a fortnight. Such bouts of failure were not approved of, but they also never earned a permanent contempt. They were too real for that.

High Street was very strong on rights. Though these might not be easily discernible to an outsider, they were very real in the life of the place, formed an invisible network of barriers and rights-of-way. It was morality by reflex to some extent, motivated often by not making the terms of an already difficult life impossible. Yet there was as well behind it a deep if muffled sense of what it meant to be a man, a realisation that there were areas which were only your own, and that if these were violated formidable forces might be invoked.

Adultery, for example, was a rare phenomenon. This was partly because the public nature of private lives and the sheer drudgery of coping with large families legislated against the contrivance of such situations. Overwork is a great provoker of chastity. But it was mainly because such a step took you on to a dark and slippery ledge, and out of earshot of the predictable. Whereas in more polite society such an action might mean the dissection of a private pain in a public place, in High Street, where a divorce court seemed as distant as the court of the Emperor must have seemed from a fortress on the Great Wall, the direction was reversed. The situation became more private, was injected to ferment in one man's skull. People averted their eyes, awaiting an outcome. The commonest one was what they called with chilling simplicity 'a kicking'. And they would have found it hard to blame a man who forgot to stop. It was simply that they understood men as bundles of conflicting and frequently immeasurable impulses, usually imperfectly contained by a fraying sense of purpose. Whoever slipped the knot would have to abide the hurricane.

For the rest, where the offence was venial, the violence was formal. Two men would go up a Sunday morning road to a handy field. Shirts off, they would punch the affair to a settlement. But such manual litigation was seldom. Relationships were so well charted through countless small daily contacts and endless conversations that there had evolved an instinctive hierarchy ranging from those with whom most remarks or attitudes were permissible to those it would be unwise to provoke. Near the top of it was Tam Docherty.

Tam was very much liked and they would have liked him more if they had known what more in him there was to like. But he was largely in shadow. Forbidding and indistinct attitudes relating to the Church and working-class life and conditions of labour obscured the clear contours of his nature, like clouds of vaguely thunderous potential. At the corner, talk of the priesthood seemed to aggravate the phlegm in his throat, so that the parabolas of spittle became more frequent, but he would say little. His name wasn't a pleasant sound to more than one pit manager in the district. He lived very much in a personal climate of squalls of sudden temper, spells of infectious pleasure that couldn't be forecast, brief winters of brooding isolation that were apparently unrelated to events around him.

Conn himself sensed this even in his early years. He learned to live comfortably among the mad swoops of affection which left him spinning in his father's hands above a ring of laughing faces, the still silences, the instant angers which his mother was expert at earthing. The anger was the more frightening for being usually incomprehensible.

But for Conn, High Street was a second mother who had secret ways of dispelling every worry. He learned the repeated moods of the place like a favourite story, savouring, dumb with delight, the parts he loved the best: the Saturday morning muster of groups of children, when the big ones were there, romantic as convicts in their freedom from school, fabulous with unimaginable experience, making involved plans that put him in an ecstasy of fear, while the week-end stretched before them like a continent; the time just before tea when the men the grown-ups called 'the heavy squad' came down from the Townholme forge and their boots made sparks on the cobblestones; when the men stood at the corner and they might box him, or his father, hunkered against the wall, would make of his legs a place where Conn could crouch and nothing could touch him; the street giving itself up to darkness, a mother leaning out of her tenement window, lassoing her son by his name in the thickening dusk.

At the top of High Street you could walk down Menford Lane, a street that died, like progress, in a factory. To its crevices clung the smell of wool and dye and human sweat, a fungus imparting dark dreams of manhood. Machines gnashed behind black windows, chewing shouts and laughter. A woman's song drowned. After its shadows, the street bruised your eyes with its brightness. The place they called The Gates was good. You went between houses, under an arch, along a causeway, through a gate. It was all grass behind the buildings where the washing was, green hummocks dropping towards the river. Soldiers bivouacked under dripping blankets. Pirates parleyed in the wash-house. Mothers came, following their own shouts.

Crouching, as if you were looking for something on the cobbles, you could see into Mitchell's pub. The door was always open. In the dimness men moved, miles away. They dipped their mouths in tumblers. Voices curled like smoke out into the street. The words lingered strangely before they disappeared, exciting and unremembered. Sometimes a man coming out would stop and laugh and look into his pockets for a penny. The window of Mrs Daly's shop was low enough to let you look in, your tongue wandering in imagination through boxes that made neat segments of colour like toy orchards. Inside she moved about in a gentle fuss of rustling clothes and sibilant words, chapping nuggets of vinegar toffee on to a scrap of paper, counting out Jap Desserts or aniseed balls, or handing over a lucky tattie into which you bit expectantly.

Opposite the Meal Market, a huge tenement at the corner of Union Street, was the opening to the park. It was down a dip, so that you had to run and, crossing the bridge in a group, you became a herd of horses. Below you, running along the backyards of High Street, the river was visible for a hundred yards of Amazonian variety. At the top beyond the mill it churned down over the Black Rocks, then planed into a pool where men and boys swam in summer. The water was black—over twenty feet deep, they said. Dripping water on the bank, they told stories of dogs down there. Flowing on, the river took blue bilge from the mill and whorled it into fantastic, vanishing shapes, broke into a thousand freshets on the rocks, before, just as it passed under the bridge, stretching tight as a skin and sheeting over a three-foot drop to a sapple of bubbles, from which in season a trout would sometimes volley into the air. Then it slung itself under the railway arch and away. The bridge led into the Kay Park, a bowl of grass with a bandstand as its centre.

In one of the yards in Soulis Street they made wheels. When you stood in it, you breathed wood-pollen, like being inside a tree-trunk. On the days when you felt brave, you could take a friend and creep into the stables under the railway arch that marked the beginning of the Foregate. Behind each door dusk was stored in huge warm slabs, veined delicately with sun-streaks. Straw fissled, inventing shapes in the darkness. A snuffle was a horse, invisibly inhabiting its breathing. A hoof threshed, and you ran. And always around were the people coming and going, a forest of faces.

Home was safety. The Dochertys were lucky in having two rooms, unlike most people in the street. There was the living-room with its two set-in beds, in one of which Conn slept, while his mother and father had the other. The kitchen which led from it was minute. The small room at the back was where Mick and Angus slept. Kathleen used the bed that folded into the press behind the outside door. The fire was a permanence and the area around it was centre-stage, where all the best things happened, where his father told him stories, where the others sat at night talking while he pretended to be asleep, where he could watch his father's body bulge from the zinc bath as the water turned black. The sheer regularity with which the same things happened every day in this house was his greatest comfort.

It was as well that he had the underlying stability of such a routine, for his relationships with his family were mainly confusing. Only his mother and Mick were always themselves. His mother's lap was the best place he knew, and usually available, and even when she was angry it simply meant that a bonus of affection was coming up. Mick was patience on legs. He would let Conn wrestle him, punch him, threaten him, and his only retaliation was laughter.

But his father was several men, not all of them nice. Kathleen frequently treated Conn's presence like a bit of accidental lumber and often tried to sweep him out of doors. Angus was the worst. Playing with him was for Conn like trying to work a machine he didn't understand. Every so often his fist would come out like a piston, and Conn couldn't tell which lever he had pulled this time. Whenever he was around Angus, Conn kept in trim for flight.

Yet even these uncertainties became a kind of fixture. And the first few years of Conn's life taught him that things were unchangeable. All there could be was his father coming in from the pit, his mother roughing his hair as she put him to bed. Time was High Street, Angus bullying, Mick laughing, Kathleen bustling.

Then he had to go to school. It astonished him that the simple expression of his unwillingness to go didn't banish the necessity. Out of the rubble of his old security he picked some weird new perceptions: that Kathleen's chest was getting bumpy, that Mick could touch the top of the door if he jumped, that Angus could lift a full pail of water off the ground. His having to go to school was just part of the general strangeness.

So he went. Very soon he accepted it. It didn't occur to him that Angus was the only other one of the family who attended the same school at the end of the street. It didn't occur to him that Mick and Kathleen were going somewhere else.

# CHAPTER THREE

Not long after he started attending High Street School, Conn came in from playing one evening, resignedly expecting to be sent to bed. But two things about the room threw routine out of joint: his father, who had come home late from the pit and wasn't long washed, stood still stripped to the waist and heating a clean shirt against the fire which faceted his body into planes of brightness; Grandpa Docherty sat beside the fire, smoking a blackened clay pipe. Conn liked his Grandpa. He was brown and thin, with enormous hands and a gentle voice that didn't belong here. When Conn's family visited his house, he would talk almost exclusively to Conn and, if his father wasn't there, would let Conn play with the strange, worn beads he carried in his jacket pocket.

Now he winked an invitation to Conn and stood him between his legs. He just sat there staring at Conn with a kind of mournful affection the boy couldn't understand. The hugeness of his hands obscured the pipe-bowl completely, so that he seemed to be grasping fire. Conn writhed uncomfortably, sensing the unfamiliarity of the room. It was as if it was no longer one place but sectored into different areas. His father was taking too long to heat his shirt. His mother was completely absorbed in folding the washing in her basket. His grandfather watched him hypnotically. Kathleen sat on the stool, staring interestedly at her grandfather.

Conn was glad when his mother said, 'Oan ye go oot, son. An' play a wee while longer. Kathleen, you watch the wean.' Kathleen tutted but took him out, his grandfather releasing him reluctantly.

With the children outside, Jenny Docherty put aside her basket of washing, pushed a loosened bang of hair behind her ear, and said brightly, 'Well. Ah want a word wi' Aggie. Ah'll see ye before ye go.'

'Right, Jenny,' Old Conn said.

'Right, nothin!' Tam's voice stopped her. 'Ye'll wait, Jen. This is your hoose. Y've a richt tae hear whit's said in it.'

'It's aw richt, Tam.'

'Of coorse it is. So jist content yerself.'

Conn's feet clattered in the entry below them. Then the room filled slowly with silence. Jenny went back to her washing, teasing and folding the clothes repetitively and needlessly. It soothed her, faced as she was with the futility of what was about to happen. This at least was something which offered an immediate return, the comfort and warmth of her family.

It was still light enough outside but the small windows acted as a filter, adjusting the day marginally at both ends, so that dawn was delayed and darkness, as now, was anticipated. The room was already drowning in dusk.

'The nichts is fairly drawin' in,' Old Conn said.

'Aye. Winter's no' faur awa.'

Jenny felt sorry for him, but it was a pity caged in the resentment she felt against the atmosphere he had created. She watched Tam tuck his shirt into his trousers and hoped that he wasn't going to be upset by the conversation that was ahead. Ladling out his enormous plate of soup and setting it on the table by the window, she felt a helpless love for him. He had been drinking. She knew that was why he had been late. It hadn't been much, but he did it so seldom that even a glass of beer showed. Each eye glowed with an almost imperceptible fuse of temper.

She had learned to recognise these times and understood them. At first she had tried to oppose them but not now. They were infrequent and, since he disliked them as much as she did, all you could do was minister to them like a nurse until the pain passed. For pain was what lay at the centre of them. Tam despised the way drink was used in High Street as a means of escaping from yourself. There were occasions when he enjoyed having a drink, and that was all right. But there were others, which both of them recognised, when the drink was a toast to his own despair. Of these he was always ashamed.

Tacitly both understood that there was in him a kind of malignancy, a small hard growth of bitterness which lay dormant most of the time but would spasmodically be activated by an accumulation of imperceptible irritations. When that irreducible nub of frustration discharged its pus, it created in him an allergy to his own life. The result was anger against whatever was nearest to him at the moment. It wouldn't last for very long but, while it did, it was like being locked in with a thunderstorm. His rage might flash out on anything, one of the children, herself, an inanimate object. They still had in the house a clock which his fist had petrified at ten past nine. It lay in a drawer as a bit of family history, an antique of anger. It had become a secret joke between them. Sometimes when his anger was swelling, she would say quietly, 'Aye, it'll soon be ten past nine, Tam.' And he would give himself up to selfconscious laughter.

Another salve she used was to say, canting her head to have him in profile, 'My! Ye're gettin' to look awfu' like Gibby Molloy.' Old Mrs Molloy's only son, who lived alone with her, two entries along from them, was the local exemplar of pointless fury. Every once in a while on a Saturday night he drank himself into a state of revolutionary ardour. Coming home, he would methodically set to work—to a stream of background noises which included an obscene roster of his personal enemies, repetitive denunciations of 'them' and 'youse', and spontaneous slogans of vaguely proletarian bias—battering down the door of the outside toilet. Every Sunday morning after such a night, he was out early, quietly and efficiently replacing the curtain on that small tabernacle of public decency.

Anyone seeing him on these occasions found him at his most benign and pleasant. He never alluded to the previous night but went about his work with pleasant forbearance, as if he was repairing damage from a very localised storm. Nobody tried to analyse what dark neurosis related Gibby periodically to his toilet in alternate conflict and reconciliation. It was a release which bothered nobody, since the toilet was out of commission for a few hours of darkness once in the space of several months. It became an accepted social phenomenon, an occasional talking-point. Someone might say, 'He's surely gettin' mair regular, is he no'? Wis it no' jist at the end o' last year the last time?' One of the communal jokes was that Gibby was working at the fulfilment of a secret ambition to be a maintainer of toilet doors.

By categorising Tam's anger with Gibby's, Jenny could sometimes negate it. But the effectiveness of her kidding was dependent on her knowing the times when it was an impertinence. She was afraid that this might be one. As she watched him sit at the table, his hair still damp from the washing, his hands tearing pieces of bread and dunking them in his soup, she tried to console herself with the thought that if he was entering one of his black phases, he would make up for it later. For afterwards his mood tended to be as expansive as a meadow, and it was like when she had first known him. Placatively, she turned to Old Conn.

'Wid ye like a plate yerself?'

'Nah. Thank ye, Jenny. But Ah'm no' long bye wi' mine.'

She went back to folding her clothes, abstracting herself from their presence. Old Conn communed with his pipe. Tam ate. The only sign that everything was not normal was that the paper, which Tam usually mouthed over painfully during his meal, lay unread on the table.

'Weel, feyther,' Tam said. 'Whit is it?'

'Oh, Ah wis jist walkin', an' Ah thocht Ah'd look in.'

'Aye. Jist the same wey as ye hivny done fur a year or twa.'

'Ah'm no' as young as Ah used tae be, Tam. Ah don't get aboot as much.'

'Naebudy's complainin'.'

The terms of their exchange were stated. Tam was refusing to meet him anyhow except frontally. Old Conn was habitually a slow talker. Every sentence tended to be the harvest of long thought. He punctuated the silences with words. His inflections, the ghost of slower days in Connemara, made even argument a wistful air, against which his son's guttural Lallans was a jarring discord.

'Ye're a sair hert tae yer mither, son,' Conn said, still wanting to seduce a response from him rather than demand it. 'She's that worried.'

'Ah see ma mither every week. Ah ken hoo she feels.'

'Do ye? Aboot the wee one?'

'Aye. Ah thocht that's whit it wis. Because he's no' et the Catholic schil.'

'Why is he no', Tam? Angus wis bad enough. Noo that's two o' them at Protestant schil. Why d'ye send them there?'

'Because it's nearer.'

'Oh, Tam!' The old man gave the words a profound sadness and at the same time a terrible finality, as if they were an excommunication. He seemed surprised that Tam, with such blasphemy scarcely cool on his lips, could still rise from the table, tear a spill from his newspaper, cross to the fire and light a cigarette.

As far as there had been a conversation, it was finished. Old Conn had come up against a familiar opacity that to him was fathomless and frightening. Whatever thoughts he had once had were long since stultified into attitudes, and these were all he could offer a situation which hurt him brutally. He retreated behind them now with a kind of glazed automatism. These formalised exchanges were an area of earned articulacy between them, being a frequently experienced conclusion to their attempts to meet each other on this issue. While Old Conn read his son the sermon of his wayward self, Tam, tying on his good boots across the fire from him, gave him the ritual responses.

'Whit's happened to ye? Sometimes Ah think Ah should never hiv left Ireland.'

'Naw. That's richt. Then we could all've starved in a state o' grace.'

'Where d'ye get yer thochts? Yer blasphemous thochts.'

'They grow in pits. Ye can howk them oot wi' the coal.'

'Nae wonder ye've had trouble gettin' jobs. The way ye talk. Ye've never known yer place.'

'Ah've still tae find it. In the meantime, ma place is wherever Ah happen tae be.'

'Look roon ye! Ye've a hoose an' a family an' a guid enough joab. Ye don't know hoo lucky ye are. When Ah came over here . . .'

'Ah ken, Ah ken. Ye chapped the door o' Kerr the builder. An' he let ye sleep in a shed fur a fortnicht. An' ye worked two weeks fur jist the price o' yer meals. Did he chain ye up at nichts, feyther?'

'Tam!' Jenny's voice as she turned from her washing surprised them both, the shock it expressed providing an objective measurement of the distance between them.

Tam stood up and when he spoke it was an indirect plea to his father for a truce.

'Luk, feyther. We've had a' this afore. Ah ken ye had it rough. An' Ah'm sorry. So there it is. But that's nae excuse fur kiddin' oan this is comfort. It's mebbe better, but it's no' guid.'

'Ye're too taken up wi' the body. Instead o' the soul.'

'So are a few folk, feyther. Ah don't see mony priests wi' malnutrition.'

'Whit aboot the wee fella? He's got a soul too, ye know.'

'Then let Goad fin' it.'

Old Conn retracted from him, as if not sure how closely God could localise his thunderbolts. He shook his head in disbelief. Tam put his white silk scarf round his neck, collected his jacket and cap, wanting to avoid further abrasion.

'Ah'm awa doon tae the corner, Jen. Ah'll no' be long. Dae ye want tae hing oan, feyther? Or wull Ah walk ye doon?'

His father said nothing. He stared at the fire, letting Tam and Jenny look at each other across a silence. His eyes looked watery in the firelight. Having sounded the depth of his bafflement, he looked at Jenny, but spoke at Tam.

'Ye never learned talk like that fae oor family,' he said softly, deliberately.

Tam's voice hardly ruffled the stillness: 'Whit does that mean?'

'It's a' richt, Tam,' Jenny said quietly. 'Forget it.'

'Whit does that mean?' Tam shouted.

The old man looked back at the fire.

'Ah mean whit Ah mean,' he said.

'Naw!' Tam was bending over him. 'That's the last thing you mean. You mean whit Father Rankin tells ye tae mean. See that.' He pointed at Conn's head. 'There's nothin' in there that belongs tae you. They confiscated yer bloody brains at birth. An' stuffed their stinkin' catechism in their place. Auld man. Whit gi'es you the richt tae think bad o' ma wife? Because she's Protestant. Damn yer stupidity! Look!' Old Conn's right hand was in his jacket pocket, and Tam yanked roughly at his arm until the hand emerged, the rosary beads he held in it spilling out roughly, like entrails. Tam took them from him. 'Bloody toays! Ye're still playin' wi' yer bloody toays!'

Tam and his father stared helplessly at each other across the rosary as if it was a frontier. On the one side was Old Conn's unassailable acceptance of his life. On the other lay Tam's personal experience, a wilderness of raw ideas and stunted dreams, a desperate landscape which this instant set before him like a map. He read in it his own despair, understood it, not rationally, but more deeply than that, because he had learned it in his blood. He saw the bleak terrain of his own life stretching before him without stint. The one oasis was his family. The rest was work that never blossomed into fulfilment, thought that was never irrigated with meaning. The absence of certitude made a moor of the future, and inarticulacy lay over everything like a blight. He felt a grotesqueness in his efforts to impose himself on the forces he was up against, the pettiness of his fights with pit managers, the ludicrousness of a family that had two religions. He had perceptions that enabled him to feel the pain, but not the words to make it work for him. He could only endure.

In this moment the rosary seemed to divide him from a mysterious contentment, perhaps brought over by his father from the rural Ireland he had never seen, born as he had been among the factories and workshops of Graithnock. Beyond that line was a safe place inhabited by his father. But it wasn't his, and he couldn't live there honestly. He realised with sudden hurt that the volume of his voice hadn't meant anger or conviction, but simply uncertainty. Gently he gave back the rosary, and it was as if he was returning to his father every gift which Old Conn had ever given him.

'Ach, feyther,' he said. His hand touched his father's shoulder awkwardly. 'It's a' wan. It disny maitter.'

He cleared his throat and made an attempt to smile at Jenny. Fumbling for a formula, he said to his father, 'Hoo's ma mither keepin' onywey?' And then as their alienation from each other swallowed up the question—'My Christ!'

He turned at once and was going out when Kathleen brought Conn back in, informing her mother, 'Mick an' Angus are jist comin', mammy.'

Their father bumped against them awkwardly. And for a second they were all floundering strangely in the gloom. Then Tam touched Conn's head in his favourite gesture of affection, and went out, leaving on Conn's scalp a message he couldn't understand and which his father couldn't express.

# CHAPTER FOUR

am didn't go immediately to the corner that night. Keeping to the opposite side of the street, he cut off down the Twelve Steps, a dark alley, the steepness of which was periodically eased by short clusters of steps that occurred like locks in a canal. It led down to the riverside. He sat on the dyke and watched the water.

He was waiting for what had happened in the house to catch up with him. What he had said to his father had been not so much a deliberate expression of his thoughts as a stumbling discovery of them, as much a revelation to himself as it was to anybody else. The confrontation had brought from him secrets he hadn't openly acknowledged in his own mind, attitudes he hadn't consciously formulated, but which had become a part of him because of the climate of his life, contracted like a virus from the slow talk of his friends, embedded like the pellets of black powder from the pit-blasts in his face. Now he had declared these attitudes in words and he had to measure himself against them.

The step of doing so wasn't an easy one to take. His mother and father had done their work well. Woven into the whole texture of his boyhood were formative memories of the crucifix on the wall, family pilgrimages to nine o'clock Mass, the catechism, priests whose casual opinions became proverbial wisdom for his parents. His three sisters had made good Catholic marriages. The four brothers he would have had if they had lived had all been baptised Catholic. He had always been told to pray for them. Now it seemed like a profanation of their infant corpses to abandon the faith which had buried them.

When he had married Jenny, it was simply because he had wanted to marry her, and the feeling was hot enough to make fuel of anything that got in its way. He had felt no conscious antagonism towards the Church. And since their marriage Jenny had never tried to influence him. When Kathleen and Mick went to the Catholic school, she accepted it. When Angus and Conn attended High Street school, it was his own decision, one made brusquely, as if he didn't want to consider its implications. 'It's nearer' was all he said.

Now at least one implication of that decision was forming slowly in his mind: perhaps he wasn't a Catholic. He felt cold without the word. It had happed his thoughts as long as he could remember. Whatever misery, anger, bitterness, despair had come to him, it had still been vaguely containable in the folds of that loose word, to be thawed to a sort of comfort. Even now he wasn't sure that the word didn't belong to him. He merely suspected that it might not, as if the deciding of it wasn't up to him. He could not make the intellectual choice. He could only sense that he somehow had to be himself, whatever that might be, and it might not be a Catholic. What he felt profoundly was the uncertainty of himself, simply that he had to meet life without protection.

The thing in him as he sat on the cold stone of the dyke, with the river flecking at his feet, wasn't a thought but an emotion. He had buried a part of himself. So he sat accepting the void, without having any good words with which to decorate it, without a reassuring thought in which to enshrine the past. It was as if above him his own cold star had come out. Ill-equipped as he was, he would follow it. Rising, he felt suddenly the complexity of the night around come over him like a blackout. He needed company.

The corner wasn't so much a place as an institution. It had its own traditions and standing orders. Small groups formed round different topics of conversation by a kind of spontaneous cohesion. In the course of an evening, a casual activity, like sparring or conundrums, would isolate certain people in it as if it was a games-room. But a precise observation or a new anecdote would be relayed from knot to knot like an announcement. The various groups remained complementary to a central unit. Solidarity was what it was all about. A typical expression of it had been the night a stranger with a Glasgow accent came to the corner.

He had been drinking, not enough to make him unsteady, just enough to activate his malice and crystallise it in his eyes. There would be perhaps two dozen men at the corner, lined unevenly along the wall of the Meal Market.

The stranger stopped at the first one and said, 'Good evenin', bastard.'

Although his voice was casual, the reaction, even among those who couldn't have caught what he actually said, was instantaneous, like an electric charge passing along them. Twenty-odd men stiffened.

Somebody muttered, 'Naw. Naw, sir,' almost pleadingly.

The stranger walked slowly along the line, mixing his insults with the measured deliberation of someone trying to brew a riot. The silence of the others was a debate. He was a big man. From his jacket pocket a bottle protruded. He might be too drunk to know what he was saying.

'Fine,' a voice said. 'That's fine! On ye go hame noo.'

'Ah'll fight any one of ye first. In a fair fight. Jessies! A bunch o' jessies!'

The main problem was a technical one. His malice was indiscriminate and they couldn't all answer it. The stranger drew lots for them.

'The Pope's a mairrit man,' he said.

He had reached the end of the line.

'A meenit, chappie!' a voice said.

It was Tadger Daly, father of ten. A champion had been chosen. The big man turned. Tadger was walking towards him.

'That's a nasty thing tae say, chappie. Noo . . .'

The big man's right hand was easing the bottle out of his pocket. From about four feet away, Tadger took off. In mid-air his head looped so that it hit the big man's nose, which opened sickeningly ('Like the Red Sea,' somebody later suggested). When the big man lay on the ground, there was a moment in which the physical ugliness of what had happened almost became dominant, until someone said matter-of-factly, 'That's wit ye call doin' penance, big man.'

And another remarked, 'You were the richt man fur the job, Tadger. As the Pope's auldest boy, ye were the natural choice.'

The incident was in perspective. Water and a cloth were brought from a nearby house. Tadger helped in cleaning up the big man. Then a couple of the men conducted him, wet cloth still held against his nose, to the end of the street, off the premises, as it were, and faced him towards the railway station. The whole thing had the quality of a communal action, and had been conducted without rancour.

That night became part of the history of the corner. Any memorable incidents, remarks or anecdotes would be frequently gone over in the nights immediately following their occurrence, like informal minutes of previous meetings. Later, they would recur less often, having been absorbed into the unofficial history of their lives, the text of which was disseminated in fragments among them. Any man who stood at the corner had invisibly about him a complex of past events like familiar furniture, the images of previous men like portraits. The corner was club-room, mess-deck, mead-hall. It was where a man went to be himself among his friends.

# CHAPTER FIVE

B ut tonight it was quiet. A dozen or so were douring the evening out. Tam joined Buff Thompson and Gibby Molloy, who were standing in silence together.

'Aye, Tam,' Gibby said.

Buff nodded and winked.

'A clear nicht,' Tam said.

And each stood letting his own thoughts feed on him.

Their silence was the infinity where three parallel despairs converged. Over the past few years Buff's whole nature had contracted. The gradual recession of his physical powers had taken with it his defensive reflex of wry humour, and left him stranded on the hard, unrelieved futility of his own life. With only a few years ahead of him, he was clenched round a frail sense of purpose that was diminishing to nothing. Gibby's natural habitat was moroseness. Living alone with his mother, held in a net of trivia, his life consisted of occasional spasms of wildness contained in a long inertia.

For Tam the moment was a funeral service for a former self. Tam Docherty, Catholic, seemed finally dead. He couldn't resist going back to memories of his boyhood, like holding a mirror to the corpse's mouth. But no strong doubts came to cloud his thought. There was in his head a clarity, a cold emptiness. The talk of the others at the corner seemed less related to him than the sound of the river had.

He still hadn't spoken by the time Dougie McMillan came up. Dougie wasted no time.

'Ah'm lookin' fur a local lad wi' a notion o' the game,' he said. He flashed his jacket open to show that he was wearing his professional pockets. 'This is a nicht that wis made fur poachin', boays. Ah' can *smell* the salmon. They're lyin' doon at Riccarton Water waitin' tae surrender. Noo Ah've a couple of vacancies. Wan oan the net an' wan tae be steerer. Who's it tae be?'

The others laughed.

'Who'll pey the fines?' Buff asked.

'Ma lawyers attend tae a' these wee things. Noo, come oan, boays. Don't make a rush like this. Form an orderly queue. Buff, Ah'm sorry Ah hiv tae turn ye doon. Ye're guid but ye're auld, son. Tam Docherty. There's ma man. The finest hundred-yards melodeon-player in Ayrshire. Tammas. Ah guarantee success. Riccarton's yer oyster. I will make youse fishers of fish.'

Since Tam's mood was unemployed, and since this was a night for picking out the lining of your pockets, he felt interested in any diversion. He let Dougie banter him into the idea of a poaching expedition. Gibby, who had been wilting with boredom for more than an hour, suddenly bloomed with enthusiasm, and insisted on offering his services. Conscious of the danger involved in using somebody subject to such unpredictable fits of not unobtrusive violence, Dougie was doubtful. He only agreed after making clear the special terms of Gibby's contract.

'Nae brainstorms,' he cautioned, as if they were a hazard as avoidable as taking matches down the pit. 'An' if we pass ony shithoose doors, fur any favour shut yer e'en. In case ye get the notion.'

Gibby nodded soberly, guaranteeing sanity at all times. Now that the outing was fully manned, there was an atmosphere of expectancy as they waited for darkness. Gibby especially was impatient. He had suggested that he should go up and let his mother know, in case she worried. But when Dougie replied that she might not let him out to play again, Gibby abandoned the idea sheepishly. Dougie had the net and a couple of rough towels in the special pockets that were sewn inside the jacket, so that there was no need for anybody to bring more gear. Even Buff caught the fever. While they waited, he recounted a long, involved story about how he had been taught the art of guddling salmon. He looked a little forlorn, mulling his memories, when they left him in the gloaming to walk down through the town.

As Tam went with them, the night that was coming seemed to mute the hardness of the town with an influence like a woman's, draped a corner with shadow, made a back lane pungent with the breath of trees. Blowsy with summer, scented with a thousand subtle mysteries, it seduced him from his loneliness and made him feel right simply to be walking towards the dark. The smells he moved among were like an aerial language, incomprehensible to him yet instinct with memory as if, could he decipher them, they would tell him who he was. He let their soundless babble break over him, feeling quicken far within him vague sensations, half-thoughts.

He remembered the summers of boyhood, not as a continuity, a part of his own history, but in one small instant ecstasy of pain, as if a bubble of blood were bursting in his heart. Borne on the air, it seemed, like dragonflies, as faint, as glimpsed, as fleet, came his regrets for what he had been, was, would never be. But they were gentle with him, as if to acknowledge them was partly to atone. Irrelevantly, the three of them walking brought back to him another night, and miners walking. He had been only a boy, ten, twelve years old, but he was there among them—miners, thousands his memory made them, walking through the darkness towards a hill. They held a meeting.

That memory still held him, when they emerged from the town along the river's edge. The darkness was waiting for them like a friend. Having made the night's acquaintance at moments in his journey through the town, Tam was still unprepared for the immediacy of its full embrace, the ripeness of its breath, the sweetness of the grass. The focus of sounds shifted, whispers magnified. The river, gagged by the town, survived its interruption to resume myriad tonal changes, like the articulation of infinity. Along the sound they walked in single file, Dougie in the lead, interpreting for them scutters in the grass, a baffle of movement somewhere in the dark.

Dougie was in no hurry to begin. He walked them long and when he found a place (a comfortably grassed chaise longue between two trees that was invisible till flattened, so that his skill had seemed to invent it), he sat down and took out his cigarettes. They smoked and talked, their voices moling gently back and forward in the darkness. It was good to listen to Dougie. He talked about poaching, stories of legendary whippets, wayward ferrets, night fishings when the catches had been Galilean. More than the anecdotes themselves Tam enjoyed the idiom in which they were expressed. Apart from the creativeness of his memory, Dougie made liberal use of expressions like 'It was that quiet ye could hear the snails breathin'', and 'The watter wis oily, throwin' the sun like arra's in yer e'en.' He was savouring the prelude to action, content to initiate them slowly into his joy in what he was doing. He didn't lech after the salmon; he loved them truly.

The first part of the ceremony over, the baptism followed. They undressed quietly, sloughing three heaps of clothes among the trees. Phosphorescent with pallor, their bodies separated, flickering like tapers through the leaves. Tam and Dougie moved down river, Gibby in the opposite direction. The uncertainty of the surface they were crossing dehumanised their progress, feet raised and lowered jaggily, arms wavering for balance, so that they seemed like three enormous birds which had never fledged. Tam felt the coldness of the night film on his body like frost.

The method was simple. Taking an end of the net each, Tam and Dougie insinuated themselves into the water, which compressed the muscles of legs, torso, and arms in turn, like a torture box, until the coldness located the genitals and clenched there like a bulldog. Then they teased the net into a gentle curve behind them and started to swim very smoothly upstream, towards where Gibby should be. A strangled gasp located him. The noise didn't matter, since his function was to cause enough disturbance to drive the fish towards them. He performed well above and beyond the call of duty. The water boiled above them and among the threshings, his curses and agonised pleadings played like flying fish. The impression was of a man acting in self-defence. Tam and Dougie felt small impacts take place within the steady pull of the river, like pulse-beats being missed. Slowly they swam the ends of the net together and hauled it out.

It was all done twice, with an interval for Gibby to offer up prayers of intercession to the god of poaching for the preservation of his manhood. They caught eleven good salmon and six or seven miscellaneous midgets, which Gibby wouldn't allow them to throw back, saying he had a client for them.

Buffing his body back to warmth under the towel, Tam experienced a profounder feeling of accomplishment than he had known for a long time. When they were dressed and walking back along the river with their catch, he watched Dougie, a cigarette in his mouth, the smoke drifting round his nostrils like incense in the stillness of the night. His face reminded Tam of the way his father's used to look when the family was returning from the Mass. Tam felt envious of the relationship Dougie had established with his life. With the chaos around him he had made his separate peace. Tam was wondering if he could do the same. The well-being he felt at the moment seemed like a promise.

Under the Riccarton bridge, Dougie cached eight of the salmon in a hole beside the river, to be taken to the back-door of the fish-shop in the morning. That gave them one each for the house, and Gibby still had what Dougie called 'the meenies'.

'Whit the hell d'ye want wi' them?' Dougie asked as they came through the backstreets.

'They're fur ma boss, see.'

'Are ye aff yer heid? They widny make a breakfast fur a bumbee.'

'They're no' fur eatin'. Mair a sorta food fur thocht. Ah'm goin' up this wey.'

Gibby made a strange, internal noise of merriment, laughter in the dark caves of his cunning. They had halted on a corner.

'Ye ken hoo holy auld Devlin is?' The other two nodded. The factory-owner's nickname was Jehovah. 'When he peys the wages, he always has a wee service. Hymns an' prayers. An' by the look o' the wages Ah think he chairges us fur them. Always talkin' aboot "The

Plan". Everythin' that happens has a purpose. Well, let 'im work this yin oot. Hauf a dozen fish lying' oan his porch at eicht in the mornin'.' Walking away from them, Gibby had started to cackle. He shouted back, 'If he disny stert buildin' an ark in the backdoor, it's no' ma faut.' He bellowed, 'Salmon! Fresh Salmon!' twice, and merged with the shadows.

'The bastard's daft,' Dougie said, not without reverence, and they walked on.

Coming in, Tam had the momentary sensation of having been away for a long time and yet felt the room fit around him like familiar clothes. After a couple of hours spent with the width of the darkness breaking across him like an ocean, the house seemed more minute than ever. Yet in some strange way this room was bigger than the night, absorbed it into itself until the excitement of the darkness disappeared.

Instantly, what they had been doing was in perspective. The vague notion Tam had had to take up the poaching seriously, to cultivate the pleasure he took in it, dissipated. He felt a little guilty, as if he had been a boy playing truant. He didn't want to be like Dougie. Poaching was a nice enough way to pass the time. But being a man wasn't a hobby. That was what they would like you to do: work your shift and take up pigeons, or greyhounds, or poaching, and hand your balls in at the pay-desk.

He looked round the room, grateful for its pokiness, its poverty. It was a place that couldn't help being honest about who he was. In the glow from the fire the moleskins shone. He listened. Every breath drawn in this house made him bigger, both told him who he was and put demands on him. He heard Conn sigh in his sleep and wanted to see him grow up overnight. What would he be? An office worker? A teacher even? He listened to Jenny's breathing, steady, peaceful—the pulse of his family. How in the name of God did she manage? His wonder was confused with her voice and her laughter and images of her body in bed. He felt an enormous upsurge of identity, and grew aggressive on it. He almost wished he could fight somebody now on their behalf.

Instead, he laughed to himself and started to make a cup of tea. The salmon lolled in the pail of water near the fireplace. There would be some for Buff and Aggie too. As he moved about, taking off his boots and jacket, buttering a piece, masking the tea, he was all the time making small superfluous noises. 'Aye', 'Ah weel', 'Uh-huh'. It was a dialogue with his own contentment. In a few hours he would be back in the pit and tomorrow night he would come home like a dead man, having paid for his loss of sleep. But for the moment time was under control, his servant. As he champed his bread and scalded his mouth luxuriously with great slurps of tea, he was startled by a noise outside, and then recognised Gibby's gentle, chuckling laughter. The sound seemed somehow lovely in the stillness, was like a rose blooming between the cobblestones of the street. And Gibby's amusement pollenated Tam's own little moment, until he found himself rocking with suppressed laughter, shaking his head, a soggy mass of bread held precariously in his mouth.

'Tam?' Sleep made the word an almost indecipherable wedge of sound.

The pressure of Tam's pent-up good humour siphoned itself off into a smile. He had someone to share it with.

'It's King Edward, Mrs Docherty. Ah jist drapped in fur a cup o' tea. The fire's oot in the palace.'

She stirred against an undertow of sleep, trying to ask about where he had been. The sensuous slowness of her movements brushed like silk against his senses. 'Ah'm no' sure,' he said to her half-formed question. 'But Ah ken where Ah'm goin'.' He rinsed his mouth out with the last of the tea and hissed the dregs on to the banked fire.

In bed he had a moment of doubt. She must be tired. But the gossamer hair of her arm breathing against his naked body blessed his urge, absolving him from choice. He won her slowly and gently from sleep, led her up out of the recesses of whatever dream had held her, to meet him. The covers tented above them, encased him with her coilings and the lush sweetness of her sweat. Only once she stinted, whispering, 'We'll waken the wean.' The words were a ridiculous irrelevance, like a naked woman trying on a mutch, and he almost laughed. He brought her to fusion and lay back quickly, muttering, 'Ah'm sorry, son,' to his spilled sperm, 'but we hivny the room.'

Out of the darkness, complete, as if it had been waiting for him there, came what he had remembered earlier tonight—miners walking in their droves towards a hill. He had been sleeping the night with his uncle, Auld Spooly. To keep him company, for Spooly was a bachelor. And Spooly had taken him with him on the march. Just about every pit in Ayrshire went spontaneously on strike. They marched to Craigie Hill and held a meeting.

What he remembered was the sheer awe of looking at their numbers. They had seemed to him enough to do whatever it was they wanted. They still were. The thought of it struck him with the force of a conversion as if he had just realised that he had once been present at a miracle. The void he had created earlier tonight talking to his father filled suddenly, wondrously, with men. He seemed to see again the opaque bulk of their bodies, massing like a storm cloud round the crest of Craigie Hill, to hear again the rumble of their voices, like frustrated thunder, to catch again the name that passed among their tight mouths like a password: Hardie. Keir Hardie. The name fell upon his mind now like a benediction. Keir Hardie knew the truth and was down there, telling it to the big ones. There was hope. Tomorrow he would go in among whatever was waiting, water, slag, bad props, and fetch his coal. And Keir Hardie would do his talking for him.

With the satisfaction of a man who has established the terms of his employment, he turned over on his side to go to sleep.

'Aye, Jenny,' he said, thinking of a detail overlooked. 'Conn goes through wi' the ither boys the morra.'

And the firelight caught his smile and showed it to nobody.

# CHAPTER SIX

Just by his moving out of the box-bed beside his parents' to the same room as Mick and Angus, Conn's life entered a new phase. The change involved no more than a few yards but in Conn's private geography he had crossed a frontier.

The strangeness of things fed his sense of exploratory excitement. The very darkness of the room was different. When he lay in it, there was no fire, no gaslight burning. For a couple of hours or so every night, he was alone in it with the voices of the others reduced to a background music, and in his house solitude was a luxury. At these times he ruled the room, his whimsy was law. His bed was ship, plateau, stockade; storms blew up out of the corner by the window; Captain Morgan boomed in whispers; the packs of wolves ran round the walls; and an enemy was beaten until exhaustion reduced him to a pillow.

Night after night his fantasy made a weird ante-room to the reality in which his family moved beyond the wall. Coming in to check on him, his mother would often find him lying on top of the covers, his body buckled awkwardly as if he had fallen from a height, an Icarus whose wings had melted into the mundanity of rumpled bedclothes, drab walls.

But most exciting of all were the times when he managed to stay awake until Mick and Angus came to bed. He shared a bed with Angus while Mick lay across from them in the isolation to which his rank entitled him. The talks they used to have affected him like a fever. Mostly he didn't really listen to their words, he simply absorbed them like microbes, until they induced in him delusions of manhood.

Mick liked to talk about places he had heard of and would like to go to. The names unfurled like bright colours in the darkness. His gentle voice, self-absorbed as a prayer, put into Conn's mind garish maps of impossible places. Mexico, he said. And Canada. The outback. Bush. Crocodiles that were mistaken for logs. Cannibals. Spittle that was ice before it hit the ground. (If you cried, would your eyes freeze?) Dancing snakes. Conn shuddered ecstatically.

Angus was more immediate. He talked most about himself. His favourite subject was the boys he had fought, closely followed by the ones he would fight. He had always seemed to be physically in advance of his age, and already he gave the impression of a man's strength compressed into a boy's body. Conn, much slighter, jocularly called 'the shakings o' the poke' by his father, listened to Angus with awe, admired him extravagantly, and surreptitiously tested his own biceps below the bedclothes.

Occasionally, Conn would say something himself. But he so often unintentionally evoked laughter, kindly from Mick, rather hooting from Angus, that he found protection in silence. The transmission of each one's secrets to the darkness, the process of almost mystically hallucinating the future—these were part of a complicated rite, in which he was only a novitiate. Letting the other two act as a filter to his own confused experience, he found a temporary perspective through their eyes. They gave more definite shape to his growing pantheon of fears and doubts and hopes. With their attitudes pontificating and his own experience giving tentative responses, there started up in him a dialogue between himself and the circumstances around him. He began, quite simply, to become himself. By trying on his brothers' attitudes he was beginning to measure himself.

At first, he was content to masquerade as them. He accepted Angus's measurement of his father just as somebody who was tougher than anybody else, who could 'easy win' any other man in High Street— which pretty well made him unofficial champion of the world. Conn enjoyed carrying that knowledge around with him like a secret weapon which could get him out of any crisis.

He faithfully filed away Mick's description of old Miss Gilfillan across the street as 'a right lady'. It didn't help much, since he wasn't clear about what a lady was, and watching Miss Gilfillan like a detective didn't clarify things. She remained a grey mystery in the funny way she walked, as if she was on wheels, her lips, which seemed to be sewn together (if you looked very close, you could see the little lines the stitching made), the special look she always gave him no matter how many other children were there, as if they had a secret. (Once she had given him a penny, coming out of her house just to do that. He had played outside quite a lot after that, but she never did it again.) Still, he kept those two things, side by side, Miss Gilfillan and 'lady', like someone memorising a dictionary meaning he doesn't understand. Knowledge is knowledge.

He took over, without modification, his brothers' opinions on a whole range of different subjects. From them he knew that football is the best game, a bee dies when it stings you. Ben Nevis isn't the biggest mountain in the world; the biggest one's in Africa. There isn't a man in the moon. You don't clipe on your friends, or anybody else.

But they also had certain positions he couldn't take up. Their contempt for school always puzzled him. He enjoyed it. Miss Anderson was nice. She told you a lot of things you didn't know. When Mick and Angus occasionally compared their different schools, taking each one room by room and scrawling their hatred across it like vandals, Conn was hurt. He was hurt for the school (especially Miss Anderson), for the way his brothers felt, and for the fact that he was different from them. The confusion depressed him.

Similarly, when it came to posh folk, he could share neither Mick's quiet dismissal nor Angus's aggressive desire to engage every boy in nice clothes in combat. Conn simply didn't see any difference in them. He was happy as he was, and that was enough for him.

Worst of all, his brothers' talk about churches took him out into chaos and abandoned him there. He dreaded the subject coming up and when it did he used to try to will himself to sleep. But their thoughts still wormed into his mind, coiling there into grotesque and fantastic shapes of fear. Though Mick and Angus exchanged Catholic and Protestant images of God with all the aesthetic preoccupation of two boys swapping cut-out pictures, their words innocently invoked in Conn a welter of lurid contradictions.

His fears were intensified by the news of God he picked up from other places in incompatible bits and pieces. In spite of the fact that Catholic and Protestant lived together harmoniously in High Street, in spite of the fact that his brothers and his sister were singularly unconcerned about any religious differences, Conn contrived to worry a great deal about whether God was a Protestant or a Catholic. He was never quite clear which side Jesus had been on. His amorphous doubts made him too vulnerable, so he crystallised them into an irrational fear of priests, who weren't an unfamiliar sight in High Street. Every time Conn saw one coming, he vanished up the first convenient close.

# CHAPTER SEVEN

It had been raining. Having become intolerable in the house, Conn was allowed out as soon as the rain stopped. For a quarter of an hour or so he had been scuffing about the almost empty street, where road and houses were still black from the rain, trying to get his idling imagination to move. Without seeming to have noticed it at any given moment, he became aware of a dark figure coming up from the Cross towards High Street. Conn paused and stared. The dull mother-of-pearl glare of the sky seemed so low as to make a tunnel of the Foregate. The figure came nearer, carrying a stick. It was a priest.

He was already spinning for cover when he saw his father standing in shirt sleeves at the close-mouth, smoking a cigarette. Wondering how long he had been there, Conn gravitated casually nearer to his father and became very interested in a chipped part of the tenement wall where the rain had softened the crumbling inside of the stone.

Sure enough the priest stopped at their entry. Conn stared in awe at the large figure. Father Rankin: a big man, in his early forties, prematurely grey—commonly known as the Holy Terror. He was said to go round certain houses where the husbands were known to lack religious fervour, and hound them out of their beds with his stick to go to Mass.

'Guid day, Father,' Conn's father said politely.

'Not for you, Tam Docherty. Not for you.'

Conn noticed his father's lips purse and his eyes begin to study his cigarette. It was a familiar moment for Tam. For years priests had been coming periodically to the house, to do battle for Angus and Conn over souls the boys didn't know they had. Usually they came in twos, a regular one and a new one, rather like an experienced doctor introducing a medical student to an unusual and particularly difficult case. Tam rather liked their visits. They always helped him to sort his own thoughts out. With a couple of them he had a pleasant, half-bantering relationship. And there was one whom he admired profoundly, Father McDermott, who called Tam 'Doubting Thomas' and insulted him pleasantly while sparring with one of the boys. But Father Rankin was different. When he was angry, his eyes beheld the damned. He felt no need of reinforcements.

'And it won't be a good day for you till you become a proper Catholic again.'

His father glanced at Conn and it was as if he was trying to explain something which Conn couldn't understand. Conn didn't know the significance of the words but the tone of them conveyed a reprimand, even to him. It was the first time he had ever heard anyone speak to his father like that.

'You're a pain to your mother and father. To your whole family. More than that. You're an affront to God.' To Conn the whole day seemed to drop dead, and they were three people standing in a desert of silence. 'Well? Have you nothing to say for yourself?'

'It's still a guid enough day, Father.'

Conn thought he had never seen anybody as angry as the priest. The stick quivered indecisively and when it suddenly swivelled to point in his direction, Conn hung where he was, impaled on the gesture.

'Is this your son?'

His father's voice came very quick and very small, its smallness measuring the force which was compressing it.

'Keep yer mooth aff the boay, Father.'

The priest's eyes enlarged, looking at Conn's father. 'Right,' he said, and moved towards the entry. Almost accidentally, it seemed, his father's hand came up to lean on the wall, so that his arm just happened to bar the way.

'Where wid ye be goin', Father?'

'To speak to your wife.'

'Ah'd raither ye widny.'

'I'm not concerned with what you want.'

'Naw, but Ah am. Slightly.'

The pressure of their confrontation was so intense that it would have seemed impossible to walk between them. Conn stared.

'I'll have to speak to her about all this.'

'She his a lot o' worries, Father. Ah don't think you wid help them any.'

The priest stepped back. The stick went horizontal in his hand. His face was tight with anger.

'Tam Docherty,' he said. 'I have a duty to perform. You're interfering with it. If you don't step out of my way, I'll take my stick to you.'

Conn's father released his breath painfully and shook his head, his eyes closed. Conn couldn't understand what it meant. Despair. Tam was suddenly exhausted by the complicated terms of his life, utterly baffled by the impossible acts of equilibrium it called for. They wanted you to respect authority when authority had no respect for you. They told you what your life meant, and asked you to believe it, when it had nothing to do with what was happening every day in your house and in your head. While your wife slaved and your weans were bred solely for the pits, like ponies, and your mates went sour, the owners bought your sweat in hutches, the government didn't know you were there. And God talked Latin. The rules had no connection with the game. You came out to your door for a smoke and a man walked up and threatened to hit you with a stick. Where did he live? Conn's father opened his eyes and looked steadily at the priest.

'You do that, Father,' he said, 'an' Ah'll brek it intae inch-long bits across yer holy heid.'

The priest seemed hypnotised by what he saw in the other's eyes. Tam's frustration had become almost impersonal to Father Rankin. The priest was no more than the catalyst for many disparate perceptions, of furtive men who turned their masonic certificates face to the wall when they saw a priest coming, drunken women who would rather send their weans to the chapel than see them properly fed, his own father thankfully embracing his life like a galley-slave kissing his oar. The priest shook his head, deciding that philosophy was the best method of defence. He nodded towards Conn.

'The sad thing is. Children tend to follow their parents. Even to the gates of Hell.'

'We'll be company fur each ither then.'

The priest shook his head again, as if Conn's father had unsuccessfully been trying to answer a question.

'What would your father say?'

'Exactly whit you tell 'im tae say. Ye've maybe made a blown egg o' the auld man's heid. But mine's still nestin'. An' ye never count yer chickens till they're hatched. Ah'll let ye know.'

The priest shook his head again, thought for a moment, turned suddenly, and walked away, back down towards the Foregate. Conn looked after the priest, elation mounting. His father had won. Turning to share his sense of victory, he saw his father's face inexplicably bleak as he flicked his cigarette stub on to the wet road and went back into the entry.

But even his father's strange lack of satisfaction couldn't curb Conn's delight. The giant who came to their door had walked away an ordinary man. The street resumed its own identity, became again simply a good place for playing in. Conn carefully lifted the discarded butt of his father's cigarette. It was damp, and spilling shag. He held it gallously between his thumb and the middle and index fingers, and walked around impressively, exhaling manly clouds of air. He felt both security and excitement. It was a stimulating mixture, a boyish version of a sensation quite a few adults had known. If you were a friend of Tam Docherty, his proximity could be exciting. It was like being friends with Mount Etna. The lava never touched you.

That night Conn had something to tell Mick and Angus. It gave him importance. They listened carefully, asking him a lot of questions, and where he didn't have an answer, he made one up. It was one of the first things he had hoarded up to share with them which wasn't diminished by their reactions. He felt as if that one incident had bestowed a status on him.

He never fully lost it again. If not yet the equal of either of his brothers, he was at least an initiated member of the secret lives they led in the darkness of the bedroom, someone with a separate identity. The separateness thrilled him, but it was a pleasure which had to be paid for. There came a phase when he lay awake at nights, drowning in waking dreams, while his brothers slept. He lost himself down strange thoughts, stared for minutes into frightening and bottomless possibilities, got himself trapped within incomprehensible fears where he wrestled for release in a sweating panic.

One night, so long after he had started to sleep in this room that he had forgotten he had once slept somewhere else, he suddenly remembered the box-bed beside his parents'. Mick and Angus were asleep, Mick restless and making strange breathing sounds like a language Conn didn't understand. Conn had been poised for more than an hour on the edge of terror. The room welled with a darkness that lived. Desperate with loneliness, Conn thought of the box-bed, the safety of having his mother and father. He wanted to be there.

Rising, he felt his way out of the room. The coldness of the floor made marble of his feet. He stepped stiffly around Kathleen's bed and saw the fire red below the dampened dross, seeing it not as a fire, something with edges and form, but just as a redness, an inflammation on the dark. Its reassurance weakened him. Wanting to cry and luxuriating in his security, he wondered whether he should just climb into his old bed and be found there in the morning, or should waken his mother and have her voice to comfort him. He had started to move into the room when a strange sound halted him. He realised at last where it came from: his mother and father's bed. But they weren't in it. It was voices which weren't voices, noises only, eerie, involved secretly with each other. He looked towards the darkness of the set-in bed, seeing it like a cave. Sounds soughed in it, a strange, underground sea whose murmurings frightened him.

Standing alone there, he was a stranger among strangers. He could hear the breathing of his brothers and his sister, whispers in the darkness, strange sounds like deformed laughter from whoever lay in his parents' bed. A train clanked and snuffled somewhere, weird as dragon. What was happening?

Cuddling his own dread to him like a doll, he went back. He lay beside Angus and a thousand miles from anyone, rigidly nursing himself to sleep, and weathered the long night like a fever.

# CHAPTER EIGHT

S trange demons haunted the edges of their small lives—periodically exorcised in print. News from chaos. For philosopher,
astrologer and shaman—the papers.

To Jenny it was all merely baffling and depressing. She sensed
portents and dangers to them all moving clumsily behind the words,
trying to break out. She wondered what it could possibly mean to her
mother and father that they should make the paper the highlight of
their day.

Every evening, Angus would come down for half-an-hour or so to
his Granny's single-end in the Pawn Loan just a few doors down from
his own house, and read the paper to them. Granny Wilson could
read, though her husband wasn't too good at it ('Ah only went tae
the schil when they caught me,' he used to say), but her eyesight was
failing, and anyway, Jenny suspected, she liked the excuse for seeing
at least one of her grandchildren for some part of every day. Before
Angus did it, it had been Mick who read to them.

They made a ceremony of it. The reader sat in front of the fire, on
the footstool. On one side sat Mairtin, smoking; on the other, hands
folded on her pinny, Jean ('Jean Kathleen', she would tartly inform
those who wondered why her granddaughter hadn't been called for
her). Custom had assigned them distinct roles. All news relating to
politics and international affairs must await the seal of Mairtin's
attitude. Taking deep puffs of worldly wisdom, he would send out his
dicta to Jean like smoke-signals. 'That Churchill's no' a freen' o' the
workin' man.' 'Turkish swine!' The human-interest stories were Jean's

province. She sighed readily for others, appended proverbs to her pity, descanted on the ubiquity of misfortune.

Perhaps that was wisdom—learning to play again like children among the chaos. But Jenny didn't have that capacity. She was too aware of how their lives were overhung with threats they couldn't control. It didn't occur to her directly in terms of what one nation might do to another, of international crises. It came ciphered into small things—prices, the mutterings of the men at the corner, Tam's growing desperation. She sensed that the small pressures they felt, the twinges that affected every day, related to something bigger, the way that tiredness can mean consumption. She didn't begin to understand it. She only knew that somehow something was wrong.

To that extent she felt older than her parents. They had a simplicity of response to what was going on around them which she envied. God knew they had endured enough themselves. Their lives had been spent among the kind of hardship that didn't exactly nurture naïveté. But perhaps they had lived so long with the imminence of dire happenings that for them it was house-trained.

They had learned to leave the bigger things to those who understood them. Unlike Jenny, they weren't fearful of the incomprehensible equations of chance that tried to resolve themselves around their lives. Jenny remembered how when King Edward died, the photograph of him which her mother kept up on the wall had been reverentially taken down and shortly replaced by the face of King George V. That was how much it all meant to them. An old bearded face melting into a younger bearded face. The numerals behind the names changing according to some ancient, inscrutable law, like a mystic calendar that measures aeons. When one guardian angel left, another took his place, staring down on them while the children read out the confusions of the times, his oracular mouth buried in his beard, his steady eyes absorbing the mystery of it all, giving it meaning. Jenny preferred simply not to hear the news, as if ignorance of the possibilities paralysed their realisation.

But tonight, being Thursday, wasn't so bad. This was the night of the week Jenny chose to come down herself for an hour or two. It was on Thursdays that her mother sent Angus to Dunsmuir's shop for *The Dundee*—a weekly paper of addictive sentimentality. In the world it depicted there were no major issues and no doubts. People were 'bodies', anger was 'Goodness Gracious!', consternation was 'Help ma Boab!', and events were what happened when the cat got lost. Bought compulsively by many families in the West of Scotland every week, its pages were a triumph of placative ignorance. It was the highlight of the week for Mairtin and Jean.

Listening to Angus read from it now, Jenny noted for the umpteenth time that he spoke as if he was repeating a message-line for the

Co-operative stores. He was fed up with the whole thing. It had been growing in him for some time. She suspected that the only reason he hadn't openly rebelled against having to do it before now was the shilling that came at the end of it. She worried about Angus. She worried about all of them, but Angus was already forcing her vague, all-enveloping mother's concern into a particular shape.

He was too hard, too much himself so soon. There was nothing frightened him, or at least nothing that would make him admit he was frightened. Not that that was bad. But just as fear couldn't be detected in him, so there wasn't much he would offer in the way of any uncertain feeling. He just returned responses. What lay behind them was his own business. Prodded, he closed up like a hedgehog. Doubt he couldn't endure. Placed in it, he would grasp a wilful decision and cudgel his way out with it, no matter what. His aggressiveness was already well known in High Street. She often felt that he was challenging something to happen to him. He seemed to get into so many fights, and win them, which perhaps was worse. He had never turned his tongue on her, and Tam's forcefulness had kept him a polite and biddable boy, as far as they knew. It was the extent of what they didn't know that worried. Even so young, he was chafing, she could tell. And soon he would start work.

Hearing his bored voice as an indirect insult to her parents, she was glad she had brought Conn along tonight. He could try to read a bit for them. He should be able to, he was doing so well at school—top of his class. She had even once received a note from one of the teachers —a Miss Anderson—saying that Conn was 'something special' and was to be 'given every encouragement'. She still kept it, at the back of a drawer, like an IOU from the future.

Watching Conn's face as he listened, she saw the difference in the two boys. The words that Angus gave out grudgingly, so that his voice's meanness seemed to make them worth nothing, were transformed by Conn's receptiveness. His expression seized them, smiled over them, went into a conspiracy with his Granny, and everything was enlarged in his reaction to it. Angus's flat insensitivity to things and Conn's vulnerability to them were a contest.

When Angus paused at the end of an article, Jenny said, 'Here, Angus. Take a wee rest. We'll let Conn read a bit.'

Angus was canny.

'There's only the Jean McFarlane bit left, noo.'

It was her parents' favourite column—written in the first person by Jean, a saga of trivia about the doings of herself and her husband, John. Helped by the name, Jenny's mother identified with the writer. Conn would be starting at the top of the bill.

'Aye. Ye've done well, son. Let Conn dae some work noo,' Jean said.

Conn became immediately excited about it. Jenny understood the momentary reluctance with which Angus handed over the paper. He was trying to calculate what proportion of a shilling the Jean McFarlane column was worth. Conn settled himself on the footstool.

'Noo,' Mairtin said, 'wan mistake an' ye're fired, wee yin.'

He made several. He started too high, had to modulate in the middle of a sentence, mispronounced some words. But finding his confidence, he read well. His voice really animated the small happenings it described. Mairtin and Jean responded well. They laughed, interpolated 'That's a guid yin'. They were like a congregation which has suffered long under a minister apathetic enough to be an unbeliever, and suddenly rediscovers an old commitment in a new voice. Their enjoyment was refreshed through Conn.

Jenny recognised a success and knew that Thursday evenings were entering a new era. It saddened her a little—not for Angus, who would be glad to get free of the duty, if not the shilling. She simply saw in this minute shift of routine another sign that her family was growing up. Which was good. But along with the growth went the loosening process that frightened her, the loss of the difficult equilibrium of security in their lives which she had somehow managed to maintain. Development meant the shifting of their postures, the need for her family to put themselves one by one into positions of danger to themselves, to move out of the range of their parents' protection.

Kathleen and Mick were already working. Kathleen was an attractive girl, getting big in the breast, subtly secretive about the eyes. She had started going to dances, being with boys. With that blank belief in the mysterious power of a faith which those who don't believe it can best indulge, Jenny cloudily hoped that Kathleen, as the only practising Catholic in the house, had special protection. Mick was least worry of all to her. He seemed happy working at the mill in Menford Lane, where Kathleen also worked. He hadn't wanted the pits, and his father was glad. Kathleen said that all the men liked him. He was so easy-going, pleasant, kind. He possessed some secret store of good nature, of unflappability, that had eluded the others. Perhaps it came from her father, whose favourite he was, and of whom he reminded Jenny.

It certainly didn't come from Tam. Tam still had, it was true, the most instinctively generous nature she had found in a man. She believed him simply the man most worthy of love she had ever met. But more often now she felt him at times recede from her, become opaque. Having seen men go mean with the pits many times before, she dreaded what might be happening in him. It troubled her how ferociously he held to certain hopes. One of them was Conn. Vaguely Tam had decided Conn would go on with his education. She feared the time when that vagueness would have to form into something concrete. She could see no way in which it was possible. Financially, they lived on the edge as it was.

That disillusionment was one of the dangers she sensed ahead. She quite frequently experienced a deep but inexplicable sensation of catastrophe to come. It wasn't something you could relate to specifics. Sometimes things were going smoothly when she felt it. It was like being on a river. The boat was sound enough. Everyone was reasonably well secured. Sometimes there were rapids, but you got through them with some fright, a bump here, a bruise there. Often there were nice times, good weather, easy talk. Yet always there was something else. A premonition. Heard faintly beyond laughter.

Conn's voice, a small complacent contradiction to her fears, finished off. There were kind words for applause. There was milk with home-made biscuits, the traditional follow-on from a reading. They all had some. In spite of Jenny's protestations, it was decided that Angus should still have his shilling, and Conn a sixpence. Both were pleased.

When Jenny told them to go straight home, Mairtin went out with them to see that they did. This too was traditional. He would wet his whistle in Mitchell's pub before coming back. Jean didn't approve of the drink. She went kirkwards every Sunday without fail and was well informed of the Lord's opinions on the subject. But short of the Lord putting in a personal appearance, nothing was likely to change her husband. Mairtin was Mairtin. She had learned to accept him as such, and he in turn, though he might tease her with it, was tolerant of her holiness, which, in truth, tended to be more obtrusive than his drink. He usually drank little, but, having been staggering drunk on quite a few occasions, he always found that Jean had wrapped cloths round the smoke-board of the fire by the time he got back.

'To protect them that canny protect themselves,' she used to say.

But he suspected that it was all meant as a wordless gesture on the degrading evils of drink, and his favourite response was to go into a parody of drunkenness, swaying her into vision, missing his footing, reaching unsteadily for things. Since she could never tell whether it was real or not, it always got her hooked.

Jenny and her mother sat chatting for an hour. Their experience was so much a common factor that their conversation was a monologue for two voices. In the quiet of the house, with the evening settling softly around them, mother and daughter talked like two women teasing out a ball of wool between them. There were only a few, brief snagging moments when one knew something which the other didn't.

Conn was coming on well, wasn't he? Jean still regretted not having been able to help at his birth. She had been ill at the time. At least she had done something by taking Kathleen out of the way and letting her sleep here.

Jenny asked her if she had seen Johnny Hose's latest poem. She hadn't. He was a milkman who came round High Street, and he pasted verses to the back of his milk-cart. While he filled a half-pint or pint measure from the tap in his churn, and then poured it into your jug, you could stand and read his most recent offering. 'Nae extra charge, ma bonny lass. Ye can't put a price on genius.' Every other morning at the mill gates, he could be seen waiting patiently, unconcerned with sales, while mill-workers crowded round his cart, some of them trying to memorise the lines they liked best. Usually they were funny, occasionally about women or nature. Jenny tried to tell her mother bits of the latest one. It was about prices.

Suzie Temple was rumoured to be ill. But then Suzie Temple was always rumoured to be ill. Miss Gilfillan almost certainly was ill, though she had mentioned it to nobody. A proud old woman. She couldn't be feeding herself.

Gibby Molloy, they both agreed, was getting worse. He should be married anyway. His mother was the only one who could control him. His brother Alec—and wasn't he a well-doing man—had an awful life from him. Wasn't that a terrible thing the last time about him challenging Alec to fight. Alec's wife, Mary, had been telling Jean the true story. There was Alec laid up in bed, his ribs in plaster. An accident at the work. Some kind of wheel and ratchet thing breaking off. Alec could tell you the way of it, Mary says. There's Alec, then, in bed. Mary sitting at the fire. The knock comes to the door. Gibby. 'Mucky fou,' Mary says. His eyes like penny-bowls. 'Sen' oot yer man,' he says. Forces his way in, is making for Alec. And Alec not able to move hardly off his back. 'A monkey fur a brither,' Gibby says. 'Too lah-di-dah fur me noo, aren't yese?' Mary's frightened Alec will try to rise. She tries to wrestle Gibby out the door. He's gentleman enough not to put a finger on her, just digs in his heels. Then he falls between sideboard and the table, roaring like a bull. Mary knows that if he rises, the house is wrecked. She puts one hand on the sideboard, one on the table. And she dances on his stomach. By this time Gibby's mother has been told. She comes round and leads him away like a lamb. The next morning Gibby's round first thing to apologise. 'The drink,' he says. And give him his due, he thanks Mary for protecting his brother, and says he admires her courage. 'Wan last thing, Mary,' he says at the door. 'Ye stertit wi' a military two-step. But wis that an eightsome reel ye feenished wi'? Ah couldny follow the steps.' You have to laugh. There's a likeable bit about him, too.

Jenny remembered Tam saying he had seen Gibby in the pub just a short while back. Tam had said at the time that Gibby was slowly going to pieces. He had taken on the daftest bet you ever heard. Matt Morrison had said, 'Your attention, please. Gentlemen, my learnt friend on the right will now endeavour to swally the sword.' And Gibby had started to chew his tumbler, spitting out glass and blood.

Brains had never been his strong point. But he was sure enough getting worse. His mother must be wishing they were back in the old days when breaking down the toilet door once in a blue moon was her biggest worry. He wasn't a well man at all.

That was Buff Thompson away then. It had been a blessing at the end. It was sad to watch when their spirit went before them. Crying like a bairn. And saying some terrible things to Aggie. She would have her own to do now, poor soul, with her son's wife not giving her the life of a scabby cat. She wouldn't be long behind him. But he had been a good man, and that was a hard enough thing to be, God knew.

As Jenny left, her mother was methodically wrapping cloths round the corner of the smoke-board. The air of contained expectancy about her gave the impression that she was looking forward to Mairtin's return. At the mouth of the entry, Jenny bumped into her father. He had had a fair amount, but seemed quite steady.

'Here, Jen,' he said. 'His she got her claiths on the smoke-board yet?

Jenny nodded.

'Aye,' Mairtin sighed. 'By the time Ah get tae the top o' these stairs, Ah'll be awfy drunk.'

'Och, feyther.'

'Not tae worry. She enjoys it fine. Makes 'er feel holy.'

He winked and went in. Climbing the stairs, he broke into loud and surprisingly tuneful song:

'There's nane may ken the humble cot
Ma lassie ca's her hame.
But though ma lassie's nay-hameless
Her kin o' low degree-hee-hee,
Her heart is warm, her thoughts are pure
And aye she's dear tae me . . .'

Throwing open the door, arms outspread, his voice rising, scouring the ceiling:

'Her heart is warm, her thoughts are pue-hure,
And aye she's dea-hear tae me-e-e-e-e-e.'

Jean looked sideways at him, lips pursed, nodding as if she read in him a moral she agreed with. He realised quite suddenly that he really was drunk, but not so drunk that he couldn't retain sufficient craftsmanship to perform his condition with some degree of style. He closed the door, came into the middle of the floor, swaying slightly.

'Ma bonny Jean,' he said, waiting for inspiration. 'Ma bonny, bonny Jean. Ah was once in Graithnock twice. Today a small boy was found lost late last night. Wearing his bare feet and his father's boots on. Hurling an empty barrow full of straw. The reward will be a fish-supper, a poke of plates, and a bottle of scones.' Sitting down. 'Ah could take a bite maself, Jean. A wee pie and a bottle o' ink wid be lovely.'

'Ye'll have the whusky-hunger, like enough.'

They took it from there. He told King George's photograph what was wrong with the country. She suggested that Mairtin himself was Britain's biggest problem. He sang 'Ah'm wearin' awa', Jean, Like snaw when it's thaw, Jean', and then gagged. 'That's me awa' noo, Jean'. She was sure she would be away before him, and he would have been the death of her.

It was a complicated ritual by two people who would never surprise each other again but found pleasure in the repeated patterns of the past—a conversational dance of death, perfected, nicely timed, delicate as a minuet.

# CHAPTER NINE

For Conn, the house at times assuming strangeness: the furniture like props that didn't fit the action, inappropriate in its cosiness and complacency; established routines giving suddenly like locks, to show the frustrations that padded in them; a frequent and sometimes frightening sense of transit—to where?

A mid-summer evening, first dark. The top halves of the windows had been taken out, left on the floor. The remains of a long hot day decomposed outside, stenching the house sweetly with the exhalations of the park across the river. In the boys' bedroom, Angus and Conn lay, steeping in tiredness. It was a Sunday. All day they had 'run the cutter', as their mother mysteriously called it, as if rehearsing for the holidays, which would be soon. Angus had been examining the hardening skin on the soles of his feet, pleased with the thought that a fortnight would bring them to their summer toughness, and he wouldn't need boots again till winter. They spoke little, content to be crooned at by soft sounds, the river quietly coughing over stones, a dog worrying distance.

Kathleen and Mick, with the privilege of earners, could be heard still through in the living-room with their parents. Jenny was sewing, making alterations to a dress which Kathleen had been trying on, and, as she did so, was talking to Kathleen. The dress was for a dance and, using it as an excuse, Jenny was gently finding out about the boy Kathleen was going with—Jack Farrell. They seemed serious about each other and Jenny wanted to know what he was like. She knew the family slightly, they were Catholic, though that wasn't important to her. To Jenny, a man's credentials were his nature, and she was concerned simply to deduce the true lineaments of the boy from Kathleen's inevitably idealised picture. Mick was crouched over the fireplace, whittling a boat-shape from a piece of wood, having ignored his father's mild observation, addressed to the room, that 'That boay does a' his work in et the ribs. He's goat the ausole like a sawmill.' Tam himself was finding his way through the paper with a kind of patient bemusement that wasn't just a matter of failing light. He finally put it down like a parcel he couldn't get into, saying, 'There's nothin' in the papers nooadays.' It was as if he half-sensed some plot to keep out of print the things that were really happening.

The street was almost asleep. Through the open window drifted the murmur of the few men who were still at the corner, their faces white, upturned blotches in the shadows.

The sound, when it came, took some time to register, it was so alien to its setting. Tam was first on his feet and over to the window, looking down.

'Aw Christ,' he said. 'No' that.'

The other three had come to stand behind him. What they saw made the sound they had heard meaningful in retrospect. A big man was crouched against Miss Gilfillan's window, visible in the faint light that came from it. His hands were held side-on to the glass with his face between, so that he could see into her house. The window was slightly lowered from the top. What they had heard was Miss Gilfillan calling for help. She shouted again, a thin whimper of a word, like the sound a hare makes when it knows the greyhound has it.

'Yer Peepin' Tom,' Tam said. 'The auld sowl'll be frichtened oot 'er wits.'

He waited, looking over towards the corner. Things seemed to have gone quiet there, as if a conference was in progress. The big man tapped slowly at Miss Gilfillan's window.

'When dae they make their bloody move?'

'She'll likely be in bed, the pair auld sowl,' Jenny murmured, and at once regretted it, for Tam was already moving.

'Tae hell wi' this,' he said as he crossed the floor.

'Tam. Ye'll stey where ye are.' She caught up with him at the door. 'There's men oot there. Let them see tae it. You're bidin' here.'

'Go in the hoose, wumman,' he said angrily and was gone.

They heard the rattle of his heavy boots as he went downstairs. Angus and Conn, who had been unaware of anything happening in the street, had caught the echo of it in their own house—first in the unnatural silence of the living-room and then in the panic of their mother's voice. They scrambled out of bed, Angus in the lead, and came through in their nightshirts—old shirts which had belonged to their father.

'Bed, you two! Bed!' their mother shouted.

But she seemed to forget about them again at once, was too distraught to follow up her threat. They stayed. And in a moment the stray particles of an ordinary night had been precipitated into imminent ignition.

Angus and Conn had arrived at the window in time to see their father emerge from the entry below them and cross towards the man at Miss Gilfillan's window. The whole family stood looking down on a scene that appeared more distant than it was, stylised, with a formal inevitability: Tam approaching the man, the men at the corner waiting and watching, utterly silent now except for one voice somewhere saying, 'Tam Docherty'. Behind the children, their mother muttering, 'Oh my Goad! Can ye no' get sittin' in peace at yer ain fire-end. Is this no' terrible?'

The stillness of the street made every sound audible. The man had turned to glance down at Tam and then resumed looking in the window. His indifference squared with the fact that he had chosen a window that faced out onto a street that wasn't empty. He seemed to believe that inches gave immunity.

'Here, sur,' Tam said. The mode of address was ominous, habitual with him when he was roused. It was the formality of a duelling challenge.

The big man turned slowly to face him, luxuriating in the action. 'Hm?'

'Here, sur. Whit d'ye mean tae be et wi' this?'

'I'm lookin' in this winda' here.' The accent was Irish.

'That's a maiden lady in there, sur. An auld budy. Ye'll be frichtenin' her tae daith wi' this cairry-oan!' Tam remained a good yard away, not wishing to provoke the big man. His voice was perfectly pleasant. 'Noo, wid ye no' be better tae go oan tae where ye're goin'.'

He looked Tam over as if measuring him for a coffin.

'Bogger off, little man. Before I fockin' fall on yese.'

Something happened instantly to the situation which was almost audible, like a safety catch unclicking.

'Noo, noo, sur,' Tam said. 'These is sweary-words ye're usin'. That's no' nice.'

The big man turned fully round now. He understood. An agreement had been reached. He looked down at the ground, shook his head, lunged suddenly at Tam. Tam ran backwards. As the impetus of the other man's rush made him stoop, so that his arms dropped, finding nothing solid, Tam came back in at full throttle, and hit him twice, flush on the cheek-bones, right hand and then left. The big man went back a couple of yards and stopped dead. He made a sound that suggested contempt and flicked one hand across his face, dismissing the blows like cobwebs.

Watching him, Tam had a revelation about what he was up against.

If this man hit him, he would be having an early night. Before the Irishman could set himself, Tam had moved right into him, hooking ceaselessly. His fists bounced the man's head off each other as if they had it on a string. It took an awful long time, and his arms were tiring, before he felt that infinitesimal relaxation, the thaw of muscles that precedes the mind's unmooring from consciousness.

He didn't stop. The man had subsided against the wall, blood spattering from his nose and cuts on his face, and still Tam punched, following his head as it slithered to the ground, rabid with anger. As the man fell, Tam kicked him once in the stomach and his leg was flailing back a second time when Jenny's voice screamed, 'Tam! Fur Goad's sake, stoap! Stoap!'

Tam's body froze. The men were round him, about five of them. They moved him back, one of them saying, 'That's enough, Tam. There's nae need fur that. That'll dae ye noo.'

'D'you want the same?' Tam was too high to recognise who it was he spoke to. He snarled at a shape. 'Ya fat-ersed bastard! Whit were you daein'? Hidin' in a bloody coarner?'

'Ye were oot before we could make a move,' somebody else said.

'Jesus. He was at it fur meenits,' Tam said. 'Beggin' fur boather. Whit were yese waitin' fur? Invitation cairds? There were enough o' ye tae move the bloke oan withoot a blow bein' struck. Ya useless bastards!' He looked down at the man, whose head rested on a pen in the road, while two of the men examined him. 'Hoo is he?'

The big man groaned and came to, as if offering an answer.

'He'll be a' richt, Tam,' somebody said.

'Who is he?' Tam asked.

'He's leevin' in the Model.' The Model Lodging House was situated at the opposite end of Soulis Street from High Street. It catered for a mixed migrant clientele, mainly labourers. 'He was in Mitchell's earlier oan. Threatenin' tae dae terrible things tae onybody that goat in his road. Then he went fur a walk. Must've came back.'

'Oan ye go in noo, Tam. We'll take 'im doon tae the Model.'

The big man had been helped to his feet, and they cleeked him off down Soulis Street. Tam came back in. Miss Gilfillan hadn't emerged and he thought it best to let her recover on her own.

The house was a strange place. The family was reduced to a stunned solemnity. The scene outside, seeming a triumph for Tam in its occurrence, had, in the retrospect of a few moments, negatived to an x-ray plate in which they saw the sinister shadows formed at the centre of Tam's self. He was aware of it, avoided their eyes, like a patient who didn't want to know the worst.

'My Goad, Tam,' Jenny said. 'Ah thocht ye hud killed 'im.'

Tam sat down suddenly, giving himself up at once to despair, and rested his head in his hands.

'Ah think Ah wantit tae,' he said. 'Oh Jesus. Why did Ah hiv tae hit 'im sa hard? It was a' bye a while before Ah stoaped. Ah widny let go. Ah widny let go.'

Jenny and Tam were only conscious of each other in the room.

'Naebudy can jist turn it oan and aff like a spicket,' she consoled him.

'But kickin' 'im. Ah've never put the boot in onybody in ma life before. Whit's happened tae me?'

He was asking Jenny, looking up at her and then down at the knuckles of his hands, bruised and beginning to swell.

'Ah better see tae yer hauns,' said Jenny, who had faith in the power of small actions to fend off big fears. The regimen of her household was a daily communion by which the amorphous forces controlling their lives were broken down into bread.

'Wid ye throw a pail o' watter ootside? There's a lot o' bluid.' The request was anxious and forlorn, as if the guilt he felt would be erased with the blood.

'Ah'll dae that as weel.' Jenny said. Her competence came up between them and what had happened. Tam sat docilely in her shelter. 'Kathleen. Pit thae twa boays tae bed.'

Kathleen ushered Angus and Conn through to the room. Angus lay talking about it for a time, paring everything that had happened to those moments of unleashed ferocity when his father had become a demolition machine. The rest appeared to be irrelevant to him. But Conn was quiet. Long after Angus was asleep and the whole house was in darkness, Conn lay awake. The night seemed menacing now. The scents of the park invaded the house like fumes. And for hours, it appeared, he could hear the voices of his mother and father. His mother patient, her indistinguishable words stroking his own thoughts to quietness. His father's voice mournful and subdued, persistent, pleading with the darkness.

Next morning, on his way out to school, he crossed to the pen outside Miss Gilfillan's window. His mother had made a good job of the cleaning. But unnoticed in the darkness, splashes of blood had remained. They showed now, several of them—big and dark, some of them more than a yard apart. As if a giant had been coughing blood.

# CHAPTER TEN

Miss Gilfillan felt the need for some gesture of thanks. She had spoken to Mr Docherty, waylaying him as he came home from the pit one day.

'Mr Docherty. I should like to take this opportunity to express my sincere thanks for your kindness in coming to my aid the other evening. I hope I didn't cause you too much trouble. And I just want you to know that your efforts on my behalf were greatly appreciated.'

She didn't say the words so much as she unveiled them. Her rehearsals had paid off. Tam's expression hid behind the coal-dust. He didn't find it easy to understand that these decorous words were the epilogue to the mêlée of fists and swear-words that had flared up on the cobblestones. He wondered how much she had heard. Tadger Daly, standing at his elbow, was frankly gaping. The expectant silence was as baffling to Tam as RSVP would have been.

'Aye. Well. Fine. Then. Eh ... That's very decent of ye, Miss Gilfillan.'

'Not at all. When that dreadful—man—' she settled on the word as a convention she wasn't at all sure was applicable in this case— 'did that, I thought my hour had come.'

Tam was ransacking his courtliness for a suitable response.

'I think I can fully appreciate what a lady like yourself must have went through.'

They were both smiling now, communication established.

'Here,' Tadger suddenly interjected. 'You two's guid. D'ye mind if Ah sell tickets?'

Miss Gilfillan flicked her smile at Tadger like a knife, and fled at a genteel pace, while Tadger took Tam's reprimand with wicked enjoyment.

She was pleased with the exchange. It was so seldom that she spoke to anyone. Sometimes she didn't come out of the house for days, just eating frugally of what she had, preserving a musty stillness where memories grew like toadstools. At first, people had tended to come to the door and check that she was all right. But she had discouraged them. Now they contented themselves with secret reassurances, the open curtains, the single flower renewing itself in the window, and most of all the table set methodically for breakfast, lunch, and dinner, with fine china and elaborate arrays of cutlery which she couldn't possibly be needing. She was never seen eating, but as long as the sequence of settings for meals was maintained, she must be all right.

Her conversation with Mr Docherty sustained her for a day or two. Sensitised by loneliness, she thought back on her few words as if they constituted an occasion, became almost heady on them, the way an anchorite's palate might be ravished by wine-dregs. As satisfaction waned, it left the appetite for more. For the first time in years, she wanted to talk with someone other than the voices in her head. She chose Conn.

She thought about it carefully before she approached him. The more she considered it, the more it appealed. He was young enough for her not to be afraid of him, as she was of most things in High Street. She would be repaying Mr Docherty in a practical way for his kindness, for she could teach Conn things he could never otherwise know about —the graces of life. From the time that she had heard his first cries on the night of his birth, she had felt specially towards him, had found out his name, singled him out from the other children in High Street, watched him play. She was already a secret godmother to him. By the time she decided, Conn had been adopted without his knowing it.

Her method had a Mary Slessor flavour to it. With the paralysing conviction of someone whose mind had closed a long time ago and in another place, wherever she looked she saw only the shapes of her own atrophied prejudice. High Street was to her just the dregs of humanity, riff-raff, scum. Even living among them, she had remained a tourist, clinging to her past like a passport. Now that she was trying to effect a rapprochement for the first time with one of them, the only role she could condescend to play was that of enlightener. She was going to do some missionary work in darkest High Street. Just as natives are lured with coloured beads, so Conn was to be enticed with sweets.

'Just a moment, please. Conn. Isn't it? You see, I know your name. Do you know mine?

'Yes, miss. You're Miss Gilfillan, miss.'

Emerging quickly from the shadow of the entry, she had seemed out of place in the sunlight. Conn wondered if he was going to get another penny from her.

'I want you to do something for me. Here's a note with some things I want you to get from Mrs Daly's shop. I've put two shillings inside it. Will you do that for me?'

'Yes, Miss Gilfillan.'

When he got back to her house, the door was very slightly ajar. He knocked as if he was afraid he might be heard. Her voice was a funny sound, like singing when the person doesn't know the tune: 'Is that Conn? Come in. But wipe your feet on the mat first. Very, very thoroughly.' He made it six wipes for each foot. 'Now close the door.' He did it reluctantly. He was inside Miss Gilfillan's house.

He felt lost at first. It was dark and there seemed to be furniture and brass and pictures and ornaments everywhere. On the other side of the room, like someone lost in a maze, sat Miss Gilfillan. She smiled.

'Aha. A gentleman to see me.'

Conn looked over his shoulder.

'I mean you, young man. Wouldn't you like to be a gentleman?' Conn nodded placatively. 'Well, you will be. I can teach you.'

She signalled him towards her. Among the things she had asked him to buy were sweets.

'These are for you,' she said. 'But I shall keep them here. And every time you come, you can have one or two. Would that be nice?'

'Thank you.'

She gave him a couple now, and he didn't like them. They were chocolate on the outside, jelly-soft inside, mushy to the teeth the way he imagined snails would be. He liked hard sweets. He wondered why she hadn't let him choose for himself, if they were to be for him.

The small gift and what it meant to him epitomised their times together.

He came quite often after that. Always before he left, she would arrange the next time for him to come. Sometimes she would have him go an errand for her. The house became familiar to him in separate pieces: the photographs on the sideboard that made their own little frozen landscape, a man with a big moustache appearing in so many of them that he conveyed to Conn the godlike ability of being in many places at once; the small table where the brass ornaments were always shining and always in exactly the same positions; the huge grandfather clock that stood forever with its hands just after twelve—noon or midnight? But the place remained in total a stranger to him, perhaps because he had to leave so much of himself at the door.

Mud on one of her frayed and fading carpets sent her into a frenzy which would have been adequate to the first signs of the plague. She conquered human nature by ignoring it, forbidding it to affront her.

Coming into her room, Conn always felt lumbered with himself, a nose that would sniff at awkward times, hands like cumbersome deformities. He didn't even breathe freely in the stuffy atmosphere, as if deep breaths were indecent. Once, awesomely, he farted. It pluffed insidiously into the cushion where he sat, and became a smell —rank as original sin. Miss Gilfillan didn't seem to notice but Conn sat surrounded by his own unworthiness.

Miss Gilfillan had noticed. But since such things didn't really exist, she could have no reaction. Like all Conn's lapses into himself, it merely seemed to render him temporarily invisible to her. There were times when she left him sitting or standing unnoticed for minutes, like a toy she had forgotten about. Their occasions together were strangely without development. What they achieved wasn't so much a relationship as the demonstration of the absence of one.

It was hopeless from the beginning. Conn was at first frightened by the ghost ceremonies Miss Gilfillan practised, whispering and moving eerily around her musty room, creating a charmed circle in which she tried to resurrect the past. She initiated him into the uses of cutlery with a ritual solemnity that suggested they were the only weapons that could reduce life to order and sense. She took tea with him as if it were a sacrament. Eventually the word 'daft' kept coming into his head like a bad angel. When she finally neglected to tell him to come back, neither regretted it, since they had never met each other.

But all those moments stayed engraved on Conn's memory, weird hieroglyphics which experience would eventually translate into some kind of sense. Looking back on it much later, he had the feeling of having been in a mausoleum.

With his departure, Miss Gilfillan sealed the door on herself. In a sense, his visits had served their purpose. His indifference to all her kindness was somehow related in her head to the scrawny, frightened boy her father had dismissed from his bakery. Conn's ingratitude absolved her father.

# CHAPTER ELEVEN

'This is Jack, mither.'

The name had for Jenny the impact of a secret formula, contained as much potency as 'Rumpelstiltskin' or 'Rapunzel'. It introduced change into their lives. Normally, a girl would only bring one young man into her parents' house. If by the end of her courting days it had extended to two, she had been flighty, and to have her married was probably a relief. Three suggested infiltration from Gomorrah.

'Hullo, Jack,' Jenny said to Kathleen's future husband. 'Sit yerself doon, son.'

'Hullo, Mrs Docherty. Thanks.' Conscious of scrutiny, Jack Farrell felt awkward, and slightly belligerent because of his awkwardness. He hung his bonnet on his knee and resented immediately the stare of the boy sitting by the window, nursing a neatly bandaged hand—that would be Conn.

'Yer feyther'll be in soon, Kathleen,' Jenny said. 'He's et the stables in Soulis Street. Wullie Manson's horse again. Takin' canary-fits. Jumpin' a' ower the place. Yer feyther's helpin' tae calm it doon.' That was a code message. Since Kathleen knew all this, she realised her mother was suggesting that Jack should still be here when her father got back.

'Jack and me's supposed tae be gaun fur a walk, mither.'

'He'll no' be long. Whit wid ye make o' this boay, Jack? He wis doon at the stables wi' his feyther. An' he wantit tae see if ferrets bite. He kens the answer noo, onywey. Ah doot Wullie Manson doesny

feed thae ferrets, Conn. We had tae clean it and bandage it fur fear
of infection, didn't we, eh?'

'The dirt that's aye oon his hauns, ye should've cleaned the ferret. It's
probably goat hydrophobia by noo.' It was a self-conscious remark,
Kathleen being smart for Jack's benefit.

'Ah've heard a lot aboot Conn,' Jack offered.

There was a pause during which Kathleen and Jack used Conn as
an escape from their embarrassment, looking at him as if he were a
picture.

'Well. Ah'll jist get ready, Jack,' Kathleen said.

'Fine, Kath.'

The shortened form of the name made a momentary window for
Jenny, through which she saw their inaccessible intimacy, a strange
area encroaching on their lives, into which Kathleen was withdrawing
more and more, and where she would eventually live almost entirely.
The experience of it was a wistful instant, happiness shaking hands
with sadness. As she ironed a semmet, she had a sense of big things
happening almost unnoticed round the corner of each trivial task,
powerful laws moving in strange conjunction with small accidents,
like a tumbril passing a house in which children play.

'Well, oan ye go then,' she said to Kathleen, who was still standing
indecisively, vaguely wanting to act as interpreter for her mother's
first impressions. 'Ah think Jack'll survive five meenits withoot
ye.'

'Huh.' Kathleen went through to the boys' room, which was
accepted as being hers in the early evening.

'Ye'll excuse me if Ah go oan wi' this ironin', Jack.'

'Aye, surely. Ah've jist left ma ain mither daein' that. Ah thocht fur
a meenit Ah hidny left the hoose.'

It was a good beginning, implied simultaneously that his mother
was a good housewife and that he felt at home with them. Jenny was
encouraged.

'Ye're never done, richt enough. Yer mither'll no be lost for somethin' tae dae. How mony in your faimly?'

'Six. Fower boays, two lassies.'

'An' you the auldest?'

'Aye.'

'An' you'll be whit?'

'Twinty come ma birthday.'

'Aye? Ah thocht ye were aulder.' (Jack understood, 'Ye'll no' be in
ony hurry tae get mairrit.') 'Kathleen tells me that ye're in the Skinwork. D'ye like it?'

'It's a' richt. As long as ye can avoid the ticks.'

'Ah thocht the ticks wid dee when the animals were slaughtered.'

'They're dour, the ticks. They hing oan. They're jist like arrows wi' bodies oan them. They stick themselves intae yer skin an' ye canny mudge them. Ye canny scrape them aff.'

Conn, tempted to go outside when they had been staring at him, was glad he had waited. He watched Jack, 'e'en an' mooth', as his mother called it.

'Whit happens then?' he asked.

'Ye light a fag,' Jack said.

He halted, enjoying the bafflement on the boy's face. Conn was trying to focus on the connection. All he could make out was a blurred picture of stoical manhood. When the ticks got a man, embedded themselves in him in their thousands, he knew it was hopeless to pluck feebly at them. They were there to stay. What could a man do but light a cigarette, and smile?

'Look. Ah'll show ye.' Jack took the excuse to light a Woodbine. 'The tick's in ma haun', richt?' He held out his hand, palm down, tapping the back of it. Conn nodded sympathetically. 'Ah haud the tip o' the fag against its bum. An' it wriggles oot . . . Ye knock it aff an' tramp oan it. The heat draws them oot, ye see.'

Conn filed away the information to pass on to his friends, having become an authority on ticks.

'The wages are guid enough?' Jenny asked.

'Guid enough. Ah can see ma mither richt. An' then save some. Ye get no' a bad wage. An' as mony ticks as ye can cairry hame wi' ye.'

It was a work joke. Not having heard it, Jenny laughed. Conn's expression was extravagant praise. Jack thawed out completely. He had arrived in the room.

'Whit's yer mither tae her ain name, Jack? Wid she be . . .'

In the next room Kathleen flinched. She knew her mother was moving on to one of her favourite subjects. Jenny carried in her head incredibly complicated interconnections of local families. She was relentlessly accurate about who was so-and-so's auldest boy, younger brother, hauf-cousin, and who he was married on to. Jack was about to be interviewed by the Keeper of the Records.

Kathleen started to get ready. Up till now, she had been sitting on one of the beds, willing the conversation to come right. She had followed its course like a game of chance, smiling to herself when Jack indicated the similarity between their mothers, grimacing when he used the word 'bum'. When she turned her attention to the freshly cleaned and ironed skirt and blouse on the bed, it meant she was satisfied that Jack had won her mother's approval. The rest was for side-stakes, though she still listened.

Checking the collar of her blouse in the mirror that sat on top of the small dressing-table, she admitted to herself the often remarked resemblance to her Granny Docherty—the same bone-structure, the same eyes that were habitually set in an attitude of startled listening.

Granny still contrived to look mildly surprised about life, as if she hadn't quite got used to the whole thing, though not for much longer. Kathleen felt guilty about all the times she had resented being compared to her grandmother, now that her grandmother was dying. She dwelt on their likeness now as a penance. For the first time, some understanding of that resentment was granted to her, like absolution.

It hadn't been anything personal to her grandmother at all. Old as she was, there was still enough left in her face to take colour from and make credible the descriptions of her past appearance that Tam and others liked to indulge in. Any comparison with their reminiscences was not unflattering. What had irked her, Kathleen saw, was that such comparisons were merely symptoms of a more serious complaint, one that affected her intermittently, so that there had been times when she came down with alienation from her family like an illness.

Sometimes the closeness of her family had almost stifled her. Even her face wasn't to be her own. They were so much involved in one another that, like grotesque Siamese sextuplets, the pain of one reverberated through all the others. She had for a time enjoyed the packed atmosphere of that small room through the wall, where so much had always seemed to be happening, where so many people carved their convictions into the air, where there was so much laughter, anger, argument and just plain talk that she had believed on occasions that her eyes must be deceiving her, and it had to be as big as a hall to be containing all this. But later, as she grew towards herself and her sexuality taught her separateness, she had felt more and more the need to deny the stridency of their demands for identification with them, the certainty of their assumption that she was just one of the family. Her desire to obey her individuality had put her at odds with them. In her family, you weren't just a member. You had to enlist.

Her father stood at the heart of her discontent. Whereas Jenny at the final level *was* the family, she still allowed within its amplitude great freedom and flexibility. There was about her something enduring, enfolding, and ultimately unshockable. You felt that whatever you did, no matter how terrible, she was the one you could tell it to. She might not understand, but she would accept it as a part of you. Her love was a gift, a necessity, yet still a form of freedom for you, and indefinitely extensive, it seemed, like air.

But Tam's proximity was somewhat more overwhelming. There was a fierceness about his affection, a relentlessness about his commitment to you. In his eyes you acquired an importance that you couldn't always live with. His love wasn't like Jenny's, uncompromised, a gently suffused warmth in which it was comfortable to move about. His was fuelled by odd, apparently disconnected fragments from other parts of his life, his rage at the man-made predestination that loomed over them, his contempt for the acceptance of it in others, his dread that they would none of them have the chance to be what they might have been. All the refuse of his experience was gathered into and consumed by the irrational belief in the worth of people which was as intense as a flame in him. In the middle of that belief, as both benefactors and victims, were his family. More than once Kathleen had been obliged to withdraw from the blast-furnace glare of his concern for all of them.

She had come to find it a burden. She had sometimes thought that if he had only stayed in the Church he would have been happier. He didn't merely live his life. He had to live it and justify the living of it simultaneously, instead of leaving that to the Church, as she was content to do. Things were neither so bad nor important as he felt them to be. Occasionally, she used amusedly to imagine him descended from an ancient line of dethroned royalty, say Irish kings. It was ridiculous, but staying in that cramped house, labouring every week in the pits, living a pot of soup away from hunger, he was still the proudest man she had ever seen. She had noticed the difference between him and Jack's father, between him and the men she worked with at the mill.

'Ye're no' ony better than onybody else, and naebody else is better than you,' he used to say. She had heard other people say that too. But he meant it differently. With them it tended to be a passive article of faith, recourse of the resigned. With him it was a battle-cry, a plea for the clearing of a space, for getting rid of false barriers and obstacles, and then they would see what happened. He seemed to believe that if you broke down the encrusted assumptions of society, each would achieve his own incalculable value.

Between her and such outrageous intensity had come Jack, and, Kathleen understood with joy, her dilemma was resolved. What she was doing now, smoothing down her skirt, fixing her hair for the third time, was a vindication of a faith which she had long nurtured and which was now being openly acknowledged by the presence of her boy-friend in the house. Sexual awareness had come on her like a secret formula for transforming the quality of her life. Before she met Jack, it had already removed her from the immediate sphere of influence of her father, had convinced her that his passionate harangues about the state of things were just a masculine attribute which didn't have any significance beyond itself, like hair on the chest. Her relationship with Jack had completed her liberation.

Her attitude now had the benignly patronising quality of the young in love. Tam, emotional revolutionary, would go on beating his life against walls that would never break. Kathleen, with the simplicity of someone in a fairy tale, had fallen in love, and the walls collapsed.

The love of Jack and herself was the force which had transmuted her life into something marvellous.

Almost ready now to go through to him, she felt gratitude as well as love, because it was through him that within herself she had made peace again with her family. By finding her own identity, she was able to give them back theirs, and saw them in a clearer perspective. Having now a choice, she could afford them the full run of their qualities, because they didn't encroach on her as they had done.

Hearing her father coming into the house, laughing about Wullie Manson's horse being 'nearly human—like a pit manager' and then saying hullo to Jack, she went through herself, hugging the thought that Jack and she had already decided to get married fairly soon. It wouldn't be long before they told their parents.

She had to wait while Jack and her father talked. It was an easy free-wheeling conversation, but behind its casualness something quite formal was discreetly happening, a mutual assessment. Through anecdote and opinion, Kathleen remained obliquely the subject of what they said: Jack coming to terms with the background she would bring with her like a dowry, Tam judging the kind of future she might have with Jack. They seemed to like each other.

Kathleen noticed happily that her father was being particularly nice. She understood his effusiveness. Gratefully, she realised that he wasn't the kind of father who was critical of his daughter's choice because he believed she deserved somebody very special. He simply believed that whoever was her choice must be very special. His wild sense of her value infused her with a sudden, deep love for him, the more intense for being valedictory. Looking at him enthroned in his chair, offering Jack his attention, his eyes an amnesty from criticism, she was taking her leave of him. With innocent arrogance, she took it for granted that the supporting role in her life to which she was assigning him was a true measurement of him. He would go on being kind and angry and discontented and concerned, and nothing much would change with him.

# CHAPTER TWELVE

When Kathleen and Jack went out, Tam winked at Jenny and said, 'That's a' richt then, intit?'

'He seems a nice boay,' Jenny said.

'He wid hiv tae be.'

Tam stood at the window, craning after them until they went through the opening to the park. He turned to Conn.

'Hoo's the wound, captain?'

'It's no sair noo, feyther. Where's oor Angus?'

'Still doon there. Wullie's still showin' him the ferrets.'

'Can Ah go?'

'It's nearly yer bedtime,' said Jenny.

'Let 'im go, Jen. He's goat tae get ower it. Ye canny hiv 'im bein' feart fae ferrets. Oan ye go.'

Conn was away before his mother should lodge any more objections.

'Ten meenits then,' she shouted to him in flight. 'An' bring Angus back wi' ye.'

Having finished her ironing, Jenny started to put the clothes away. Tam sat down again and lit a dout. It was unusually still with only the two of them in the house, a momentary insight into the future. She knew the thought his silence held but would let him wait his own time to unwrap it. In the meantime:

'Mick didny say where he wis goin' the nicht.'

Her voice was faintly edged with annoyance.

'Did ye ask him?'

'Ah did. "Over the hills and far away," he says.'

Tam laughed.

'Jist preuchin' aboot. Lukkin' fur some place tae pit his energy.'

'He should've said.'

'Jen. He's no' a boay. Ye canny keep them in shoart troosers a' their days.'

'He's no Methuselah either. Though times he seems tae think he kens as much.'

She sat down for a minute.

'That Jack's a sensible boay, Ah think.'

'Aye.'

'Ah hope they're baith sensible enough tae wait a while yet.'

'Aye. They're auld enough tae ken ye canny leeve oan kisses.'

His mood hobbled discussion. There was much more to be said and she knew that soon, tonight in bed or tomorrow evening by the fire, they would exchange reactions at length, and establish their common response to the situation and its immediate implications. But not now. He threw the stub of his cigarette in the fire. She realised his question before he put it.

'Hoo is she the day then?'

'Much the same. Maybe a wee bit lower. It's no' long noo.'

'Ah'd best go roon.'

'Aye. She'll luk fur ye.'

He sat on. She appreciated his reluctance. It wasn't just the pain of looking at his mother die. It was that salted by his surroundings, aggravated by its happening in the complex of disappointment and rejection which his family had become to him. Lizzie, his eldest sister, would be there. It was her turn tonight. She was a strong Catholic, to whom lapsing was just a flabby self-indulgence. She had never forgiven Tam for hurting his parents. Jenny she managed to tolerate as someone who had been born benighted, though Lizzie did believe that she should never have married the man if she wasn't prepared to worship with him. And there would be his father, accusing with silence.

His mother herself had never remonstrated with him about leaving the faith. Unlike her husband and two daughters, her religious conviction was for her just the way she had learned of getting the world to talk sense. There were bound to be other ways, just as there would be other languages. She was Catholic because she needed to be, as she needed clothes for winter. But Tam's desertion hadn't diminished him a centimetre in her eyes. When told about the shocking things he had said about the Church, she would say to Lizzie or Mary, the youngest of them, 'A man is mair than his words.' She was quite often inclined to follow this up by describing Jenny as 'the best wee wife in the toon' with the assurance of someone announcing the result of a poll.

Jenny, going to the house every day lately and quite a few evenings, felt bad enough about being an intruder on everyone except old Sarah Docherty herself. It was almost unbearable for Tam. He saw families as little fortresses of loyalty and sanity and mutual concern, set defiantly in a landscape of legalised looting and social injustice. Yet here was his father untouchably distant from him, his sisters strangers, his brothers-in-law having little to say to him, and among the ruins of their relationships his mother dying, her eyes enlarging on their half-shut faces, her death demeaned by the politics of their pointless disagreements.

He stared into the fire and said, 'Aye, then. Ah'll go roon.'

Old Conn and Sarah lived in Boyd Street. Waving to the fellows at the corner, Tam walked along Union Street. The evening was mild but clouds hung sluggishly in the air. Turning right at the end of Union Street, Tam climbed the cobbled hill to the house.

What was happening there drew him immediately into the inevitability of itself, its gathering stillness. His mother was neither better nor worse than she had been. Only perhaps the eyes had frozen a little more, her thoughts and fears dim blurs beyond them. Lizzie's busyness hopelessly sought purpose, a candle against a glacier. Old Conn's fingers led him along his rosary's braille. Tam stood at the bed, his mouth a mockery.

'Hoo are ye the day then, mither?'

She smiled and nodded. Her answer was incomprehensible, a knead of soft sounds. She smiled again, stared at him, and closed her eyes. She seemed to understand that he had come.

He crossed to the window and looked out. Through the gaps between the houses opposite, and rising above them, he could see the infirmary. She had refused to go there. The ominous bulk of the building on its hill, overwhelming their houses, was partly an explanation of her doggedness. It looked like offices, a network of long corridors and big, strange-smelling rooms, where the initiated watched over the dispensing of fierce laws which their subjects would never understand. Appeals were made obliquely, long and complicated hassles entered into, reprieves won, a limb conceded, a sentence deferred, and some came out acquitted. Others stayed, bewildered into submission. It was as if Sarah knew that to go in there was to surrender herself, condone her dying.

Her unwillingness to do that was typical. Arbitrariness was her element. The only shape that could be imposed on her life was a time-span. She hadn't matured in any definable sense. She had simply grown older. Her past was a rubble of contradictions from which no coherent pattern could be salvaged. She was a Catholic who was secretly rather impressed that her son had stopped being one. She had accepted Old Conn's passivity in the face of whatever happened without ever agreeing with it. She had been a woman who could be a careful solicitous mother for months and then be genteelly drunk for a week at a time with her friend, old Bella Duncan.

Tam remembered some of those times, when his mother and Bella would sit at opposite sides of the fire, rocking slightly and cackling in a private, preoccupied way, like witches who had found a charm for annihilating every concern but themselves. There wouldn't be a bite to eat in the house, and his father, coming home, would banish Bella and put Sarah to bed. They would have to try to confine her to the house till the impulse passed from her, like a temperature dropping. With false recoveries and relapses, a bout could last for days. Once, not long after he had started in the pits, Tam came in to the two of them smirking together. He changed, stood among the men at the corner for a while, and then went down to Ayr to enlist in the army. But he was kept waiting so long that his mother and Bella had arrived before he could do it. One of the men at the corner, who had been talking to him, had gone to the house and informed his mother what he was doing. Since he was cheating his age to get in, he had to come away. His mother had been very contrite. It was the last time she went seriously on the drink.

Now it seemed right that she should die outside the walls of understanding and explanation. She had never wanted to come to terms with the factors that governed her life, to understand what lay behind her hardships. She had simply been herself from day to day. Her death was similarly going to be her own event, uncompromised by official explanations. The only intermediary she needed was a priest. The tumour secreted inside her was uniquely her own, like a birth-mark. Like everything else in her life, her family, her poverty, getting married, having children, it was just something that had happened to her, not significantly related to causes, and certainly not to effects.

Standing at the window, Tam endured a garbled pain that became confused with the shape of the infirmary, the cruciform frame of wood in the window, the oppressive shabbiness of the room behind him, his father's posture, Lizzie's fussiness, the very placing of the furniture, it seemed, as if they were all somehow the cause of it, all of them together, and as if the altering of one of them would make things different. In the illumination not of thought but of experience, one word came to him with visionary suddenness: unnecessary. All of it. Not in the fact that it happened. But in the way that it happened. Like an army, the members of which never reach the battle. But die not for a common cause. Separately, and to no purpose. Choking on a fishbone. Contracting gangrene from a skelf.

He turned and tried to talk to his father. But the priest would be coming tonight and Conn was more or less postponing himself till he should arrive. Lizzie had always seemed to be talking round the edge of some preoccupation, ever since he had ceased to call himself a Catholic. Tam crossed again to the bed and looked at his mother. She didn't open her eyes. For the last few nights it had felt strange coming round here. She had now become more a process than a person. You simply came and looked on, at an event.

'Ah'll luk roon again the morra,' he said.

As he left, he heard Lizzie complaining to her father that Mary wasn't doing her share, had missed a turn.

At the corner he stood silently. It started to rain and they all stepped back against the building. He hoped that Kathleen and Jack had found some shelter.

# CHAPTER THIRTEEN

'Auld Swig? They used tae say it wis only Communion wine he drank. The drunker he goat, the holier he goat. Ye mind that, Jessie?'

'Hiv Ah no' jist. His sister Peggy could tell ye aboot that. She gi'ed him a plate o' soup ance. When he had the drinker's hunger on 'im. Twa plates he took. Smacks his foag, says, "That was guid!" "So it should be," says she, "wi' a pun o' guid beef stock in it." He went white. "God forgi'e ye, wumman. It's Friday." He went ootside like a whittrick an' put his fingers doon his throat. Twa plate o' soup doon the pen.'

'He wis an awfu' drinker.'

'Young Sconey's no' sa bad, is he?'

'Naw. He can take a dram wi' the next man. But no' like his feyther. He went at it like a day's darg.'

'He's an awfu' case, the Sconey.'

'It wis him that stole the candyman's cairt at the Taury Raws. Did a cavalry charge up the street wi' it.'

'Aye. Shoutin', "Weans, weans, gether banes, an' Ah'll gi'e ye candy."'

'Here, Andra. Whit wis it he did in the street yon nicht wi' you?'

They all waited, some watching Andra expectantly, because this was part of the Sconey legend that they hadn't heard of so far.

'Och, it wis jist a wee thing,' Andra said. 'We were walkin' doon the main street. A summer's evenin', like. Ah wis quite prood o' maself. Done up like a dish o' fish. An' Sconey says, "A meenit, Andra. Ah'll catch up wi' ye." He nipped intae an entry. Tae tie his lace, as

Ah thocht. So. He catches up richt enough. An' we walk oan. Quite jocko. But Ah stertit to notice folk sniggerin'. As they went past. An' lookin' back et us. Ah looked doon tae check maself aff, ye ken? An' here's Sconey wi' wan trooser-leg rolled up tae 'is thigh. Stridin' along, his face sober as a judge. Whit a leg, tae! As if he'd done a clean swap wi' a spider.'

The story gained by context: Andra Crawford sat looking, as people always said of him, as if he'd just stepped out of a band-box. An ex-regular soldier, he still dressed with a military neatness and precision. For him, a walk was a one-man parade. Set against his punctiliousness, Sconey's behaviour took on a satirical edge with Andra as involuntary straight man in a double-act.

Their laughter was measured, formal as a response, hardly more than a chorus of amplified smiles. It washed gently round the coffin that sat on trestles in the centre of the room. The talk was all of local people, things they had said, what they had done, caught living in a luminous phrase or a definitive action. Sarah Docherty herself featured in some of them. But there was no attempt to talk particularly of her. When she appeared, it was because she naturally belonged in what they happened to be saying. She was, in any case, inseparably a part of all they said. Oral scriptures, the stories absorbed her into them, saving something from the corpse in the box.

The people sat against the walls of the room. Since Sarah came originally from Cronberry, none of her brothers or sisters or their children had managed to be present. They lived too far away, but would come in for the funeral. Even without them the place was filled, with neighbours, relatives, friends of the family. All the borrowed chairs, which had been set round the room against the walls, were in use. Some of the men sat on the floor. All evening people had been coming and going, some waiting only an hour or so, others staying. Clay pipes and saucers containing Woodbines and teased tobacco had been put at various places, and people helped themselves. The conversation too was communal, like a hookah.

'Miss Gilfillan's keepin' herself by herself these days.'
'Aye.'
'She's always done that, mind ye.'
'Aye, but mair so lately.'
'Pair sowl.'
'Is she no'!'
'Aye. But she's got mair in her heid than the kaim'll take oot. The same lady.'
'Goad aye. D'ye hear whit she did wi' the fellas at her windy?'
'Ah heard aboot that.'
'Whit wis that?'
'Two or three o' the fellas late at night.'

'Ah wis wan. It was jist afore we a' went up hame. We stoapped tae hiv a word ootside her windy. An' we plants oor bums on the ledge, ye see. Well, we wis talkin' quiet but it must've annoyed her. Afore we kent whit wis happenin' wur bums is soakin'. She'd eased up the windy awfu' quiet an' poored watter richt along the windy-sill. No' a word spoken, mark ye. But we goat the message.'

'Whit did ye say?'

'Whit could we say? Good nicht.'

'No' bad, richt enough.'

'Oh, she's a winker.'

Andra Crawford rose and crossed towards the door of the house. It was open and he stepped out into the upstairs lobby of the tenement. He wanted to stretch his legs. As he walked up and down slowly, smoking, he could still hear their voices, though the words had no meaning, muffled by the wall. It was pleasant that way, like listening to a muted, improvised music. A Protestant himself, Andra preferred the atmosphere at a Catholic wake. Perhaps it was because he had been a soldier that he responded to the sense of orderliness, the way in which the Catholics present carried in their hands the means to reduce the whole thing to a prearranged pattern. At midnight, someone would kneel down and say the rosary and their words would range themselves in drilled ranks against the fear that surrounded them.

He had come because it was Tam Docherty's mother. He hadn't known the old woman very well but he talked to Tam at the corner quite a lot. Old Conn he saw quite often on the streets and he had been watching him tonight, sitting like a monument among them, older than his age, quietly tholing the amputation of a large part of himself.

Andra went down the few stairs to the middle-landing and stubbed his cigarette out on the ledge of the open window. Throwing the stub, he watched it roll down the roof of the wash-house and settle in the guttering. The aimless action, felt suddenly against the size of what was happening in the room above, was plucked from continuity, fell from him slowly, it seemed, suspended upon void, like the descent of a feather measuring a chasm. That fragment of an evening which had come to rest minutely and invisibly among the complex of roofs and buildings below him like a dust-speck on a prairie was himself. He looked above the buildings to the trees in the darkness of the park, fortuitously remembered Africa. Strange rivers. Land that never held a print. A quarrel that was nobody's. Thoughts drifted in his head like the dust that settles after motion. None of them seemed to belong particularly to him. Except Anderson. A Galloway man lying on a kopje. His chest caved in on one side. The paybook and the photos blown to bits. He thought of Old Conn, weathered and alone, washed up on a single-end in Ayrshire, not having come here, but having been brought. Sarah dead. His own children going to work in the mill. His youngest son with a heart as weak as paper. Six medals in the house. Anderson's face, the eyeballs hardening. His own father, remembered sitting by the fire, waiting somehow, as if his life was an anteroom to a place he never reached. Andra stood, his mind submerging slowly, drowning among currents he couldn't overcome.

Into his foundering thoughts came voices. His reactions were unfocused for a moment until he realised that people were speaking quietly, urgently in the lobby above him and that they couldn't see him because of his position on the landing.

'It his tae be decided noo.'

That was Lizzie, Sarah's daughter. Among the consenting murmurs he picked out the other daughter Mary's voice and what he took to be both their husbands.

'The auld sowl canny afford tae stey himself,' Mary said.

'But we've nae room.' One of the men.

'Nae mair hiv we.' The other husband.

There was a silence. It came to Andra as the sound of shame. He wanted to leave, felt as if he was spying on people in the lavatory. But he was unwilling to betray his presence with noise and held in spite of himself by the hypnotism of other people's dilemmas.

'Then it'll maybe hiv tae be the Home.'

Lizzie had been the one with the guts to say it. Andra's mind automatically translated her euphemism—The Pairhoose—then instantly substituted another more common euphemism of his own—The Hoose wi' the Wan Lum.

'We jist couldny possibly manage wi' him.' Mary's voice was canvassing support.

'Nane o' us could.' Lizzie's husband it sounded like.

'Whit does Tam say?' the other man asked.

'Where is oor Tam onywey?' Mary said.

'I telt him tae step oot a meenit. He's comin',' Lizzie replied.

They took refuge again in silence. Lizzie broke it.

'It'll a' hiv tae be seen aboot richt awa.'

The others muttered.

'Whit's this?'

Andra recognised Tam Docherty's voice. Lizzie was the obvious spokesman.

'It's aboot ma feyther, Tam. Whit's tae be done wi' him? We've nane o' us got room. An '. . .'

'Jesus Christ!'

'Noo listen. Oor Tam . . .'

'Listen? Ma mither's no' richt cauld an' ye're pittin' the auld man up fur auction.'

'Ye've nae richt tae be talkin' that wey, Tam,' Lizzie's husband said.

'Ah've every richt. It's ma feyther ye're tryin' tae parcel up among ye.'

'He's mine tae, ye ken,' Lizzie broke in.

'By Christ, ye hide it weel.'

'Tam!' Mary was angry. 'It'll hiv tae be the Home.'

'Naw, naw.'

'But there's nae room.'

'Then we'll make room.'

'Hoo? Jist tell me hoo!'

'Listen! Whit's gaun oan here? Ye should be fightin' tae take 'im. No tae get rid o' 'im.'

'Och. Talk sense, Tam,' Lizzie said. 'We hivny room!'

'It's a bit late fur sense. Hoo mony weans hiv you goat, Lizzie? Five. An' Mary's three. An' Ah hiv fower. If sense came intae it, that wid be twelve weans less tae feed fur a stert. If ye want tae be sensible, take yer weans up tae the market oan Friday an' sell them. Because that's what we are. Fuckin' cattle. Unless we can prove different. Well Ah'm different. An' Ah'm damned if Ah'll leeve ma life according tae *their* sense. Whit's mine belongs tae me. An' Ah'm no' askin' *thame* tae come an' collect him like a bit o' rubbish. He's fur nae "Home". D'ye ken whit it's like in there?'

'But d'ye . . .'

'It's feenished. He steys wi' me. Whit are we talkin' aboot this fur? Can ye no' see? By the time somethin' like this gets tae talk there's nothin' tae say.'

They all said nothing. Andra heard somebody else come out into the lobby.

'Lizzie!' It was a woman's voice. 'They're jist goin' tae say the rosary noo.'

'Right, Agnes,' Lizzie said.

Andra listened, but nobody had moved.

'Whit's Jenny goin' tae say?' Mary asked.

'Jenny'll have him. Ah ken her.'

Andra heard them move along the lobby back into the room. He wouldn't be going in after them, not just because they might know he had heard them. It was mainly from a desire to keep intact the feeling that was in him. He thought he understood why it was he had always liked Tam Docherty so much. He was more than anything in his life showed him to be, and he knew it. The effect on Andra was as if he had come across some powerful animal in a cage, kept fit on its own frustration, endlessly restless, knowing instinctively that the bars are an invention, nothing final, and feeling contempt for its keepers. Andra sensed quite simply that Tam was not defeated. And if Tam wasn't, neither was he.

'Our father who art in heaven . . .' A single voice began, continued, was joined by others: 'Forgive us our trespasses as we forgive them that trespass against us . . .'

Andra slipped quietly down the stairs and went home to his private faith.

# CHAPTER FOURTEEN

The rocking-chair interested Conn—worn, discoloured, chipped at parts, it somehow conveyed to him a sense of other places as well as other times. Whenever he had the chance, he liked to sit in it, gathering speed, as if it were a means of transport. But he didn't very often get the chance. It was the only piece of furniture his Grandpa Docherty had brought with him and the old man almost lived in it, like a private room. When Tam started to call it 'the jaunting car', Conn was puzzled, until he noticed how often his Grandpa talked about Ireland from it, as if he was still seeing it.

The chair was the last prop for the old man's pride. Hurt by the knowledge that it had taken the family renegade and his Protestant wife to save him from the poorhouse, he continued to convince himself, with commendable inventiveness, that as long as he had the chair he was less a non-paying lodger than a sub-tenant. Swaying gently in it, he would disappear for an hour at a time into martyred silence on which the inscription read: 'Far be it from me to be a nuisance to anyone.' It was precisely at such times that his presence tended to irritate. A question met with a response the tired gentleness of which was a remonstrance. Carefully judged attempts to bring him into the conversation were foiled by the deafness which afflicted him in unpredictable phases, sometimes coming and going by the minute. Tam diagnosed him as suffering from 'politician's lugs'.

Jenny was best at dealing with him. Her success lay in the way she combined a readiness to accord him privileges with a refusal to grant him concessions. Miraculously, she managed to keep him supplied from the housekeeping with money for tobacco and the clay pipes he smoked it in. She didn't buy them for him. Every other day, the money appeared on the mantelpiece, and was enough to get him the occasional glass of beer he took as well. It was never mentioned after the first evening when she told him what it was for, and she never handed it directly to him. It might as well have come from an anonymous benefactor. At the same time, she wasn't inclined to spend a lot of attention on his huffs. Her ability to ignore them made them happen in a void, so that he was glad to come out of them.

When others wanted to complain about him, Jenny would remind them of his hands, as if they were justification enough for any mood. Before, Conn had always been conscious of the hugeness of his Grandpa's hands. Now they were crippled with arthritis, making him unfit for work. Grotesquely gnarled and knobbed, they seemed only distantly related to his arms, projecting from them like pieces of monumental sculpture. 'It's in the breed,' Old Conn would explain. But Tam, who in his wilder moments would have blamed the weather on the wealthy, claimed they were the result of his work with Kerr the builder. There was a certain amount of proxy justice in Tam's statement. Kerr had worked Old Conn for a pittance all his life and, when he couldn't work any more, had dismissed him with a handshake in which all that changed hands was sweat, not Kerr's. When his father was dead, Tam used to say, they should have the hands mounted and presented to Kerr. 'For above his bloody mantelpiece.'

Once settled in, the old man came to seem not so much a new presence as the acknowledgement of one that had always been there, as the figure of a madonna merely locates an already existing influence. With him ensconced every day beside the fire, the mystique of venerability had difficulty surviving the manual clumsiness, the hoasting, the simply boring repetitiousness of his talk.

Only Conn perhaps felt something like awe, for a short time. He was fascinated by the hands filling the pipe, moving separately like misshapen crabs, the small swirl of sound that began somewhere inside, enlarged slowly, broke in a storm of coughing, the complete stillness which the old man could achieve within the motion of his chair. Also, he was the one his Grandpa liked to talk to. Secretly, Old Conn was paying for his keep by being subversive. Indoors, he talked of Ireland to his youngest grandson, trying to convey to him the sense of Connemara, which had become the landscape of his own mind— those miles of unremitting barrenness through which the rocks rise up like headstones. But outside, on the frequent walks when he took Conn 'up the country', he was trying to save the boy from the Protestant limbo in which he lived. He catechised him in the nature of God, spoke familiarly enough of hell to have been there, kept putting the rosary into his hands. Always before they came back to the house, Conn would be reminded of the need for secrecy, as if God were the head of a cabal.

It would all have affected Conn more deeply if it hadn't been for the counter-influence of his Grandpa Wilson. He too, needing to tighten his grasp on something before it loosened forever, moved closer to Conn, like a rival planet. His love of town rather than country exerted more power.

To walk through Graithnock with Mairtin was to be ambushed at every corner by the past. From the fluted pillar inset in the wall of the Old High Kirk 'To the memory of Lord Soulis AD 1444' (of whose murder Mairtin was able to give an eye-witness account) to the house of Alexander Smith in Douglas Street ('a genius wi' words' of whom Mairtin hadn't read a line) the town came alive with ghosts. The industrial school was still to him what it had been—'The Place', Graithnock House, residence of the last Earl of Graithnock, executed for his part in the '45 Rebellion after having unsuccessfully demanded that the citizens of Graithnock supply him with their arms. Mairtin liked to repeat how the local people had informed the Earl that if they gave him their guns it would be 'with the muzzle till him.' Graithnock, Mairtin said with pride, had always been loyal to the crown.

From Mairtin Conn learned of 'The Soor Mulk Rebellion' of almost a hundred years ago, when housewives drenched baillies and farmers in milk at the Cross, rather than pay the increased prices the farmers were demanding. He discovered who Tam Samson was. He found out that thirty people had once been crushed to death in the old Laigh Kirk during a panic when the congregation thought the roof was falling in. He memorised, like a mystic message of grandeur, the words: 'Here lies John Nisbet who was taken by Major Balfour's Party and suffered at Graithnock 14 April 1683 for adhering to the word of God and our Covenant—Revn. XII and II. Renewed by public subscription AD 1823.' 'Who was taken . . . and suffered'—the words haunted him.

The best story of all was the one Mairtin told about the Foregate. When he was a boy, he said, there had been a two-storeyed thatched house there. When they were knocking it down, one of the workmen had found a leather pouch concealed under the thatch. As he lifted it out, it burst, and in seconds people were scrambling in the street for the hoard of silver coins that had scattered. The coins belonged to the reigns of Charles I and Charles II. How had they come there? 'Only the grave kens,' Mairtin would say.

With that ability to conjure exotic past out of mundane present Grandpa Docherty couldn't compete. Conn found himself joining with Angus in a conspiracy of mild laughter at the old man. They liked him but got into the habit of not taking him seriously. Angus was inclined to bait him a little, encouraging him to talk about Ireland.

He would have done so more often if Mick hadn't been aware of Angus's tendency and stifled it whenever he saw it asserting itself.

Mick was almost certainly the one affected most by his grandfather's arrival. It clarified his understanding of himself and his family. Mick was naturally an accepter of the way things were, not spinelessly, or mindlessly, but just because he believed that was the only way you could make anything of them. He had a capacity for refining the raw shape his life had inherited into a personal pattern, and enjoying it, so that the drab necessity for work, for example, heightened his leisure-time rather than stultified it. Consequently, the discontent of someone like his father occasionally irked him and frequently puzzled him. Through countless long arguments with Tam, which Mick had incidentally enjoyed, he had tried to formulate what he meant, to explain why he didn't share his father's fervour for change. He had never quite succeeded.

But in his grandfather, when he came to live with them, he saw his argument incarnate. Mick admired the old man very much. In everything from his arthritis to his love of Ireland, Mick found the same quality—the ability to accept necessity and make it a part of himself. It didn't matter if you didn't believe that Catholicism was true. Mick himself had stopped going to church because it had come to mean nothing to him. But the point was that it was true for Old Conn, as everything about him was. There was nothing that for Mick could imaginably have been different. He felt his grandfather had become what he inevitably had to be. Accordingly, he lived amicably with himself, the pain in his hands, his poverty, his exile. By accepting his troubles, he was able to extract daily from their bitterness, as by an age-old, secret process, the dram of comfort that made his living worthwhile.

His insight into Old Conn gave Mick a perspective on the rest of his family, he felt. He saw his grandfather as having inherited from his early rural life the talent for enduring as simply as a tree, twisted by the winds, perhaps, stunted even, but still there. What his father lacked, having been born in an industrial town, was that simple acceptance. To Mick, Old Conn had a patriarchal authority, offered a way of life to them, not through his words, which were often almost nonsensical, but by being as he was.

But it was an authority to which Mick's young brothers seemed impervious. There was a brief spell not long after Old Conn came to live with them when their disrespect threatened to become open. It took one of Tam's cauterising expressions of anger to cure them.

Old Conn had been talking about Skibbereen. He did that a lot. It held some obscure but fundamental significance for him that made him invoke it every so often. When someone mentioned present hardships, Old Conn had a habit of saying 'Aye. How are things in

Skib then?' as if that somehow put everything else in perspective. He referred much to the mass grave there and sometimes would allow you to persuade him to sing 'Revenge for Skibbereen', lack of breath erasing half-lines, garbling words. The effect was of listening to someone far away in a shifting wind.

On this night he talked himself towards a peroration: 'The blight, ye see. But the blight wisny jist in the grund. It wis in the folk as weel. The nabarry. Their leavin's wid've saved lives. But naw. Fur want of a tattie they died.'

Angus and Conn could hardly stop laughing. Apart from the natural tendency of solemnity to induce hysteria in them, there was the fact that Angus had been doing a secret imitation of the old man's expressions and gestures. Conn, trying to swallow his amusement, noticed Angus coming nearer and nearer to the state that his mother called 'Gettin' above yerself'. As if to demonstrate the accuracy of Conn's observation, Angus spoke.

'It wid hiv tae've been an awfu' big tattie. Wid it no', Grandpa?'

Angus brayed once with laughter and Conn irresistibly echoed him.

'Hey!' Their father crumpled the paper he was trying to read. 'D'ye ken who ye're talkin' tae?'

He stared at them steadily. The rain falling beyond the window behind him slicked the room in grey light. Conn felt the charge of shock that meant incontrovertibly they had crossed a border, trespassed where they shouldn't be.

'Dae ye?' He paused, his eyes angry. 'This is a man that kens whit he's talkin' aboot. He's had times when there wis nothin' tae eat but air. An' he came through them. An' if he hadny, you two widny be here. Show them yer hauns, feyther. Show them! Ye see that? Ye ken hoo they goat like that?'

'Workin' wi' the bricks,' Conn suggested.

'Wi' pittin' the bite in ma mooth. An' that means yours as weel. An' don't you forget it. That's a man ye're talkin' tae. No' a bloody bit o' furniture. Ya pair o' yelps!'

'Och, feyther,' Kathleen said. His anger was becoming ridiculously disproportionate. 'Ye've said yerself ma Grandpa goes oan aboot Ireland at an awfu' rate.'

'Whit if Ah have? An' you're another yin. Lady Muck. Ah've heard ye complainin' aboot the mess o' the fire-end wi' him. This is a hoose. No' a hotel. An' if Ah fa' oot wi' him aboot Ireland, well, that's a private argument.' He looked round them all. 'An' jist all of ye remember. He's where ye come fae. An' whaurever ye go, ye'll have tae take 'im wi' ye.'

They sat welded into a group by his words, the rain corroding their silence. Having turned a casual evening into a family manifesto, Tam smoothed out his paper and resumed staring at it. Angus watched him opaquely. Kathleen huffed. The old man rose slowly.

'Well. Ah'm doon the entry-mooth fur a breath o' air.'

When he was gone, Conn remained hypnotised by the rocking of his empty chair. Its motion without presence gave it a quality of mysterious power. By the time it was still, it had impressed the image of itself on Conn with a force greater than words, a part of his personal heraldry.

# CHAPTER FIFTEEN

'Docherty!' Less a voice than an effulgence of sound falling across their suddenly stricken silence. Outwith its paralysing glare, others freeze. Conn stands up slowly, carefully doesn't look at anybody else, as if a glance might prove infectious. They all wait. 'Simpson! Would you two creatures come out here.'

They are allowed to stand on the floor for a moment, to become the relief of the others, a moral.

'You'll excuse us, Miss Carmichael. I wouldn't want to get blood on your floor.'

Some titters are gratefully offered, withdrawn. Silence is safest.

'Certainly, Mr Pirrie.'

They pass into the next room. Their small procession isn't a unique sight but they gain a brief attention here too. Beyond this room, a small cloakroom area, where they stop.

Conn almost swoons with the staleness of the place. It is a small passageway, foetid with forgotten children, a knackery for futures. He sees the drifting motes as clear as constellations. Two coats hang damp. Their quality of sadness haunts his inarticulacy. Mr Pirrie inflates, enormous in the silence, hovers like a Zeppelin.

'Well, well, well. Who started it?'

On one of the floorboards an accentuation in the grain makes a road. It runs winding, vanishes under Mr Pirrie's boot.

'It doesn't matter. You'll both be getting the same. What's wrong with your face, Docherty?'

'Skint ma nose, sur.'

'How?'

'Ah fell an' bumped ma heid in the sheuch, sur.'

'I beg your pardon?'

'Ah fell an' bumped ma heid in the sheuch, sur.'

'I beg your pardon?'

In the pause Conn understands the nature of the choice, tremblingly, compulsively, makes it.

'Ah fell an' bumped ma heid in the sheuch, sur.'

The blow is instant. His ear seems to enlarge, is muffed in numbness. But it's only the dread of tears that hurts. Mr Pirrie distends on a lozenge of light which mustn't be allowed to break. It doesn't. Conn hasn't cried.

'That, Docherty, is impertinence. You will translate, please, into the mother-tongue.'

The blow is a mistake, Conn knows. If he tells his father, he will come up to the school. 'Ye'll take whit ye get wi' the strap an' like it. But if onybody takes their hauns tae ye, ye'll let me ken.' He thinks about it. But the problem is his own. It frightens him more to imagine his father coming up.

'I'm waiting, Docherty. What happened?'

'I bumped my head, sir.'

'Where? Where did you bump it, Docherty?'

'In the gutter, sir.'

'Not an inappropriate setting for you, if I may say so.'

The words mean nothing. Only what happens counts.

'I'm disappointed in you, Docherty. You'll soon be coming up to the big school. And I'll be ready for you. I used to hear nice things about you. But not any more. You might've had the chance to go to the Academy. You still could. Do you know what that means? But what's the point? I wouldn't waste the time of highly qualified men. But while you're here you'll behave like civilised people. Brawling in the playground!'

His voice shudders the wood around them. The words have worked, mystically invoke his anger. It possesses him. The veins in his nose suffuse. The strap snakes out from its nest under the shoulder of his jacket.

'Simpson first!' It is a ritual. He holds the strap in his right hand, drops it over his shoulder, reaches back with his left hand, flexes the leather, begins. 'I will *not*. Have. Violence. In my school.'

Four. Conn can prepare.

'Docherty!' One. Conn recites to himself: *Ah bumped ma heid in the sheuch*. Two. *Sheuch*. 'You're getting as bad as your brother was.' Three. *Fat man*. 'I was glad to get rid of him.' Four. Conn's hands drop, stiff as plaster-casts. 'Up, Docherty, up! Two more for insolence.' Five. *Bastard*. He is watching for signs of tears. Six. *Big, fat bastard*.

He has become his hands. His will huddles round them, containing the radiations of their pain, refusing them the salve of tears. The two of them are led back to the room.

Mr Pirrie says, 'I've just been tickling these two's hands. As a little warning. The next boys I catch behaving like savages won't be able to use their hands for a week.'

The room is dislocated by his departure, becomes for a moment no more than his absence. Patiently, Miss Carmichael shepherds their attention. Her talk moves delicately across the film of her own thoughts, a fly walking water. Her sympathy, limed by circumstances, flutters half-heartedly and subsides. No doubt Mr Pirrie knows best. He comes from a working-class home himself, he says. He isn't afraid to admit what his father was—a pig walking upright. Troughing it at the table. Swearing. They're all the same. Afraid to better themselves. They need the comfort of the herd. They have the place they want. They have to be taught to keep it. He blesses his mother, who married beneath herself and found that you couldn't convert them. No wonder Livingstone left Blantyre. Africa was an easier proposition. But she at least managed to save her son. He will be forever grateful for what she has helped him to become.

A dull sense of irony exists in Miss Carmichael's mind without the hardness of conviction to sharpen it against. Her thoughts shift to High Street. There is a family there that she visits. From them she has heard about Conn's father. Once he was pointed out to her in the street. The stories about him have fused in her head with the white gash of a face, the hard-heeled walk. The image has occasionally troubled the demureness of her thoughts, like an uncouth and uninvited guest at a tea-party, and has become the extension of a vague unease in her own life. A brief confrontation of pictures occurs in her mind. Mr Pirrie seated in his own house, a book in his hand, people listening, his words incontrovertible in the atmosphere of the room, the whole scene held in a self-generated luminosity, bright and delicate as a soap-bubble. Tam Docherty walking down a street. The bubble bursts.

Briefly there comes to Miss Carmichael a swamping and frightening sense of chaos, thousands of uncontradictable and contradictory opinions, unimaginable ideas, invisible angers, millions of directions, pains, all hopelessly entangled. What is there that can possibly be done? She teaches spelling.

In the room there is a snuffling sound, contained, private. Alan Simpson is crying. Conn, on the brink of tears himself, is sorry but grateful. Poor Alan. He lost the fight too. Conn knows now that he won't be crying. Alan Simpson is doing it for him.

It was an unimportant incident and yet significant beyond itself, the hundredth sparrow alighting that snaps the twig. Within minutes, Conn was taking an almost aesthetic interest in the look of his wrists, pebbled lightly with blisters. Inside the puffiness of their pain his fingers hardened again. He flexed them. The rawness of the experience had already refined itself into separate constituents, not without their uses. The blisters weren't unimpressive. There would be the admiration of the boys, the sympathy of the girls. He would have to enlist his mother's help, though, in making sure that his father didn't take it any further.

Conn's conscious adjustment to what had happened didn't go much deeper than that. But more important, registering beyond the reach of his awareness, the small incident in the cloakroom was like a crucial digit affecting an immensely complicated calculation. Relating to it, realignments were already taking place in him. He was coming to understand through his own experience the attitudes Mick and Angus had expressed towards school. More and more he was beginning to envy Angus his escape and involvement in what was to Conn the real life of his family, work and the bringing in of a wage. He knew his father's contempt for the way they had to live and his reverence for education. But against that went Conn's sense of the irrelevance of school, its denial of the worth of his father and his family, the falsity of its judgements, the rarified atmosphere of its terminology. It was quite a wordless feeling, but all the stronger for that, establishing itself in him with the force of an allergy.

While Miss Carmichael gave him sympathetic exemption from her questions, he took a stub of pencil in his fingers. Slowly across a scuffed piece of paper a word moved clumsily. Opposite it another word was manoeuvred and settled, the way he had seen in a dictionary Miss Carmichael showed him. His hand shook as he did it. It was a painful and tremulous matter, like an ant trying to manipulate stones. He sat buried inside himself while the words spread themselves across the paper. Minutes later, he was stunned into stillness, looking at the big awkward shapes they made before him.

| | |
|---|---|
| *sheuch* | *gutter* |
| *speugh* | *sparrow* |
| *lum* | *chimny* |
| *brace* | *mantalpiece* |
| *bine* | *tub* |
| *coom* | *foot* |
| *coomie* | *foolish man (Mr Pirrie)* |
| *gomeril* | *another foolish man* |
| *spicket* | *tap* |
| *glaur* | *muck what is in a puddle after the puddle goes away* |
| *wabbit* | *tired* |

| | |
|---|---|
| *whaup* | *curloo* |
| *tumshie* | *turnip* |
| *breeks* | *troosers* |
| *chanty* | *po* |
| *preuch* | *anything you can get* |
| *I was taigled longer* | *I was kept back* |
| *nor I ettled* | *for a more longer* |
| | *time than I desired.* |

One side of the paper was filled. He didn't start on the other side because he now wanted to write things that he couldn't find any English for. When something sad had happened and his mother was meaning that there wasn't anything you could do about it, she would say 'ye maun dree yer weird'. When she was busy, she had said she was 'saund-papered tae a whuppet.' 'Pit a raker oan the fire.' 'Hand-cuffed to Mackindoe's ghost.' 'A face tae follow a flittin'.' If his father had to give him a row but wasn't really angry, he said 'Ah'll skelp yer bum wi' a tealeaf tae yer nose bluids.'

Conn despaired of English. Suddenly, with the desperation of a man trying to amputate his own infected arm, he savagely scored out all the English equivalents.

On his way out of school, he folded his grubby piece of paper very carefully and put it in his pocket. It was religiously preserved for weeks. By the time he lost it, he didn't need it.

# CHAPTER SIXTEEN

Mairtin stood translating everything into himself. The glass in his hand took wilful reflections from everything around him. The bulge of his belly was satisfaction. One foot danced in stasis, his family moving threaded on his thoughts. In the moustache years were held in arrested avalanche.

Each dance was a relationship. The steps created a convention within which they could celebrate themselves, uncles, cousins, aunts, neighbours, friends, advancing, receding, intersecting, pivoting on one another, all conforming to patterns whose law was whimsy. The music quickened the whole thing into compulsion.

In the flare of sudden movement, round the corner of a comment, faces bobbed, piked on exertion, a group sat in an alcove of private conversation. Privacies became public.

A fat man's galluses burst. He had taken off his jacket and waistcoat to be comfortable. One strand of the braces twanged over his shoulder like a fractured harp-string. One side of his trousers drooped, revealing the tops of home-made drawers of scarlet wool. Tadger Daly stood bowed in the middle of the floor, lockjawed with laughter.

Jenny's Uncle James revealed the secret of how to put water and whisky in the same glass and keep them separate. While the younger children played at sliding along the edge of the dance-floor, Angus, hiding at the end of a corridor, showed Conn how to smoke, and drank an inch of stale beer from a tumbler which had been left below a chair. The Co-operative Hall was a masque of faces lurid with enjoyment, luminous with sweat. Even Jenny's mother, in the presence of so much drink, kept a festive smile clenched like a fading rose between her teeth.

The dress, an heirloom starched and laundered specially for Kathleen, shed radiance wherever she went. At half past seven in the morning, she had stood in the living-room, imprisoned in its stiff whiteness, waiting for the cab to take her to chapel. Her strange presence muted the rest of the room, made it seem drab, a cocoon that had belied its contents. Her father and brothers were almost shy, embarrassed by what they hadn't seen before. Her mother fussed gently, possessing for the last time. Kathleen asked plaintive irrelevant questions about her appearance, innocent of her own transformation. It wasn't beauty, or anything that could be objectively named. It was simply Kathleen, the blackness of her hair blued subtly by the whiteness of the veil, her eyes deepened into an awareness of what she thought the day meant to her, her body's ripeness, her oval face achieving the brief perfection of itself.

Conn's Uncle Sammy dropped a glass. Having been accused of being drunk, he offered to stand on his hands to prove sobriety. To have his hands free for demonstration, he put his glass down on a chair that had been taken away minutes ago. It was the beer he didn't take that finally couped him. Seeing the exploded shards of glass, he dismissed any suggestion of a brush and shovel.

'Nae man that wisny sober could pick up a' these bits withoot an injury. Right?'

His wife escorted him home five minutes later, handcuffed with a bloodstained dish-towel.

Old Conn enjoyed himself with his pipe and a little beer. All evening people arrived at his chair to talk, laugh, and go away. He smiled much. Reflected in his gentle eyes, the dancers whirled and flung across a desert.

Jack said, 'Ah never expected tae enjoy ma ain waddin' as much. An' the best o' it's tae come.'

He tried to make sure he spoke to as many people as possible. He moved among a minefield of suspicions and survived. Older women watched, waited for him, listened, nodded.

'He seems a nice boay.'

'A guid wey wi' him.'

'Aye. At least they're beginnin' weel enough.'

The children gave way first, so that the evening died slowly and piecemeal among them. One lay asleep on a window-ledge, cushioned on a jacket. Another slept across two chairs, another on his mother's knee. Two small brothers niggled each other half-heartedly, wrangling with their tiredness. The songs grew sadder. 'The Nameless Lassie' was strangled at leisure. Only a few couples still soft-shoed around the floor, as if caught up in a habit they couldn't break. A woman sat staring across the bleakness of tomorrow. The empty glasses covered two trestle-tables. Three men, caged in their own agreement, picked fleas from one another's egos. The band were taking longer between tunes. The dark silence of the town outside was seeping into the place like gas, deadening them.

It was a bright moon, the cadaver of daylight. The unusualness of being abroad together in the early hours of the morning heightened their awareness of one another. They were more a family for being alone in the lunar emptiness of the town. Angus walked slightly ahead of Jenny, whose hand was on Conn's shoulder. Mick and Tam came behind them, talking Tam, proud of the social ease and straight-forward likeableness he had seen in Mick this evening, was pleased to let him do most of the talking, while Tam himself silently memorised his happiness so that he could keep it with him after tonight. Kathleen, he thought, was well married. Jack should make a good man. Every-thing had been fine—the meal, the drink, the dancing. They couldn't really afford it, except that you had to be able to afford what your children deserved. There wasn't any other way to live.

He had enjoyed seeing so many people together, in contact with one another. He felt like a man who had successfully expressed what he wanted to say. He felt somehow reconfirmed in his love of people. As he passed a decaying tenement building, he took the flower from his button-hole and stuck it in a crevice of the brick.

The sunlight Conn wakened into was disappointing. The day ahead defined itself negatively: it wasn't the day of Kathleen's wedding. Mick and Angus were already up. Conn could hear the sounds of the others through in the living-room. There were just the same small things as always waiting to be done. But as he rose and pulled on his trousers, he found that fragments of the previous day were still with him, usurping the dullness of the room like sunspots. The horses had been marvellous. He loved the way the skin moved like water over the hardness of their muscles. The priest. Frightening in his bright clothes. Moving his hands as mysteriously as a magician. The high coolness of the church. The variety of faces. And the noise. Angus with the beer, saying he bet he was nearly as strong as his father. The richness of the whole day gave Conn a terrible impatience to take part in things.

With his nightshirt off, he crossed to the mirror on the dresser. He crooked his arms and squeezed. The biceps came up like small bubbles below the skin. Shutting out the sound of his mother laying out the dishes on the table, he carefully achieved the expression he wanted, glared a challenge at himself.

# CHAPTER SEVENTEEN

Miss Gilfillan was dead. It was in this form High Street first became aware that anything was different with her. Decorous as ever, she hadn't appeared to public knowledge as one of the undignified dying, but merely passed invisibly from a gentle life to the perfect gentility of death. With faultless etiquette, she had become a corpse quietly and in private.

Disbelief followed the news to every face that heard it. She had never allowed them to become a part of her life, but—perhaps largely because of this—she had become a very special part of theirs—intractable, perennial, an enduring posture from the past, like a local version of the Albert Memorial. For her to die seemed a needless refinement. An era had been erased.

Meeting this incredulity, the facts found themselves affected by it, formed into minor legend. None of the ritual signs of her existence had changed while she was dying. She hadn't been seen on the street for some time beforehand. But that wasn't unusual. Old Mrs Molloy vouched for the fact that the setting of the table had continued regularly, except perhaps for the day before, when she herself hadn't been out of the house because she was 'chesty'. Nobody had seen her eating during this time, right enough. But nobody ever saw her eating.

Mrs Simpson, who lived upstairs, had been the first to sense something wrong. She realised that for days she hadn't heard a sound from Miss Gilfillan's house. It wasn't that she had expected to hear much. Miss Gilfillan was the quietest neighbour anybody ever had. But now and again you could hear her moving about, and sometimes talking quietly to her own loneliness. Mrs Simpson put a piece of dumpling on a plate, took it with her, and knocked at the door. The dumpling was an excuse. She knew Miss Gilfillan wouldn't take it. She wouldn't take anything from anybody. There was no answer.

When Mrs Simpson told her husband in the evening, he said she had likely been out. But Mrs Simpson had tried three times since that and, anyway, where was there for Miss Gilfillan to go? Next morning, before her husband went to work, he tried as well. Getting no answer, he went outside and looked in the window. He could see a vague shape lying in the set-in bed, fully clothed, it seemed. He broke in the door.

It was a thought, as they said, that Miss Gilfillan, who would have polished the doorknob after somebody's hand had been on it, should have her door burst in and not move a muscle. It was enough to make her come alive again. She was found lying dead on top of the bed. She was wearing what must once have been an expensive dress, and was perfectly composed, except one leg had slipped so that her foot rested at an angle on the floor in a most unladylike position. Around her the room was perfectly neat and tidy, marred only by dust that had settled since she stopped moving. The table was laid for dinner.

From all of this her last days were reconstructed. She was said to have died of starvation. She hadn't once asked anybody for help and she had been found in a room cluttered with objects which would have brought a good return from the pawnshop just across the street. She had to be imagined daily dusting these very things with the last of her strength, unfailingly setting a table on which food never arrived, sacrificing herself for a roomful of objects.

For the men at the corner the room took on the charisma of a shrine. But it didn't last. Not long afterwards, relatives who had never been to see her when she lived arrived to despoil, haggle over relics, and peel the place to the bare walls. A bricklayer and his family moved in. He soon acquired a reputation for knocking the wife about.

For a month or so her absence had a reaction on the life of the place, precipitated that intensified sense of oneself that an unexpected death frequently brings. It expressed itself obliquely. At the corner the small preoccupations of the men became defensively more strident, like dogs barking at strange noises in the dark. Using their gathered presences like a verbal gymnasium, they shed the sluggishness of winter, rehoned old commitments, vaunted a bit, and with plans and forecasts took out each a personal lease on the coming spring.

Gibby Molloy greeted the burgeoning year with a conviction strong enough to suggest that he had had an equinoctial vision. He was, he had decided, a formidable fighting-man. All things considered, this was an interestingly original interpretation of his experience so far. It was true that he had always been subject to unforeseeable fits of violence, but these had almost invariably involved him in conflict with inanimate objects. More than one man had seen this as proof that his shrewdness as promoter exceeded his shrewdness as participant. As Tadger Daly had used to say, 'Gibby wid fight wi' his shadda. An' he wid stert second favourite.'

But though the source of Gibby's conviction was secret, at least one of its effects was obvious. It brought to an end those uncontrollable outbursts of aimless destruction that had dogged his life. He was like someone who, having been mugged by the same footpad for years, finally hires him as a bodyguard. By formalising his tendency to violence into open challenge, he managed to contain it.

Unfortunately, Gibby's first action in his new role was not an auspicious one. He challenged Tadger Daly. This went beyond courage so far as to encroach on fantasy, being roughly equivalent to a boy who has been given a pair of boxing-gloves for his Christmas matching himself with the heavyweight champion of the world. Tadger had long ago earned High Street's accolade—the designation 'hard man'. Not quarrelsome by nature, he was content to let his past speak for him. Occasionally, he offered a mild reminder. With his hands in his pockets and wearing his pit boots, he would turn a complete somersault on the causeys. He was reputed to be able to put the head on a man from six feet away in one acrobatic leap. His truncated body was fitted with the preposterously long arms of a much bigger man, as if borrowed from the Brownie of Blednoch. Sometimes, hyperbolic with drink, he would claim to be the only man who could tie his laces without bending down.

Against this, Gibby ranged the full force of his impertinence, like a sparrow trying to intimidate a buzz-saw. Perhaps it was the very outlandishness of the challenge that inspired Gibby to make it. There certainly seemed to be no more mundane explanation.

It happened at the corner. They were talking about football players when Tadger remarked that Paterson, a local outside right who had gone senior, had no idea. 'If ye put icin' on the baw,' Tadger said, 'he wid eat it.' It suddenly occurred to Gibby that Andy Paterson had once walked out with his sister and there had been talk of their getting married. Therefore, Andy Paterson was, in a sense, nearly Gibby's brother-in-law.

'Ye'd better take that last remark back, Tadger,' Gibby said with quiet menace.

'Ah've goat naewhere tae keep it, Gibby,' Tadger replied, and went on to talk about something else.

'Tadger! Ah'm talkin' tae you.'

There was a puzzled silence. Gibby grew on it.

'Ye better take that back.'

'Whit back?'

'Aboot Andy Paterson.'

Tadger reflected.

'A' richt, Gibby. If ye put icin' on the baw, he widny eat it. He wid maist likely divide it oot among the weans. Fair enough?'

Gibby shrugged with the air of a man who has done his utmost to avoid the inevitable and seen his efforts scorned.

'Right,' he said. 'Come oan. Ower the park.'

Scenting a jocular conspiracy, Tadger looked round the other men at the corner. But the incredulity on their faces was unmistakably genuine. It came very slowly to Tadger that Gibby meant business. It wasn't possible but it was happening.

'Och, away tae hell, Gibby,' Tadger said. 'Whit dae ye want? Buried under the band-stand? Wi' full military honours.'

Everybody appreciated the humour of it except Gibby.

'Ye'll come. Or ye'll get it here. Are ye comin'?'

'Ah'm fine here, Gibby. Thanks a' the same.'

'Are ye comin'?'

'Gibby!'

Tadger spread his arms in appeal. Gibby attacked. Tadger's left arm shot out and took a handful of Gibby's lapels. Keeping his arm absolutely rigid, Tadger stood side-on to Gibby's assault. It was a heroic moment—Tadger standing holding a frustrated tornado by the scruff of the neck, while he reasoned with its fury.

'Gibby, Gibby. This is ney wey tae be gaun oan. Folk'll think we've fell oot. Could we no' discuss it?'

Gibby's answer was to increase his efforts, his ferocious fists savaging Tadger's armpit. After some more pleas for peace, Tadger turned to the others, bringing Gibby with him like a gaffed fish.

'Well, boys. Ye see hoo Ah'm placed. If Ah let him go, he'll kill me.'

There were sympathetic murmurs. Without warning, Tadger's arm compressed like a spring and he applied his bowed head to Gibby's inrushing brow with the precision of someone administering an anaesthetic. There was a crack like a rifle-shot. Tadger held on to Gibby as he sagged and solicitously propped him up against the wall. Three-quarters of an hour later, Gibby came to.

But those who had assumed that the matter was closed had failed to understand the new Gibby who had emerged from his winter sleep. Two days later, he challenged Tadger again. This time he made the stipulation that Tadger's head constituted an unfair advantage and only fists should be used. Tadger agreed. Three days after this defeat, Gibby issued his third challenge. His tactics were now becoming clear. He admitted that his intention was to wear Tadger down and he expressed the belief that he would finally be victorious. He was, in a way, proved right. When he demanded a fourth contest, Tadger shook hands with him and apologised for any remarks he had made about Andy Paterson.

Gibby was content. Thereafter he kept his antagonism for those outside High Street. He had achieved his identity among the men at the corner, hewn out his own small niche in the annals of High Street. Like the inventor of gunpowder, he had devised a devastating new mode of combat—the ability so to sate the enemy with victories that he surrenders. As Tadger admitted, nursing bruised hands, made wise by experience, 'Ye canny beat Gibby. He's too cute fur us. He's goat a system, ye see. He keeps pittin' the heid oan your hauns till yer knuckles brek.'

Tadger himself was too involved with other thoughts that spring to be much concerned with Gibby. He had carried out his three demolition jobs with a casualness that was almost absent-minded. He had his own worries. With his family nearly large enough to be declared a separate state, he and his wife had decided there would be no more. When he let this be known, it became a temporary pastime to make jokes about it. There were hints of panic in the Vatican, commemorative medals being struck, suggestions that he had lost his faith, counter-suggestions that that wasn't what he had lost. None of this bothered Tadger. What bothered him was the fact itself—they would have no more children. Though there were some families whose large numbers weren't entirely unrelated to the promptings of local priests, this wasn't the case with Tadger's. Both he and his wife were besotted with children. They had produced fourteen not so much in defiance of their circumstances as indifference to them. Eleven were still alive. Things had been made slightly less impossible by the fact that four of them were now working, while Tadger's mother, with her small shop, was able to help. Two of the children lived with her. But a sense of economy had finally overtaken the manic creative urge of Tadger and his wife.

The effect on Tadger was a gentle melancholy that lasted for a few weeks, rather like a one-man wake for the unborn. The familiar thought of children to come had become so central to his life that he missed it badly. For a time he made up for it by telling stories about the children he had. Every day brought a new chapter in the saga of his family. His tendency to be boring about them was accepted by the others as a natural phase.

Not all forms of boredom were so benign. Josey Mackay, long absent from the corner, reappeared regularly to issue up-to-the-minute bulletins on the Boer War. Much older than most of the others, Josey was conscious of his irrelevance to what was going on around him. His answer was to make everything irrelevant to him. Catching a lull in the conversation, he would suddenly say, 'Aye. D'ye ken whit they used tae dae?' An account of the unbelievable machinations of the

Boers would follow. Between such urgent messages, Josey filled up the void of other people's conversations with whistling. Fortunately for the others, Andra Crawford, though a good deal younger than Josey, had fought in the same war. It was one of his functions to confound Josey's impressive powers of boredom by contradiction of facts, disruption of sequence, and by generally defusing the point of what Josey was saying, although this wasn't always easy to locate.

While Josey marched eternally on Mafeking and Andra out-manoeuvred him with ambush, the spring, almost unnoticed by them, proliferated into new forms around their barren and disputed tract of past. One of Wullie Manson's ferrets, obeying some primal urge, chewed its way out of its cage and escaped. It was duly arrested at the Cross by the prodigiously fat policeman they called Fifty Waist-coats. 'The chairge is vagrancy,' he told Wullie when he reclaimed it.

Dougie McMillan talked of one day owning a fleet of motorcars that could descend on well stocked rivers such as the Stinchar and cull salmon 'like getherin' buttercups'. He wouldn't travel himself, just sit in a wall-mapped office, directing an army of poachers. Alec Simpson talked of emigrating. Sconey developed the habit of buying a bag of grapes at the Barras so that, standing at the corner, he could throw the rotten ones up at Auld Jimmy Sticket's window. What he enjoyed was disputing with Auld Jimmy when he had shoved his bald head out of the window: 'We've seen nothin', Jimmy. Ah'm afraid yer evidence is very flimsy. Widny stand up in a court of law. In fact, yer argument widny haud wee tatties.'

Johnnie Allison believed he was going to have a good year at the horses. Danny Mitchell cured his wife completely of her tendency to neglect her household chores. Home from the factory one day, he threw up the window and screamed, 'Fire! Fire! Fire!' When a crowd was gathering below, he added at a bellow, 'In everybody's bloody hoose but mine.'

Andy Dunlop's greyhound bitch had three pups from a good strain, and Andy saw a fortune up ahead. Tam Docherty felt inexplicably that things were going to be all right, as if hope came to him in the air, like pollen. Four of the men formed themselves into a barber-shop quartet, giving corner recitals. Night after night as they stood there, songs, ambitions, small, private hopes, careful plans, were revealed, and released like pigeons into the evening air.

It was March 1914.

# CHAPTER EIGHTEEN

'Trees talk' his Grandpa had once said. And around Conn lay a countryside brimming with dangers, peopled by all races, mountained wildly, amok with monsters.

Other people called it 'The Bringan'. Conn knew the name but had frequently managed to forget it. It was applied to the stretch of countryside lying north east of the town, between the Dean Estate on the one hand and the Grassyards Road on the other. Built above the Barren Red Coal Measures, Graithnock was an industrial town under siege from farmland, so that Bringan was only one of many areas of rich greenery, but to Conn it was what 'the country' meant.

Introduced to him by his Grandpa Docherty, it became more than a place and assumed the importance of a relationship, establishing in him a growing and shifting complex of responses which partly measured and partly influenced his development. Seeing it first through the druidical eyes of his Grandpa, he was frightened, deliciously stirred. Trees were brooding presences, soughing incantations. Every bush hid an invisible force, frequently malevolent. Just to walk was to invade all sorts of jealously held terrains and you had to avoid taboos and observe placative rites.

But it wasn't long before deliberate misdemeanours without retribution undid the old man's enchantments, and Conn was able to imbue the place with his own more enlightened and manageable mythology. There was the Crawfurdland Estate, wooded with a luxuriance unlike any other part of Bringan, in summer dark and dense with undergrowth. Anyone with any knowledge of these things could see that it was Africa.

The familiar part of the river where the land shelved down dramatically towards it for fifty feet or so, balancing trees, was Indian country. You had to move warily there, for—Indians will be Indians—they had that habit of whooping suddenly over the crest of the hill to sweep down on you among the trees. The trick was to keep your nerve until they were on you, crouch swiftly, and, straightening unexpectedly, catapult them on down the slope where they drowned in a huddle of broken bones.

Just beyond the main bridge on the other of the two rivers, which ran through the Bringan before converging in the Dean, the forest became fir. There, among the pine-cones, trappers moved, swaddled warmly in fur-lined jerseys, their bare feet defying the snow as they fought off the ravening wolves. Perhaps best known of all was the hill he had discovered by himself, coming on it suddenly round a bend in the river. It was uniquely ribbed, a huge semi-circle of grass like an eroded stairway. For whoever dared to climb, the rewards were great. Standing victorious on its summit, you could see the world spread out like a map twenty feet below.

Little by little, though, the forces of practicality reclaim their own. The man absorbed in trapping the passing seasons in his field is a persistent presence. It's all right if you can remain invisible to him so that he becomes unknowingly a part of whatever landscape you put him in. But seeing you some days, he tames the tumult, atomises all reivers with a look. The war-paint fades, the whoops of pursuit wane into sunlight, and you're left standing small beside a hedge, looking at a man ploughing, legginged in mud, who waves and laughs with a jauntiness that is no way to treat a warrior. At least the horse is beautiful.

It was a slow and patient process, by those who worked the land, lived on it, used it, this reclamation for ordinary purposes of country usurped by fantastic intruders. For Conn, some salutary moments, which measured his acceptance of reality rather than provoked it: being chased from the Crawfurdland Estate by the gamey, who, while Conn dodged among the trees, remained an invisible pursuer, enraged Zulu, but, seen from the safety of the road beyond the gate, emerged from the trees middle-aged and jacketed, and disappointingly out of breath. Falling into the river while defending a fort, so that he had to sit naked on the grass while his clothes 'dried' and Angus and some other boys engaged in wild battles. When he arrived home shivering in damp jersey and trousers, he was given a mustard bath by his mother, who kept muttering 'pneumonia'. Meeting poachers, whose preoccupied movements and bulbous jackets hinted at real adventures taking place around him which made his own imaginary ones seem silly.

Gradually, then, the Bringan became itself for him, no longer strange. Over several years, visiting it frequently, first with his Grandpa, then with others or alone, he made of it the opposite pole to his life from High Street. The Bringan was where he could escape from the arbitrary and frequently harsh identity which High Street impressed on him. It was more gentle, flexible, yielding easily to mood, and, in its timeless folds of field and aged conclaves of trees, it held places that could absorb any grief, soothe any hurt.

Two places in particular were special for him, drew his injuries to them like foxes hunted to their earths. One was the lake in Crawfurdland, the better for being forbidden—a big stagnancy of water, mocked frequently into small waves by the wind, haunted fitfully by wild ducks. Sedge made inroads into it, lilies drowned. Trees grew thickly, making colonnades of gloom along its edge.

The other was Moses' Well. He didn't know why it mattered so much to him, but its hold on him was potent as a shrine's. How many times he slid precariously down among the trees that overhung the river to reach the niche hollowed from the rock by the water— polished and slippery like green glass, damp and vapoury, largely screened by ferns and fronds of weed. The water didn't fall but hung, bright and still as an icicle which is melting from within, so that it seemed to shiver inwardly in a tremor of light. It was only at the base of the niche that you were aware of movement, as the water broke itself across a sycamore leaf (who kept renewing it?). The frozen length of water melted onto the leaf, delicately filming its intricately grained texture with the finest veneer until it channelled to the centre-tip, spouting into the air. That was where you drank.

But these places themselves, like the fantasies in which he had once clothed them, became residual. The lake and the well turned into the past, as if they contained sloughed selves. As he grew, the Bringan, which he thought he had used, had really been using him, had taken over a part of him. Always inclined to be withdrawn, he had allowed himself to become so addicted to the silences of Bringan, the shelter of its trees, the languor of its fields, that set against the demands which High Street made on his growing, it caused a conflict in him.

Holding him in a vice between them, Bringan and High Street squeezed him into puberty. In his emergence, what was left behind was what Bringan had meant to him. What stayed with him was High Street. Later, when he thought of his boyhood, it was Bringan he would remember. But, ageing towards work and responsibility within his family, his times in Bringan came more and more to seem like truancy from himself, the person he had to learn to be.

So, as time passed, returning in many dusks from Bringan, he was burying his boyhood, not once but again and again, as if it was a corpse which had to be disposed of gradually, limb by limb. And each time High Street took him to itself more firmly, claimed him as part of itself. Scattered throughout Bringan, buried several autumns deep like the traces of distant picnics, lay hopes of an impossibility such as only a boy's heart can encompass, preposterous ambitions, fragile dreams.

Instinctively, he had come to know that this was who he was. The geography of his future would be discovered among these things that greeted his return: the massive women folded like sphinxes on their window-sills; the pub that burst with laughter as he passed it; the dark archway where coopers hammered—the three men returning from the day; welcomed by a dog, a bundle of barking chained to their iron heels. One day he would be one of them. And he was glad.

*BOOK II*

# CHAPTER ONE

Londön and Berlin were two places but one scene. On balconies appeared figures, too distant from the crowd below to be recognisable to them. In the streets surged people, too distant from the figures above to be recognisable to them. The people cheered. The gestures enlarged the cheers, the cheers enlarged the gestures. The languages were different but, since no words were audible, the sounds became identical. Straw boaters, waved aloft, pitched above the abandoned faces like the heads of lopped off flowers.

High Street was less hysterical. As a mere distant province of the truth, it received the news already modified by its having happened, as if the distance it had travelled from the capital had left its regal livery stained a little, as if the things that lay between, the sheep rooted in their hillsides, the factory-towns preoccupied with their smoke, the rivers thin with summer and the farms, had all given it accretions of their disbelief, indifference, dismay. Like a messenger who has come so far that he forgets exactly what his message is, word of the war limped stammering into High Street, barely audible above the shouts of children, needing to repeat itself to housewives sleeved in suds, having to wait for a man to turn from his loom and listen.

That evening men gathered at the corner in large numbers. Their muttered conversations were a council, for, faced with the alien presence of a war, they had to relate it communally to what they understood, and what they understood best was one another, the accidental interweaving of their pasts tightening under pressure to the necessity of dependence on one another. Their ignorance and bafflement made their proximity mutually unenlightening but all the more compulsive for that. At least to have your incomprehension shared was some kind of comfort. In any case, they had nowhere else to be.

Josey Mackay was out early. He brought with him a paragraph cut out of the *Daily Mail*, quoting the Foreign Office announcement, and pasted—in accordance with some dark, unfathomable purpose—on to a piece of plain cardboard with his name in pencil on the back. He kept passing this out to people as they arrived. Although everyone knew the content by now, they would each read it, as if the words might contain an escape clause they had missed. But the message remained as inflexible as an epitaph: 'Owing to the summary rejection by the German Government of the request made by His Majesty's Government for assurances that the neutrality of Belgium would be respected, His Majesty's Ambassador in Berlin has received his passports, and His Majesty's Government has declared to the German Government that a state of war exists between Great Britain and Germany as from 11 p.m. on August 4.'

'Of coorse, 11 p.m. London time is midnight Berlin time,' Josey said every time he got his card back, glad that he had had the foresight not to include that piece of information in his cutting. He offered the remark always with the air of a man putting the entire complex of international affairs in a new and illuminating perspective. Then he would move along to somebody else, being somehow proprietary about the whole thing, as if the war was a newly discovered and underdeveloped area and he was establishing a stake in it. That weird fragment of officialdom bearing his name meant something to him. It was as though history had visited him personally and left its calling-card. He was to keep it and subsequently, in his seemingly endless old age, take a strange pride in showing it to people, scuffed with the thumbs of men who died in the war. He would nod with the senile complacency of a man who has managed to fingerprint fate.

They found themselves searching the recent past for significant events, like the torn pieces of a picture they had carelessly thrown out. When they had been so busy with what had seemed important, what really had been happening? With the masochism of nostalgia, they tried to confront the ravaged face of that summer they had veiled in a selfish innocence which, it seemed, would never again be possible. It was obvious that Britain was in the war because of Belgium. Somebody pointed out that Belgium was really just a road into France. Another voice was sure that the French were allied in some way to the Russians. But Russia would never have been in the war if it could have helped it. Hadn't the Russians tried to keep the peace? But Germany had declared war on the Russians on 1 August. That was because of Serbia. Serbia had an alliance with Russia. The moves and counter-moves multiplied themselves into the incompatibility of a game for which they didn't know the rules. Their attempts to under-stand what was going on broke down into expletive frustration. 'That daft bastard wi' the gun in Serbia,' Wullie Manson said. 'He must be aboot as wise as Gibby Molloy.' 'An' where the bloody hell is Serbia?' somebody wanted to know. 'Turn left at Knockentiber,' Tadger said.

The sky, grazing its peaceful clouds above them, was a camouflage that fooled nobody. The mother who shooed her two children home to safety was ironic. A bird sang its idiot song in the eaves of a tenement. Tomorrow was the war. Each wondered what it was going to be like. Only Josey Mackay knew. 'Oor cavalry'll rin them intae the grund. The Jerry canny handle a horse the way that oor boys can. An' then again, we're in better trim. We've focht mair recently. Against the Boers. Ah've seen oor men dae things . . .' Even Andra Crawfurd let him rave. It was not an unpleasant sound, like a song that reminds of an almost unimaginable past. All Andra himself would say was, 'It'll be like nothin' that's been afore.' They understood. Their pasts lay like obsolete maps.

Uncertain who would be eligible for enlistment, wavering among conflicting impulses of fear and patriotism and duty and common sense and a feeling of exhilaration in their lives becoming strange, they achieved a temporary equilibrium in angling their reactions towards fantasy. Mock tactics were discussed. Wullie Manson inspired some revolutionary military concepts. His enormous bulk ('Ah just don't ken ma wecht. The last scales Ah wis oan surrendered at twinty stane an' gave up the joab') had long accommodated barbs without complaint. Told about the unbelievable dimensions of his rump, he would pleasantly reply, 'Ye need a big hammer fur a nine-inch nail.' Andra Crawford had once remarked, 'Big Wullie doesny go fur a walk. It's a mairch-past. If ye're waitin' fur him tae pass, it can take ye quarter o' an 'oor tae croass the road.' Now that remembered image was generously embellished. 'They'll probably make Big Wullie intae a regiment,' Tam Docherty suggested. 'The Manson Light Infan-try' was someone's ironic name for it. Tadger foresaw Sir John French deploying his forces skilfully and blocking the French frontier with Wullie Manson.

Having exhausted Big Wullie's potential, their fancy went further afield, considered Gibby Molloy as Britain's secret weapon, created Field-Marshal and reducing the enemy to victorious collapse. They saw Josey Mackay as the dreaded talking-machine that would secure German surrender in return for two days' silence. But, their laughter thinning to a frenetic flippancy, they yielded more and more to the stillness that was growing in each of them as the evening ended.

Opinions were proffered like motions for the future to consider. 'It'll a' be ower in three month.' 'Mair like a year, Ah wid say maself.' 'They're too much in the wrang no' tae loass this war.' Tam remarked,

'D'ye think Asquith's got some kinna pull wi' Goad?' Tadger thought, 'They should've sunk the bastards when they had the chance at Kiel in June.' 'Ach, we'll maybe be laughin' aboot this six months fae noo,' Danny Hawkins said. 'There's no' much we can dae aboot it wan wey or the ither, is there, then?' That was Dan Melville. 'Jine up, Ah suppose.' 'Aye.' 'Aye.' 'That's aboot it, richt enough.'

The talk gave out. It had all been irrelevant anyway. But, like the nervous words of those awaiting a birth, it had served its purpose of being merely a means of letting something happen. Now, in the darkness constellated with glowing cigarettes, the war had become a fact. Like a minuscule separate state, unmappable except in the perspectives of its people, High Street had declared itself at war with Germany.

Goodnights were muttered. A fist flicked its farewell at a shoulder. Someone lobbed an empty cigarette packet over his arm and back-heeled it into the gutter. The group of men moved in slow, disintegrating vortex, surrendering its solidity in ones and twos. Like all conversations, theirs had been a measurement of the area of their respective silences, and it was silence, now more defined, that each took home with him.

For the war, after all, external artefact though it seemed, accomplished and immutable enormity, would be a different war for every one of them. Having no more than the natures that they stood in, they weren't fixed in the marble pages of history and it didn't inhabit its invented logic. They were only themselves, inhaling a troubled and incalculable air. They must compute on their pulses as it came, each as he could. Such computation would involve unknown quantities of eccentricity and trivia, the stink of a trench made more tolerable by the memory of a particular woman or conscience anaes-thetised by patriotic slogans or the sufferings of Europe obliterated by the loss of a son, until the war assumed uniqueness in the experience of everyone who lived it.

For them that evening war wasn't politics or geography or the mobilisation of forces. It was, as they entered their houses, a special diffidence in the eyes of some of their women. It was a sharper etching of objects around them, as if a film had been scraped from their eyeballs. It was how the kettle was a comfort, the battered chair luxurious, the collapsing of a coal-husk in the fire inexpressibly elegiac.

# CHAPTER TWO

'Ah'm gonny jine up,' Mick said.

Around his words the casual evening congealed to an event. They passed from a number of people who happened to be in the same room into a family group, frozen inside his statement. The absence of Angus and Conn became immediately inappropriate.

'Aw, naw,' Jenny said.

But it was a reflex, the way people shut their eyes on an imminent blow, which doesn't mean they expect to avoid it. Jenny had known he was trying to decide. She had hoped without conviction that this wouldn't be his decision. She had been glad he had survived the first fever for enlisting at the start of the war. Otherwise, he might have been dead by now. Some from High Street were. Ypres had already been naturalised to Wipers by the weight of its British dead. But he hadn't escaped the fever. It had merely been incubating in him.

'Ah've made up ma mind, mither.'

'But why, Mick?'

'Ah just think it's whit Ah should dae.'

'Ah don't see why it is. Ah don't see that at a'.'

'Ither folk jine up, mither.'

'You're no' ither folk. It's different when it comes tae yer ain door.'

But it had come and they all knew it, even Jenny. Her voice had been from the first brittle with hopelessness. You couldn't talk to the war. As Mick put on his jacket and picked fluff from his cap, they seemed already to be spectators in his life, their own lives having become derivative. For the first time, the war was visiting their house.

The past few months had been a pretence that had collapsed. They had gone on with their lives in desperate conclave, as if the more determinedly they remained themselves, the less chance the war would have of reaching them. They half-believed it would be over before it became personal to them.

Now they were left staring stupidly at their small preoccupations, the means by which they had tried to effect the magical exorcism of big events turned into trivia in their hands. Jenny, sewing a patch on Angus's moleskin trousers felt her fingers sore with trying to force the needle through, and wondered why she was bothering at all. She had spent her life amassing tiny, patient skills against the weather, accident, disease. She knew what to do when faced with most troubles from a burnt hand to suspected pneumonia. And there didn't seem to be much point to any of it.

Tam, cutting wire and looping it into snares for Wullie Manson, decided the last bit he had cut was too short, and threw it into the fire. Old Conn stilled his rocking-chair, erasing himself into silence. Kathleen was the only other person there. Since she had become pregnant with her first, she had tended to look in on her mother several times a week. ('Jist in case it's eicht month early,' Tam had kidded her at first.) Now even she became fully aware of a world beyond her belly.

Mick was ready to go out but knew he had to wait. Their silence was still talking to him.

'When did ye decide this, son?' Tam asked.

'Ah've been thinkin' aboot it for a while. Me an' Danny Hawkins.'

'Does Danny mean tae jine up tae?'

'Aye.'

'My Goad,' Jenny said. 'He's everythin' that Mary Hawkins has.'

'It's the HLI we fancy,' Mick told his father.

'The Highland Light Infantry', Old Conn confided to the air in front of him. He had developed a disconcerting habit of acting as a kind of neutral commentator on conversations, as if interpreting events for invisible friends.

'They're jist sully boays.' Jenny offered the remark to Tam like advice.

'Ye say ye've thocht aboot this?' Tam asked.

'Aye. A lot.'

'Ye ken whit Keir Hardie says?'

'Whit's that?' Mick fretted with his cap, feeling pestered with irrelevances. He had expected his mother not to understand but not that his father would invoke Keir Hardie even for this, although he had long been used to that name which his father used with the familiarity of a friend.

'He says it's a dishonourable war. A capitalist war.' He put the stress on the second syllable. 'An' he disny think there's ony place in it fur a workin' man.'

'Did he tell that tae the Germans?'

'By Christ, son. Don't try tae take yer watter aff that man. You'll dae whit ye think ye hiv tae dae. But don't make jokes aboot it. Whitever it is, it isny funny.'

'Ah don't mean it that wey, feyther. But if it's no' a guid war, the best thing tae dae is get it feenished. Is it no'?'

Jenny looked up at him, shaking her head.

'An' you an' Danny Hawkins'll see tae that, wull yese? My Goad, son. Ye don't ken whit ye're daein'.'

'Och, mither. Credit us wi' some brains. We're no' kiddin' oorselves. But we'll help a sicht mair by enlistin' than by hidin' in the mull. Wid ye like us tae let ither folk dae oor fightin' fur us? Is that whit ye want?'

'Ah'll tell ye whit Ah want. Ah want ye the wey Goad made ye. Wi' a' yer faculties. That's all Ah want.'

Tam was quiet. He felt his position compromised by the fact that he and Tadger Daly had both secretly taken steps to find out if they were fit for the army. Suspecting, in any case, that their age was against them, they had paid a local doctor to examine them. The idea was that they would have their decision made easier for them without causing any worry to their families. Both had been declared unfit. Tam's eyesight had been described as 'atrocious'. Tadger was asked what he was using for lungs. These melancholy reassurances should have helped more than they had done. Financially, it was unthinkable that they should leave their families, and the doctor's findings should merely have added a moral sanction to the economic necessity of staying at home. Also, constituting as they did a revolutionary caucus of two, they should have taken solace from being absolved from helping to fight a war they felt had nothing to do with them. They both believed profoundly in Keir Hardie and though they couldn't have access to his comprehension of the situation, they had faith in the pronouncements that emerged from it. But still they shared an irrational sense of guilt. Younger friends of both were in the war and no number of ideas would ever alter that. Both Tam and Tadger wished they hadn't disqualified themselves from trying to enlist, since any attempt now would have been a safe and empty gesture.

Jenny said, 'An' hoo are we supposed tae manage wi' you awa'?'

It was a remark so desperately untypical of Jenny that the rest of them were embarrassed. It showed her prepared to hobble Mick's freedom of choice by any means.

Mick said, 'Aw, mither,' and she looked away at the fire.

'Ah'll no' be a burden tae onybody,' Old Conn said suddenly, busking for sympathy along the edge of their attention. 'Ah'm no' afraid o' the pair hoose,' he confided to his secret brotherhood.

'Behave yerself, feyther,' Tam said. 'Ye wid bring a tear tae an iron bed.'

Mick put on his cap.

'Ah'm gled Jack has a limp onywey. Ah'm gled.' The childish simplicity of Kathleen's interjection put the whole scene in perspective instantly, for they knew their own responses were no more sophisticated than hers. Jenny's protectiveness, Tam's confusion, Mick's determination to be a soldier, all were revealed as naïve and arbitrary reactions in the face of an ungraspable complexity.

'We'll talk mair aboot this when ye get back, son,' Tam said.

'Right, feyther.' Mick went out.

Jenny could hardly believe that this was all. She knew that something very serious, perhaps terrible, had been decided. Yet it had taken no longer than it would to discuss buying a new suit and there seemed even less to be said about it. Aware of the masculine assumptions around her—Mick's that he must fight, Tam's that Mick must be allowed to make an untrammelled choice, she despaired of the stupidity of things. She remembered Wullie and Annie Manson's only boy. Ill in infancy, desperately wanted, willed into health by Annie who hoarded his every breath and fought for each hour of his life until he became a big, sonsy boy that everybody liked—and then, after Annie had put fourteen years of his life together, illness and health, like a hand-stitched quilt, he was drowned in the Black Rocks because his foot slipped on a wet stone and there was no man near enough to get to him in time. God had to be a man. No woman could ever be as wasteful.

Tam found it hard to concentrate on what he was doing. The sequence of more than this one evening was broken. The sense of continuity he had always clung to in their lives was lost, had been for some time now, but Mick's decision had demonstrated it with a clarity he couldn't hide from. The slow evolution towards improvement which he had kept his faith in was interrupted. The intrusion of the war showed the naïveté of his beliefs, the triviality of any contribution he could make to his own life. He had noticed the feeling of self-importance there was in Mick, as if history had just called out his name, and while Tam couldn't share his son's conviction, it did make the converse real for him—that the rest of them were living in parenthesis.

The room was becalmed in aimlessness. Old Conn rocked, nursing his martyrdom, Kathleen knitted, Tam looped a snare and tested the speed of its contraction. Jenny ran her thumbnail along the moleskin, softening a path of easier access for the needle. Against the ravening insanity of nations, a cunning skill for keeping out the damp.

# CHAPTER THREE

Abranch was creaking, close, intimate, like the sound of a shoulder-strap. A peeweep haunted the area, its plaintive pretence of defencelessness combing back and forth persistently. Beside them the grass was slowly straightening again, absorbing their love-making. Where they sat was a hollow beside two trees and among long grass, so that they had no sense of location, all fixity diffused among the lazy whorlings of the sky, adrift on an ocean of land. Drugged with country fumes, Mick smoked heavily, watching the grass scars heal on the back of his hand and remembering the same marks on her thighs and arms when they were finished, as if they had both just newly been amputated from the earth. Tuned into small sounds all around them, their voices found a low key, naturalised themselves to an insect softness.

May was saying, 'Ah don't want ye tae go. Whit if ye get killed?'

Mick said, 'Ah'll no' get killed.'

'Whit if ye did?'

'Weel, it'll no' be ma worry then. Will it?'

'Naw. It'll be mine.'

Her voice was sad but the sadness was overlaid with something else, a deliciousness almost. Mick put his hand over hers and the gesture allowed them to think of themselves as lovers sadly parting. They needed a convention within which to enact what was happening in them. May fumbled for words.

'Ah'll wait fur ye,' she said.

'Wull ye, May?'

'Of coorse.'

'Ah want ye tae dae that. But we don't ken whit can happen.'

'An' Ah don't care.'

'Ye'll maybe chinge, May.'

'Maybe you wull.'

'No' the way Ah feel fur you. That canny change.' His kiss wasn't something willed but a formality that both of them expected, like punctuation. 'Ah'll still want you.'

'An' Ah'll want you. Ah'll wait. Ah don't care hoo long it is.'

'But whit if Ah get killed?'

'Ye'll no get killed.'

'But whit if Ah did?'

'Then Ah'll never mairry.'

'May.' His voice was solemn. Both of them managed to ignore the fact that a passing bird had dropped a shit on the grass beside them. Perhaps they hadn't seen it. 'Ah want ye tae promise me something.'

'Naw, Mick, naw.'

'Ah want ye tae promise me that if Ah don't come back ye'll mairry somebody else.'

'Naw, Mick. Ah'll no'.'

'But, May. Ye hiv tae.'

'Ah'll never want tae mairry onybody else.'

'Maybe ye wull.'

'Hoo can ye say that? Wull you?'

'Naw, Ah'll no'.'

'Then why are ye sayin' that aboot me then? Oh, Mick, whit dae ye take me fur?'

Before she had a chance to cry, he had embraced her, being careful with his cigarette. It was easier without words. What made talk doubly difficult was that both of them were acting, trying to evoke with words a reality that was inconceivably alien to this place and time that they were sharing. What was war to them? Meaningless statistics, awesome principles that had never before occurred to them, the rantings of the press. They only knew that it was there and Mick was going to it. They had to try to match the simplicity of their relationship to the complexity that had compromised it. In the effort they stopped being themselves and became the roles they thought circumstances had cast them in.

The truth was that they found it impossible to believe seriously in any of the possibilities they entertained in words. The likelihood of Mick dying was to them a stage-prop, merely a means of establishing more firmly the fact that he was alive. Their commitment to each other was as yet too immediate and direct to realise the feasible disintegration of itself.

From the beginning their relationship had been a natural and remarkably uncomplicated phenomenon. Meeting May at a dance,

Mick had walked her home to the farm where she was in service. The ease with which they were able to talk left them with an unfinished conversation, and they met again. What they learned about each other gave them a private area that nobody else had access to, like a furnished room only they knew about. May was an orphan who didn't like the farm where she worked, and her loneliness made her especially confessional with Mick. He in turn put the intensity of his family into perspective through her eyes. Neither had told anyone else about themselves. Tam and Jenny were left to surmise that Mick was walking out with somebody and the family at the farm were left not bothering to surmise what May was doing.

In this way, free from any social pressures, their times together taking place mainly along empty roads and among the anonymous sounds of the countryside, there was an animal naturalness about what happened with them. When they eventually began to make love, it was as a simple progression in themselves, a further discovery. Marriage seemed inevitable at some time and if May were to become pregnant, it would only change later to sooner, nothing more. But the easy spontaneity that had attracted them to each other was also what was causing them to part, for it was that quality which made Mick decide without too much thought to join the army and which made May accept his decision without more than a token resistance.

Mick disengaged his arm in order to drop his cigarette butt on the grass and grind it with his foot. He stood up, put on his cap, and helped May to her feet. As they brushed the grass from each other, it was as if they weren't alone. The war was like an onlooker and, self-conscious of the pleasant ordinariness of what they were doing, they felt they should be doing more. They suddenly embraced fiercely, hurting themselves with the impact, and clung.

'Let's get mairrit noo, Mick,' May gasped.

'Before Ah go away?'

'Aye.'

'Where wid ye leeve?'

'Ah don't know.'

'If only we could.'

'Why can we no'?'

'It isny poassible.'

Mick had given the right response. If he had said anything else, neither of them would have known how to go on from there. But at the moment of saying these things, they believed in their own sincerity, identified with the spurious intensity events were imparting to them. Infected by that delusive sense of stature history sometimes causes, as if private lives could be enlarged by public events, they seemed more than just themselves. They strove to assume virtues of constancy and self-awareness, which until now their relationship had been too innocent, too pure to need. Unconscious of their own pathos, they half-believed, standing there in a clumsy embrace, that they had somehow become more important. The grass soughed romantically, the trees mourned, and three or four birds foundered around them in the wind like personal omens.

Then, turning to walk, Mick tripped on a tree-root, was hit on the bridge of the nose by a low branch, fell on his knees, lost his cap among the long grass. He crouched there, looking up at her as his eyes watered. There was a moment of disbelief before they both started to laugh. Mick collapsed on to his back. May finished leaning against the tree, moaning for mercy.

As they walked along the road, laughter came on them from time to time in small ambushes. They were themselves again. Passing a derelict cottage which they had often seen, Mick had an inspiration. Lifting May, he carried her through the ruined doorway.

'It's a surprise,' he said. 'Ah've bocht this fur us.'

He set her down among the grass of the earthen floor, littered with rubbish, a burst and rusted basin, a weathered boot, the remains of a fire, and in one corner excrement. The windows had no frames. About a third of the roof was gone, admitting sky.

'Well,' he said. 'Whit dae ye think o' it?'

'It's in a good area.'

'Of coorse, it still needs one or two things done tae it. Ah thocht we'd maybe get a door, fur example. An' cut the grass. But there's advantages.' He lifted the basin. 'Ye've yer kitchen utensils. Plenty o' fresh air. An inside toilet.'

She was giggling and he put his arm round her, dropping the basin. They had forgotten what was going to happen, too full of themselves to avoid for long transforming everything into a private pleasure, secreting optimism.

'Whit Ah really like,' he said, 'is no' needin' tae go oot the hoose tae dig the gairden.'

# CHAPTER FOUR

Conn became more important to them. Kathleen was married, Mick was going to be a soldier, Angus was becoming more and more separate. The war made everything seem different, temporary. Only Conn remained the same, the ignorance of his youth an exemption, his life obedient to an older rhythm that nothing seemed able to interrupt. They informed him with that adult nostalgia for their own childhood which tends to make the childhood of others mythic. The small pulse of his activities became the centre of the family, like the heart of a hibernating animal. The same questions and answers were litanised into their evening conversations. 'Whit's he been up tae noo?' 'Ye'll no' believe whit he did.' 'If Ah could tell ye that, Ah'd take up fortune-tellin'.' 'He's an awfu' boay.' 'Whaur's the wee yin?'

Everywhere, it seemed. He still had his duties: dauding the pit-clothes against the wall outside, bringing up water, collecting worms for Angus's fishing, running errands. But he performed them with such practised speed that he seemed hardly to be engaged in them at all. They created the illusion of attendance behind which he was missing for hours at a time. Where he found to go remained mysterious. He travelled like a puffball. Sometimes he came surprisingly to their attention in a posture so exotic that they felt they had unknowingly been harbouring a changeling. So Jenny stumbled on him one rainy day in the wash-house. He was reclining on an upturned tub, smoking two Woodbines simultaneously (since time was short) and tutoring another boy in swear words. In that half-light slicked with rain and sinuous with smoke, Jenny felt as if she had come upon one of the side-rooms of hell. Conn was cuffed and hounded supperless to bed, although later, with the connivance of his mother, Angus took him through some food, whispering and glancing over his shoulder with an operatic display of secrecy.

Another time he was discovered hanging about fifteen feet up from a piece of machinery in Lawson's mill. News of that found his family incapable of assimilating it all at once into the ordinariness of what they were doing themselves. Tam was at his paper, Angus putting more oil in his pit-flask, and Jenny elbowed on the sill when wee Sammy Haggerty was fired out of Menford Lane as if it had been a cannon. He spun dizzily at the top of High Street before turning to face the Foregate and running, his feet treating the cobbles like coals. Jenny said later she felt at once that he was headed towards her. She wasn't in doubt for long. From about fifty yards away, wee Sammy was shouting, 'Mrs Docherty! Mrs Docherty!' He stopped below her. His eyes were like penny-bowls. Trying to speak, he swallowed his news in mouthfuls.

'In the name o' Goad, calm yersel', son,' Jenny said. 'Whit is it?'

'It's Conn, Mrs Docherty. It's Conn. Up in the air.'

His words carried in through the open window and Tam and Angus crowded there for details of the portent. But Sammy wasn't about to supply them. When Jenny asked him what he meant, he danced crazily, whining, 'In the mull. In the mull. Oh come quick, Mr Docherty,' seeing Tam's face.

By the time the three of them were in the street, the few men at the corner had come over to Sammy and were trying to decipher what had happened. The only fact that emerged clearly was that Conn was in Lawson's mill. The small knot of people started unevenly up High Street, Tam in the lead, running full tilt. One of the men had the foresight to stop in at the house of old McGarrity, the watchman, so that he arrived with the keys to unlock the main gate as Tam was climbing over it. After several desperate arguments of keys with locks, they reached where the flat-machines were kept. As the door was opened, somebody deliberately got in front of Jenny, in case what was there wasn't for her to see. The others craned through the door behind Tam.

Sammy's message took on meaning. Conn was suspended miraculously in mid-air, a rod of metal having caught itself in his jersey, which was gathered above him and pulled up to his armpits. Below him were the teeth of a machine against which the force of his broken fall would have gutted him. Over his head was the jagged hole he had made in the glass roof. Spreadeagled on the glass, like someone on thin ice, Rab Ritchie was edging towards the hole with a piece of slender rope in one hand.

Conn said, 'Hullo, feyther.'

Two ladders, a lot of advice and a visit to the infirmary later, Conn was home. His only injuries were a glass-splinter in his bum and an abrasion on his spine. Facts were slowly assembled to show the logical machinery of the fantastic. The boys had been playing at tig. To make it more exciting they had established as boundary-lines the roof of the mill, with all its outcrops. The rest of them were barefoot but Conn still had on his boots. When some of them moved onto the glass-covered section, Conn's involvement in the game had caused him to forget one significant circumstance, and he followed. The rope had been Conn's idea. He had shouted up at the ring of incredulous faces to throw down a rope and he would climb up it. Jenny shuddered at the thought of what would have happened if they hadn't arrived when they did. Tam said, 'That wee boay Ritchie. He wisny absent when they gave oot guts. Ye could pit a room-an-kitchen in his hert.' Jenny said, 'His brains seem tae take up less room.' 'A bit like yerself, Conn, eh?' Tam suggested. 'That bit o' gless must just've missed yer brainbox.'

But incidents as arresting as that were becoming rare. Conn tended more and more to happen offstage. His favourite place was in the Kay Park, a den in a copse of trees beside the lake. There he met his friends. Having sloughed his private fantasies of Bringan, he moved on to almost daily sessions of vaunting talk among the trees when they all engaged in a kind of group hypnosis, hallucinating manhood. Screened with leaves, they kept vigil for the future with the dedication of medieval knights. Their profanities were relentless. They smoked with dutiful persistence, ignoring the watering of one another's eyes. Grass was chewed, leaves dismantled vein by vein, twigs skinned to willow wishbones. With the gravity of a committee specially appointed for that purpose, they worked on the definitive concept of a man.

The final version was bound to be eclectic, being a compound of all their experiences. There were certain obvious basics that none of them could doubt. To be a man it was necessary to swear without noticing, to spit long distances now and again, and to smoke. All had already passed these initial tests. Beyond that, areas of specialisation naturally emerged.

Cammy, Dougie McMillan's youngest boy, was the expert on poaching. He always had with him some fragment of the craft like an identity card—a white scut, a wire snare, the teethmarks of a ferret on his hand. He knew how to cover one end of a burrow before releasing the ferret into the other so that it would chew the rabbit's backside till it broke. He knew that guddling was the technique of tickling a fish out of the water with your bare hands. He had seen a whippet catch a hare. He could recognise which birds' eggs were worth eating. His father had promised soon to sew a special pocket inside his jacket. For him his clearest image of the future was that pocket, out of which, like a magician, his manhood would draw endlessly game, excitement, amazing skill, numberless days among dark woods, bright rivers, fields whose principal crop was rabbit.

Rab Ritchie was waiting to be a soldier, probably a general, though he knew this wasn't a job you could just step into. It might take years. Meanwhile, he prepared himself. His memory was an arsenal of every known gun and explosive. He could recite the names of regiments like an epic poem. He throve on dares. Once when some older boys stole a posh boy's jacket, symbol of effeteness, and threw it with great difficulty over a hornet's nest in a tree, Rab had volunteered to retrieve it. He passed through the Kay Park like a motorised cloud, jumping fully clothed into the lake. Hanging over his life in the manner of a tragic destiny was the likelihood that the war would be over before he was of age.

Conn's province related mainly to fighting and girls. He had, in fact, fought but a few times, and wished they had been fewer. Nevertheless, he had so far always been successful. It wasn't so much that he had won as that he had stayed around until the other boy decided he had lost. Also, he was called Docherty, and in High Street that was enough. The authority Tam imparted to the name, so that it had the force of a prohibitive notice, had been enlarged by recent stories of the strength shown by Angus in the pits. Conn's reputation for knowing about girls was only slightly less justified than that for knowing how to fight. It was founded primarily on the fact that the year before, when the writing of love-notes had become a seasonal preoccupation in his class, like collecting chestnuts, he had received four declarations of profound affection in one day. Since then he had done no more than conduct the usual tentative experiments with girls much in the same spirit as he had examined stationary motor-cars and, once, having been allowed into the mill with Mick's forgotten piece, the workings of a flat-machine. But it didn't matter. His name was made. When he let it be known that a girl could only have a baby every nine months, the others saw it had to be true.

The only non-specialist among them was Sammy Haggerty, whose chief contribution was a talent for awe. Almost everything astounded Sammy. Each dawn seemed to take him by surprise. 'Away ye go!' was his habitual response, breathed with the reverence of a prayer upon the myriad forms of an unfathomable universe. It was invoked in acknowledgement of the incredible truths the others were possessed of, that women's breasts were used for holding milk, rabbits could change the colour of their fur in winter, a gun could kill a man half-a-mile away. It also served as a measure of his astonishment when his own researches were declared erroneous, such as his contention that sleeping with your knees up gave you curly hair. It caused waves, he had thought, in the bloodstream.

In relation to the others, each rather jealous of his area of expertise, Sammy's naïveté was invaluable. It guaranteed at least one heartening response to any new discovery and gave to the others' knowledge a hint of vastness. With Sammy's help, their meetings remained essentially harmonious. Though each might secretly know that his own sphere was the most important forcing-ground for manhood, there was a loosely-held agreement that the only complete man was a soldier who spent his leaves poaching, fighting and giving a girl a baby every nine months.

Other boys sometimes visited their smoking-room among the trees but the permanent membership remained at four. From there they made their sorties, armed in an identity that only themselves were aware of. They spat over bridges, noted pubs for future reference, appraised oblivious women, stood talking rough at corners, cased the entire town. They were a casual fifth-column. Everybody else thought they were just four boys. Nobody knew who they really were. At times they only had to look at one another to laugh, and the laughter was in code. Pacing out their property, they strolled. It seemed that they could feel their muscles grow.

Yet the surrender of the streets to them was illusory. They lounged in sights that they had never known were set. The town was a carefully organised trap. The first to fall was Cammy. His father having obtained him exemption from school, he went to work first, in a factory near the bottom of the town. It was a place the four of them had often walked past, tempted towards its cavernous entrance, unaware that it could close. Once the three of them thought they caught his face at a window, but he didn't wave. Later, meeting one of them, he would grudge hullo, as if they had betrayed him, or he them. His silence left a root in each of the others.

And Conn, the night after Mick had left with Danny Hawkins to join the HLI and live for the time being with an aunt of Danny's in Glasgow, came home to his big brother's absence. As it had been when Kathleen was married, Conn's sense of loss was physically felt, as actual as an illness. He knew the end of something. Mick's smile, which had for years been to Conn like a night-light, had gone out. His kidding, his almost invariable patience, his reduction of any fear to something ordinary were gone. The war was real. The reality of things was hard to deal with.

Mick had carved a boat especially for Conn before he left. Conn kept it beside his bed to look at at nights. To have more influence with God, he gave up smoking.

# CHAPTER FIVE

'Unions!' Angus said. 'That's just a wey o' gettin' strong folk tae work fur wake yins.'

Tam's answer was a roll-call of abused men and bitter places until Angus was stubbornly at bay before a regiment of the oppressed past.

'If Ah wis Auld Conn,' Angus said, 'Ah'd take a quiet walk intae the Black Rocks wi' the heavy bits oan. Whit's the use o' just draggin' yerself aboot day efter day?'

Jenny said that was his grandfather he was talking about and she'd thank him to call him that and it was his grandfather's house as much as it was anybody else's and blood was thicker than water and death wasn't great company and he would be old himself some day, though not if his father heard him at that, and if he did it wasn't Old Conn would finish in the Black Rocks.

'The beardies ye had in that jeelly jaur?' Angus said. 'Ah used them fur bait. Don't be daft! Whit did ye want tae keep them fur? Ye've a bool in yer heid.'

Conn's fist could only make contact with Angus's elbows and forearms and the pain of it was salted by seeing Angus's face crumpled with laughter, as if he was being tickled.

'Ah want tae make masel' that strong,' Angus said, 'that naebody can stoap me daein' whit Ah want tae dae.'

The young men he stood among kept their enmity quiet. Their motive was partly caution, perhaps, but to a greater degree and much more importantly it was also a reflex of consideration, like not referring to the deformity of a friend. For they all saw Angus's excess of egotism in the wider context of his generosity, his capacity for enjoyment that could be contagious, his even temper. In any case, they were all familiar with those fascist impulses which pass erratically through the emergent young like electric charges, because they were all subject to them. It was just that Angus was more subject than most, not surprisingly, since his strength stirred in him like a continent still to be colonised. Who could tell the extent of it?

Angus had to explore. His exploration tended to create border disputes with everybody around him. He said things that encroached painfully on the long established attitudes of others, he was cavalier about accepted principles of behaviour in the family, he provoked retaliation, and he seemed thoroughly to enjoy the exercise. Only at one boundary-line did his attitudes pass from being self-sufficient manoeuvres into something more serious, and that was between himself and his father. In the pit, Angus didn't work so much with his father as in competition with him. While Tam cut the coal, Angus loaded and drew the hutches. It was always his endeavour to achieve such speed that Tam would be unable to keep him supplied with coal. At home he had a habit of saying provocative things in Tam's presence, waiting for a reaction. It was comparatively seldom that Tam resorted to invoking his absolute authority in his own house. Usually, he tried to confront Angus on his terms. He sensed that it was something deeper than could be contained by protocol, bull versus bull. Consequently, while he might oppose Angus, he respected that part of him which was already impatient for manhood. It was Jenny who would say every so often, 'Are ye no' goin' tae dae something aboot that boay? He'll be gettin' too big for *your* bits, never mind his.' Tam had once replied, 'The day he can take them aff me, he can wear them.'

In the meantime Angus was a boy who gave the spasmodic illusion of being a man, so that preconceptions about what someone as young was like would give way, like a garment that was too tight bursting. Every so often an incident occurred that caused people to check on his age. One of these had happened in the pit when he was fifteen.

He had gone into a disused working, looking for rails. They laid their own rails as they progressed, using flat forearm and hand plus three fingers of the other hand as a gauge, and the practice was to pull up rails from exhausted workings and relay them where they were needed. Angus had found the lengths he wanted and was emerging from the working into the main tunnel.

The ground there was at a cant. Opposite Angus was a working from which coal was still being cut by Tadger Daly. Tadger had just filled a five-hundredweight hutch and braked it with a piece of wood jammed in a wheel. He was walking down the slope away from the hutch as Angus came out and saw the wood slip from the wheel. The hutch started to roll.

'Rin, Tadger, rin!' Angus shouted, and as Tadger turned, he saw, like a negative he would only have time to develop later, the hutch coming at him with Angus hanging on to it and scooping something off the ground—'the wey ye've heard aboot in thae cowboy-shows'.

Tadger ran—'Ye're no' goin' tae stop an' argu wi' a quarter ton o' coal.' The workings led off the tunnel at thirty-yard intervals. 'Ah put oan a year for every fit.' Behind him, involved with the thudding of his feet and the rasping of his breath, he was aware of the rumble of the hutch. 'Like daith's empty stomach.' By the time he had made the next working and thrown himself into its shelter, he could only lean against a prop for a moment, until the silence came home to him and he saw Angus looking at him. 'Aw right then, Tadger?'

From that time Tadger appointed himself official keeper of Angus's legend. The truth was that Angus had caught hold of the hutch before it had moved very far. Staying with it, he never allowed it to gain anything like full momentum and acted as a partial brake until he could get the wood wedged once more into the wheel. It was an impressive demonstration of strength mobilised by courage in somebody so young but Tadger in gratitude enlarged it into a wonder. The story of Angus's twenty-five-yard wrestling match with a quarter ton of coal circulated swiftly and confirmed the reputation Angus already had of being a physical prodigy. 'That's no' a boay,' Tadger had said. 'He's three men dressed up as a boay. He's awfu' clever et disguises.' By the time the men came off their shift, there weren't many who didn't know about it. Angus came out among ungrudging acknowledgements of what he had done. As they all tramped away from the pit-head, roughly together for the first couple of hundred yards like an undisciplined army, Angus walking beside his father and already a couple of inches taller, there was a lot of banter and somebody shouted, 'Who's that wee boay ye've goat workin' wi' ye, Gus?' Tam laughed and shouted, 'Well. They say guid gear comes in wee book.'

In the house Tam told the others. He was very proud and it wasn't until Angus was reconstructing the event for the third time that Tam started to play it down. Then when Mick arrived for the night from Glasgow, the whole thing was gone over again. Seeing the talk shift from himself to Mick's experiences of military training, Angus said he wouldn't mind faking his age himself and joining up.

'That's richt.' Tam was laughing. 'You cairry oan. An' the Germans'll no' need tae kill ye. Ah'll save them a joab.'

Angus's dour reaction to Tam's remark, as if it were a serious one, was a sudden reminder of how young he was still. The man's strength became something innocuous again, a boy's plaything, for the time being. To ease his awkwardness, Jenny pressed Mick for details of what he was doing.

'Och, we don't even hiv uniforms yet. We spend the time mairchin' aboot the streets. Playin' at sojers.'

# CHAPTER SIX

They were so tightly knit that just one of them leaving affected every relationship, meant that he heightened not only the others' sense of himself but their awareness of one another as well. That was the effect Mick's departure had on them.

It was a rowdy evening, full of strained laughter, noisy with masculine anecdote, secretive with the snifflings of the women, repetitive with sententious takings of leave.

'Mick, son. Ah want tae tell ye this.' That was his father. What he wanted to tell him wasn't important. What mattered was the hand on his arm, the tremor in his voice he kept under control. Mick indulged his father's sentimentality. He knew what he meant all right and at least it was better than kissing, which, according to some of the men in the Company he was shipping out with, was how the French would have done it.

'Mick. Ye're young yit, son. But jist you remember this.' It was Tadger's turn. He seemed to have dropped round specially to tell him. All Mick would remember would be Tadger's expression smudged with the drink and the renewed awareness of how much Mick liked him.

'Goad bliss ye, boay,' was Mairtin. Jean said, 'the best gran' wean a wumman ever hud.' 'Ah'm tellin' ye that's seen it. Noo jist you remember, son.' That was Andra Crawford. Where had he come from? Jean and Mairtin's house, where they had gathered, was a chaos of comings and goings, like a railway station.

In the middle of it was Jean, propped up in bed. It was because of her illness that they had all come here. 'Trouble never comes its lane,'

Jenny had said. Jean had been going to get out of bed and come up
to their house, and the only way they could stop her was to bring the
goodbyes to her. You only had to look at her to see why she had to
be stopped. She was very ill. Some said it was her last illness. Her
heart was bad. Mairtin had not had a drink for weeks, though now
she was always urging him out for a pint.

But tonight she somehow rose above her illness. She still looked
unbelievably frail but she achieved that preternatural brightness sick
people sometimes have. She glowed with the company. She had even
consented to have some drink in the house. That was in tribute to
Mick, whom she watched all the same and carefully counted his beer.
He had two glasses. Mairtin himself would have none, in spite of the
coaxings. It had become very important to him not to take drink. It
was as if he somehow believed her illness was deliberate and, by
abstaining, he could coerce her to get better.

His abstinence wasn't out of place, for the drinking wasn't much.
But given the amount of emotion in the room with which it combined,
it was enough. Mick was an awful provocation to sentiment, standing
there in his kilt and his khaki tunic, looking fresh and young enough
to be a boy dressed up for Hallowe'en but going to a war that was
very real.

Jenny found him almost unbearably moving. Along with Kathleen,
he had always seemed to her less obtrusive than the other two. Angus
just had to be noticed, he demanded worry. Conn, being the youngest,
had concerned her most. But Mick had always seemed so even and
somehow safe. Yet here he was, fully fledged from the training he had
told them so little about, dressed up like a stranger and preparing to
face a threat that her thoughts hardly dared to guess at.

She felt a little guilty, as if she had let it all happen behind her back.
But she consoled herself with the thought that she had never smothered
any one of her family. She genuinely had no favourites. She had always
tried to let the needs of her family dictate the expression of her
concern. And Mick and Kathleen had demanded her attention less
than the other two.

Seeing them all together tonight was a vindication. Kathleen and
Jack had been in earlier. Jack had had to leave to see about something.
But Kathleen had stayed to talk for a long time to Mick. The way she
was fighting off her tears meant more to Jenny than if she had cried
outright.

Angus had come in late but he was still here too. Jenny understood
the lateness of his arrival, his slightly bragging brotherhood with
Mick. Angus had to create his own night within the main one.
Wherever he was, he was for himself the centre. That was just Angus.

And Conn had been there all night, watching and laughing, his eyes
enlarging everything into a wonder. She saw how he kept making sure

that he was standing beside Mick, as if the magic of Mick's presence might be catching. She was glad that Conn should do that. At least in Mick's leaving, Jenny could see that she had made a good family. In the moment of knowing that, she looked for the man who had made it with her.

Tam was talking to Old Conn, and to Jenny it seemed typical that just as she was thinking something gentle and nice about him, Tam should be making her falter in that thought. Unconsciously, he was shrugging off her compliment. For he was annoyed. Sensing trouble, she crossed towards them in time to hear the end of what Tam was saying.

'Fur Christ's sake, feyther. The boay is goin' tae France. Can ye no' at least hing oan till he gets the train?'

'Ah'm only goin' oot fur a pint.'

'A pint, bejesus. Ye'll get a' the drink ye want in the hoose here.'

'It's no' the drink.'

'Whit the hell is it then?'

'Ah aye go oot fur a pint at this time o' nicht.'

'Feyther. Ma son is goin' tae the war. That's your grandson, in case ye've forgotten that. Ye'll get yer fuckin' pint the morra. An' the next nicht. But oor Mick'll no' be here then. Ah want ma faimly roon 'im while he's here. An' you're pairt o' ma faimly, feyther. Christ, if the King wis here the nicht, Ah'd expect 'im tae wait.'

'Let yer feyther hiv his pint, Tam,' Jenny said.

Then Mick was there.

'Oan ye go, aul' yin,' Mick said and he winked. 'Hiv wan fur me while ye're there then, eh?'

'Ye ken whit Ah mean, son,' Old Conn said. 'Ah aye go oot at this time. Ye ken whit Ah mean?'

'Ah ken whit ye mean. Ah'll be seein' ye, gran'feyther.'

'Aye, richt, son. A' the best, Mick. D'ye hear? The very best.'

Old Conn was going.

'Christ,' Tam said. 'Ye'd think ye were goin' tae the Croass.'

'Och, feyther. He's an auld man. It's jist his wey o' workin'.'

Tam started to laugh.

'When ma feyther dees,' he said, 'he'll be awa' oot fur a walk before onybody's noticed.'

As Mick moved off to talk to his grandmother again, Jenny said quietly to Tam, 'There's nae sign o' that lassie Mick tellt us aboot.'

'Naw.'

'Ah thocht she wis maybe comin'.'

'Aye, Mick said she micht be comin'. She wid likely hae boather gettin' intae the toon. She's workin' oan a ferm, is she no'?'

'Aye, richt enough. It's a peety she couldny a been here, though. It woulda meant a lot tae Mick.'

'Still,' Tam said. 'There's wan or twa did manage tae make it. Hoo are ye managin' yersel', Jen?'

'Ah'm a' richt the noo.'

'Ye're daein' awfu' weel. Jist try tae keep it goin' fur Mick's sake, hen. If you greet too sair, he'll be leavin' the maist o' himsel' here. An' he'll be needin' everythin' fur whaur he's goin'.'

'Ah'm a' richt, Tam.'

Surprisingly, she was. She had been outmanoeuvring her tears all night. Mostly it meant keeping on the move, not speaking for too long to any one person and making sure that she wasn't trapped into talking to her mother or Kathleen. If they had got together, each would have undermined the other. She did remarkably well until she saw Danny Hawkins come in. Then she knew it was only a matter of time before she embarrassed Mick. With Danny were a couple of friends and his mother. It was seeing Mary Hawkins that softened Jenny. Unlike Jenny, Mary would be completely alone with Danny gone. Having been stern with her own feelings, Jenny allowed herself to emote for Mary, found release by proxy. The two of them sought each other out immediately, like friends recognising each other in a roomful of strangers.

But their mutual sadness was submerged for the moment in the increased tempo of the evening. Danny's arrival meant that he and Mick would soon be going for the train and everybody came together frenetically in last attempts to say what they had been wanting to say and to touch and to extract a final essence from the occasion. In the scrum of affection the form of what was happening was lost, and then suddenly Mick and Danny were among the men and moving towards the door. Jean was lying back on her pillow, lips compressed and wet with her own tears, the sensation of Mick's embrace still warm on her cheek. Kathleen was standing herself, just crying. Tam was gently easing Jenny out of Mick's arms and Mary Hawkins was being prised away from Danny. Then the men receded like a tide and left the women stranded in an empty room.

The group collected more men at the corner. By the time they reached the station, they were a small battalion. On the platform they stamped and jostled, waiting for the train that would take Mick and Danny on the first stage of the journey to their camp on the east coast. Their breaths fluttered around them, a cluster of small pennants. Their voices were raucous, trying to match the size of the situation. There was a lot of determined laughter. People laid hands on Mick and Danny till they bruised.

The train just saved the whole thing from hysteria. Seats were found and the men who had been carrying the kitbags left them while everybody piled out again and Mick and Danny stood at the window. With about a minute to go Kathleen, pregnant as she was, came running along the platform. They had forgotten the fags which were to be shared between them as a parting gift. Also, Mick's grandmother had been meaning to give them a clothes-brush each as an extra item of kit.

'We've goat wan,' Mick said.

But they had to take them.

'No' somethin' else,' Danny said, laughing. 'Christ, ma mither wantit me tae take the chist o' drawers. But it widny fit intae ma kitbag.'

Those were the famous last words of their departure. The train was moving. In spite of all the careful preparation that had gone into the evening, the heart of it was in that suddenness, the clank of the wheel-rods, the chuff and lurch of the train, the wrench of distance. The rest of it had only been a ceremony for discovering that surprise, for savouring it by contrast. The real farewell was in those slightly shocked expressions, the words deflected by the wind, the gestures that fell into the distance.

# CHAPTER SEVEN

'War's Remedy. Let the soldier be abroad if he will, he can do nothing in this age. There is another personage—a personage less imposing in the eyes of some—perhaps insignificant. The school- master is abroad, and I trust to him, armed with his primer, against the soldier in full military array.

Lord Brougham
Speech, 1828'

Conn's voice had baulked on the name, his hesitation advancing and receding like someone contemplating a jump. Finally he had settled for Bruffam, pronounced almost inaudibly. In compensation he declaimed the date with impressive sonorousness.

His father said, 'Read that again.'

While Conn did, slanting the book towards the window to snare the last of the light, Tam's lips moved silently in pursuit of the words.

'That's true, son,' he said. 'That is true.'

Conn recognised in his father's tone the implication that it was especially true for Conn. Before Conn had said anything, his father was already arguing with his silence, because he knew the stubborn attitudes that lay behind it. Conn found himself wishing that his grandfather hadn't gone to bed so early or that Angus would come in or that his mother hadn't found it necessary to go down to Kathleen's house. Why did Kathleen need to be having a baby anyway? Feeling himself in the familiar position of being betrayed by a conspiracy of adult whims, Conn surrendered himself to the inevitability of having to confront his father's mood alone, to undergo a 'serious talk'.

Tam was lighting one of the many clay pipes he had started recently to use. As the shred of newspaper flared in his fingers, face and throat inhabited for a second the poetry of the flame, achieved in the half-dark a vivid isolation of line and texture held focused in the concentration of a trivial act, like a luminous painting instantly destroyed. Tam fluttered the charred paper, serrated like a feather, into the fire.

'Is that no' whit Ah've been tryin' tae tell ye a' along?' Conn waited. 'It's education, son. That's whit ye've got tae hiv. You're clever enough tae go oan et the schil. Ah ken ye are. Yer mither's got a note there fae a teacher. A lassie. Whit's her name?'

'Miss Anderson.'

'Miss Anderson. That's who it wis. Miss Anderson. She says ye're capable. An' so ye are. But why are ye no' interested?'

Conn shuffled in the chair.

'Ah jist want tae work in the pits.'

'Christ, son. The pits! Ponies work in the pits, son. That's as mony brains as ye need tae work in the pits. They go blin'. Did ye ken that? They're doon in the daurk that long that they canny see. An' they're no' the only wans. Ah've been blin' fae Ah wis ony age masel'. That's whit it does tae ye. When Ah wis your age, Ah had ideas, son. Things Ah could see that Ah wid like tae dae. But the pits took care o' that. Ah'm jist a miner noo. Ma days don't belong tae me. Ah'm doon there. An' Ah canny see beyond the seam that Ah'm tryin' tae howk.'

Tam spread his arms and shook his head, as if offering the image of himself to Conn as irrefutable proof of the failure he couldn't find words to convey. Paradoxically, what Conn saw were the forearms bulging from the rolled up sleeves, the hands that looked as tough as stone. The whole person emitted an aura of impunity as cautionary as an electric fence. Sitting there, self-deprecating man and hero-worshipping boy, they made an irony of each other, Tam imparting to his son a conviction he had no words to counteract, Conn interpreting his father's silence against itself.

'Ye see that pair auld man through there? He's leeved a slave an' he's deein' a slave. They can gi'e it ony ither name they like. But that's whit he is. An' ye ken why?' Tam jabbed a forefinger against his own temple. 'Because they took ower in there. That's the only wey ye'll ever bate them, son. By findin' oot the truth fur yerself an' keepin' it in there. Yer gran'feyther's nearly seeventy. An' he's waitin' tae leeve his furst day as his ain man.'

Tam sat looking into the fire, his head cocked delicately as if he was listening. He nodded to his own thoughts and, watching him, Conn experienced a moment that had the eeriness of a seance. He became conscious of the shadows emerging from the fire's meeting with the approaching darkness, and they were assembling themselves around him in the room, like ghosts with whom his father was communing. A minute jet of gas burst from a break in the coal with a sound like a centuries old moan, before it ignited to a separate incandescence within the fire's burning.

'Yer Uncle James. Ah've never telt ye aboot him yet. Hiv Ah, Conn?' Conn shook his head, his boredom animating for the first time into interest at the prospect of a story, at the thought of hearing about a man instead of all this incomprehensible talk about 'them' and 'education'. 'He wis fae Cronberry, then. Yer Granny's nephew. Ma cousin, Ah suppose. Worked in the pits as weel. But a clever, clever boay. Ye ken whit he did? Every day he did his shift in the pits. But at nichts. He studied and he re-studied. Tired tae the marrow o' his bones he wis. Aye. But every nicht, right reason or nane—the studyin'! It wis a' . . .' Tam's rhetoric lost course for a moment in an absence of facts—'the rocks an' that. You ken. Stanes an' the earth. Whit is it?'

'Geology.' Conn felt casually and impressively knowledgeable, a state of mind he was careful not to spoil by dwelling on the fact that he had only learned the word from the teacher the day before.

'That's the wan.' Tam paused as if about to repeat it but didn't bother. 'Oot in a' wathers. Wi' his trooser-legs rowed up. Wadin' the burns. Lookin' fur jist the special stane that he wid be efter at the time. Chappin' them up wi' a wee mell. Makin' his notes. The names he had fur them! He could come oot wi' a name that wid choke a horse. An a' it wid be wis a wee thing like a causey. Ye've nae conception, son. Well. He persevered. An' he wisny stuffy, either. In fact, he knew that he wis deein'. An' him jist in his twinties. But he went oan. He wis efter some kind o' qualification thing. Like letters ahint his name or that. He took his examinations. An' ye ken. The week he dee'd, the word came through the post. The boy had passed. A certificate kinda thing. His mither his it in the hoose yet. Twinty-seeven when he dee'd. An' she his a drawer there in her big dresser that she keeps the wey he left it. The first time we're up, Ah'll get her tae show ye it. It's a thing tae see. Jist fu' o' stanes every colour o' the rainbow. Every wan found by James himsel'. An' every wan wi' its wee caird, an' oan the caird the special thing they ca' it. Names ye never thocht were poassible. By, that's some drawer. It's no' a drawer, son. It's a monument.'

There was a silence of some seconds for the legendary James. Tam was remembering holding that certificate in his hands. The name on it was James's but the official wording was relevant to all of them, an amnesty from the inevitability of the narrowness of their lives. Conn was imagining the drawer. He saw the stones like jewels, heaped fragments of blinding iridescence, having no point in his mind beyond their own beauty, a dead man's treasure trove.

'The man's richt.' Tam nodded at the book, 'A Treasury of Prose and Poetry', resting on Conn's knee with his finger keeping the place. 'Hoo can war help *us*? We'll be in the same mogre when it's a' by. Poor Mick. He's daein' whit he has tae dae. But it's no' gonny make ony difference. That's the thing, Conn. Yer brither's life's at stake. An whoever wins, it canny be us. We loast before it stertit.' Caught in the renewed intensity of an old realisation, Tam looked for hope. 'Conn. Why will ye no' see the sense o' goin' oan at the schil, son. Why no'?'

'Ah jist don't want tae, feyther.'

'But whit is it? Why no'?'

'Ah don't like it.'

'Is it the teachers? His somebody goat it in fur ye?'

'Naw. It's no' that.'

'Ah don't understand ye, son. Ah mean, that's where ye could make somethin' o' yerself. See Mr Pirrie. He's aff the same kinna folk as oorselves, Ah hear. An' ye see whit he's made o' himself. Noo is that no' an example fur ye?'

Clumsily, Tam had activated Conn's antagonism towards school, which had so far remained in the lethargy of long-established attitudes. Now, mobilising against that name, past convictions mustered confusedly in his head, the more determined for being inarticulate. So irrational as to be anonymous forces, those convictions nevertheless represented areas of real experience for Conn. They related to truths he had earned for himself, no matter how incapable he was of proving his right to them with words, to the fact that nothing he was taught at school took the slightest cognizance of who he was, that the fundamental premise underlying everything he was offered there was the inferiority of what he had, that the vivid spontaneity of his natural speech was something he was supposed to be ashamed of, that so many of the people who mouthed platitudes about the liberating effects of education were looking through bars at the time, that most teachers breathed hypocrisy, like tortured Christians trying to convert happy pagans, that the classroom wasn't a filter for but a refuge from reality. His indignation came in a welter of incoherent images, a mob of reasons that drowned reason, and the only expression of it all he could achieve was a dogged, sullen silence.

'Mr Pirrie. Noo is that no' somebody ye could look up tae an' try tae dae the same?'

Seeing his father so mistaken in his estimation of himself, Conn couldn't let it pass. It was all right being silent on the question of staying on at school. He had made up his mind on that one. Nothing short of being taken there in handcuffs every day would have induced him to stay on after he was fourteen. But it depressed him to see the way his father was so misled about the school. Mr Pirrie. Why did his father reduce himself to an admiring boy in front of someone who wasn't a match for him? Conn struggled to say something he knew. What came out, like a hiccup after long meditation, was:

'Och, feyther. Ye could easy win him.'

Conn didn't just mean it physically. There was in him a hazy desire to express the result of some ultimate and ideal confrontation of the two men. The words were an attempt to convey a deep faith in his father, something which had survived in spite of what they had taught him in the school, an unshakeable commitment, not unlike 'I love you'.

His father's response was to burst out laughing, shake his head in a patronising way, and then to seem saddened by his son's remark. Conn held in his hurt.

'Whit are ye talkin' aboot, son? Whit's that got tae dae wi' onything? Life's a bit mair complicated than a fist-fight. Ah've maybe goat muscles. But maist o' them are in ma heid. Naw, son. Ye need education.'

They sat hopelessly together in the darkening room, their shapes unfinished sculptures in the firelight, affirming the worth of each other and injuring each other in the affirmation. Conn turned the book over in his hand. He had always loved the feel of it, bound in soft leather and on the front two circles, one within the other, embossed in gold, like a medallion, inside which was the figure of a lady in a wide, sweeping dress. But at the moment he resented it. Running his fingers over the braille of that design, it was as if the gesture taught him he was blind, as if the book could only be a tactile object for him, and he and his father were locked out from the rest of it, rejected by the complex patterns of words which it contained. The sensation which his fingers casually imparted to him now was never entirely to leave him, like a burn that mutes all subsequent touches to a partial memory of itself, one of those perceptions that remain precisely because their truths outreach our rational comprehensions, have no need of it, though our comprehension will repeatedly come back to illumine them, intensifying the mystery.

So, in later years, holding again this book, Conn as a man was to understand this evening better, and so many others like it. He would realise how much it had meant to his father, to have this, the only book in the house, given to him at the corner by somebody whose possession of it remained unexplained. He would understand the balm his father felt in listening to the words Conn read from it, those extracts which were often incomprehensible to both of them but which had another meaning for his father, the statement that there were men who understood what was happening to them, that somewhere out there there was meaning. He would even appreciate his father's respect for that leather parcel of words, so that, passing it to his son, he handled it as if it was TNT. But all these laggard insights would only deepen the mystery of what the book had been for both of them, conceal in more impenetrable shadows what it was they had really been trying to say in those evenings of stumbling talk among the carefully cultivated words of strangers.

For Conn later understood what was so obvious, that his father couldn't have afforded to keep him on at school anyway. It had never been a serious possibility. It did, in fact, take all of Tam's tenacity not to accept exemption for Conn, by which he would have been able, due to financial circumstances, to start work at twelve. So why had his father taken so much trouble so often to try to convince him of the wisdom of staying on? Was he perversely hoping that Conn would convince him that it was better to leave, and so assuage his guilt? Or did he console himself with attempting to establish in Conn at least the principle of continued education if he couldn't present to him the fact of it? Was he teaching Conn to condemn his own inability to keep him on at school by way of an apology?

It was to seem to Conn that those evenings, so apparently incidental at the time, their content totally unmemorable, contained the baffling essence of his relationship with his father, that their shy attempts at thought and hobbled gestures held a communication which no eloquence could have paraphrased, and the irrelevant book, which had fallen accidentally between them, was a bridge across which they had trafficked with themselves. The constraint and hurt that traffic had sometimes involved wasn't to be regretted, because it was real.

'Read us somethin' else, son.'

Conn crouched forward in his seat, holding the book almost vertically towards the fire. He flicked the roughly cut pages, looking for a bit that wasn't too big. The heading 'Nature's Records' attracted him. He read aloud:

'Nature will be reported. All things are engaged in writing their history. The planet, the pebble, goes attended by its shadow. The rolling rock leaves its scratches on the mountain: the river its channel in the soil; the animal its bones in the stratum; the fern and the leaf their modest epitaph in the coal. The falling drop makes its sculpture in the sand or the stone. Not a foot steps into the snow or along the ground, but prints in characters more or less lasting a map of its march. Every act of the man inscribes itself in the memories of his fellows and in his own manners and face. The air is full of sounds; the sky, of tokens; the ground is all memoranda and signatures, and every object is covered over with hints which speak to the intelligence.

R. W. Emerson
*Representative Men*'

The room had now abandoned the definition of its contours to the darkness. Only the fire salvaged them a space. But Tam made no move to light the mantle. His face was tightened on itself in concentration, as if the words were a knot he couldn't unravel.

'Read that again, Conn.'

While someone released a flare of laughter in the street outside, Conn read again, wishing his mother and Angus would come back, the strangeness of some of the phrases occurring like discomfort in his mouth, and his father listened in utter stillness, as if they were the pagan scriptures.

# CHAPTER EIGHT

The two columns passed each other in the street. Some of the men going out waved and shouted, 'Leave some mam'selles for us.' 'Whit size dae ye take in a German? Ah'll bring ye wan back.' They were clean and brisk. The men coming back were mud-stained and walked as if they were still up to the ankles in foot-sucking clay. Their smiles and gestures happened far in the wake of the remarks they were meant to answer.

Together, the two columns were like parts of the same conveyor-belt. It was like being back in the factory, Mick thought. But he didn't think it for long. Today it wasn't his war. The day after tomorrow it would be again. That was soon enough.

He levered water from the pump in the yard and savoured it. Water was a marvellous thing. Stripped to the waist, he luxuriously splashed his body, finding delight in the simple fact that it was still all there. He dried himself with a towel that felt like sand-paper, lovely agony, and went back up the stairs.

This time in Bethune they were billeted in a loft above an archway leading to a carter's yard. The only two still left in the place were Danny Hawkins and Auld Jake.

'You took yer time,' Jake said. 'Whit were ye daein'? Coontin yer fingers?'

'There's only wan thing Ah coont,' Danny said. 'Every mornin', first thing. Ah check tae see 'e hisny desertit. An' he's always there. Standin' tae attention. A regiment o' wan.'

'Ah like it here,' Mick said. He was dressing beside the one small, dusty window.

'Ah don't want ony medals,' Danny was saying. 'Ah jist want ma auld man hame wi' me. He's gonny hiv his work cut oot when this is by.'

Mick buttoned his shirt. This place reminded him of the Foregate in Graithnock except for the noise. Danny hated the noise. It went on day and night.

'Come oan, Mick,' Danny said. 'Let's get oan wi' it. Ah jist want tae pu' some wumman ower ma heid an' forget aboot it.'

'You go oan. Ah'll see ye roon there.'

Mick watched Danny walking up and down. He wondered how many folk from High Street would recognise him now. Sometimes Mick himself wasn't sure he knew him. Terror had reduced him to what Jake called 'a porter fur his prick' and whenever they got a few days from the trenches Danny spent the time plunging off in whatever direction it pointed. Mick felt the life in the trenches that was waiting to ingest them again intrude briefly like a horrible machine but he didn't want to think about it. This place, with the sun-motes in its stillness, was to be taken as itself, like an antidote. Only, noticing Danny, he couldn't help wondering how the war was reducing himself, into what simplified shape he was being whittled.

Like the wood in Auld Jake's hands. Mick couldn't make out what it was going to be yet. An animal of some kind, because Jake only made animals. He had been a farm-labourer. He sat in the only chair in the place, beside the small window to have the best of the light, carving patiently at the wood.

'Come oan, Mick,' Danny said.

'Naw, you go oan. Ah'm gonny take a walk furst.'

'Whit fur? There'll be a queue a mile long. Well Ah'm awa'. Ah'll see ye.'

'Don't come moanin' tae me wi' yer coack in a soack,' Jake said.

Mick finished dressing and didn't want to go out just yet. He didn't want to displace the stillness of the room, the peace it gave him. He checked that he had the letter on him. Then he sat down on the old mattress that was his bed.

'Whit's that gonny be?' he asked.

'Hedgehog.'

'Why dae ye jist make animals, Jake?'

'Ah like them. Ye learn tae make somethin', some o' whit it's goat micht jist rub aff oan ye.'

'Whit's a hedgehog goat?'

'Caution. Disny take too many chances, this bugger.'

'Whit aboot yon badger ye made?'

'Well. Hoo mony badgers huv you seen?'

Mick laughed. He lit a cigarette.

'Whit age are ye, Jake?'

'Ah'm foarty-wan. Comin' oan fur ninety.'

'An' ye've been in fae the stert.' Mick shook his head, smiling.

'Whit's the secret o' yer long life?'

Mick was trying to coax Jake out because he had only once heard him talk at any length and it had been good. Jake, cultivator of long country silences, felt a conversation emerge.

'Releegion,' he said.

'Whit church did ye go tae?'

'The holiest place Ah go tae is ma bed. Naw. Ah mean Ah'm that feart, it's a releegion wi' me.'

'Oh, if that wis whit it wis, we'd a' leeve furever. We're a' natural cowards.'

'Aye, but youse boys is amateurs et the gemme. Ah'm a devout, devout man. Ah've hud tae be.'

'Hoo dae ye mean?'

'Ah'm mair feart than you, that's a'. It's hard tae think o' onythin' Ah'm no' feart fae.'

'There must be some things.'

'Oh, Ah huv lapses, richt enough. We're nane o' us perfect. But Ah'm workin' oan them. There used tae be a lot o' things Ah wisny feart fae. A cat, a moose, a tablespinfu' o' watter. A needle in a heystack. Ah wisny a very releegious man. But Ah've studit a bit an' thocht a bit. An' a cat can sit oan yer face when ye're sleepin'. Snuffed oot. Watch oot fur the cats.'

Mick laughed. Outside, the noise was unceasing of the rattling of a gun-carriage or the whine of a despatch-rider's motorcycle or the guns rupturing the air in the distance or the throb of an ambulance, leaving empty, coming back loaded with injured—what Jake called the butcher's van. Inside, Jake's philosophy was an ironic descant.

'Mice is vermin. Their wee paws is daith warrants. A septic needle can poison the bluid. Deid in a matter o' 'oors.'

He whittled on, knowing Mick would have to ask.

'Whit aboot the watter?'

'That. Get a tablespin' o' watter up yer nose an' ye'll droon. Ah read that ance. Ah ken ma scriptures.'

They sat on in the room, silent except for the scraping of Auld Jake's knife. Mick got up to leave.

'Watch oot fur the earthquake,' Jake said.

'Whit earthquake?'

'The wan that's due here.'

'There's never been an earthquake here, Jake.'

'That's whit Ah mean.'

Coming out of the yard, Mick found the war confronting him like a poster. The British observation balloon, moored about a mile outside the town, hung nudged by air-currents, the white puffs of spent shells occasionally occurring around it. It reminded him that the war was everywhere. The realisation renewing itself brought back to him Jake's words. He understood them, that conversation stylised as a vaudeville routine. He made a juggling act of his fear because to let it come to rest was to be finished. It wasn't bearable as itself. You had to use it in some way, make a style of it.

You had to have a way to hold things at a distance. Mick had his.

He walked until he came to the Grande Place, found a table in the open air, sat down and ordered a beer. A military band was playing. He waited until the beer had arrived before he began, because for him this was a ceremony.

He took a sip of the beer and replaced the glass on the table. Then rather surreptitiously, as if it was a passport somebody might try to impound, he took out the letter from his mother. He spread the two sheets side by side on the table. He kept a finger on each in case the wind would catch them. By this time he had read the letter so often that all the words had assumed a uniform texture, had become a single object, something from home. Therefore, 'about Conn getting a start in the pits' had the same weight as 'your grandfather Mairtin's death the old soul didny seem to want to go on without my mother he caught a chill and that was it and as your father was saying he seemed to think that was as good an excuse as any'.

From something else she said, 'sorry to be telling you this your father was saying you cant be short of worries yourself and this is the second time in a row with bad news like this first my mother now my father', Mick knew that he had missed a letter. He grudged it bitterly. Every letter was a transfusion. Both getting them and sending them, he connected temporarily with a livable life, re-entered a context where the individual happiness and pain were meaningful. When he wrote to them about the trenches, the things he told them became a way of coping with his experience here. His need to lie came to seem like a kind of truth. If he could pretend so effectively that it wasn't so bad, perhaps it wasn't so bad.

He folded the letter up. The fact that it moved him so little wasn't a problem. He had had it for some time now. What mattered was that when he had first received it, it had moved him very much. His own sense of grief had amazed him.

He took another sip of the beer, aware of the letter in his tunic pocket, his identity, his proof that he could still feel things.

# CHAPTER NINE

Empty, the room acquired a simple dignity. Edited of incidentals, it made a small, firm statement. It could be seen for what it was, space formally distinguished from space by a geometry of stone, a walled pocket of air set in mid-air, a private climate hung on faith among wind and rain. Two places polarised the area, gave axis to its void. One was the set-in beds, stripped now to two stained mattresses. The other was the fire, cleaned, sepulchral with black lead —beside it, the empty soup-pot. 'Fire's hauf meat,' Mairtin had often said.

The bland anonymity of the rest was touched here and there with the past. The wall-paper, its vaguely urn-shaped pattern faded to thread-lines that the light erased completely from certain angles, showed fresh where a calendar had been pinned beside the fireplace, preserved the shape of the dresser, was mapped with grease in places. The brown linoleum, like a digging, suggested the shape of what once had been there. Smooth patches were where the furniture had been, the symmetry of the one at the window marred where feet had rested under the table, the two at the fireplace defined by four torn places each, revealing the floor, where the legs of the chairs had sat. Scuffed passages ran between the door and the fireplace, between the fireplace and the table-area.

Mairtin's pipe rack was still nailed beside the fire, containing one broken clay-pipe, bowl and half the stem, baked brown with the burnings of tobacco. Below it lay a little mound of objects to be thrown out: a pair of Jean's old shoes, ridiculously small, the uppers polished to the yieldingness of chamois, the broken soles counteracted from the inside by two pieces of brown paper, folded several times and each having at its centre a darker brown stain that expired outwards in jagged white spirals; Mairtin's 'museum' trousers that Jean had threatened to cut him out of someday ('They wid dae fur makin' soup,' she used to say); a burst tobacco-pouch; a broken willow-patterned saucer; a shepherdess figurine, roughly glazed and beheaded. Above the fireplace, King George was still enthroned.

Among so many mementoes, Jenny moved in an oblivion of practical involvement. The occasional sighs were a concession to physical effort, nothing more. The brush-head knocked sometimes on the skirting as she swept and around her dust sifted, vortexed briefly in the sunlight and resettled. Pinnied, sneezing now and again among frenzied motes, alone in an afternoon that seemed already decaying in this room, although it was still bright outside, she was performing her family's last traditional act of possession of the house. Her friends had helped. Ornaments and clothes had been disposed of. The husbands had co-operated in getting the furniture out, some taken to their houses, other parts sold to the second-hand shop in the Foregate. This final cleaning wasn't being done for the factor, but from pride, because, no matter how shabby the house, it had to be left fresh for who came next.

When Jenny had brushed the entire floor, she negotiated the dust in one crackling, furry heap on to her shovel. She placed the shovel in the hearth. She turned to the pail of warm water she had brought up with her. She was unwrapping the cloth that held the scrubbing-brush and rough soap when she remembered the beds. She took the brush again and knelt to sweep under them. The brush head chimed on a chamber-pot below her parents' bed. She brought it out, dusted it with the dry cloth, and replaced it. Under the second bed her brush struck something else. After some difficulty, she managed to hook it out on to the floor. It was a small, wooden box, sealed with dust. Wiping it, she slid the lid off.

The contents, long untouched, had fused with time into one another and their container. The inside of the box yielded them reluctantly, like membranes of itself. She picked their delicate organisms apart, into a ribbon, a folded picture, a piece of paper, a square of cloth, a doll's eye and a ring. The cloth, heavy as brocade, was still fairly bright, and the centre of the ribbon, where it had been folded on itself, retained the original sharpness of its yellow. The picture was in colour, the painting of a house idyllic in a garden where flowers of different seasons bloomed together. The piece of paper said in clumsy capitals 'I love Peter' and then the name 'Peter' written many times. The ring was from a lucky-bag. Putting it on her pinky, it stuck across her nail. The doll's eye had been a jewel. She realised with surprise that they were hers. It was like finding your heart when a child preserved in a box.

She replaced the lid and put the box in the hearth because she wanted to use the water before it went cold. But as she scrubbed, the room in spite of her had come alive. The action of disturbing that small cache of rubbish in the box had activated the pity of the past like a taboo broken. Determinedly, she netted more of the lukewarm water in the bristles of the brush, skinned the soap across them, scraped at the floor. But moving across the empty surface on her knees, she couldn't contain what she was doing to a trivial practicality. It became in part a conjuration of her past. While she made around her wide circles of white froth and then removed them with the wetted cloth she was tormented with thoughts of who she might have been, as if tugging at her arms was the child who had hoarded those bits of dreams like promises, asking unanswerable questions, hurt with silence. Her vigour became an exorcism.

Finished, she put the shovelful of ouse carefully into the fire to be burned, and then remembered she had no matches. She thought of leaving it because she wanted to get quickly out of the house. But it wasn't right to leave your dirt behind. Then it occurred to her that her father had for years been in the habit of hiding away odd matches against the emergency of needing a smoke some summer evening, when the fire wasn't lit and he was out of matches. They had found his cautiousness funny, especially since he could never remember where he had hidden them. Searching, she grew conscious of how the light had changed since it had started to rain, and now lay like a lacquer on the floor.

She finally found one stuck behind the pipe-rack. The phosphorus was neutralised with a covering of grease. Leaving over to light it, she saw on the fireplace the small, runnelled area where her father always struck his matches. In her vision, the place took on the isolation of an object held in her hand, a pathetic fragment. The sight of it halted her, brought home to her freshly what had happened, linked with the events of the past couple of weeks like a connective that makes instant sense of what had been gibberish. She knew her mother and father dead most clearly in that moment. She felt the funeral, the emptying of the house, the cleaning, as somehow conspiratorial, erasures of the truth before it should impinge too strongly. The pathos of the two bodies stashed hastily into the dark struck her.

She was bitter. They were dead and it was incidental. Their own family had hardly noticed. The war, she thought, the war. It had changed everything and nothing would ever be the same again. Things used to have their place. For her mother and father there had been a way of dealing with life that didn't work any longer. She thought of Mick, one of those seconds of concern for her family that came at random every day like heartbeats missed. It was the war. Everything was the war. At another time it would have been different. But there was a sense in which their lives being lost by the way like other people's small change had a ridiculous appropriateness external to the war. She looked at the photo above her. That was, she suspected, how they all died. The shape of her own life became momentarily grotesquely accidental.

Remembering the box she had found, she wondered how she had become the woman she was. Memories almost came to her, like wind-gagged cries. She felt revulsion from her own body, which seemed to her an amalgam of heavy breasts, distended stomach, legs ruinous with veins, a violated promise from her past, used by husband, mouthed by children, caricatured maliciously by work. Dead hopes lay heaped in her like a mass-grave. She was still standing there, memorial to herself, when Conn came in. He was wearing an old jacket of Tam's, cuffs upturned, drooping shoulders pulped with rain. His shabby presence angered her.

'Whit dae you want noo?'

'That's ma feyther an' Angus in fae the pit, mither.'

'Well?'

'Ye said Ah wis tae tell ye.'

She knew what they would be doing now. For half-an-hour or more they would lie down before the fire, as they did every evening after work, filleted with fatigue and groggy with black damp. The image of them there rehearsing death made her want to hurry. She felt her regret for herself as selfish. There were things to do. The water to be brought up for their bath. The pit-clothes to be taken out and dauded against the corner of the building to beat out the coal dust in them. The soup and bread to set out on the table. There would happen what always happened. Tam would let Angus have the first of the water. She would help them to wash. Angus would let his back be wiped except for a ridge of coal dust down the middle because, in spite of Tam's contempt for the superstition, Angus was afraid of weakening his spine. Tam would say, 'This watter's aye like bluidy treacle when Ah get ma turn.' Then they would eat.

She had to wear off the oiliness with several strokes before the match flared. Ceremonially, as if it represented her parents' past, her own self-pity, Jenny applied the match to the ball of sweepings in the fire. In a second its substance was flame and then a shadow of grease across the grid.

Feeling remote from her, Conn said, 'Ah'll say ye're comin', mither.'

'Jist a meenit, son. Ah'll come wi' ye.'

She looked round the room, noticed the photograph of the king and took it down.

'You cairry this, Conn.'

Conn took it, held it out to study it.

'Whit fur?'

'Fur the hoose, of coorse.' She needed something but couldn't have explained. 'Fur luck.' The irony of it only occurred to her once she had spoken.

'Ma feyther'll no' thank ye fur it,' Conn said solemnly.

She started to laugh, her eyes softening as they looked at him. 'Is that a fact? Come oan.'

She gathered the rubbish beside the fire, putting the box on top of it. Conn took the pail containing scrubbing-brush, soap and cloth, as well as carrying floor-brush and shovel. She had some trouble helping him to negotiate the doorway. She locked up and put the key in her pinny pocket to be handed in to the factor. Downstairs she threw everything she was holding in the dustbin.

At the mouth of the entry the pair of them paused, looking out at the rain. She pulled up the collar of the jacket he was wearing and tried to tighten the lapel across his chest. In the end she had to secure it with a pin taken from her apron. His head nestled on his father's shoulders. 'Like a pea oan a drum,' she laughed, as he wrestled away from her fussing hands. 'But ye'll fill it yet, eh, Conn?' Knowing he would want to go at his own pace and not hers, she took the brush and the photograph back from him, and said, 'Rin then, son. An' if ye fa', don't boather tae get back up. Jist rin oan.'

He ran. Coming out into the rain behind him, she watched. The pail bumped clumsily against his gangly legs. The jacket was like a cloak on him in width. But it was amazing how well he took up the length. He was getting big. Big enough for the pits, unless a miracle came. For Tam's sake as well as Conn's, she hoped it would.

Passing on the other side of the street, Mary Erskine called, 'Guid wather for folk wi' gills this, Jenny, eh?'

'Aye, Mary.'

Her inability to move fast gave her a galleon grace that seemed contemptuous of the rain.

# CHAPTER TEN

Everything had been prepared with the care of an organised
evacuation. Old Conn had set out first to walk to the station
because he couldn't move as fast as the rest. He carried the
dumplings Jenny had made. Tam and Angus, having finished the early
shift, washed and ate in relays. Conn dauded the pit-clothes and saw
that the clean shirts were there for them. Jenny did half-a-dozen things
at once.

Calmly, measuredly, systematically, they arrived at chaos. The
neatly drilled and interweaving movements became a traffic-jam of
cross-purposes. The voices that had been saying quietly, 'Ye can get
in noo' and 'Thanks', went off like horns. It started with the realisation
that thirteen minutes before the train was due Kathleen still hadn't
arrived with Alec, the baby. Jenny sent Conn down to the close-mouth
to watch for her and, as he ran back up every other minute to report
her absence, each time as breathlessly as if it was a new phenomenon,
he was able to catch scalding glimpses of the confusion among which
the others threshed. His father standing before the sideboard with its
drawers hanging out at different angles, his arms outstretched so that
the dangling shirt-cuffs gave him a vaguely priestly appearance, calling
'Studs! Studs! Whaur i' the bloody studs?' Angus running for a cloth,
head averted and hands up to prevent the scattering blood from going
on his shirt, while his father, embittered by his own failure and still
at the sideboard as if he expected a stud to appear to him any minute,
was saying, 'Ya sully bugger. Ye're supposed tae wait tae the hair
grows onywey, before ye shave. Whit are ye tryin' tae dae? Frichten

it awa' before it comes?' His mother fixing her hair while she told his father where he might find a stud while she advised Angus to wet a piece of paper with his tongue and put it over the cut. They joined Conn at the close-mouth just as Kathleen trauchled out of the Kay Park with Alec in her arms. Haste strung them out, Angus in front, running with his mother's message-bag, Conn consoling himself for second place with the thought that Kathleen's bag of baby-things must be heavier. Tam took Alec. Jenny and Kathleen came last, burdened with the weight of being women. It wasn't until they had found the compartment, just in time, with Old Conn already a part of it, the dumplings beside him, puffing his pipe in that way that made a hearth of wherever he happened to be, that they started to laugh.

The remembered moments cohered into a ridiculous composition, The Flight of the Five Dochertys. One of the handles of Kathleen's bag had snapped, throwing a nappy on to the pavement. 'That auld wumman's face,' Tam said. 'She lukked as if she wis thinkin' Conn wis the maist backward boay she'd ever came acroass.' Jenny checked on them all as the train shuffled off houses and streets, a woman shaking a duster out of a window, a group of boys foreshortening in the park, Graithnock and the war, and butted its way into the countryside.

They got off at Barrahill and waited. The station had an abandoned outpost atmosphere, the platform raided by couch-grass, the window of the single waiting-room cataracted with dust. Nobody else was there. Bird-sounds threaded silence and a few cows ate a field.

There, with his father teaching Alec wood and flowers and stone, his mother and Kathleen miming conversation through the dirty glass, Angus doing a miner's crouch in the middle of nowhere as if he'd located the corner of the wind, his grandfather filling his pipe, Conn suddenly entered the day for the first time. It was as if he had passed through a doorway in the wind. The banal facts that had brought them to this place shelved away and he felt not so much come here as grown. He stood drenched in daylight, almost gasping with happiness, lost among acres of sunshine. He laid his hand on the hot stone of the wall beside him, like someone who needs support, and the porous imprint of it seemed fused on palm and fingers. Without looking at anything in particular, he seemed to see it all, from the iceberg clouds and trees and fields hung out along the horizon to the group they made in the middle of it and the stalk of grass that bobbed in Angus's mouth and his father's buckled shadow on the ground. The acrid crackle of his grandfather's lighting pipe seemed big in the hanging stillness, a hayrick burning.

In his mind a word rose for no reason like a fish and fell: 'mysterious'. He lost it but the ripples it left went on, touching everything around him. The placings of the others, casual yet related, fascinated him inexplicably. His father had hung his jacket on a fence-stake. Shirt-sleeved, dappled with leaf-shadows, he was a stranger, holding a child Conn seemed to be seeing for the first time. Through the glass Kathleen smiled and stroked her forehead with two fingers. What she and his mother might be saying was unimaginable to him. His grandfather was a riddle—an ancient man sitting in sunlight on a broken bench with two cloth-wrapped dumplings beside him. Conn looked at the bag he had carried, lying against the fence, and wondered where it had come from, who had made it. Because Angus's hair was ruffled by a faint breeze, Conn couldn't understand why he had so often resented his brother.

He stood dumb with love, ravaged with joy. He felt caught up, carried along, like being involved in an incredibly complicated dance the steps of which he didn't know. He only knew that he wished to share in it more fully, desired to have the casually preoccupied poise of the rest, to be like them. He was almost unbearably filled with what seemed an unstoppable energy and he had nowhere to put it, no means to release it. He wanted to express it and all he could find to do was to lift a lopped branch of a tree and, spinning, whirr the air into scars of sound that healed instantly. He whirled and stopped, lashed and rested, and the more vigour he expended the more he had, while his people and his place became more marvellous, and the day, in huge fragments that seemed burning, that were both mystery and revelation, fell all around him.

And kept on falling. That train was no train. It could never have appeared on any timetable. Yesterday or tomorrow or any other day you could wait at the same time and only a train would come. But today they stepped into a fable—a jostle of giants with blackened faces being conveyed through the unsuspecting countryside from one secrecy to another. Conn smelled the dank earth-smells caught among their clothes betraying them as no ordinary men. They didn't fool him with the disguise of their casual talk or their attempts to wear unexceptional smiles. Not listening to their words, he heard their voices, harsh, electric, swelling and muttering, like storms conversing. He noticed the unnatural whiteness of the teeth against the darkened skin, so that every smile was an unexpected brightness quickly cached. They might deceive others but he knew all right that nobody knew who they really were.

When some of them got seats for his mother and Kathleen and his grandfather, and recognised his father, Conn felt suddenly taller to think that he had connections with them. Their conversation fell on him like a magic formula releasing him into himself.

'It couldny be Tam Docherty.'

'Hell, it couldny be onybody else. Tam Docherty.'

The name rippled among a few of them, causing looks Conn couldn't understand at the time, that lens-adjustment by which the blurred hearsay of the past is crystallised into present fact.

'Hoo's it then, Tam? Hoo's yer knuckles fur bruises?'

'Ah hear ye're leevin' quiet, then.'

'Retired undefeated. Bob Fitzsimmons the Second, eh?'

Somebody made a corner of a seat for Conn, saying, 'Here y'are, son.'

'Aye,' somebody else said. 'The auld dug fur the hard road, the pup fur the pavement.'

'Ye'll hiv tae learn tae staun' awa' fae yer feyther, onywey, son. He's a wee man but he makes a big shadda.'

Sitting, Conn felt even more a part of them. As if he were a prince to whom they couldn't bring enough gifts, the man who had spoken turned from him to his mother.

'Whit's yer secret, Jenny? Ye're aulder but ye're no' less braw. Mind when ye used tae come up tae the village? Nae maitter whit time o' year it wis, ye were bloomin'. Ye were a wee summer all oan yer ain. Ah wid've mairrit ye maself.'

One of the younger men shouted, 'Ye see hoo lucky ye were, missus,' and there was laughter. Jenny was laughing too, embarrassed but not sorry to be so.

'Away, ya skelf,' the man went on. 'You young yins think ye inventit men an' women. But Ah've seen the real breed, son. Hauf o' youse widny make a pit-piece fur a man. Ah could get a better man in a lucky-bag. But Ah've seen men.'

'We've heard it a' afore,' the young man shouted.

'Aye, ye hear it but ye don't listen. An' Ah've seen weemen, like Jenny here, that didny hiv tae buy their faces ower the coonter. A complexion straight fae Goad, son.'

'In the name o' Goad, man,' Jenny said involuntarily.

'Ah'm sayin' that, Jenny. But ye were wise. Ye mairrit the richt man. Wan o' the best wee men in Ayrshire here.' He announced it like a town-crier. 'If ye've never seen this yin in action, ye've never seen an angry man.'

'Here, sur,' Tam said. 'Ye're talkin' like a book withoot batters.'

Their laughter finally quelled him and he joined in it. The young man didn't pursue the comparison of generations, out of deference to Jenny, but the implied challenge had made a buoyancy among them that kept afloat the sense of expansiveness they felt in work being over. Conn had his own reasons for catching the contagion, having just discovered who his mother and father were.

'Ye're up fur the jing-a-ling then?' somebody asked.

'Aye, it's pairtly that,' Tam said.

'It should be a guid yin.'

'Some richt guid teams.'

Conn experienced awe of what was ahead. His father had tried to convince him that a jing-a-ling was just a night when a few mining communities got together in one village for a five-a-side football competition and maybe a few games of quoits and whatever else could be organised. But he knew now that whatever it was, a jing-a-ling wasn't as simple as that.

'An this'll be Mick.'

'Naw. Mick's in the sojers.'

'Oh, aye. He wisny in the pits. He's no' exempt, like.'

'He didny want tae be. Naw. This is Angus.'

'Gus. Of coorse. Gus. Ah can hardly credit it. Whit dae ye feed him oan then, Jenny? A hoarse between two mattresses? Whit age are ye, son?'

'Ah'm sixteen past.'

'An' Kathleen there. Hoo are ye, hen? That's guid. A mither as well. Ye're a gran'feyther, Tam, like me. Ah canny get used tae it. It's no' me that's gettin' auld. It's jist that mair folk are gettin' young nooadays. An' that's yer youngest.'

'That's Conn,' his father said.

'Ye hadny lost yer touch, Tam. He looks a likely boay.'

The man turned away to make faces at Alec, having just bestowed a kingdom upon Conn. He had always believed in himself as someone special and now he knew it. The train moved through country that he owned, bringing him nearer to the capital of himself. He had been to the village before but always just as nobody in particular. Now he seemed to see it.

The walk from the station lay through wonders. Conn just had time to take in the bleakness of the country that he found to his liking, the small school and the playground where he wished he had played, and at the end of the miner's row the low house with its rain-barrel under the eaves, before, in getting there, he found his sense of place transformed into a sequence of events.

People exploded on them from all sides and the week-end became for Conn a daze of impressions. He was poked and talked at, his hair ruffled, his biceps felt. Gusts of indecipherable laughter kept taking place. He met bizarre clusters of unknown features and was taught to call them Uncle and Auntie, only to find behind their formidable fronts unexpected recesses of kindness where shillings were kept for weans and sly jokes hoarded.

His new-found Auntie Chrissie kept him in front of her for a while, shaking her head and saying, 'My oh my, Jenny. Ah canny get ower it yit. Sarah! Wha is that like? Wha is that boay the image o' staun'in' there? See the boattom hauf o' his face there. It's Tam as a boay. Here, Tam. You'll never be deid while he's leevin'. That's a fact.'

Then she gave Conn a shilling, for the bottom half of his face as far as he was aware.

His Uncle Airchie showed him a trick with a penny and a handkerchief. His cousin Chairlie ('Ah'm really jist yer hauf cousin but it doesny maitter. Ah'll jist tell the boays ye're ma cousin.') took him out to the woods to show him places where men poached. Chairlie was a year older but not snobbish with it. In bed at night, while the talk of the grown-ups rose and fell in the big room, the two of them lay in the dark, exchanging their ideas about things. For two days they were friends for life.

For Conn there was so much that was new and yet expected, as if he had at last found an expression of himself that matched his imagination. It wasn't just in the sense of belonging which the affection of so many adults gave him, nor in seeing for the first time his cousin James's fabled collection of rocks and being able to say that he knew about them already. It went wider than that. He took to everything that was happening with a naturalness and an enthusiasm that suggested he was discovering his element.

The jing-a-ling typified it. He loved it all. Seeing it, he developed a different ambition every half-hour or so. He would be a football-player. The roughness of the game played in tackety boots, that crazy stramash of strength and energy, charged him like a dynamo. He *knew* that was what he would be like. He knew he was the same as these people.

Then he was going to be a quoiter. He was allowed to lift one of the heavy iron-rings and then marvel at the distance the men threw them, wrapping them round a metal stake embedded almost completely in the mud. Then he wanted to be a marker, one of the men who crouched over the mud-patch, holding a piece of paper where the quoit should land. Some of them would stay like that, unmoving, until the quoit brushed the paper from their fingers. The bravado of it thrilled Conn. He couldn't decide whether he wanted more to be the man who could casually show that depth of trust or the man who inspired it.

He was bewildered with potentialities. In the course of the weekend his imagination contracted a kind of fever, so that by the time they were coming back on the train he was no longer sharing the same reality as the rest of his family. They talked banally about things, and outside Graithnock station, his father told a friend who had stopped to talk that they had been up at Cronberry for the weekend. To them that was all that had seemed to take place.

Conn took his own truth home with him. It sustained him through the evening. After Kathleen had gone home and Angus was out for the night and Old Conn was away for his walk, Conn lay alone in his room, glad to have the place to himself. There his fragments of ambition formed themselves into one. He was going to be a man like his father and those uncles because to be that would include all the other ambitions. The feeling suffused him like a passion and so impatient was he, so determined, that the time he would have to wait seemed like forever. Without warning, he started to cry. He cried quietly because between him and where he had to get to it seemed such an endless and ridiculous waste.

Hearing his mother coming in, he covered his face quickly with his arm as if he had fallen asleep in that position.

'Conn? A'right, son?'

He breathed evenly and didn't answer. He listened to her going out again and heard her say to his father, 'Ah thocht Ah heard the wee yin greetin' there. Ah goat sich a shock. Ah kent there couldny be ony reason fur it.'

'Whit's wrang like?' Tam asked.

'Naw, it's nothin'. He's sleepin' fine. It musta been ma imagination.'

Conn stopped crying and took his arm away. He lay still for a long time, being a miner. Then with his hand he wiped the damp patch on the pillow where the last of his boyhood had drained out of him.

# CHAPTER ELEVEN

It was lined paper. There was a grease-stain in the top right-hand corner. The stain was not unlike a face in profile. The candle was resting on a flat piece of tin. The run grease made small, white, frozen waves. The pencil was small and snub-nosed, its tip disappearing under the prongs of the pared wood, like a small stone in a setting too big for it. The delicately flapping candle-flame made an area of dimness in the dark, a light that almost seemed breathing fitfully, inhaling to take in the humped bodies of two of the men, exhaling to leave them in darkness again. The centre of it was the paper. To Mick's troubled sight the page looked hardly solid, a shaft sunk, a wall of whiteness.

It was like being back at school. A pencil, a paper and the obligation to write. It was a test. Could you move the words across the paper and say what you were expected to say, without breaking the rules, without being wrong? Without wandering into what wasn't the point?

He no longer found refuge in letters. At first it had been good to write them, but, like a course in which the exams get progressively harder, he found the problem more and more difficult. It seemed impossible to manoeuvre the words on to the paper from the great waste that surrounded it. There was nothing he could say.

'Dear mother and father,

I'm fine as usual. No worries.'

He saw his hand. It was abraded along the back where it had scuffed a sandbag. The candlelight floated it at him separately, a huge complex of knuckles and bloated pores. Like a planet watched through a telescope. He seemed a long, long way from what was happening there.

'But there's something I have to tell you.'

He rested. And Jake made a baffled noise in his sleep. Mick wanted to tell his mother and father what the faces of some of the men looked like in candlelight as they lay in tiredness which sleep could barely touch. But that would have been pointless.

'Danny Hawkins was killed yesterday. He died very brave.'

He had barely time to get the words down before they were buried in images of Danny dying. The 'milk-can' coming through the air. The scrambled panic. And Danny running towards it instead of away. It must have been deliberate, Mick thought. The scream that was Danny disembowelling. The few animal whines that admitted him to his death.

'Tell Mrs Hawkins she can be proud of him. He was a good soldier.'

Filthy. Troubled with lice. Living in a permanent state of hypnotised fear. Suspected syphilis. Private Hawkins, deceased.

As one of them had said, 'Ah wonder if he really had the pox. Or jist the gun.'

The mocking horror of it swarmed up at Mick through the words he had placed on the paper, memories of men dead, of sad laughter, flies buzzing in an eye-socket, assaulted him. The lines of the paper became the bars of a cage through which terrible images reached for him. He took the page and held it to the candle, cauterising his mind. The fire flared against his hand but he hardly felt it. He hardly felt anything. He blew the candle out and sat in the dark.

He had failed.

# CHAPTER TWELVE

Jenny temporarily developed the habit of saying, 'Ah canny believe it. Time seems tae pass that quick,' to which Tam said nothing. Kathleen frequently shook her head and said, 'He seems too wee.' Angus offered his pit-hanky as a means of transport. At nights Jenny seemed always to be sewing at the same things, taking them out and folding them away again with mesmerised preoccupation, so that one of Angus's working shirts was short of a button for more than a fortnight, which had never happened before, and a hole in Tam's moleskins was allowed to get bigger. Once Tam looked at what she was doing and said ambiguously, 'Aye'. Once she asked him, 'Whit aboot the gaffer?' but Tam just kept looking into the fire and she didn't ask again. Small economies occurred and nobody mentioned where the extra butter and the second egg had gone. The signs of change were absorbed discreetly into the rhythm of their lives without very much open reference to what lay behind them.

The object of them was Conn. When he was out of the house or in bed, the sewing and the talk and the silences went on around him like a conspiracy. He animated them by his exclusion. But the suppressed nature of the activities that related to him wasn't solely due to a desire to keep them secret from him. Jenny also didn't want what was going on to intrude too strongly on Tam. In his lengthening silences something was being interred.

Both of them spoke little about it, merely lived with it in an oblique almost shamefaced way, rather like parents obliged to arrange a Black Christmas for their child and ashamed to be giving him nothing but a stockingful of ashes. Yet Conn knew what was going on and was secretly happy. As a child will who knows what is being planned for him but doesn't want to spoil it for his parents, he too remained discreet. For a month or so, they lived in an irony of gentle, mutual deceptions. Behind the deceptions, their real feelings were their own.

One night when they were both together by the fire, Jenny said suddenly, 'Hoo long is it that we're mairrit, Tam?'

Her sewing fluttered on to her lap and she was staring into her own question as intensely as if she were trying to count her way back through every chore from the one in her hands till then.

'Twinty year?' Tam asked.

'Oh. Did we hiv Kathleen before we were mairrit?'

Tam came out of his preoccupations and together they gathered clues with a concentration that suggested the answer was more than itself.

'Ah wis in the Barchan Pit at the time.'

'It wis jist efter ma Auntie Chrissie dee'd. Ah mind she said fae her bed she wid dance at ma weddin'. The sowl!'

'Ah wid jist be twinty-three. Or twinty-fower.'

'Ye mind the rain?'

'Christ, ye were braw.'

'You looked younger than Ah'd ever seen ye. Like yer ain wee brither.'

'Aye, it wis twinty-three year ago.'

'Naw. Twinty-fower. Oor Kathleen's twinty-three past.'

Tam pokered the fire against the hard frost and the grey thoughts. Jenny didn't resume her sewing. The fogged window still showed very faintly where Tam's hand had minutes ago rubbed a spyhole on the pane, but their breaths were sealing it again. With Angus and Conn asleep and themselves drawn tight to the heat as if only the fire could see them past approaching midnight, the silence appeared to stretch away from them like something vast. The house, becoming the architecture of their thoughts, seemed not two rooms but a big emptiness.

'A' that time,' Jenny said.

'An' ye never failed them fur a meenit o' it. Nane o' the fower o' them.'

'A' that time. It seems funny tae think aboot it noo.'

'Aye.' Tam had the fire settled for the night. 'But we better no' laugh too lood. We'd waken the boays.'

Standing in front of the fire, he stripped for bed. As he bent, the firelight picked out the blue of the coal-scars round the shoulders. His left biceps had acquired an ineradicable dusting of black powder, shadow of an explosion. Saying, 'Ach aye,' Jenny rolled up her sewing in agreement. The rest was simply unsayable.

But they thought it, touching beyond talk in their awareness of each other the learned weaknesses and hurt parts. Jenny knew why Tam didn't want to see too much of the work she was doing, although he loved and admired the thoroughness with which she did it. She understood without words the growing resignation in his eyes, just as she would have understood the expression of a devout believer who has come back for the umpteenth time from Lourdes to find the same deformities, and can't imagine where he can find the strength ever to go back.

Tam sensed Jenny's feelings, the pride that was tinged with melancholy, so that her natural business gave way every so often to brooding stares, like someone who had just realised that she has been eagerly sewing her own shroud. For a part of her life was ending and with it came the awareness that she would never be as necessary again. From now on the extent of her involvement could only diminish. Halting from time to time in her work, she went over the realisation again and again, committing a hard lesson to memory.

Conn, though not oblivious to the fact that this time affected his mother and father in some ways sadly, was too absorbed in the richness of his own reactions to take those of his parents very seriously. As the day he had been living towards came near, his thoughts grew more callously self-centred. When the night arrived for being given the results of his mother's work, he was so far out of himself in an almost mystical transport that everybody else was just irrelevant, except perhaps as mirrors of his mood.

It was Christmas Eve. Several objects were carefully arranged on the table: a pit-bonnet with the leather patch sewn on to the skip to hold the lamp; a pit-lamp bought by Tam; an oil-flask acquired second-hand and burnished for days by Angus; a working-shirt bought by Kathleen; working trousers and moleskins Jenny had made a fit for Conn and a pair of pit-boots that had cost her more than she could afford. Over a chair-back was a jacket she had modified as much as she could towards Conn's build. Their presence on that evening was due to a double insistence of Conn's: that he wanted nothing for his Christmas except what would help him in starting his work; and that, since he wasn't a wee boy any longer, he would take them on Christmas Eve instead of Christmas morning. Also on the table in an attempt, which was lost on Conn, to soften the implications of these things, to make them seem more a gift, were a pen-knife and a second-hand book, both given by Tam.

Returning from the unnecessary errand he had been sent on, Conn had given his mother the matches before he noticed the stuff on the table. His expression was a prerogative of the young, unfakeable as a sunrise. He said, 'Great!'

The family watched, enjoying the importance with which he imbued everything he touched. Angus had stayed in and Kathleen had come up ostensibly to ask her mother's advice about Alec but more importantly to witness the ceremony. Having still not achieved a sense of family in her marriage, she found in the occasion a temporary renewal of conviction in the possibilities the future held.

'These are great,' Conn said.

'The lamp hooks in here,' Angus explained.

'Ah ken. Ah've seen ma feyther's an yours often enough.'

'An' ye fill it oot o' this.'

'That's a beauty. An' moleskins tae. Can Ah try them oan?'

Kathleen helped him to carry them through to the room and then left him. Putting the things on was for Conn a confused, fevered experience, haunted by half-remembered stories of magical garments and astonishing transformations wrought in seconds and secret truths stunning those to whom they were suddenly revealed. The nearest thing to clarity in him was a sense of the defeat of the stifling narrowness of school, the negation of its lies. But the feeling didn't occupy him long, for school was instantly and utterly irrelevant. When the frog becomes a prince, he bears no malice towards rodents. The bonnet gave him a new identity. The shoulders of the jacket drooped like inconspicuous wings. The boots were seven-league. He emerged to awe the others.

Angus's suppressed laughter became a tight smile on Kathleen's face, as if it had to find an outlet somewhere. Jenny held her feelings in balance with difficulty. The clothes were an intrusion on his youth, gave the impression that adulthood was abducting him. She could have cried except that, if he had to go to work, there was consolation in his being so well prepared. A lot of families had to beg or borrow the means for starting a son in the pits. At least they had provided by themselves for Conn and he owed nothing to anybody. With long-acquired skill, she fended off vague, disturbing emotions by concentrating on practicalities. The boots were a good buy, the moleskins fine. The jacket wasn't too bad. The bonnet was the only problem, the fact that it was too big emphasised by the weight of the lamp. She would have to cut a panel out the back.

'That's quite a bunnet ye've goat there, Conn,' Angus was saying. 'When ye're no' wearin' it, ye can aye rent it oot as a single-end.'

'A' ye've goat tae dae, son,' Kathleen countered, 'is learn hoo tae be as big-heided as yer brither an' it'll fit ye fine.'

Looking on, Tam accepted Angus's mockery as if it were aimed at him. He regretted the two pressures that had made him agree to this: Conn's insistence and their poverty. He couldn't have felt worse if he had given Conn a suicide-kit for Christmas. But more hurtful than the immediate irony was seeing in front of him the incarnation of the inevitable. That he had refused to face the fact that it was inevitable until now made him more ashamed. He could never have afforded to keep Conn on at school. It had been a silly dream for a grown man to allow himself. Now Conn had made him admit the obvious. He had fathered four children and all he had ever been able to give them was their personal set of shackles. He went over suddenly and put his arm round Conn, slapping his shoulder. He winked at Conn and started to laugh.

'Aye, ye'll dae, son. You can stert onytime. Hoo aboot this man, eh?'

His laughter established a mood. They closed on Conn, getting him to show them things, making him important. His mother said, 'Ah wish oor Mick could see ye noo.' He felt his father relaxing towards him, as if he accepted who Conn was in a way he never had before. The feeling was to grow, establishing between Conn and his father a deepening relationship, and Conn was at that time unaware of what lay behind the removal of the tension that had existed before with his father, was too young to appreciate the pragmatism experience teaches us, so that, once the desperate hope that had seemed a vital organ is removed, we can learn to live without it.

Later that night the objects were again set out on the table where Conn had insisted on leaving them when he went to bed. Only the boots were on the floor, because Jenny had said it was unlucky to have them on the table. She wasn't normally superstitious but this was not a time for taking chances. She was for propitiating even the gods of strangers.

In different rooms Tam and Conn remained awake, the one too tired, the other too eager to sleep. In the darkened house, the invisible pit-lamp glowed in the minds of both. For one, the mocking past, absurd precipitate of twenty-four years of struggle. For the other, the promising future.

# CHAPTER THIRTEEN

An advanced field dressing station in a trench called Harley Street. And other names: Glasgow Road, Strathcona Walk, Finchley Road. Edwardian Britain stripped of its stucco morning-suits. Dug-outs became villas, christened Mary, Violet or Nancy. Kensington Palace stank of unjustifiable suffering. In The Picture House the deaths were genuine. Burlington Arcade and the Leicester Lounge had human limbs for mortar. Kelvingrove Mansions frequently caved in.

Set down in an ironic metaphor of Britain, Mick accepted it, learned its topography thoroughly. His horizon became the back of the man in front of him. From dug-out to sandbags and back again was a shift. Lice were natural. A sliced petrol-can was a fire. Army biscuits were a form of fuel. He questioned nothing. Yet there occurred in him dim implications, a vague need for reprisals. His postponed anger was a kind of politics.

For the moment it didn't reach the length of coherent thought. There wasn't time. He lived from sleep to sleep, an ache of small necessities, to hunt for lice, to scavenge heat, to avoid being killed. He pared himself to the starkness of the place. Beyond his reflexes he was void. He lived in the taste of biscuit, through a fag, as a listening for the sound of the look-out's whistle.

'Bomb to right!'

He forced himself to look, to wait till he could see and judge and run and throw himself flat. The detonation juddered under him, seemed to lift him on a wave of earth and throw him into space. His eyes still closed, he span. His hearing was a plangent agony. He drifted in a waste of terror from which he didn't believe he could ever come back, until he heard a voice saying, 'Fuck this fur a coamic song.' He opened his eyes and the world was made again. In the beginning was the word.

And the word was with man. The men were the only identity he had left. He survived only as one of them. The others were the only sanity each of them had. They had evolved their shared esperanto for the truth: na-pooh, san-fairy-an, nae bloody bon. They transformed the machinery of hell into contemptible jokes: coal-boxes, whizz-bangs, pip-squeaks, milk-cans, old boots. They purified enormity into obscenity. They enriched the mud with swearing.

In the old barn they'd had a sing-song. Mick had watched their faces, feeling what he imagined some religious people must have felt at a revivalist meeting. For the moment he was saved. It wasn't the heroism of men singing before a battle. It was the opposite of that. The singing was mostly lousy. It was their recalcitrant ordinariness, their refusal to be heroic. The horror that they had come from and the terror they were going to were both earthed in their faces into something bearable. Mick saw men who would have to count themselves lucky if they lived another two months and they were unselfconsciously casual. One of them winked in acknowledgement of a cigarette. Another wiped his nose across his sleeve. Another sang obliviously in the wrong key. Confronted by the ravaged face of history, they nodded wrily and worked out how to make the fags last and concentrated on keeping their heads down. Their secret was their inability to pretend to be more than themselves, the distinct reality that belonged to each of them separately, like moles or warts. They became what Mick had in place of a religion.

Big Tosher had crystallised it for him. Waking one night to someone talking, Mick tried dimly to focus on the sound. They were back from twelve days in the trenches and sleeping in some kind of outbuilding on a farm. Nobody knew exactly what kind of building it was because it had been dark when they came to it. Mick located Tosher lying on the ground along from him. Apart from the troubled breathing of the men, Tosher's voice was the only sound. He was speaking quietly, saying, 'Naw. Ye'll have tae go, freen'. Tae hell wi' this. Must be removed.'

Mick's first reaction was a chill of apprehension. He thought Big Tosher had snapped. He had known it happen often enough before. You couldn't always foresee it. Sometimes a man sat down quite casually, throwing out a remark, and he wouldn't get back up as himself. That remark would prove to be the last coherent news, like a message sent out from a transmitter that mysteriously breaks down. Some delicate balance had shifted in him and he would sit gleying ahead of himself. You would have had to sink a mine to get to him.

Others went out in a sudden fragmentation of hysteria. Mick listened in awe, wondering if he was hearing the first bulletin from Tosher's madness.

'Must be removed! Bloody interlowper.'

Tosher was moving quietly into the darkness. His self-absorption was total.

'Leevin' aff the back o' the worker, eh? Nut at a'. Oop, ya bastart!'

It seemed to Mick that Tosher was taking off his clothes.

'Ye micht as weel gi'e yersel' up. Ye've nae chance. Must be removed.'

Just when Mick was considering intervention, the truth of it came to him, Tosher was on a louse-hunt.

'Whit dae ye think this is? The bloody Pairish. Ah'm no charity.'

Listening with understanding, Mick found himself laughing noise-lessly into the darkness. Hearing Tosher's moment of triumph, 'Goat ye, ya Hun!', the noises of satisfaction, the gradual subsidence, Mick experienced a small revelation. Like Tosher's campaign against the louse, Mick's war was a private one.

He understood what had so often jarred his sense of honesty in the way the papers talked about the war. They said things like 'honour' and 'self-sacrifice' and 'indifference to personal danger'. They didn't understand. What the war taught was selfishness, a flame of pure necessity through which each man had to pass. And something strange happened to most of them who went through it. It connected them to others. They became so expert in caring about themselves that they comprehended that same care as it existed in others, could judge it with an emotionless neutrality. The result was that they discovered true generosity.

If a man gave up a share of rations to another or took over early from him, it was simply his expertise in the pressures they lived among telling him that he could afford to do that at that time and the other couldn't. That was all. The gift carried no obligation. It was just an acknowledgement of both their natures. They existed beyond the power of stimuli like principles or ethics. Virtue and necessity were the same.

As the war progressed, living among these specialists in being human, Mick had learned. More and more he shed any unnecessary luggage of thought or speculation. He honed himself down to just being there. His sense of himself was in the third person.

So he tried to avoid what he knew he couldn't handle. All the time he was experiencing things which he couldn't allow to take place in him just then but which would have to happen later. His mind recorded them like undeveloped negatives. 'Stretcher-bearer to the left!', and later the man with half a face was carried past him. The feet of the rats across his body coded future nightmares into his mind.

The trench in moonlight printed a plate of leprous beauty on his memory.

Survival could only be partial. What was happening didn't happen to individuals. Catastrophe had nothing to do with being you. It was the result of fortuitous positioning, accidental decisions, momentary orders. It was what happened to people.

He moved beyond all sense of time, among what only his body could comprehend. Mindlessness was his routine. He was someone. Disaster was what would probably happen. When it happened, it would happen to someone. When it came, it came. The shell exploded. Something was moving through the air. The ground was battering someone. Someone's pain was splitting the sky.

# CHAPTER FOURTEEN

When they left the road, the ground seemed harder, conveying the strange sensation that asphalt was a cushion on the earth. They climbed a banking ferrous with frost and began to cross a field. It was still dark and shapes were different densities of black. Grass skinkled, the frozen filaments snapping as they stepped. Denied a visual perspective, they felt themselves defined by a sensory braille. A foot that had to adjust to an angle of the ground affirmed the bulk of the body. The weight of the things they carried, bumping, measured the motion of their walking like a metronome. Cold etched at their faces. Breath froze.

Not much was being said. Sliddering down another banking, they could see against the sky other shapes converging. They hit a dirt road where the struck stones didn't budge. The crunching of their boots was absorbed in moments among the multiplying versions of itself. The sense of space was lost, first through sound.

The feet just a yard ahead of him took Conn by surprise. He looked behind and then to the front again. He was part of a crowd. Again his determination to take in every part of this day stage by stage had been defeated. His expectations had been ambushed so often by unpredictable realities that his powers of assimilation were scattered. So much had happened already.

There was the eeriness of Tadger's whistle, calling his father and Angus, and himself for the first time, out into the darkness. The drugged movements of the men in the small roomful of ashen light, as if compelled to obey what they couldn't control. The scalding porridge, his mother whispering, 'That'll stick tae yer ribs.' The harshness of new lace-thongs on his fingers, gouging him awake. Angus with boots and trousers on but still in his vest, slumped forward asleep in a fireside chair, his elbows on his knees, his forehead resting on the backs of his clasped hands, the shoulders bulging like a deformity, while his mother brought him food and shook him gently alive. His father pulling on his trousers, his lips crinkling to keep the cigarette in his mouth as he started to cough, the cigarette taken out as the cough became a seizure, and his father leaning on the smoke-board, his body working like a bellows, until he spat a knot of phlegm into the fire and his breathing subsided to a noisy wheezing. His mother saying, 'Ah wish tae Goad ye widny smoke oan an empty stomach.' Familiar things that seemed strange: the bottled tea, dark red; work-jackets over chairs, stiff-armed like suits of armour. The enjoyment of them walking with Tadger and his three sons through darkened empty streets, sentries guarding other people's sleep. His mother's last remark, 'Goad bliss ye an' the devil miss ye,' and her smile that was almost shy, as if she was sorry to be saying something so silly.

The remembered fragments were confused with others. Coughing that broke out among the walking men, moving from one to another like a password in the black morning air. The lights at the pithead thawed the darkness into bleak random patches and gave what had been mysterious figures grey, ordinary faces. His father talked to a man whose eyes measured Conn disinterestedly.

The cage took four. In the blackness with only his stomach as a guide, Conn thought they were going up. A darkness enveloped them.

Tadger's voice said, 'Thank Christ we'll hit some watter-leaf the day.'

His father's voice wasn't his father's voice. It said, 'Splint we're oan. The hale bluidy country's made o' splint.'

'Except fur the stane.'

'Hiv ye some Alfred Noble?'

'Aye. Ye can hiv some.'

Angus suddenly shouted, 'Get ready, fower-an'-a-hauf! They're comin' up!'

'Keep yer wind fur breathin',' Tam said.

'Aye, if ye've ony spare,' Tadger said, 'jist pass it along.' He put his hand lightly on the top of Conn's back and thumbed the hair on the back of his neck in a gesture he would never have allowed himself in the daylight.

Somebody opened the door of the cage at the bottom and said, 'Aye, boays.'

One big light burned near the cage, blue, gently palpitating, a poisonous flower. Like petals fallen from it, the lighted pit-lamps swayed away, settling into darkness.

'Haud oan, ye'll be pasted before ye stert yer shift.'

Angus held his arm to stop him. His father went on. Tadger was gone. Angus and he just stood.

'Noo ye're sure ye've goat everythin'?' Angus asked. 'Ye haveny left yer muscles in the hoose?'

'Where's ma feyther?'

'Don't greet, son. He'll be back. That's when it'll be time tae greet.'

Angus leaned against a prop. Their father's lamp appeared again and they followed it.

Coal was strange, more various than could have been imagined, black only sometimes, inclined to mimic rock, a place, an architecture, a record, an opposition, a measurement of time. His father muttered to it occasionally, 'That's aboot us.' 'Come oan, ya bastard.' The swear-words were as soft as endearments. Dust was so much that you forgot it. The hutches were deceptive, not looking big but feeling like wells when you tried to fill them. Angus, cutting coal, loading a hutch, pushing it, was alone with his exertion. Bread tasted marvellous. 'Pit-breid', his father said, 'is the only guid reason fur goin' doon a mine.' Behind the chink of axes, the infrequent dull explosions, the rumble of the hutches, the pit was secretive. Props sighed. Water whispered in inaccessible places. Rats leapt away from lights.

Learning to work there, Conn became part of a time-scale different from any he had known. The pit was something separate, an entity on its own. Anything that happened on the surface was just punctuation. Here the continuity was unbroken of hewing and propping and hutching and drawing. Day merged with day and events followed a sequence not dependent on time so much as an internal logic of their own, the cutting of new workings, the driving of props, the counting of hutches, the laying of rails, the lifting of rails, something as abstruse and self-extending as a mathematical equation. It was a self-justifying involvement, an expertise the purpose of which was itself. Day after day he mastered the skill of the others, the art of constructing tunnels that led to blank walls, like entombed men studying the aesthetics of escape. Behind them they left a Lascaux of dripping passageways, roughly sculpted chambers, perilous with water, foul with gas, upheld by rotting timbers, a folk-monument that undermined the earth. There, like a primitive religion most people had forgotten, they had practised painful genuflections, hard prostrations, lain in water, wrestled with rock, while the pit left its message in them like stigmata. Later, Conn thought there must have been a time when it was all new to him, but he couldn't remember it.

The boy's wonder petrified into facts, and they were all the man was left with of what he had been, like stones on which fern-leaf shadows can dimly be made out. The Blue Dan was the light that burned at the bottom. Water-leaf was the best household coal. You could see your face in it. It brought most money and was easiest to get out. Alfred Noble was explosive used for blasting. 'Fower-an'-a-hauf' was the weighman for the pit. He never allowed more than four-and-a-half hundredweight per hutch, though a lot of the men claimed they held nearer five. There was a check-weighman to act on behalf of the men, called 'Leg-an'-a-hauf' because he had lost a foot in the pit, but he was known to be the other weighman's echo. Each day the bottomer opened the cage for Conn.

Like a dogma accepted beneath the level of questions or comprehension, his experience there became a central influence on his life. Because of it, much else followed naturally. Like the others, he developed a love of the open air, green country. Washed, his first instinct was to get out. Whippets interested him, the chase became inexplicably a part of his heraldry—greyhound on a field verte. The old stories he had heard so often of the closeness of the men who worked down the pits took on new meaning. Even the superstitions that he had listened to his father dismiss seemed to him not stupid at all but like a code only the miners themselves understood.

Two or three weeks after starting in the pits, he saw Tadger stop in the chill morning air.

'Hell,' Tadger said. 'Ah've forgotten ma piece.'

The seven of them stood in a dark, empty street. Tadger was thinking. There was still time to go back. It was a moment or two before Conn realised the problem, that it was unlucky to turn back for anything, that if a man had to return to the house, he should stay there. 'You three'll no' be leevin' as fat at piece-time the day.' The others laughed, not without relief, and they all walked on.

In step with them, Conn thought of the pit they were headed towards, soughing, black, dangerous. He understood the place where Tadger had been standing. With gladness he realised that his wish had been granted. He was one of them. The implications of that wish were something he still had to learn, but for the moment his new experience was complete and absorbing in itself, so absorbing that when the official word came about Mick, Conn felt a small shock of surprise that real things were happening outside the sphere of his own life.

# CHAPTER FIFTEEN

The best way to make the room was to start with the gable-end. That gave you a mainly blank surface, regular in shape. The two windows, it was true, were a difficulty. But by being careful not to focus on them directly, you could reduce them merely to shapes made of light, acting not as clarification but as a baffle to whatever was beyond them. This meant you had a rectangle inset with two smaller rectangles, and the effect was one of strengthening the sense of rigid form.

On such solidity you could build. Progress would now give the impression of being not lateral but vertical, for this was your foundation. Speed was variable. Sometimes you could move with quite surprising quickness from one familiarity to another, from the remembered dark brown stain on a brass bedstead to the indentation on the polished floor beside it. On such occasions you had the feeling that the entire structure was already there and only waiting for you to make use of it. But at other times the problems seemed insurmountable. It was so hard to maintain what you had made until it acquired the strength to stand by itself. An unanticipated noise could make rubble of half-an-hour's work. The hump of bedclothes, carelessly allowed to intrude before the rest of the room was ready for it, could become a complex of ridges, where you were lost. This was frightening because there was no way of telling what you might meet there. To lose total control of the present was to stumble again on to that wilderness where events from the past survived like crazy anchorites, nurtured on their own monstrosity and hungry to impose their lunacy on whoever was foolish enough to come across them. The only refuge was the room, or rather not the room but the work of making it. There was even a way in which the mildly disgruntled consciousness of futility, that awareness of dealing with intractable materials, was not a bad thing. The need to go on with it was always there.

It was generally the case that progress was slow, for the room was a very long one. It could take Mick, say, a couple of hours of painfully sustained patience to complete the place, an achievement which was, indeed, remarkably rare. Mostly he was content simply to go on with the attempt as long as he could. Success was most validly measured in time passed. This attitude became so familiar, not to say comfortable to him that he frequently forgot altogether about the very possibility of completion. This probably didn't matter, or if it did was most likely helpful, since the best thing that could happen wasn't that he finished but that the burden of what he was trying to do was realised afresh as being intolerable and his mind, achieving an intense moment of recoil, shuffled the entire problem instantly, and won void—not that terrifying wilderness that pressed so often against the very walls of the room, but silence bland as unguented bandage, a glacial emptiness in which he was at peace. After that, the work could begin again.

Every day it was the same. The need to start anew was not un-pleasant, had something almost of excitement in it. There was a recurring moment that he loved especially. It happened most often in the morning but could occasionally be found at other times of the day, as if a time-lock had occurred and a new day was beginning in the middle of the old one. It was when he was at just the right distance from the room to see the sunlight and nothing else. Along the room large windows faced each other, and the sunlight took place at regular intervals, lying from window to window in vast, unbroken blocks. The room then derived a purpose, was purified simply into contours for containing these—like a hangar for stored sunlight. That was the time. The sunlight lay waiting like great luminous slabs of Carrara marble, from which he could with patience tease the shapes and presences already implicit in it. It felt almost like hope.

There were even days when hope seemed justified. The room was completed. The whole preposterous structure was painstakingly built up fragment by meaningless fragment, teetering with absurdity. Achievement had gone beyond that. In moments of particularly intense concentration, he had managed, still keeping everything in place, to know the room in its horizontal solidarity, a firm projection of stone. The grass beyond it was also permissible. In the last of those moments the word 'hospital' firmed in his mind through a series of almost insensible jolts, like a recently erected building settling.

These times became more common. Then it was that he fully rejoined his body, became properly a part of the words he said every day to whoever happened to be sitting beside his bed. The room ceased to be a collapsing collection of things and resolved itself into a continuing and actual place with beds and people and occurrences that were sequential. But the attainment of this condition, as he discovered, did not necessarily mean its permanence. Days still came when his mouth was left to carry on a charade of conversation, his body to profess a firm certainty in which he himself couldn't share. And even though the actuality of the room became more easily realisable, though it became more natural to see it solid, even to identify the people in the various beds, to say their names, to talk to them—the most hazardous part of all remained. This was not to locate the existence of the room, but to locate the existence of himself within the room.

It was long and lonely for him trying to catch up with his body on the bed. How many times he returned to terrible events, still sheeted in the flames of their happening, how many times sheered off in remembered terror, only to lug himself back again and again, in an attempt to find lost pieces of himself. Between the fear of his past and the fear of his present he shuttled, desperate to salvage what was left of him from his experience.

His own body was his only certitude. It was the best way to come at what had happened, meant the past. Frequently he would inventory his wounds, without pity or, indeed, feeling of any kind, but with the mechanical repetitiveness of a prayer recited under stress. The sight of one eye was restored. The other was permanently useless. This in itself was to be counted as a gain, since he had been for a time totally blind. Besides, as had been pointed out to him, the ruined eye was not significantly disfigured. A slight scar showed near the temple. All it meant, he had been told, was the need to take special care of the eye that functioned. The leg, he was assured, would heal. 'Complete mobility,' the doctor said. That left only the arm, the right one. The surgery on it was finished now. They had begun by taking off the hand, then part of the forearm, and had finally stopped above the elbow—an almost shy progression, as if the truth were diffident. And thus, the map of his recent past was made complete.

With its help, his experience almost became possible. It wasn't so much that his wounds measured what had happened to him but rather that they indicated what hadn't happened. He hadn't hung on wire, discharging a refuse of guts and moaning till one of his own men shot him from a trench. He hadn't stepped back from the parapet, saying mildly 'fuck it' to nobody in particular, and sat down gently dead, a sardonic medal of blood on his tunic. He hadn't run screaming in an attempt to put himself in the path of the mortar that cartwheeled clumsily through the air. He hadn't ended as a talking torso, like some remnant of statuary unfortunately damaged in transit. He was simply going to be blind in one eye and minus an arm.

That wasn't bad. The biggest immediate disappointment was probably that he was less relieved than he had expected to be, that he felt less of everything than he would have imagined in his desire to get out of the trenches. Incapable of formulating an explanation for himself, he nevertheless remembered an incident when he had arrived at understanding, not as a rational process but as an observed fact, physically enacted. It had been when he was wakening after one of the operations. At the foot of his bed a doctor was talking to someone else about him. The doctor's voice was pleasantly matter-of-fact. Mick felt for his hand and it wasn't there. Another time, if he had been more himself, he might have responded with anger or outrage, adopting the common enough stance of resenting being treated as a number. But, too weak to have an automatic reaction, he was obliged to have a real one. He saw that he felt not the slightest offence at the way the doctor was talking. He saw that he wasn't being treated as a number—he *was* a number. And the doctor was merely another one. Outside the walls, the machinery was clanking on, and whether it needed your hand or your eyes or your legs or yourself to run on made no difference to anything. That was simply what it needed. That was all that mattered. You didn't. Personal responses were irrelevant.

The building he was in was only one of countless throughout Europe, temples to the modern mysticism. To them came those who, regardless of race, had managed to attain the new Nirvana. They had gone through the novitiate's visionary instant in the falling flare, understood the words exchanged in darkness, been purified with mud, and reached the final sanctum. Their prophet's promises hadn't been in vain. The gods that controlled their lives had admitted them to their presence. Who would be petty enough to quibble about what must be lost in order to gain so much? They returned blind or legless or having left their minds behind. Transformed, indeed enlarged by decimation, they were led or were wheeled or limped among their endless private visions, unutterable to others—therefore, how great. The new elect, they had been placed above the confines of a private life, the folly of ambition, the silliness of ordinary love. Their future was the past.

Absolved of himself, he lay in bed, feeling nothing, waiting for nothing. When he saw the two of them come through the door at the end of the room, recognition didn't occur to him at first. The orderly pointed. As the other man advanced, Mick's own tears told him it was his father. The tears meant nothing to him. They just happened, like a wound that was supposed to be healed reopening. They touched his cheeks strangely, as if belonging to someone else. He couldn't remember when he had felt them last. He wondered if in some way he was crying for his father, for the terrible naïveté of his presence, coming forward now, one hand crumpling his bonnet, staring towards him, looking too physical for the place, and somehow contaminating that clinical atmosphere, awkward as a human being in heaven. He didn't know. He didn't realise that he was weeping through his father's eyes, that, empty as an angel, he could only come alive through the suffering of another.

# CHAPTER SIXTEEN

T am returned from the military hospital on a Saturday evening. He was tired from the journey, and that helped. It softened the directness of his meeting with the family. He was a man back from a distance and familiar roles could be adopted until such time as they all felt able to face the uniqueness of the situation. Kathleen helped her mother by putting plate, spoon and bread out on the table, while Jenny pretended the soup wasn't quite ready. Conn stoked the fire and Angus brought more coal. Wee Alec, asleep in the plaidie, lay on one of the set-in beds. Tam himself took off his collar, untied his boots, and talked about travelling on trains, as if the whole purpose of his journey had been inspection of the railway system.

The news of Mick waited among them like an awkward stranger against whom their deliberate intimacy was a defence. They took their time, waiting for it to find some way of introducing itself into their lives. Jenny and the others were one multiple presence, the fears of one a part of and intensified by the fears of the rest. She didn't know, for example, if Conn could hear what Tam had to say, while Conn, absorbing without comprehension his mother's misgivings, enlarged them, was prepared for the unspeakable to be spoken. His very real dread was compromised by a growing curiosity. All anxious for word of Mick, their anxiety became so neurotically intense that it paralysed itself. The war, for so long a terrible thing that happened, like death, to others, had happened to them. It was an event Mick would have to live with for the rest of his life. And they were Mick.

Tam's hesitancy wasn't a decision, merely a fact. He had arrived ahead of his understanding, still didn't know what it was he had seen.

There were things he had to say, of course. But these were all so closely involved with things he was determined he wouldn't say that to his usual problem of articulacy was added that of suppression, which was a new experience for him. His home had always been to him the place where he existed with a kind of absoluteness. From swearing to religion he allowed himself full range. It wasn't tyranny in him or lack of consideration for his children, but simply that he believed children had the right to exposure as well as protection. The only legacy he could give them was himself. Even outside, a reluctant, chafing silence was the closest he could get to compromise. Now this ignorance of the art of pretence irked him.

'Well,' he said, taking his soup. 'Ah seen the man.' The gallousness emerged from his search for an idiom. He was assessing their preparedness. Jenny had found some clothes to fold. It occurred to him how often she did that. Under pressure, it was habitual for her to move about building up those small mounds of cleanliness like sandbags. The realisation hurt him. Kathleen fussed needlessly over the soup-pot, as if broth were a potion against the powers of change. Angus sat with the paper. Conn just sat. 'He seems no' bad. No' bad at a'. Considerin'.'

'Will he be a' richt?' Kathleen's voice inched open their apprehension, afraid of what it would admit.

'Ah'd say that. He wis mair annoyed aboot hoo things were goin' wi' youse that aboot himsel'. He says dae Conn an' Angus still fight as much.'

'He's no' shell-shocked or anythin'?' It was a term Kathleen had merely heard, a name for the nameless.

'He's come through a lot. But he's come through. He's goin' tae be a' richt.'

Tam looked round them as if what he'd said wasn't a statement but something to be decided by vote.

'When will he get hame, feyther?' Conn asked.

'No' that long, Ah'd say. Maybe a month or two. But the great thing is that his war's bye. The Docherties have declared peace on the Kaiser. That's whit he said.'

Kathleen and Angus encouraged each other into a smile.

'Tam!' Jenny held a rough pit-towel folded square in her hands, staring at it. 'Ye'll tell us noo, Tam. Aboot oor Mick!'

'That's whit Ah'm tryin' Jenny.'

'Ah need tae ken hoo he is.'

Tam felt ashamed of his attempts at going round it. The simplicity of her stance chastised his pretence. She demanded her grief to be given honestly.

'He's woundit in the leg. But that'll get better. His sicht is back. In wan e'e, onywey. An' he's lost an airm.'

His voice trailed to a whisper. Jenny sat down almost formally on one of the high-backed chairs, her hands restlessly smoothing the towel on her lap. She emitted breath in one long, sustained shudder. 'Aw, Mick,' she said, 'Son, son. Whit've they done tae ye, son. O my Goad. Whit've ye been through, son. Whit hiv you been through.' She started very quietly to cry, her body hunched, her head sideways as if trying to turn away from something. The tears fell on the towel. 'He's jist a boay. He's no' twinty yet. Aw. No, no, no. Ye're a' richt noo, Mick. Ye're a' richt, son.'

None of the others moved or tried to speak. The room was held in the trance of Jenny's grief. She keened on, communing with nothing, seeming to see what wasn't there, like a priestess in a terrible ecstasy. Very slowly, she subsided. When she rose, the room became normal again. Tam finished his soup and sat by the fire. They all talked quietly, making tentative plans against Mick's coming back. But Tam remained taut, his mind clenched on what he had seen. Jenny knew it. About half past eight, she said, 'Why no' go doon an' hiv a pint, Tam?'

'Ah'm fine, hen,' he said.

'Oan ye go. It'll ease ye.'

After some persuasion, he went down to Mitchell's pub. As he drank, his meeting with Mick hung brightly in the centre of his thoughts, an icicle unthawed by beer or conversation or the whisky Tadger Daly bought him. Reflecting against the hardness of that scene, the smiles were tinsel, the friendliness was mockery. He saw them all like children capering around the stillness of his son. He remembered Mick's eyes so bright that they looked wet, but Mick didn't cry. Mick talked quietly, kidded just a little. The two of them had played successfully towards each other. It was only when he came away that Tam thought over Mick's remarks and found in every one of them a wound. Every joke contused in him. One memory was the core, in which in reaching for his son he had touched stone. Mick said, 'Whit's happened tae me isny important, feyther.'

Tam felt his mind dilate, admitting darkness, and he seemed to become no more than a part of his own anger, like flotsam on a tide. Possible reasons, explanations for what had happened to Mick shivered to aimless fragments, as distant and irrelevant as stars. In all of it there was no sense and no direction. It was only by coming back that Tam discovered where he had been. Here, in the warmth and custom of Mitchell's pub, he finally managed to hear what Mick was saying. Around him voices eagerly gleaned chaff, heads nodded like so many glove-puppets. The comfort he had so often found here was gone. Tonight was a wake for it. Composed in death, its features became clearer.

The comfort had come from a faith he experienced here, a sensation of being inexplicably recharged. At the heart of his refusal to admit futility had always been a tacit awareness of something irreducible in himself. Circumstances could take whatever shape they liked, they finally had to come at him on his terms. Secreted so far inaccessibly inside him had been an undefeated sense of purpose, a private place where he had his dignity, that no happening could pillage, no failure violate. Through it, everything could be transformed. The unfair conditions of his work became the triumph of his physical strength. The lack of opportunity open to his children measured the remarkableness of the people they managed to be. Poverty became the defiance of itself.

The key had been a deep physical pride. He had believed himself capable of confronting any man or any situation and surviving intact. He had once lost a fight to big Dan Melville. But when Tam, the skin around his eyes still gentian and pouchy from subsided swellings, went looking again for Dan, Dan didn't want to know. He said he had been lucky to catch Tam when he stumbled in a rut of the field where they fought, their bodies shipping sweat and stained with the dirt of their falls. And Dan had apologised, because defeat had made Tam stronger. There were a lot of men he knew he couldn't beat. But there was nobody he wouldn't have fought. Similarly, there had been no situation he felt unable to face. From that pride radiated the force that had given his life any sense of purpose it possessed. He felt at least able to give his family the protection of himself and at the same time to pass on to them an awareness of the importance of themselves.

Now he stood at the bar, where before the company of his friends had approximated to a congregation, a confirmation in mass of his personal conviction, and he felt himself participating in a useless ritual, mechanically lifting and lowering a glass, savouring the sourness of his past. He saw Mick as a son abducted and dismembered, and he was without response save anger, without recourse not just to defence but even to understanding. Tam felt redundant to his own life. His previous authority over his own experience was a joke. He was like a gunfighter, practised to perfection, unafraid, heroically hard, and pitted against germ warfare. That evening standing there, smiling now and again, being patted on the back by a passing friend, a terrible erosion began to happen in him. Having withstood the bruisings of despair for years, at last he began to haemorrhage. What had always been his own was invaded, broken up, trampled on, his past certainties demolished, his hopes gutted. His dreams were raped. Tam had come home.

In the house they waited for him. Old Conn had come in from his Saturday evening walk and the pint which he took in a different pub every week. He was told about Mick and would be praying for him. He had reached a point where he no longer had any private griefs.

His only perspective on events was a formal one, the important and the trivial distinguished by the number of Hail Marys and Our Fathers each received. Experience had become for him an endless circular journey round his rosary. Kathleen had waited on, uncertainly wanting more before she went home. She needed for them to fix among them what had happened to Mick, to give it a more definite shape. Alec had been wakened and been fed, and Jenny nursed him for a long time in the shawl, reluctant to let go, reliving through the weight of his small body the time when her own children had been safe. She was still holding him when Tam came in.

Jenny saw at once that what she had expected had taken place. Tam was deliberately drunk. Unwilling to admit the extent of his hopelessness, he had given himself the excuse of being drunk. Putting his jacket over a chair, he sat down by the fire and took off his boots. He set them beside the chair and, although tomorrow was Sunday, automatically reached over for his working boots and put them next to the hearth. The gesture shackled him to the week ahead, to all the weeks ahead.

Watching him, Conn saw the pit-boots quite suddenly as objects in themselves, was made aware of their familiarity enlarged into strangeness, so that he seemed to see every scuff and scratch, to understand the polished corrugations the laces had made, drawn how many hundred times across the dull stiffness of the tongues, to realise the record of bruised bones, humped hutches, sweat lost in the windings of blind workings, all etched indecipherably upon the leather. The boots were in some way a pathetic testimonial to the nature of their lives, a testimonial that Conn could see without being able to read, like a tablet inscribed with a lost language. They represented an insight the meaning of which was that its meaning could never be understood. Disturbed by the atmosphere of lost security which his home had held all evening, he sensed a reason that was outside of comprehension—the utter isolation of one man's life. His heart took on a knowledge which his mind would never have, the realisation that in each of our lives everybody else is just a tourist.

'Ah've been hearin' aboot Mick, Tam,' Old Conn said.

'Aye,' Tam nodded, looking into the fire.

'Ah'll pray for 'im, son.'

As Tam turned to stare at his father, his expression was brutal, the eyes a rejection of sight. But slowly the eyes came alive with self-doubt and the hardness of his face gave way around them. He looked at the floor. He nodded, nibbling his lip.

'Aye,' he said. 'You dae that, feyther.' All his family were looking at him and Jenny saw him dredge his drunkenness for something to say. 'He'll need a' the help he can get. He's been faur'er than we can imagine. It's up tae us tae help 'im.' The tone was quiet and unfamiliarly constrained, not a personal statement so much as an attempt neutrally to articulate circumstances. The room was charged with the sense of Tam's tiredness and coercion. It was the first time in the experience of any of them that he had renounced his ascendancy over the future. He was divesting himself of the image they had always given him, and in the moment of losing it their dependence on it became clearer than ever. It seemed intolerable that he was just another bloke. 'Things'll soart themselves oot some wey. He'll maybe be able tae work at somethin'. An' we can a' chip in. We'll see whit happens. We'll jist hiv tae help each ither. We'll see, we'll see.' It was his abdication speech.

Jenny made a masking of tea, leaving Alec on the bed. They all had some and then found themselves becalmed in their own thoughts.

'Kathleen, hen,' Tam said at last. 'Yer man'll think ye've left him. Angus'll see ye doon the road.'

'Richt,' said Angus.

They walked slowly because Kathleen didn't want to jostle Alec awake in the plaid. Only odd sounds came, a couple of men murmuring in shadows, a door closing, a phrase drifting through an open window, a soundflake melting on silence—the town talking in its sleep. Once they passed two people, a man and a boy, struggling out of an entry with a small ornate dresser. The man said, 'Shurrup! We've as much richt tae it as yer Uncle Harry has.' The boy said, 'Wull ma granny dee?' The darkness behind them absorbed the scene like a fragment of irrational dream.

Kathleen didn't relish returning home. She was late. She had been to hear news of her brother, it was true, but Jack wasn't likely to see that as much of a justification. Lately, the source of his responses to her had become even more muddied, more opaque than it had been in the second year of their marriage. She couldn't trace it, must just bewilderedly wait for its manifestations in the dourness of his moods, the bitterness of his talk. Was it because of Alec or his failure to be accepted by the army or the loss of his job in the skinwork? He was in the dyework now, and didn't like it.

She hoped he wouldn't hit her tonight, for she was pregnant again. She had been going to tell her mother after she missed the second period but couldn't. Jenny had enough worries. Kathleen had never told any of her family about the times Jack had beaten her. Twice it was. Fortunately, she had managed to keep the marks concealed under her clothes, shameful as leprosy. She had been afraid of what her father would do. The beatings were the worst of it, denying her attempts to pretend to herself that things were all right by imprinting the ugliness of what was happening to them on her body. Jack's unmotivated viciousness had caused her to gravitate more and more back to the solace of her family's company, and this in turn gave him the pretence of a reason. She cared more about them, he said, than she did about her own husband and son. Thus, the means of her defence became the terms of his accusation. It was hopeless.

Tonight, even the refuge of her family had been lost to her. She had felt her father's sadness perhaps more strongly than anyone else because this evening she had needed his firmness and certainty more than any of the others. With that gone, there wasn't much she could rely on. Still hardly able to believe it, she tried to talk to Angus about it.

'Aye,' he said. 'He's gettin' auld, isn't he?'

Angus sounded sorry but neither deeply moved nor especially surprised. It was the pronouncement of a man moving towards an impressive physical prime. The animal force in him projected itself innocently into a law for everything. The strong won; if you didn't win, it meant you weren't strong enough. Anything else was an irrelevant complication. His words were so far from what she had experienced they came to her like a foreign language, and this was her brother speaking it. She felt alienated from him, from everyone, it seemed, except her mother. In the moment of saying goodnight, she thought she understood her mother's capacity for endurance. Faced with such a variety of masculine wilfulness, with the naïve indifference she was leaving and the calculated callousness she was going in to, what could you do but endure.

On the way home, for no reason he could think of, Angus tested his strength.

Passing beside the river, he unearthed an enormous boulder, struggled it chest high and heaved it into the water. It was a considerable feat of strength, witnessed by no one, the splash profound. Its only record was the ripples. Coming back into the house, he found his mother and father preparing to go to bed. Conn and his grandfather were already in the other room, where Angus joined them. He still shared a bed with Conn, while the old man used Mick's.

Stripped to the waist, Tam sat down again, aimlessly staring at the fire. Jenny left him for a moment, then said, 'Tam. Come oan tae bed.'

'Uh-huh.'

He rose, stood a second, bent and lifted the pit-boots to put them somewhere, stopped. 'O-O-O-Oh,' he said. Instantly his face had tears. Jenny looked at him, the desire to go to him and the desire to turn away and cover her eyes holding her paralysed between them. She had never seen him cry before and she didn't understand what was happening in him, but she knew that he was finally at bay. The sound of pain which he hadn't managed to stifle had broken the sequence of trivia behind which he was hiding, behind which he would hide for the rest of his life, and exposed momentarily to the truth of himself, he acknowledged the pointlessness of what he had been, was, would be. He looked blindly round the room, cringing slightly as if it were attacking him. He looked at the boots in his hands as if he would never understand how they got there. He shouted, 'Damn them!' but the shout exploded soundlessly back into his throat, like someone trying to scream under water. His right arm flailed and the boot crashed against the picture of the king salvaged from the house of Jenny's parents. It hit the corner of the frame. Glass tinkled to the floor, its musical whispering a mocking of his fury. The picture lurched wildly to one side, then to the other, achieved a motion of diminishing pendulum, was still. The king stared out a moment longer in innocent benignity, then slowly, with unchanging dignity, toppled forward on to the floor. The frame hung empty.

Into the following silence came the sound of bare feet in the next room. Tam moved swiftly to the bed, sat down on it, turned away his head.

'Don't let the boays see me like this,' he said.

Jenny intercepted Conn at the door, saying, 'It's a' richt, son. There's something fell. A pictur. That wis a'.'

Conn back in his room, Tam said, 'Jenny, Ah'm sorry, Jen. Ah'm awfu' sorry. Whit ye must think o' me. Christ, Ah'm ashamed.' He was genuinely the victim of his own event, completely baffled by the chemistry that transformed the depth of his passion into a farce in the instant of its occurrence, made the absolute truth of what he felt a source of shame as soon as it was expressed. He knew himself ridiculous, a silly man, his grief good substance for an anecdote. Shame precipitated his drunkenness protectively into stupor. 'Ah'm sorry, love. We'll be a' richt. Ah'll soart things oot.'

Jenny soothed him, gathered the glass, crumpled the picture, snapped the frame, wrapped the lot in a newspaper for disposal tomorrow, finding the deepest sadness in the fact that the ashes of the righteous anger of the best man she had ever met should make so small a parcel. Both in bed, Tam havered on, the certainties growing more empty, the promises wilder, till they expired in snores. Jenny lay very still, knowing how much he needed his sleep. She thought of Mick. She thought of Tam, of Kathleen, Angus, Conn. Her small plans patiently nudged their way towards the future, moled unstoppably into the empty dark.

In the other room, Angus said, 'Hey. Whit wis that?'

'A pictur fell,' Conn answered.

'It musta been a big yin. Whit pictur? There's only two.'

'Ah don't ken.'

Conn had heard his father's voice coming through tears. Through that one fissure of sound he knew the significance if not the form of what had happened. He had never before been able to contemplate such a thing and he now thought that the war must indeed be something of incredible terror if it could make his father cry. His grandfather must have heard the noise, since he slept so light he said he could waken with a feather falling, but he hadn't stirred.

The old man *was* awake and he had heard. But he lay inscrutably still in the mysterious shroud of himself. He was thinking himself through a part of Connemara. Angus fell asleep at once, wondering how many people could have lifted that rock. Conn imagined German soldiers in the street. The ways in which we acknowledge the disintegration of those we love are legion.

# CHAPTER SEVENTEEN

The next morning Tam was up early. Not alluding to the night before, he had made a cup of tea for Jenny before he would let her get out of bed. He was brisk, pleasant, talking about Mick getting home. His words threatened constructiveness rather than achieved it, like a scaffolding erected on a waste lot. He was making plans for making plans. Significantly, he didn't make any attempt to come to terms with last night's despair. He merely reacted away from it, so that a counter-reaction would be inevitable. A syndrome was being established. He had become the victim of his life instead of its exponent.

Not that anyone could have noticed. Leaning over Jenny, a dawn the colour of unfired clay on his shoulders, he was laughing with the tea-cup in his hand, calling himself 'Jessie Tinney', which was his term for a hen-peck. You couldn't have told that he was lifting one morning too many. Jenny, with so much reason for faith in him, would have been betraying what they had made together if she had appreciated the poignancy of that moment. She was right to believe that last night would be overcome and that he would survive intact. It was only in retrospect that she would see that night as an earthquake in the annals of her private life.

The extent of the damage was to be learnt only slowly. Over the next few years she would find broken parts of him, disseminated widely in time, come upon in a casual conversation, nudged accidentally in an aimless rummaging of her thoughts beside the fire. In them she would understand the hurt that had been done him. Piecing them together, she would reconstruct the man that he had been before they broke him and would wonder at his stature. Augmenting her failed memory with love, she would make him preposterously bigger than anyone else had ever seen him, but no bigger than he had been.

What Jenny was to gather in the years ahead, to hoard in herself like mementoes of some important person, would be small perceptions, observed perhaps by others but rendered worthless by their ignorance or thrown aside by their indifference or crushed like archaic pottery to powder by the clumsiness of their unearthing. For they would be very fragile things, the truths about a man, for long ignored, buried like refuse under what *was* refuse, secreted like ancient gold under layers of error and misunderstanding. She alone would have the faith to find them, the skill to keep them intact, the love to understand their meaning.

In this way she was soon to notice how impossible Tam's promises became, how his certainties went no deeper than his voice. Hearing his desperate convictions brag themselves alive and die of their own intensity, like fireworks leaving the darkness blacker than before, seeing the emptiness that welled out of his eyes in some moments of calm, she knew that they measured not just the defeat of what he was becoming, but the almost unbelievable victory of what he had for so long been. Observing how his natural generosity developed into something more wilful, an unpredictable squandering of his time and what little money he had on aimless acts of kindness, so that paradoxically he seemed to some people more of a man than he had been, she knew it for a weakness, but a weakness stronger than the strength of many others. Having lost the purpose of his own life, he distributed it frantically among those he cared for, as if they might have a use for it.

But no one else would notice much, except Jenny. The only thing that struck some people was that Tam Docherty was more heavy on the drink. There were those perceptive enough to say, 'Aye. Since his auldest boay wis in the war. A funny thing that. Tam wis aye that sober.' Jenny herself was to date roughly from that time the pattern Tam evolved of Saturday night drunkenness and Sunday morning plans for an unrealisable future. She understood it was an arbitrary choice of time to some extent. He had been drunk before that. He had often enough before had depressions so black as to make his presence all but uninhabitable for other people. And after that night he was to remain as formidable as ever in the eyes of outsiders. In some ways he was to seem more so to them, because his anger and his concern and the frequently rivetting instantaneousness of his responses could operate more dramatically, their deployment no longer inhibited by the need to conform to a central and continuous control. Only Jenny was gradually to grow aware that these had become more gesture than action and that the almost primal sense of unchallengeable selfhood that had animated them had now abandoned them. Nobody else could have realised that Tam, still forceful and outwardly intimidatingly hard, had forsaken any future. There was, after all, no visible wreckage but a broken photograph, which Tam himself threw out that morning, as if he didn't want Jenny to have to touch it.

But Jenny, ignorant at the time of that Sunday's implications, was to come back to it so often later in her life, enlarging it with her understanding. It was to be the uttermost fulfilment of her love that she would know all of him in the part of him that remained. She would record in herself, incommunicable to any other living person, the importance of a courageous living and a secret, terrible, consuming grief of failure that would otherwise have had the permanence of smoke, been as conspicuous as the death of a wild crocus in a forest. This she would achieve not with words or by reasons, which other reasons could have refuted, but with a mute tenacity of belief that only death could relax. Her love would show her this, the magnitude of his experience, not as a matter of exclusive arrogance, but as a law for all here, where even the agony of the dying ant is seismic.

Yet that morning was at that time just itself. Surrounding himself with imprecise plans, Tam seemed genuinely hopeful, nothing like a man immuring himself alive in his own past. The cups of tea he gave to Jenny and his father and to Conn and Angus were incidental thoughtfulness, hadn't become a part of his pathetic future generosities, those errant kindnesses purposely done, like seeds planted in stone, as if he were Johnny Appleseed lost in a city. Washed and dressed and mending the fire, Jenny smiled over at him, blessedly without understanding, which never arrives except in time for the headstone. The day was going to be fine.

'We'll hiv a walk in the afternin, Jenny, eh?'

'As long as its no' too faur,' she laughed.

# CHAPTER EIGHTEEN

Mick didn't come home to the place so much as the place came home to him, in suddenly found fragments, like broken pieces of a mirror he would have to try to fit together. In them he found distortions of himself.

Wullie Manson said, 'It wid be hellish, wis it, son?'

'Well. It wis bad.'

'At least they say it'll no' be long noo tae it's ower. Ha'e some mair beer.'

Wullie didn't seem to know that it wouldn't be over. Not for Mick and not for any of the people who lived through it. Mick wanted to convince Wullie of the men who would die twenty years later of gas. But it wasn't possible.

And Tadger thought, 'There's wan thing, Mick son. You've did yer bit. Everybody in this room's owin' you. They'll no' forget in a hurry.'

Not in a hurry. It might take a year or two. Already Mick had overheard himself referred to in Mitchell's as 'him wi' the wan wing'. In a couple of years, he'd just be a curio. Anyway, he didn't think they owed him anything. He hadn't done it for them. He didn't know why he had done it. That was what made it so hard to live with.

'Ye a' richt, son?' His mother's hand touched his shoulder.

'Ah'm a' richt, mither.'

'They're a' that gled tae see ye. It's great jist tae hiv ye sittin' there. Thank Goad ye're back.'

But he wasn't back. He was among strangers. When they thought they were touching him, he could feel no contact. He looked round the room. There were his family and friends. They had gathered without forewarning to welcome him. He knew they were kind and generous, and he felt a bitter black anger towards them. No matter what happened, all they could offer against it was their warmth. Their goodness seemed to him impossible. The only connection he could make was sometimes in the eyes of Conn, as if he was honestly trying to work out who Mick was. That gave Mick and him something in common.

Mick endured that occasion and it gave way to others like it. Most of the time he felt at best uncomfortable and clumsy, as if his life didn't fit him. Only rarely could he find any resemblance between what happened outside and what was going on in him, like the first time he visited Mary Hawkins.

It was a strange event. He had gone because he felt he had to. He had no idea of what to say or do. He just went. When she opened the door, she looked at him, put her hand out and touched his face, and said, 'Och.' She walked back to her chair, sat down and started to cry. He came in and closed the door.

The two of them sat like that for a long time, Mary crying and Mick just being there. He thought at first he should say something, had a moment of guilt because he let this happen without trying to console her. But he remembered Danny and consolation seemed ridiculous. Her tears were right. Danny's death was making something happen. Someone was admitting what it meant. It would have been false to deny that admission.

Outside, Mick could hear people passing in the street. He remembered Auld Jake's voice in Bethune—Danny had been living then—telling a human truth in counterpoint to the military pretence going on outside. It seemed to him that Mary Hawkins was answering the glibness outside in the same way. He had brought his utter bleakness to her and she acknowledged it with crying. Together, they made up a kind of truth.

Later, she got up and made him tea. It seemed to him a ceremony of immense dignity, an old woman ordering her grief into politeness. They took the tea and talked a little, and he tried to tell her nice things about Danny. But his respect for her sorrow made him tell her only true things, very small, momentary things, which were in any case all that was left of her son which she would have recognised.

Leaving, he was thanked by her for coming. He said he would come back. He did, partly because he felt closer to her than almost anybody else. It wasn't that Danny had meant so much to him. It wasn't that Mary Hawkins's grief affected him so deeply. It wasn't what she felt or for whom she felt it—it was the pure fact that she did feel it. She wasn't able to hide from the reality Mick was experiencing, as even his own family appeared to him to do. She shared it with him.

His home wasn't a place where he liked to be. The others felt it.

But the more they tried to help him the more they irked him. Every acknowledgement of what he was going through was for him a diminution of it, every action just a gesture. He went out a lot.

His walks were aimless. Mostly he noticed the changes even in places. Though they had taken place before he had joined up, he saw them now as if they had a new personal significance. The Meal Market had become 'The Scotia'. Sometimes he went in there to hide and let the piano music and the pictures blot out his thoughts.

Once in the street he met May. She was pregnant. She stopped and said defiantly, 'Hullo!' He noticed that she didn't wear a ring. She told him she was pregnant to the farmer she worked for. He was a recent widower and he couldn't marry her just now because his family would have been too offended. But he was good man and kind to her. She kept Mick standing for a long time while she justified herself and he listened absently. What puzzled him was that she thought it mattered.

How long he would have gone on living in limbo he didn't know —perhaps for good. But his father arranged it differently. He usually did. There were a lot of things you could feel about Tam Docherty, but indifference wasn't one of them. His presence was an invasion. You had to react to survive. And Mick reacted.

There were the three of them in the house, Mick and his mother and father. Angus was at the dancing, obeying his blood in a way Mick could just about remember and almost envy. Conn was wherever Conn was. You couldn't tell with him. He often set out for a place and never got there. He was always being ambushed. So many things seemed to interest him. Old Conn was out for a walk.

Jenny was watching him. Mick had felt her watching. His father was reading the paper.

'Christ!' Tam said. 'Whit wid ye make o' that? This is a learnt man talkin'. Yer JP nane the less. "The theft of this pail of coal . . ." This wee lassie o' eleeven. Her feyther's deid. She stole the coal fae a railway yaird. Tae keep the faimly warm. "The theft of this pail of coal is a serious offence. The more so that it takes place in time of war. Responsibility—", Tam stumbled over the word, "for the nation's plight belongs to all of us. This offence cannot be overlooked. We are all in need in this war." Aye. An' Ah hope yer choke on yer roast beef. Ye can write tae that fella care o' Mars, by Christ.'

Mick was willing his mother not to watch him. He dreaded that she was going to be concerned for him. He didn't want her to speak. She spoke.

'Mick, son. Dae ye no' fancy the picturs? It's Charlie Chaplin in the Scotia.'

'Yer Chairlie Chaipleton,' Tam said.

His father's attempt at levity made him grue.

'Naw, mither. Ah'm no' fussy.'

'Ye're sittin' in too much these nichts, Mick. It's no' healthy fur a young man sittin' in wi' us.'

He couldn't explain that he felt older than them. She didn't understand. He just wished she would keep quiet.

'It's a nice nicht, son. Wid ye no' like a walk?'

'Mither. If ye want the hoose tae yersel's, then Ah'll go oot. Is that whit ye want then? Is it?'

'Aw, Mick. It's no' that, son. It's jist . . .'

'Mither! Fur Christ's sake, gi'e it a by. Stoap worryin' yersel'. Fur ye ken damn a' aboot it. Jist gi'e us peace, wumman.'

He heard his father's paper lowering.

'Hey, boay.' Against Mick's will, the intensity of his father impinged on him. 'It's time Ah tellt you somethin'. Ah don't care you've been tae hell an' came back. Ah don't care you loast three fuckin' airms. Ye talk tae yer mither like that an' Ah'll take yer wan airm an' wrap it roon yer fuckin' neck. Ah'll fell you deid. Noo unnerstaun' that, son.'

'Tam,' Jenny said.

Her head was lowered. Mick looked at her and for the first time for a long time he touched the quick of himself. He was feeling shame. He shook his head. He saw his father's eyes bruise.

'Aw, Mick,' Tam said. 'Forget it, son.'

That wasn't possible. Tam's anger had precipitated a mutual awareness in which they were caught. Jenny saw in the two of them the bafflement of her love. Her great gift had always been for loving people. She had sublimated everything else into that and now it was all that she had, she saw that it wasn't enough. Incarnated in Tam and Mick that love merely intensified the terrible contradictions in their lives and made them fiercer. She saw the life she irrevocably had to inhabit. She was nailed to her love for them and though that love might offer temporary happinesses, the end of it was pain.

Tam saw the strangeness of his son. Mick sat shaped and partly broken by an experience Tam could never imagine, and Tam felt ashamed of his own anger. His need to connect with Mick had made him say what he had no right to say.

But it had worked. For Mick's protective shell of bleakness had been breached. Somewhere in him an icicle thawed. He was beginning to feel again. He admitted to himself who his mother was—not some petty nuisance but a woman with an awesome ability for love. There was no way you could stop her loving you. In reacting against his father, he was obliged to try to see him honestly. It seemed to Mick that his father quite simply didn't hold with privacy. Experience was for sharing and people only happened in one another. That was what gave him that force which made his very presence seem a happening.

He forced people out of themselves and into events. As had happened now.

Mick felt almost substantial again. He had a hazy sense of perspective on himself. He saw his mother and father as very simple people, dangerously simple, but at the same time he knew himself unmistakably a part of them, in part defined by them. They gave him no choice. In that, he thought, he saw a way to go on living. There had to be a way to connect the truth he felt he had glimpsed to their own lives, a way that would protect them from their own simplicity, a way that would give purpose to the desecration of folk like Danny.

For the first time since his wound, he wanted to participate again. But the terms would have to be his. Carefully, with precise calculation, he decided to make it all right for their sakes. His war was not with them.

'Ach, Ah'm sorry, mither.'

'Aw, Mick. It's a' richt, son. It's jist that Ah've been worryin' aboot ye lately.'

'Mick, son,' Tam said.

'Naw. It's a' richt, feyther. Ah ken whit ye meant. Ye're richt enough tae. Don't worry aboot it. Ah'll soart masel' oot.'

It was a tentative contract. Their obvious relief showed that they didn't understand the terms of it. Not long afterwards, Mick fulfilled his part by taking the job that had been on offer to him for some time, since old McGarrity was dead. He became the watchman in Lawson's mill. Seeing him come and go, like any other worker except that the hours were staggered, Jenny and Tam were convinced that Mick had settled for a limited version of his past. Mick let them think that because his personal life was no longer the area where he expected his sense of truth to happen. He was looking for other terms.

He became a kind of recluse among them. His thoughts were seldom shared. The part of him they were aware of, sitting at table, reading the paper by the fire, talking occasionally, concealed the most of him, that deep fifth-column which was examining their lives very critically. The only two he saw hope for were Angus and Conn. The rebelliousness of Angus answered something in Mick himself. Angus opposed the way he had to live. But his opposition was fitful and always wilful. Mick saw the need to pick his way more carefully. Conn seemed to him too young to be sure about. But Mick had hopes that he would question things at least.

Mick was asking his own questions. Almost every night now he was reading. Not much of it was fiction. Painfully, he acquired a certain skill. His compulsion to find out, to understand what was happening to them, sharpened his intelligence to the point where it operated with a force that belied his education. He sifted, he underlined, he put together.

Painstakingly, he was trying to construct his own maps of where they were. The areas towards which his father had all his life just made desperate gestures Mick was trying to penetrate, to chart. He acquired a certain authority, even with Tam. The very unpredictability of his responses they found arresting.

When the peace finally came, Mick dampened their delight by showing no elation. Somebody in the street had shouted up, 'It's by, it's by!' Mick had only said, 'Naw. It's only jist stertin'.'

He imparted to the house a sense of waiting. He read the papers as if they were personal letters in a code only he understood. When the terms of the Treaty of Versailles appeared there, he nodded over them as if they were the answer to a problem he had been working out and he'd got it right.

'The bastards,' was his summation.

'The Jerry asked fur it,' Old Conn was saying. 'He deserves everythin' he gets. That'll teach him a lesson.'

'Naw. But it should bloody well teach us wan.'

'To the victor the spoils,' Old Conn announced.

'Hoo much o' the spoils are you gettin', gran'feyther. Can ye no' see? They're playin' at medieval bloody knights. Still! A' richt, they've had their fun. Noo fur the real war.'

The others waited for him to explain it. But he didn't. He just sat there staring at his paper, and waiting, it seemed.

# CHAPTER NINETEEN

The moment might well have had solemnity, the year becoming monument. But too many people were busy claiming the last available space for personal graffiti. Two strangers drank to the fact that they had never met. A man leaning out of a tenement window shouted, 'Goad bless ye if ye're no' a Catholic.' A woman in her fifties sang 'Sweet Sixteen'. A man fell and, feeling the inside of his jacket wet, said, 'Ah've ruptured ma whusky.' Three friends were harmonising. As the clock struck, the crowd at the Cross overwhelmed the weight of its announcement. They cheered, shook hands, juggled toasts, kissed, embraced. For some time the small area at the centre of the town churned confusedly with people and the impression was that everybody there was determined to shake hands with everybody else and everybody had lost count. People were wished Happy Hogmanays, Hogmaloos, Houghmagandies. A big man clamped his friend at arm's length, stared at him and said, his voice tremulous with reverence, 'Ya auld bastard.'

Dispersal was slow. People who had already gone came back, vaguely moved around as if looking for something. Gradually, the place cleared, the last promises pronounced, the last improbable assignations made. The only surviving residents of the Cross were a man, leaning over to boke prodigiously into the gutter, and his friend, who had waited behind, loyal to him in his time of need, and was singing 'Should auld acquaintance be forgot' with an improvisational brilliance that made the absence of lyric and tune a minor problem. Between harmonic experiments, he would say, 'Oan ye go, son, get it up' or 'Ring out the old, ring in the new'.

The others had moved off along the streets that led from the Cross. They took away with them a part of what had happened, a piece of the warmth, and for another hour or two, small groups would carry their elation like a torch through the streets.

In the house, Jenny and Kathleen had been preparing, knowing that their hospitality would soon be under siege. The house had been cleaned with an almost superstitious thoroughness, as if in propitiation of the New Year. Beer and whisky were on the sideboard beside shortbread and black bun. Extra chairs and glasses had been borrowed. The fire reflected brilliantly on the black-leaded surfaces around it. In his rocking-chair sat Old Conn, his first Ne 'erday dram cached like a gold nugget in his enormous, buckled hand. Through the room Alec, and Jennifer, a few months old, were sleeping. Jenny, Kathleen and Old Conn had wished one another a Happy New Year and now they waited, listening to 1920 squall itself alive in the street outside.

Jenny didn't like Hogmanay. It was one of the two times of the year she would have wished to cut out of the calendar. The other was the Grozet Fair. Asked why, she would say simply, 'Things happen'. She could have recited a whole catalogue of accidents, deaths and other private misfortunes relating to one local family or another and all filed in her memory under one or the other heading. Hogmanay was the worst. It was in the nature of men to be trouble-makers at any time, but at Hogmanay they seemed to declare a fiesta for their capacity for bother. Drink circulated carelessly in crowded rooms. Small men imagined themselves bigger. People said wild things and then tried to measure themselves against them. The songs, the laughter, the jokes, the bragging, they were harmless in themselves but they were like fireworks set off among powder-kegs. The result was that even if they escaped the almost mystical malevolence Jenny sensed in those few hours when the calendar was suspended, people were all too likely to improvise a minor disaster of their own.

She remembered years ago visiting with her parents the reunion of another family at Ne'erday. The members of the family had begun almost formally, not having seen one another for some time. But by midnight they were wallowing in communal sentimentality. At half past one they were ranged behind past grievances, hurling accusations. By two o'clock it was civil war. The father sustained a broken nose, the oldest son had his head split with a pail. As her father said on the way home, 'A guid New Year tae yin an' a', an' mony may ye see.'

Yet, much as she dreaded it, it would never have occurred to her not to celebrate it. Every year her house had what it was traditional to offer and was open to anyone. Tonight she expected Tam and Tadger Daly would be in first. They had just stepped down to the Cross to bring in the New Year, Tadger was by long usage her accepted first foot. Jack should be with them. He had said earlier he would meet them at the Cross at midnight. Jenny looked at Kathleen, who was still soft in the belly from carrying Jennifer, and hoped, as she did several times a day, that she and Jack would sort things out all right. Mick had gone to see old Mary Hawkins. Mick was settling down now that he had that caretaker's job in the mill. Where Angus and Conn were was anybody's guess. Jenny had wanted Conn to stay in the house but Tam had said to let him go out. He was too young, though. Jenny reflected how Tam was becoming more lax with the family, as if to make up for what he felt was happening in himself. She hoped Tam would be happy tonight.

There was a knock at the door. The ceremony was part of the occasion. Smoothing down her clean pinny, Jenny crossed and opened it. Only Tadger stood there, a bottle bulging in his pocket, a wee raker of coal in his hand. 'Jenny,' he said, 'a Happy New Year, hen.' 'Happy New Year.' They embraced lightly. Over Tadger's shoulder, she saw Tam come into view, his expression a licence for her to forget about him and get on with her own enjoyment. Wullie Manson was with him.

They eddied briefly in the middle of the floor, happy-new-yearing. Before they were finished, Jack came in, explaining that he had missed them at the Cross and almost managed to catch up with them before they reached the house. His breathlessness acted on them like an epigram on the brevity of pleasure. Greetings exchanged, drinks were given out. The men had whisky, Jenny and Kathleen had ginger wine. Tadger gave a toast to 1920.

The occasion began to generate its own chronology. Talk gathered momentum, remarks thrown in from all sides like simples being mixed to induce a vision. Tam and Jack compared the things they had seen at the Cross. Tadger told an anecdote about his children. Jenny told the story she had thought of earlier about the family battle she had once attended at Ne'erday. Eating black bun and shortbread, they scattered crumbs as they laughed, like an allusion of plenty. Tam took resonance from the company of his friends, as if his nature, so often tautened to discord, was tuned by their presence to evoke its deeper reaches. Their talk struck rich responses in him of laughter, comment, pure enjoyment. Their pleasure in one another transmuted the meanness of the room, the way music can put the sleaziest public hall where it's played into breathtaking orbit. Things happened, words took place with tropical suddenness and seemed natural. Old Conn sang:

> Oh father dear, I oftimes hear
> You speak of Skibbereen,
> Of lofty scene and valleys green
> And mountains rude and wild.

His voice was a reed, year-fretted, saliva-stopped, played fitfully by his age, mocked with ironies of unintended silence. Seen through the song, a place more real than Skibbereen, a private landscape of sound, hard fields, unpeopled houses, bleak acres whauped by dead injustices, bright-flowering moments, a long way come alone. He didn't sing. More than seventy years sang themselves in. Before he was finished, Conn was home, standing motionless at the doorway, acknowledging the nods and winks without a word, because he had been taught that you might as well interrupt a prayer as a song.

> Ah father dear, the day will dawn
> When in vengeance we will call
> And Irishmen from near and far
> Will rally to that call.
> I'll be that man to lead the van
> Beneath the flag of green.
> And loud and high we'll raise the cry
> Revenge for Skibbereen.

'Guid, auld yin.'

'An' where've you been, young-fella-me-lad?' Tadger had unconsciously anticipated Jenny, burlesquing what would have been her question. 'This is some cairry-oan. Ye go oot the hoose wan year an' don't come back tae the next.'

'That's right.' Wullie Manson took it up. 'This is the first Ah've seen o' 'im since last year. He's grown since then.'

'No' as much as he seems tae think,' Jenny said. 'Ye're gey late, Conn.'

'Aye.' Tadger was grave. 'Ye'll need tae take that boay o' yours in hand, Tam.'

'The young folk nooadays,' Wullie offered. 'Ah didny get oot tae play efter eicht o'clock till Ah wis twinty-wan.'

'Stane?' asked Tadger.

'Well, Conn?' Jenny asked.

The men were a mock jury, the flippancy of their affection relentlessly neutralising the seriousness of Jenny's concern. Caught in the blatancy of all their loves, Conn's annoyance at being treated like a wee boy shrivelled. The excuses he had been trying on like a man's clothes seemed suddenly not to fit, their glib casualness embarrassing, their throw-away authority ridiculous, and he stood exposed in a sheepish smile.

'A wis jist wi' some o' the boays,' he managed.

'Boays o' yer ain age, Ah hope.'

'Hiv ye goat their birth certificates oan ye, son? Yer mither wid like tae see them,' Tam said.

Among the laughter, Tam put up his arms, defending himself against
Jenny's wrath. Her look flashed on him for a second before her own
laughter extinguished it.

'He's jist new turned sixteen,' Jenny reminded them.

'Since first I saw the lovelight in your eyes.' Tadger's inspiration
became a duet with Wullie Manson. They all went on about Conn,
roughing him verbally in a clumsy, animal affection. Woven in with
their remarks, each heightening the other, Conn was still vividly
conscious of where he had just been. His memory of saying cheerio
to his mates an hour ago was involved with the gentle heavings of
Wullie Manson's enormous frame. His father's laughter sheered like
a light across the place where he had met Jessie Langley in the
darkness.

'Where exactly've ye been, Conn?'

How old was Jessie? In her thirties, he had heard people say. For
him, a fabled distance away. Legendary as Jezebel. Murky with the
past, veiled in whisperings. She walked among bitter mouths, 'tail',
'hoor', 'the merry widow'.

'Say nothin' till ye see yer lawyer, son.'

The suddenness of her appearance in front of him. Wearing shadow,
making an accessory of darkness. The innocence of her deception.
'Could ye tell me the way tae Fleming Street, son?' The strangeness
of talk. Her words leading him, manoeuvring him with threads until
he came incredibly to be standing on the wasteground with her.

'Jist roon' aboot.'

'Where's roon' an' whit were ye aboot?'

He welled where she touched him. And his own hands, led along
her, discovered continents among her clothes. Breasts and thighs
distended on his palms, undulated from him, became journeys he must
make.

'He's no' drunk, is he?'

Her softness was the past, the residue of other men. How she
underpinned the welter of his feelings with ceremony, made the
savagery gentle. She forbade the final meeting. Smiling, shaking her
head. Why? Stories of disease stirred, caved within his head. Taking,
she was giving. She left him himself as a gift.

'All Ah've drunk is watter.'

'No' guid fur ye.'

'All right in moderation.'

He laughed among their faces, and hers was one of them. He felt
defined by all of them. All the furtive stories, the jokes told in the
park, the impossible facts relayed by boys who wanted to know from
his reaction if they could be true, the haemorrhaging shames, they
were a code translated into benignity on her body. The secret examinations of himself, the desperate masturbation in empty places, they

hadn't been dirty, but ordinary and innocent. Prayers about to be answered. He sensed that, if nobody else knew, what had happened between him and her was good. It was just their own.

'Ye still hivny told us, Conn,' his mother said.

He looked at her, laughing.

'Well, mammy. Whit it is, me an' ma' gang broke intae a' the shoaps oan the richt haun side o' the main street. Next week we're daein' the left side. There'll be somethin' in it fur yerself, mammy.'

The reaction of the others demolished Jenny's last chance of seriousness. All she could manage was, 'There'll be something in it fur you tae. A guid hidin'.'

His father said, 'If ye come in as late as this again, Ah'll skelp yer bum wi' a tea-leaf tae yer nose bluids.'

Chaos was restored. Given something to eat ('He's loast his appetite. An' fun' a hoarse's', 'Aye, hunger's guid kitchen.'), Conn was allowed a glass of ginger wine and the privilege of staying up. Jack sang. Tam coaxed Kathleen to sing 'The Donegal Wedding'. Mick appeared with old Mary Hawkins, she had no one to spend Ne'erday with.

The situation's intensity became like an abstract of the way they lived, a celebration of themselves, a persistent buoyancy flexible enough to pass through retrospective calms, shallows of tiredness, bleak and sudden memories of the future, and stay intact. Their present transmuted past and future without seeking to deny either. They became philosophical with the same naturalness as they laughed, sadnesses being controlled by the fact that they could give them shape.

For a time they talked about people they had known who were now dead. And even that was pleasant, not remotely morbid. They moved through that area with conspiratorial nods and nudges and muted laughter, like a procession of dignified drunks revisiting in secret catacombs that weren't officially known about. Their shifting words illumined a face here, a posture there, and all around them the dead seemed defiantly themselves, presenting gestures that mocked the accepted heraldry of death, winking in their shrouds.

Only once did their deft conversation, knowing its way by instinct in the dark, uncover not a reassuring facsimile of death, made homely by familiarity, but a real dying, the echo of the scream still on its face, still close enough to living to be its obscene parody. In spite of Jenny's careful charting of their direction, somebody inevitably mentioned the peace, and the peace meant the war. Mary Hawkins broke down, instantly and noisily. Her self-control, like something she had carried around till it became too heavy, fell from her, shattered, and the room seemed immediately awash with her grief.

The shock of it froze Conn. The only feeling he could get hold of was embarrassment. It was the first time he had seen an adult cry so openly and the physical impact of it obscured everything else. It was an ugly performance. The dignity of her face unseamed, the eyes crumpling, the prim mouth retching up astonished sobs of pain. His surprise was enlarged by the calmness of the others.

His mother said, 'Aye, Mary, aye.' Tadger and Wullie Manson looked stoically into the fire. Mick, sitting beside her, put his hand on her shoulder. His father, leant forward, his elbows on his knees, his hands loosely clasped, watched her, his eyes moist but unblinking. She was saying wild things that never fully formed, words ill-shaped and changing and meaningless yet measuring something of elemental force, like cloud-wracks in a big wind. It was 'Ma boay, ma boay' and 'They took him awa' fae me' and 'The finest son that ever Goad put braith in.'

'Talk it oot, hen,' Tam said. 'Talk it oot. He wis a guid boy.'

'He wis the best boay,' Mary said. And as she went on, the embarrassment no longer mattered for Conn, became like his reflection in a piece of glass he was looking through. Through the others he simply accepted that this was happening. What people ought to do is a feeble affront to what they have to do, like a lace handkerchief held against a wound.

Mary wept. She was old, alone, her husband long dead, her relatives far away, and every day rose on the absence of her son. Her natural inarticulacy refined by events to utter incoherence, she raved against everything, the war, 'that swine Haig', shells, growing up, having sons, the aimlessness of her accusations indicting the accuser, like a madwoman trying to formulate charges against those who have made her mad. Having withstood so much, she had at last been bewildered into a child again in her sixties.

Mick understood more than the others. He had learned to hate the simple way in which a person became a fact in the army. Now all those statistics which governments had neatly stacked away as if they were finished with, must breed like bacteria, able to find a real existence only in the private lives of people like Mary Hawkins. Mick let the others feed Mary's sadness till it glutted and then he started to talk about Danny, as he had done to her often enough before. His description of their friendship in the army with some of the things Danny had said normalised his death for her to some extent. It was Mick's betrayal of his own experience, something in which he was already practised, something that would help to define him as he grew older. Faced with someone like Mary Hawkins, all you could do was protect her from the truth. Like most returning soldiers, for the rest of his life he would be fighting a rearguard action against admitting the truth of what he had experienced into their private lives.

Together, they all made an ikon of Mary's son for her. She became calm and their talk, eddying for a while, finally moved on to other things. But it wasn't until Angus came in that the mood she had induced was left behind.

Angus had friends with him, a retinue of three, and he didn't so much come in as he entered. He had reached that stage where the lambency of first maturity can make the most ordinary features striking, and he was in any case not unhandsome. Tonight his mood seemed to put him in primary colours, the black hair blued with health, the greenishness of the eyes heightened. A couple of glasses of beer had set him on stilts. He shucked his jacket on to one of the set-in beds and slipped tie and collar over his head in a piece. The shirt, collarless, with sleeves rolled under the elbow, was an effectively simple frame for his torso, offsetting the firm neck, the tapering forearms.

'Hoo are we daein'?' he said into the greetings of the others.

He went first to his mother, hugged her, embraced Kathleen, gently shook hands with Mary Hawkins, was deliberately respectful in shaking hands with Jack, kidded progressively through his good wishes to Mick, Wullie Manson, Tadger and Conn, until he reached his father. With Tam his handshake had the prolonged quality of a reluctant farewell. Both did a very brief double-take and it was as if the automatic gesture had accidentally been charged with something real, a small shock of recognition of something they had both known but had needed this formal moment to admit. Angus's shrug and smile seemed to suggest that's the way it goes. It was the kind of smile a victorious boxer gives the loser.

Angus's friends followed him round the company. They were all respectful enough but their self-confidence was somehow so gaudy that they couldn't help making the others feel that they were bystanders at a procession. Like the soldiers of an army that has never been defeated, they didn't know how to come into a place without taking it over. They were still finding stray bits of laughter among themselves that must have stayed with them from wherever they had been, like ticker-tape caught among their clothes. They contrived innocently to convey the impression that the rest had only been waiting for their arrival.

'Oh, Ah can place ye noo,' Jenny said to the young man who was shaking her hand. 'You're *Rab* Morrison's boay, no' Alec's. Yer mither wis a McQueen tae her ain name.'

'That's richt, Mrs Docherty.'

'An' your name's . . . ?'

'Rab as weel.'

'Goad aye. Ye're just yer feyther ower the back. Ye couldny lift wan an' lay the ither.'

'Except for acroass the e'en, Jenny,' Mary Hawkins said. 'He's goat Lizzie McQueen's e'en. He's goat her e'en.'

'Hoo's yer mither gettin' oan withoot them, Rab?' Angus asked.

They all laughed, but Angus and his friends laughed differently, together making a schism of their amusement, a private joke about the quaintness of their parents' generation. The others felt their separateness, each being partly defined by not being one of that vigorous group who wore their smiles like badges. Angus Docherty, Rab Morrison, Johnny Lawson and Buzz Crawley seemed to have taken out a joint lease on the 1920s. Conn was impatient with his own youth, feeling a couple of Hogmanays behind the place where things were happening; for Jenny and Mary, tracing the features of the parents through the children, it was as if their pasts had been relet; Kathleen felt she was almost as old as her mother; Mick nursed his arm as if he had just lost it; Jack remembered what he had been like a few years ago and was glad that they wouldn't be long till they learned. The older men felt that the room was crowded.

It was a moment ordinary yet profound, such as are found in long-established rituals. For implicit in their casual coming-together in that room was the acknowledgement of the ruthless terms to which they were contracted, the hard philosophy that underlay their lives. They were physical people, their bodies almost all they had—to a degree that could have been called ascetic, except that they were too ascetic ever to have needed the word. When the body started to go, they had no recourse in the occupational therapy of art, the bathchair of intellect, the artificial stimuli of theories.

Their only tenable reality was themselves, and it was a harsh one. There was childhood, brief as a dragonfly. After that men worked, women had children and kept house. The closest thing to freedom lay between, in those few years before they put their bodies into hawk for their families, when the young men paraded in loud groups, poached for the hell of it, went to late dances looking for girls and fights, when the girls couldn't walk down a street without knowing they were desirable, found many things exciting, were happiest waiting to find out who would be their husband.

In having a choice between different forms of the same necessity lay the illusion of freedom. It was the best time, when they could imagine that the intensity with which they burned presaged continuance instead of its opposite, penny-candles with delusions of galaxies. After it there was a lifetime's darg and the struggle of each to retain as much of that imagined amplitude as possible. And every successive time the mystery renewed itself, as it did tonight in the persons of Angus and his friends, the older ones could measure against them how much they had lost.

Tadger was measuring, not bitterly or spitefully, just honestly, with a seriousness that was a compliment to the young men. They would have understood his thoughts and appreciated them. In this game the one rule was that you were beaten when you believed you were. They were young but he had learned some things. Mentally, he confronted them in the pit, in bed, in a fight. He would, he decided, hold his own. Not bad considering he was giving away a twenty-odd year handicap.

But he had to admit to himself that he wasn't counting Angus in his calculations. He didn't even allow himself to plead age as an excuse. Baulking at the thought, he imagined a team battle, old versus young. They might pull that off. But Big Wullie only needed to fall and it would take a couple of Clydesdales to get him back on his feet. There were problems there.

Finally, Tadger chose champions. Angus against Tam. It was a brilliant piece of matchmaking, he saw at once, a contest for connoisseurs. He thought his way around it, gathering form. At first it looked all Angus. He was young. You could be hitting him for a week. He must be faster. He was one of the strongest men Tadger had ever seen, and that made him very strong. He could lift Tam off the ground and throw him away. But then what would Tam be doing in the meantime? And where could he throw him that was far enough? It would have to be off the face of the earth. Tadger remembered them talking about Tam once at the corner after he had fought the Irish labourer. Sam Connell had said what was possibly true. 'Tam Docherty? Ah could bate Tam the morra. But whit aboot the next day. An' the day after that? Ah'll take Tam as an opponent any time. But fur Christ's sake don't gimme 'im as an enemy. Ye've goat tae bury that kind tae bate them.' Tadger decided he knew which way he would bet.

It wasn't too long until his odds looked more than speculative. Angus had filled out beer for his friends and himself. Talk had slowed a bit, like a vehicle that has taken on an extra load. Angus's mates tended to glance towards him a lot, as if nudging him with their silences. After a time he stood up.

'Heh, listen,' he said. 'We were at Rab's hoose there. An' they sterted tryin' a thing. Somebody sits in a chair an' ye have tae lift the lot, man an' chair. Who's gemme?'

Standing there, his eyes bright with challenge, he crystallised instantly the vague sense of competitiveness most of the men had been feeling. It was definitive Angus. He had always had a talent for creating borders across which to confront other people.

There was a pause in which the need to do something slowly expanded, pushing them out. Tadger looked at Tam. Benign with beer, he was smiling. Wullie Manson rose deliberately.

'Right ye are, son,' he said quietly. 'You called me oot. An' here Ah come. Up a meenit, son.' He took Buzz Crawley's chair, placed it ceremonially in an empty space. 'Ah'm gonny lift this chair wi' a man *and* a wumman oan it.' There was silence. Wullie placed two figurines on the chair and hoisted it with one hand. As they laughed, he said, 'Conn. Rin doon tae oor hoose an' bring up the wally dug an' the cheeny cat. Ah'll lift the hale bloody menagerie.'

While Angus tried to re-establish the seriousness of the feat, Tadger said, 'Richt, Angus. Ye can show us hoo it's done.'

Clearing away the ornaments, Tadger sat Wullie Manson on the chair. The others laughed.

'Aw, noo,' Angus said. 'Ah said *wan* man.'

'Aye, ye're richt enough, son,' Tadger agreed. He knocked lightly on Big Wullie's chest. 'Come oot wan by wan. We ken ye're in there.'

But Angus had the patience of an assured victor. In the end he had Buzz Crawley, the smallest and lightest of his friends, on the chair. Slowly, tensely, he lifted the whole thing fractionally off the floor and set it back down, showing more veins in the process than Conn would have thought they had among them.

'Oh my Goad, son,' Mary Hawkins said.

'Ye'll damage yer hert wi' that cairry-oan,' his mother said.

Knowing the others had disqualified themselves, Angus turned to Tam. 'D'ye fancy a go, feyther?'

'Son,' Tam said. 'Ah've mair in ma heid than the kaim'll take oot. Ye never play at somebody else's gemme. If a man says, "Richt, we'll fight wi' wan haun tied behint wur backs," don't entertain 'im. He'll hiv been practisin' fur years. Stan up a meenit, Buzz.'

Tam placed his right hand round the seat-edge of the empty chair and then positioned his left hand carefully on the ridge of the chair-back. With a flick of his feet, he was standing on his hands on the chair, right arm rigid, left arm bent so that his left shoulder almost rested on the chair-back. Instead of equalling Angus's achievement, he had neatly shifted the terms of the contest. It was a victory for politics over force. From his position of authority, Tam talked.

'The question is, son. Can you dae this? Muscles don't mean much. Hoarses hiv them, but they don't dae *them* much guid. It's whit ye can dae wi' them.'

'Well, that's no' goin' tae solve a lot o' problems, either,' Angus said, and Tam laughed agreement.

Angus felt cheated. The chair trick was a family fixture. All the sons had had it before them for a long time, like a wall mark of their father's height. Since none of them had ever been able to do it, its irrelevant persistence annoyed them, like a physical equivalent of 'When you're as auld as Ah am, ye'll think different.'

'Ach, ye ken Ah canny dae that,' Angus said.

But since it was new to the other men, it effectively diminished Angus's show of strength. His friends were particularly impressed by the way Tam seemed able to hold his position indefinitely, as casually as if this was the purpose to which he always put a chair.

'Ah feel guilty daein' this when the rest o' ye hiv tae staun',' Tam said. 'Come oan. There's plenty o' chairs in the hoose. Take wan the piece.'

When he descended among them again, they wanted to try it. With each successive attempt, advice grew more general, assisting hands more numerous. 'It must a' be connectit wi' yer centre o' balance.' 'Naw, yer left haun's at fault there.' 'Ah'll haud yer feet till ye find yer hauns.' 'Swing yourself up, man. Yer arse must be made o' cement.' But at the end of it, all they had achieved was a working knowledge of how not to stand on your hands on a chair. Johnny Lawson had been unable to get his feet more than a few inches off the floor. Wullie Manson was forbidden to try, on the grounds of cruelty to chairs. Tadger came nearest, so near that he swung right over, bruising his shinbone.

They sought compensation in other ploys, each introducing the contest he thought he could win, until they had spontaneously devised the indoor Olympic Games. The women talked among themselves, prices and wayward husbands and strikes and illnesses, their talk an ominous gloss on the garbled noisy nonsense of the men. The competitions grew defiantly more ludicrous until they were all engaged in a knockout version of hand-wrestling. Tam and Angus met in the final.

As a generator runs down, the jocularity died, and in its absence, like a sound always present but not fully heard till now, seriousness occurred. The women were no longer talking.

'Gi'e folk a chance, Wullie,' Tadger said. 'You staun' at the back.'

'Whit dae ye think Ah'm daein'?'

'Hell, man, when you staun' at the back ye're still at the front.'

But nobody laughed. Tam and Angus joined hands, elbows pressed down on the table where empty glasses had been pushed back unevenly to make a space, among the dried beer-stains and the crumbs of black bun, for serious business. Tadger was official. 'The final's best o' three,' he said.

The first was over instantly. Angus powered his father's forearm down until the knuckles of Tam's hand cracked on the table. The second lasted longer, until Tam, who still hadn't forgotten how to be a bad loser, had laid the back of Angus's hand, almost pore by pore flat against the wood.

There were mock cheers. Angus nodded, bored his backside into the chair, checked the angle of his body. Tam's eyes ignored everything around, waiting for his determination to set. Their hands ingratiated themselves one with another until Tadger gave the signal, when they locked. The expectancy of the others was first a pause, then a wait, finally a wonder.

The tension in the two hands grew like a glacier. They inhabited a six-inch axis as absolutely as if it had been fenced, and the areas beyond were private property. The pressures were more than physical. Angus was utterly unyielding but there played across the hardness of his eyes a kind of bafflement, as if he knew that there could never be any discoverable reason why his father's arm didn't buckle. Perhaps for the first time in his life his idea of what strength was, lost its certainty, became too complicated for his understanding. Around their clenched hands, their eyes moved thoughtfully, taking in the table, their wrung knuckles, the wall, as if looking for where the most strength was. When they met, Angus's were questions, dilating with incredulity. Don't you know I'm stronger? Don't you know I'm younger? Don't you know you can't keep it up? When will you accept it? Tam's were strangely absent, black as all the pits he had worked in, bleak as slag. He hardly seemed present as himself, had become his arm.

Anxious to catch the decisive moment that must come, the others stared till everything else went out of focus, and only those crossed arms remained with the clarity of an emblem, cabbalistic handshake, reducing everything else to a setting for themselves. They assumed the stasis of sculpture, making it seem silly to expect a resolution. Tadger stepped forward, putting a hand on each wrist.

'It his tae be a draw,' he said. 'We canny a' be here tae next new year.'

The onlookers didn't plead the rules because it's only games that have rules. Angus looked angry for a moment then let his hand twitchingly prize itself open. He said, 'A' richt, feyther. But ye canny get ony better. Wi' me the longer the stronger.'

Tam rubbed his hand gently, as if thanking it, and smiled. 'That's richt enough,' he said, really looking at Angus for the first time since they had started. 'Ah'll no get ony better at playin' gemmes. But we'll no' aye be playin' gemmes.'

The night had found its core. The commemorative urge that hides in parties, that magi-complex that haunts the edge of situations, hoping that if it waits long enough it will witness their miraculous transformation into events, was satisfied. Something had taken place. As always, the ability to infuse the trivia with a vision lay in their common past and wasn't communicable. But they had all been a part of that ambiguous nexus where the muscles of the two men were simultaneously opposed and complementary, measuring mutual strength.

At first they had been partisan, Rab Morrison wanting Angus to prove something, Tadger needing to go on believing in Tam. But in the end watchers and protagonists were together in a conspiracy, an experiment to prove how formidable they were. For them what had happened was the equivalent of a poem or a play—like those, over-simplified, but still a celebration of themselves. For a moment they could innocently believe that those joined hands squeezed everything into irrelevance but their own joint strength, that that was all there was. They could almost convince themselves that they weren't just dupes, that they didn't spend their lives in self-defeating conflict with one another merely because they were stupid but because they were themselves the only ones worthy of their own antagonism, that they were set apart not by their ignorance and their folly but by their honesty and a knowledge from the bone, abjuring as they did every day any meaning but a life.

Their satisfaction in this pointless contest had the same ancestry as their love of gambling, drinking, fighting. It wasn't only, as the socially conscious were inclined to say, the pathetic desire to escape from their condition. They were, much more profoundly, the expression of that condition. They gambled to gamble, they drank to drink, they fought to fight.

The mystique of habits they practised went beyond reflexes conditioned by capitalist oppression, came closer to primitive rites for exorcising the power of the bastard god, economy, originated in an impulse that antedated Factory Acts. Like the adherents of a persecuted faith, they had endured long enough to acquire the sense not just of the unmerited privileges of others but of their essential worthlessness as well. Many of them, like Tam, felt militant in the face of these injustices. But it was difficult to mobilise that just resentment because so many carried deep inside themselves, like a tribal precept, a wordless understanding of the powerlessness of any social structure to defeat them. Their bondage admitted them to the presence of a truth from which their masters hid, because to live with necessity is the only freedom.

It wasn't surprising that the champions of reform, calling them to their cause, found them intractably engaged in inconsequential arguments over a pint, stealing a hare when they could have had the acres that it ran on, pursuing private vendettas. For they believed that the hare was all they would be needing till the next time. It was a fundamentalism frustrating to the more sophisticated, whether he was the owner elevated by his interest in painting or the political theorist baffled by their reluctance to animate his theories. What the socially superior failed to see was that they were the least conditioned members of society.

Like the inheritors of an ancient black art, they could conjure real presences out of very thin air. A place behind a pit-bing and two pennies made a sport. A corner and some men was everywhere, debating-chamber, funeral-parlour, coffee-house, confessional, where they gave thoughts, hopes, laughter, words directly to the wind. Any open space was where two men could finally come to terms. Since they had learned how to become themselves under any circumstances, the exact nature of those circumstances was something they found it hard to care continuously about.

That they were going to have to learn to care, perhaps only Mick, of all the people in the room, fully realised. For the rest, nights like tonight were their own meaning. The abrasiveness there had been between Tam and Angus was already receding. What stayed was the moment they'd made out of it. They all drifted away into their own thoughts and conversations like a crowd dispersing.

The rest of the night was improvising elegies. Somebody sang 'John Anderson, my Jo'. Andra Crawford came ('Ah saw yer licht in, Tam.') and wanted to talk about Keir Hardie. Into a growing silence Big Wullie Manson gently interjected, 'Ah uset tae be ten stane nine.' Angus's friends all left. Mick saw Mary Hawkins home. Kathleen and Jack went with them, one of the weans in the shawl and Jack carrying the other one wrapped up, with Tadger saying, 'Hoo much wid ye take fur wan o' yer weans then, Kathleen?'

Standing in the doorway before going through to his bed, Conn looked into the room and the image halted him. He saw its texture. It was as rich and strange as a painting. He took delight in the room for its own sake, the dying fire, the glow of the mantle, Wullie Manson meditating slimness, Tadger sprawled in comfort threatening never to go home. The scatter of empty glasses formed a mysterious pattern, a rightness that could never have been achieved deliberately.

Conn found himself wishing that the completeness of that room with those people in it could be kept, that it could somehow be a self-sufficiency. He found himself wondering why it wasn't enough.

# BOOK III

# CHAPTER ONE

The men coming out of the dyeworks were walking briskly, their preoccupied faces stamped with a private destination. Each of them carried his wages in his pocket, like a map of the week ahead. It was bleak terrain.

Some of them noticed him as they passed, standing against the wall as still as a statue in a niche, a stance they could have captioned: 'This is a claim.' The realisation held them momentarily before, checking the features and finding them impersonal, they moved on. Quite a few felt the vague sense of relief that comes when an accident happens to somebody else.

He knew what would reach his recognition first. He waited patiently until he was aware of that limping walk from yards away, before it came into the lamplight. The swagger was enforced, he knew, but he let it feed his purpose, pride before the fall. Without moving, he called pleasantly, 'Jack.'

Jack swivelled. The man who had been walking with him went on a few paces before turning round. There was a pause. Then the man said, 'Ah'll see ye, Jack.'

'Gus.' Jack used the shortened form of the name unintentionally. He had never called him that and he knew himself it was placative. In his confusion, his mouth had led the way, taught him what he was feeling. He admitted to himself that he felt guilty and that he understood exactly why Angus was here.

'Ah want tae talk tae ye,' Angus said and started walking. Jack walked with him. They turned the corner to where the river ran on one side of the narrow lane and the factory buildings overhung the other. Angus stopped on a patch of wasteground between two buildings. Gas-lamps made a lunar landscape of it.

Jack understood. They were standing on the terms Angus was offering. They could talk and something might be settled that way. If it wasn't, they would have to go on to something else. Like someone finding himself in a blind alley, Jack thought back through the recent turnings he had taken. He couldn't pretend to be surprised that this was where they led.

'It's aboot Kathleen.'

'Whit aboot her?'

'She's no' happy.'

'Whit's happy?'

'No' whit she is, onywey.'

They waited in the pale light for something to happen, a meeting to take place. The words they had said were like the noises people make in a mist, trying to locate each other. For Jack what was happening was still confused with the conversation he had been having coming out of the works. Angus listened to somebody's footsteps, wanting them to disappear, as if he needed silence to unravel whatever was knotted in him. Across the river a dog barked distantly. They were as far from it as from each other.

'She disny hiv much o' a life.'

'Who telt ye that?'

'Ah'm tellin' you that.'

'Ah think she's a' richt. Ah'm maybe no' makin' as much money as you. But we manage.'

'It's no' jist the money. Ah've seen bruises oan 'er.'

What affected Jack was the innocence of Angus's knowingness. He had seen bruises on his sister and it was something terrible. Through Angus's reaction to some grains of sand, Jack had a fresh perspective on the desert he was living in. He saw how unimaginable it must be to Angus, who was still young enough to be shocked at the infringement of a principle—you never hit women. Jack had been taught that too. Even now he couldn't have argued against it. It was just that he had been beyond argument, to places where such principles seemed about as relevant as brushing a corpse's teeth. There was no way for him to convey how he and Kathleen lived, how circumstances had taught them to be. Nor could he understand how they had got from where they started to where they were. But wordlessly a part of him were long evenings when they sat through their marriage like a wake while their past illusions reflected their present as in grotesque, distorting mirrors. So he drank and Kathleen hid behind religion, like a married nun. Often they quarrelled. He blamed himself. Certainly Kathleen had tried. She was miraculous with money. In her hands its value doubled, though it still wasn't enough. He sometimes wondered if it was because he had missed the war. But nothing answered the void in him. It would have been like trying to explain why someone had a weak heart. He had no hopes beyond today. Even anger seemed futile. He had nothing to say to Angus, who stood luxuriating in his own feelings like a boy who stands in a cemetery mourning the carcase of a mouse.

'It'll no' dae.'

'That's fur Kathleen tae decide.'

'Whit dae you say?'

'Ah say it's nane o' yer business.'

'She's ma sister.'

'She's ma wife.'

'Ye hide it weel.'

In the realisation that their words were going nowhere, Jack saw what was going to happen. It seemed pointless. While Angus wound himself up, Jack was aware of a rusted bicycle wheel lying near them. Some spokes had sprung. He felt vaguely that it was as much involved in this as he was, that it and the river coughing quietly near them were a part of his predicament.

'She deserves better.'

'It's no' jist ma fault.'

'It's nae way tae treat a wumman. Ye've nae decency. It's no' richt.'

Jack said nothing. In this place Angus's words seemed empty, even to himself. The concept of some kind of morality that he had been stumbling towards, to which he had been trying to bring Jack, had seemed important, even impressive. Now that he had got there, it was like a ruin that houses only shit and clumsy slogans. People used to live here, that was all. For the first time the place impinged on Angus and he felt as if the rubble among which they stood was shifting under his feet. He lost his hold on what was happening. He felt that, in some way he couldn't understand, it was Jack who was aggressing on him. Just by being there and waiting passively, Jack was exerting a pressure.

Angus's assurance divided, and what had started in him that evening as a proclamation of intent became an argument. He began to wonder why he was here. It occurred to him wilfully and shockingly that it wasn't so much Jack he was confronting as his father, because he knew that Tam should have been the one to do this, and by Angus's doing it he was demonstrating something about his father, putting a date on the headstone. Angus hesitated. He felt himself involved in a contest the rules of which were secret. So how could you ever know if you were winning?

'Jack. You're gonny hiv tae treat her better.'

His voice was as near to a plea as it could go.

'Ah'll treat her the wey Ah treat her.'

'Christ. It's goat tae be different. Ye'd better promise tae try.'

'Why?'

Angus was faced with a moment he thought he would have relished. It had come down to bodies, and there he knew quite simply that he couldn't lose. But with the two of them alone on that amphitheatrical patch of ground, he waited for the familiar sensation that made the blood surge like a crowd, and nothing happened. He was aware only of a deafening silence, a baffling sense of pointlessness as if those who had arranged the contest were unable to attend. Dimly, he felt used, hired to carry out something he didn't understand. What did it matter what he did? Fifty yards away beyond the wasteground, he saw a woman's shape move behind a tenement window, and he was afflicted by a nightmare sensation of people mysteriously doing things in rooms, as if the front walls of every building in the town were made of glass. He realised that he didn't know what was happening.

When he hit Jack, it was less an event than the expression of a need for one. Jack rocked and stood. It was as if both of them felt nothing. Angus looked into the set hardness of Jack's face and struck it again. Jack's head came down and his hands waved slightly. Something bounced out of his breast-pocket and fell on the ground. A trickle of blood came out of the corner of his mouth. It was finished. Angus's arm atrophied.

'Okay?' he said, not knowing what he meant himself.

Jack nodded. Angus bent down and picked up what had fallen. It was Jack's pay-packet. It felt about as heavy as birdseed and the amount scrawled in pen on the front of it was an insult. Giving it back, Angus was embarrassed, and he couldn't get rid of the feeling that he had lost a fight. Jack took the packet, wiped his mouth, and walked away.

Going in the other direction, Angus was hesitant, walked slowly, as if he had inherited Jack's limp. But the further away he went, the more positive his stride became. He had acted, he had done something. He had dispelled his own misgivings by going right through them, and as far as he was concerned they were finished. He had no need of the erratic gas-lamps to find his way through the maze of grubby streets. He carried his own certainty with him like a lantern and, knowing where he was going, the darkness all around didn't bother him, and the feeling that what he had almost met on the waste lot, the thing that had almost pinioned his arms, padded patiently behind him, was no more than a slight unease.

# CHAPTER TWO

The house had gradually changed for them. Tam had felt it settle round him like a shroud. It wasn't just that it was old in itself but that it was worn with them, used. As well as the simple overcrowding of so many adults in such a confined space, it was replete with a past that oppressed the present. It had contracted from a refuge to a cage.

Jenny still scrubbed and dusted and polished it as thoroughly as before but what had been an action became a tic. Her work enshrined its own futility, preserved the ugly furniture scars in polish, wore down the linoleum it cleaned. And following her as she went, like dust she could never be rid of, was the growing sense that the family, which was what gave everything purpose for her, didn't really live here any more.

Angus and Conn used the house like an inn, stopping in it en route from place to place, exchanging travellers' tales. Mick was often a stranger. Old Conn was always there but he had changed too, as if all his past acquiescence had been a means of forming an alliance with the house. Physically, the house was more his than anybody else's. His rocking-chair had become the basic rhythm of each day, like a clock the monotony of which sometimes threatened to drive Jenny mad. He remained pleasant but utterly intractable, wanting tea at certain times, the paper read to him at others. Like a monument set in the middle of a busy thoroughfare, his presence brought the persistent annoyance of having to re-route all traffic round it.

At times Jenny had tried to talk to Tam about what was happening to them but it was difficult. For one thing, it was something that surrounded them, like an element, too much a part of them to be isolated and examined. For another, Tam didn't want to talk about it. He tended more and more to let incidents glance off him instead of facing them frontally as he had used to. It was seldom that his anger exploded as it formerly had so that in the middle of an otherwise ordinary evening he was haranguing their lives into militancy against the forces he dimly felt crushing them. Now he was more likely to take a sudden frenzy for some intense but apparently unmotivated activity. For a week he would be painting the doors in the house, defiantly. But the drabness of the place seemed to absorb his and Jenny's efforts more quickly now. Or he would take to going round the dog-tracks, or poaching, or try the pitch-and-toss, as if the key to what was wrong was somewhere around and he'd better find it quickly. But all these substitute actions left the centre of his life more empty. Like Jenny, he knew his house was dividing and, like her, he couldn't understand it.

Both of them shared with other members of the older generation in High Street the wide conviction that things were 'no' the same'. This wasn't merely an expression of that hardening falsification of the past to which people over a certain age are subject, like cataracts or hair in the ears. They were aware of something new in their lives, tangible if incomprehensible. It was as if the Spanish ''flu' had developed a social counterpart, and just as, although that virus had been invisible to them, the corpses it left had been proof of its existence, so now the obsolescence of attitudes they had held for so long conveyed to them the strangeness of their circumstances. Women at the close-mouth relayed the latest account of how a son had insulted his father, a daughter was smoking. Older men at the corner heard yet another story of a young man attacking somebody with a weapon, and of the time when a man might pulp his opponent's face but only with a clenched fist they talked sadly, as if mourning the death of chivalry. The strange virus was everywhere and parents waited for their family to catch it and bring it into the house.

So Jenny knew the symptoms when Angus said, 'Ah'll work a few weeks mair, feyther, an' then Ah'm leavin' the pit. Tae go tae Number Eicht.'

The remark interrupted what Old Conn had been saying. But that wasn't significant. There were certain nights when if you wanted to speak, chances were you would have to interrupt Old Conn. He took periodic talking fits, lengthy flushings of the mind. They were always about the past and the same stories occurred irregularly. Tonight he had been talking about the priests blessing the fishing boats on the west coast of Ireland. He had been stuck for the name of one of the priests. Names eluded him and he would never go on without them, believing that if he surrendered one he might lose them all. 'Always let yer memory ken who's boss,' he said. He had been busy trying to establish the mastery when Angus spoke.

'When did ye decide this?' Tam asked.

'Ah've been thinkin' aboot it fur a while.'

'Ye never said.'

'That's whit Ah'm daein' noo, feyther.'

'Nice o' ye tae let us ken, richt enough.'

Immediately, Jenny and Old Conn were spectators at something that involved the other four, who were no longer just separate presences but were each a part of the same small tension. She saw them very clearly defined by their own unselfconsciousness. The dominant impression she had was of how they filled the room, how bulky they were in its tightness, how they couldn't help bumping one another if they moved. Tam sat in his chair beside the fire, legs stretched, shirt sleeves rolled up, thumbs tucked behind the big buckle of his belt, so that his forearms rested heavily on the arms of the chair. Angus was making his usual gesture towards reading the paper, which meant he was leafing through it, giving it the chance to arrest his attention. Mick, the only one who hadn't eaten, since he came in after the others, was sitting at the table and had begun to take his soup more slowly, like an actor who knows his cue is coming soon. Across the table from him sat Conn, and Jenny noticed again how fast he was filling out, bringing home another muscle from the pit every day. Though he had long since finished his meal, he had scavenged a piece of Mick's bread and was chewing it dry. His jaws were distended, holding the mouthful of bread motionless while he watched his father and Angus.

'Ay, Ah'm a nice fella.' Angus was laughing.

Tam wasn't. He got up and crossed towards Angus, bending suddenly towards him. Angus stiffened. Tam tore an unprinted edge off the newspaper, folded it, went back to the fire and lit the cigarette stub he had taken from behind his ear. The paper flared in one sudden flame so that Tam seemed to be lighting the cigarette with his own burning fingers. He sprinkled the charred flakes into the fireplace and sat back down.

'Whit's wrang wi' the pit ye're in?'

'It's a bad pit.'

'Ye mean there's guid pits?'

'No' enough money.'

'You're gonny make mair?'

'That's richt.'

With thumb and middle-finger Tam massaged the area above his temples where the hair had receded.

'Whit's different aboot Number Eicht?'

'Ah'm contractin' fur the coal.'

'Whit dae ye mean?' Jenny asked.

'It means Ah contract tae get so much coal oot for so much money. An' Ah pey the squad that works wi' me.'

'It means we've goat a capitalist in the hoose,' Tam said.

Angus appealed to the ceiling.

'Och, feyther.' Mick looked as if his soup had gone sour. 'Ye should visit the twentieth century some time. That's where the rest o' us are leevin'.'

'Ah don't trust a man who pits himself in a position tae make money aff his mates.'

'Me make money aff them! Listen, feyther. The men who're comin' wi' me want tae come. Because they ken Ah could work them intae the grund eicht days a week. They canny lose. Because Ah'll dae ma share, a' richt. An' maybe a bit o' theirs. That's whit they're thinkin'.'

'An' whit are you thinkin'? No' the same. When did you become a public benefactor?'

'Ah'm thinkin' Ah can work alongside ony man Ah ever met. An' maybe a bit in front o' 'im. An' Ah want the money Ah deserve. They'd heard o' me at Number Eicht.'

'Christ, ye're famous. Did they tell ye whit they had heard?'

'Aye, richt, richt.'

'Maybe that yer heid's just fu' o' muscles. An' that yer only freen is yer pey-poke.'

'Feyther, feyther!' Mick was holding the severed stump of his arm in its pinned-up sleeve, in what had become a habit. He was crouched slightly in his chair as if holding in the pain. 'Whit is it wi' you? Whit are ye angry aboot? Ye've been doon there long enough tae ken whit it's like. Why should Angus no' move somewhere else if he can make some money? Ye talk as if he had some sacred duty tae knock his pan oot fur pennies.'

'He should ken who he is by this time. That's whit Ah've learned doon there. Ye don't make contracts wi' yer enemies.'

'An' whit have you done?'

'Ah've asked fur nothin'. Ah've met ma life at the pit-face every day that Goad sent. An' Ah took whit they widny gi'e me. An' Ah showed them that they couldny invent conditions Ah couldny meet.'

'Oh, that's guid.' Mick had his eyes closed, shaking his head. 'That is very impressive.'

Angus stretched out his arms like a crucifix and said, 'Could Ah supply ma ain nails, please?'

'Dae ye no' see whit that means?' Mick was trying to be patient. 'That means you're no' even worth a contract. Who needs tae make a contract wi' folk like you, feyther? The miners sterted as slaves. An' the chains are still in your bluid. Why no' hiv a contract? For Goad's sake, jist tell me why!'

'Because it's agreein' tae whit is rotten in the first place. It's shakin' hands with shit. An' that makes you the same. Clever Ah'm not. Ah'll grant ye. But Ah'd have tae be helluva stupit no' tae hiv learned wan thing. Where we leeve, it's too late fur arrangements. A copper here, a bit o' paper there. Contracts? There's wan contract they'll get fae us. Tae get the hell aff oor backs ance an' fur all. Less than that, Ah'm no' interested in.'

'An' whit hiv you been daein' tae get them aff yer back? Ye've been feedin' the bloody system a' yer days. Proppin' it up.'

'Ah've been waitin'. That's whit Ah've been daein'. Ah've kept somethin' alive that they've been tryin' tae kill. An' that's ma joab. Tae deny them every day o' ma life. Tae show them they can neither brek us nor buy us. Fur oor time's comin'.'

'When?' Mick's laughter was just a noisy exhalation. 'Ye widny happen tae hiv the date oan ye, wid ye?'

'When it comes. Ah don't ken when. When the yins that ken aboot these things can make it happen. An' they will. Me. Ah'm jist keepin' the accoonts clean. A kinna tallyman. Ah ken hoo much is owed. An' Ah'm no' settlin' fur less.'

'Ye canny believe that, feyther.'

'Son. Ah canny no' believe it.'

'Dear Goad,' Mick said gently. 'Fifty-odd-year-auld an' still playin' at Peter Pan.'

'Mick!' Jenny called as if he was moving out of earshot.

'Let 'im talk,' Tam said.

'Aye, let 'im talk,' Mick shouted. 'Because there's nae wey you're gonny stoap 'im. Because the truth's been lukin' in that bloody windy since Ah wis born, an' we've still goat tae pretend it isny there. Ah've listened tae you, feyther. Fur years Ah've listened. Ye've said it that oaften, Ah sterted tae think it wis true. Feyther. Oor time isny comin'. Oor time's here. An' your time's past. An' they're baith o' them the same. Why have ye fed us this tripe fur years? D'ye ken ye made me that backward Ah wis eichteen before Ah wis born? Because an airm's the least o' whit Ah loast. Ah loast the inside o' ma heid. An' Ah'm havin' tae grow a new yin. An' it's sair, feyther. It's bloody sair! Because ootside this room, the rules are different. An' you've never learned that yit. Well, Ah had tae learn. An' whit Ah learned is that we're a joke. No' a very funny joke, but a joke jist the same. Naebudy is aboot tae set us free, feyther. The folk you're waitin' fur don't ken ye're born. If you want somethin', ye'd better learn tae get it fur yerself. An' you've never stertit tae fin' oot. Whit offends you aboot Angus is he's no' goin' tae shove his heid in the same halter as you. You are pathetic.'

The silence that followed made Conn wince.

'Is that whit ye' think?' Tam's voice had the gentleness of fingers touching a wound.

'That's whit Ah bluidy well think!'

'Is that whit you think, Angus?'

'Ah think ye're hidin', feyther. Ye're hidin',' Angus said. 'An' ye've been hidin' fur years.'

Unsmoked, the cigarette stub had burned out in Tam's fingers. He threw it at the fire but it fell in the hearth. The moment was a long recoil from the irrevocable, like watching the subsidence of an assassinated body. For Conn, what was dying was the sense of family he had. During the argument he had been siding mentally with his brothers, adding the weight of his silence to their words. Now he was like a conspirator who realises what unified as intention separates as event. For he felt with chilling certainty the separateness of them all, his family as an eccentricity. They weren't so much brothers as they were a man with one arm, a muscular bully-boy and a worried nonentity. In rejecting their father, they had also rejected one another.

'As ye sow, so shall ye reap,' Old Conn said, not without a certain contentment. 'Ah've warned ye repeatedly. And the son shall raise his hand against the father. That's whit comes of keepin' a godless house.'

Conn felt a profound hatred for the old man. He had sat in this house almost as long as Conn could remember, through how many endless conversations, desperate arguments, watching hope starve and dreams decay in his own son, waiting to pronounce the epitaph he made up before he came. Nothing had made any difference to him. Nothing could change him. He had sat through it all like a stone idol no offerings could move. In the silence Conn wished his father could resurrect himself as he had been.

'Luk, feyther,' Angus said quietly. 'If it's the wages that's worryin' ye . . .'

'Oh here, though,' Tam said, but Angus was too busy being generous to understand.

'Ah'll still be helpin' oot in the hoose. Ye'll no' be the loser. Ah'll see . . .'

Tam was suddenly on his feet.

'You'll see tae yerself,' he shouted. 'You offer me so much as tuppence o' yer charity an' they'll be usin' them tae haud yer fuckin' eyelids doon. When Ah need you, son, bury me. Ye've ma permission. Put a pit-axe through ma heid an' bury me. Ah'm better aff deid than needin' the likes o' you.'

'Hey, feyther.' Conn was starting to speak when the pain of his father's whirling look made him feel as if he was holding a knife.

Mick made a tutting sound with his mouth and shook his head.

'An' you, son.' Tam turned on him. 'You've had yer say, an' Ah don't want tae hear it said again. You've had hard times. An' ma life hisny been a holiday. An' years an' years ago, Ah made a line. An' you're the furst man that's came acroass it an' walked back. The rest hiv a' been cairrit. An' don't dae it again, son. Don't dae it again.'

He took his jacket from the chairback and walked out, leaving a silence behind. It was an impressive performance. A stranger would have been awed. But Conn had known him when he would have stayed. And he knew what it meant.

'Well then. Well then,' Angus said.

The sons sat still. Jenny rose and cleared away Mick's plate and made fresh tea.

'McCann,' Old Conn said.

Conn looked at him.

'McCann. That wis the young priest's name. A big dark-heided fella. He took tae the drink in the end, Ah mind.'

Jenny poured Mick's tea and sat back down.

'You will respect that man,' she said, 'or you will not be in this house.' She said it formally, to the wall that she was facing. 'That's the best man ye'll meet in a week's walk. An' you'll respect him.'

Nobody else spoke. Conn was surprised to find himself thinking quite calmly that he did respect him, but not as much as he had done. In a way, it was his father's fault for having been so impressive before. Now you couldn't help but see the difference. Like a boxer who was once fearless but has learned to be afraid, he might seem himself to those who didn't know him. But appearance had been encroaching more and more upon the substance and he could no longer bear to live within the range of other people's force, for he couldn't any more stand hurt.

'He wis the best man ye could find,' Jenny said. And added as if correcting herself, 'An' still is.'

Conn knew this time that she was looking at him. But he was too embarrassed to look back. For she must have known herself she didn't believe it. Her words had become just a formula, something to say. The King is dead. Long live the King.

# CHAPTER THREE

What was happening in his house no longer affected Conn as deeply as before, for the polarity of his life had shifted. He had discovered girls. He'd always known of them, right enough, but the difference between his present experience of them and his past was the difference between dreaming over a map of the Amazon forest and being dropped blindfold into it. He had known the terms but now he was visited by them as palpitating presences. Mystic breasts descended upon him. He saw visionary thighs. The most mundane objects were capable of growing female parts and whole stretches of his life became surrealistic.

He often wondered why his family didn't notice. They would look at him the same way as before, or more frequently not even bother to look, as if his solidity could be taken for granted, whereas he was ferociously in flux, a teem of pressures and urges and needs that his skin seemed hardly capable of containing. He had recurrent dreads that somebody would accidentally gain access to the locked room his thinking had become. One of these took the form of a fear that some night, when he was sitting in his house as if he was just another human being, the dirty words that orgied in his mind would force an exit from his mouth and dance obscenely across the room like nude chorus-girls. Another was that one of his erections would never subside and he, as the first recorded sufferer from lockjaw of the scrotum, no cure known to medical science as yet, would have to walk through life advertising his enormity and having special suits made for him.

He lived in a private time-scale. A week was a weekend with some other days hanging round it. His sense of himself had become uncertain and he was now someone he only met up with fitfully. There was one favoured meeting-place—the dancehall. He pursued himself wherever a dance was held, going most often in the company of Bert Crawford and Jock Finlay, either in the town or trekking to the villages around. The location didn't matter, a five-mile walk was nothing. For the dance-hall wasn't a place but a continuing event in which the rest of the week was just the intermission. Nowhere else could he find the heat and noise and hustle and the swarming sense of possibilities to match what was happening in himself. There you could be as many people as you wanted.

So he said, 'Because Ah'm thinkin' o' emigratin'.'

'Where wid ye go?'

'Maybe Canada.'

'But why?'

'Why no'.'

She looked at him as if his daring was unanswerable.

'Ah widny hiv the nerve.'

As he danced, everything took on vividness from his imminent departure. He noted the colours and the faces and the sounds, recording his future nostalgia. Too far away to be heard by the others, ships bleated their foghorns.

'When wid ye be goin'?'

'Nothin's fixed yet.'

But for five minutes after the dance, he felt as if it was, moving with quizzical vagueness among his friends, wondering how much he would be missed, an emigré from his own future.

And he said, 'Hiv ye ever thocht o' gettin' mairrit?' 'You look like Mary Pickford.' And, 'Ye like readin'? Ah read an awfu' lot maself. Ah come fae a readin' faimly.' And, 'Maybe Australia.'

'Why that?'

'Because there's lots o' opportunity oot there.'

'Whit wid ye dae?'

'Whitever comes up.'

'Ah wish Ah had your courage,' she said, squeezing his arm as if to feel his muscles.

And an hour might have passed before he realised that he wished he had his courage too. By that time he was lost in compensations.

Bert Crawford was saying, 'Ye hear aboot Tadger, then? Well, he's helluva constipated, right? Wance went eleeven days withoot a passage. Had coabwebs oan his erse by the time he made the grade. Well, when Mickey Ray an' Andy Cunningham begged 'im fur the price o' a gemme o' snooker, he gi'es them it oan condeetion they drink a boattle o' castor ile an' a boattle o' cascara. He had the stuff in the hoose. An' they did it. They managed to poat a red.'

Or Jock Finlay was counting the number of blokes' heels he could click in the course of a dance. Or the three of them were agreeing to pick partners only from a back-view, and see who came out best. Or Conn was playing the eye-game with every girl within range, chalking up victories against defeats.

The dancehall was a factory for sensations. Conn loved to go there and let himself be ambushed by whatever happened. Situations kept breaking over him with visionary suddenness. A girl with black flecks in her eyes, like sedge below the surface of a lake. The soft flesh of a girl's back rippling under his hand as she moved. The smell of them was infinitely diverse. Everything was so various that at times it seemed to him that he could happily spend the rest of his life moving among dim noisy rooms like these, being accosted by sensations, dallying with touches, contemplating eyes.

His enjoyment of it all made him understand Angus a little better, brought them nearer. Not that they were much together, but they were caught in intersecting orbits. Now Conn saw how Angus, so often out of place at home, wore this context like something made to measure. Here he looked so relaxed and yet alert, his passing ruffling the attention of others slightly, his eyes assessing both the men and the women.

Once Conn watched him in deep conversation with a girl. It looked very serious. She was talking at him desperately, a hand touching his jacket. Angus leaned against a wall, his hand resting flat on his head. His eyes moved steadily among the people dancing past. When he answered her, his face didn't change and he spoke evenly, measuredly, saying something with a shake of the head that nothing was going to change. It occurred to Conn that it looked like trouble which they would eventually hear of in the house. But whatever extensions there might be of this situation seemed to him inevitably irrelevant. What struck him was just the poignancy of that scene, the pity that it should have to mean more than itself, the two of them beautifully pre-occupied, with the music round them, the girl's suffused, delicate face making Conn envious of his brother, Angus leant there electric with health.

Moments like those admitted Conn to Angus's sense of the importance of yourself. Politics, history, strikes seemed marginal pastimes. What were they supposed to be all about? Conn was too busy prospecting himself. For him real problems were things like how to copulate standing up—'the gentle art of the knee-shaker' Bert called it. He was obsessed by the physical difficulties that broke in upon his dream-like experiences with girls, the cold awakenings into bleak fact that were like an anchorite finding his knees chafed at the end of a religious ecstasy. And always haunting him was the dark underside of rumour, the apocrypha of sexual horror. Who could care about the state of the nation when he might have galloping syphilis?

Looming larger and larger in his life was the subculture he and his friends were evolving among them—Jock Finlay, who got washed and cleaned every evening so that he could be out early looking for a fight; Bert Crawford, much of whose conversation was concerned with refining his sense of the ideal set-up with a married woman. Conn made up the third of a triumvirate that was secretly at work realigning the priorities of the world.

Only sometimes, coming home from an evening left smouldering behind them like a pillaged city, he would think guiltily of his mother and Mick—together in the house. Like the legless man who sat at John Finnie Street corner and to whom he sometimes gave a tanner, they spoiled his pleasure. And you couldn't buy them off with a sixpence.

# CHAPTER FOUR

'Ah'll awa' doon then,' Kathleen said, and didn't move.

She stood in the middle of the floor, twisting a button of her coat. Jenny, on her knees beside the fire, averted her face from the heat as she brushed the hearth. Finished, she heaved herself up and sat in the fireside chair, staring into the warmth. She was becoming more addicted to her 'wee rests', like someone acquiring a taste for old age.

'Ah've left Jack in himsel' wi' the weans.' Kathleen seemed trying to justify her leaving, though nobody was arguing. 'He'll be grey in the heid by the time Ah get back.'

Old Conn was still asleep in his rocking-chair. Jenny had already eased the clay-pipe from his fingers, the bowl still warm, and put it on the mantelpiece. Mick, seated at the window with a book on the table, nursed the stump of his arm. Jenny's breathing settled itself and her flushing subsided.

'Ah suppose Ah better get doon, then,' Kathleen said.

Reluctantly, as if she still hadn't drunk enough of its strength, Jenny took her eyes from the fire and looked at Kathleen.

'Hoo is he, then?' she asked, not because she wanted an answer but because she knew that Kathleen needed the question.

'Whit? Jack? He could be worse.'

'He disny lift his hand tae ye?'

'Naw. No' noo.'

'It's a thing yer feyther's never done tae me in his life.'

'Where is he the nicht?'

'Jist oot.'

They looked at each other, a deep inarticulacy of childbirth shared, men coming home drunk, an experience branded on their hands in callouses, a message whose meaning was that it couldn't be expressed. The words were substitutes.

'So ye're managin' a' richt,' Jenny said.

'He's workin' still. That's a lot.'

'Aye.'

'He's awfu' restless, though.'

'They're a' restless. The hale world's restless.'

'If he strikes, Ah don't ken hoo we're gonny leeve.'

'A day at a time. A day at a time. It's hoo we've always leeved.'

'It canny go oan.'

'It never could go oan. But it always his.'

Jenny watched the fire. The clock grew dominant. Old Conn's mouth sagged: a well that was running dry. Mick rocked gently over his book. Mother and daughter were a meeting in void, a brackish oasis. Future was past and past was future—nothing more to happen.

'Ah'll get awa', mither.'

'Bring the weans up soon, hen.'

'So Ah wull. Goodnight, Mick.'

'Night.'

Old Conn stirred, gulped, subsided. Jenny watched Kathleen age towards the door. The room clammed on itself. With Kathleen gone, Jenny saw her. Ah, she was older. She was too old. Jenny remembered a station somewhere and Kathleen beside her, talking, raising a hand to her head and the finger seemed to point out the lines on her brow. In the instant Kathleen had changed from being a daughter to an event, something Jenny was helpless to assist. She could no longer remember where and when it had been. But that station stayed with her, not as a place but as a fact.

It had been deserted, overgrown. It was, she wondered to realise, where they all were now. No trains stopped here. Yet they went on waiting. Kathleen was right. It couldn't go on. But it went on.

'Look at them,' Mick said. 'Wid ye luk at them.'

Jenny raised her eyes to him. He was looking through the window across the corner, shaking his head.

'They're playin' at fitba' wi' a fag packet.'

She heard the bitterness in his voice and she put her silence to it like a salve. Poor Mick, poor Mick, and he would have been angry if she'd voiced what she felt. But she had watched him trying to put himself together again, sore piece by piece. He dreamed a lot. His angers were often wilful, unrelated to anything around him. Once, sitting at the fire, he had said simply, 'Ah ance shot a man that wis caught oan the wire. Ah wonder who he wis.'

Mick sat very still, a strange mood on him. He sensed himself that his anger was displaced, belonged somewhere else. But he couldn't help himself. These days his past was delivered to him piecemeal, like anonymous letters. He was caught in his own escape-hatch: the only way to survive some of his experience had been to deny it and now it would express itself in a kind of cipher. His anger grew.

'Luk at them! Big grown men. Like wee lassies playin' at peevers.'

'They're daein' nae hem, Mick.'

'Are they no'? They'd make ye sick. They'll dae onythin' but think.'

'Can ye blame them?'

'That's Gibby scored a goal. Listen tae them! Is that no' pathetic?'

'They're guid men,' Jenny said simply.

'Ach, mither. Why dae ye only see whit you want tae see?'

'Naw, son. You're maybe nearer tae daein' that than me. When Ah luk oot that windy, Ah see mair than a bunch o' boays et the coarner.'

Mick pretended to be reading again. Jenny was looking back at the fire, speaking quietly.

'Have you heard Tadger Daly singin' at the coarner oan a summer's nicht when he wis twenty-five? It woulda broke yer hert. A voice as clear as a bell. Or did ye see Deke Dorns when he wis eichteen cairryin' his wee brither hame deid fae the pits? Or Eck An'erson gi'in' his feyther a backy tae the pair hoose. Ye mind the summer ye were jist a wean? We had only Kathleen an' you. An' a hale squad o' us went up the watter fur a picnic. The boays went in the watter. Yer feyther could swim like an otter. We had a day! Talk aboot laugh. An' it wis afore Wullie Manson had the bother wi' his glands. Near invisible in his bathin'-suit. Ye coulda threidit him through a needle. They're no' jist whit they luk tae you the day.'

'Ah hope tae Goad they're no'! Can ye no' see hoo stupit they've been a' their days, mither? Lettin' themselves be tramped oan? Dae they never get fed up waitin'? Can they no' see it's got tae chinge? Fur Ah can see it. An' the quicker the better.'

'Ah hope ye're richt, son. An' Ah'm gled ye can see it. But wherever ye're goin', don't tramp oan thae men's names tae get there. For there's naewhere guid tae get tae by daein' that.'

Mick said nothing. He watched her looking at the fire and he felt utterly despondent. You couldn't change her. You couldn't argue with her. Faced with her evidence, God wouldn't have dared condemn them. But the quarrel wasn't with God.

Jenny moved restlessly in her chair. The room had become oppressive, ironing not quite finished, the pit-clothes to be laid out. Tomorrow she could face them. But tonight, as sometimes happened, she had for the moment lost her faith. She couldn't endure the demands of this room because they were final demands. This, she accepted, was as far as any of them were going. She would go on cooking and washing and scrubbing and Conn would be in the pits till he died.

They were all trapped. All they could do was wait, while the government invented the weather, visited crises on them like hurricanes, out of nowhere, never to be understood, and somebody's son took ill and another took to the drink and one husband was carried home from the pits and another took up with a fancy woman. And the best you could do was survive.

'Ah think Ah'll go doon an' see Mary fur an 'oor.'

She liked talking to Mary Erskine. Their conversations were a coven, a gentle witchcraft of involved genealogies and esoteric anecdote and endlessly repeated names, spells for placating history. She rose and pulled a shawl over her shoulders.

'If yer feyther comes in, tell 'im Ah'll no' be long.'

She went out into the dusk of the street. It was a sad night, with a sluggish wind that nudged round her as she walked. But when she reached Mary's there was a good fire going. The kettle was put on and the two of them sat down to talk.

Tam was drinking in Bailey's pub and accepting a challenge to stand on his hands on a chair. Kathleen was nursing the youngest on her knee because the children had wakened crying in an empty house before she got back. She was trying not to cry herself. Angus was walking in the main street with Buzz and looking for events. Conn was laughing in Bert Crawford's house.

Old Conn woke up and lit his pipe. He started to talk about his life with Kerr the builder. 'A fine man,' he was saying. Mick didn't answer. He was reading about Russia. He loved the power he felt in the book that rested lightly and dangerously in his hands, like a time-bomb.

# CHAPTER FIVE

J enny found herself dovering over her paper and snapped upright to show that she was, as always, wide awake. She tended to be embarrassed by how often she was doing that now and she glanced round quickly to check if anyone had noticed. She needn't have worried. Instead of being self-conscious, she became engrossed in looking at the others.

They were totally preoccupied and she saw them with that strangeness just having wakened imparts, where you're still not sure exactly where you are. They looked very strange. She remembered that Angus had only been out for an hour or so tonight. Now everybody was in. It was unusual to have everyone in the house this early in the evening, but it shouldn't have been as unusual as it looked. Jenny felt briefly like a sane person who has discovered that sanity is a lonely state.

Angus had his shirt off and was doing exercises in his vest, watching himself dully in the mirror just under the gas-mantle. Old Conn was asleep, his mouth sagging open like a cave. Mick was crouched over a book and rocking gently with it in that way he had, as if he was nursing something. Conn was staring vaguely into the fire. Tam had a little mirror on his knee and with a small pair of scissors was setting about trying to trim the hair growing out of his nose. Jenny started to smile.

'This place is like a madhoose,' she said.

But it was a pleasant one. They were all relaxed and the atmosphere was easy. It was a time for fraternising.

'Christ, Ah doot Ah've swallied a boattle o' hair-restorer,' Tam was saying. 'There's hair growin' oot o' me everywhere. Ye canny see inside ma nose. Luk. It's a' bloody overgrown.'

'Watch whit ye're daein' in there, feyther,' Angus said. 'Ye micht never be heard o'.'

'Sen' in David Livingstone,' Conn said.

Tam snittered and then said, 'Ooh, tae Christ! Ah nearly left maself withoot a nose tae luk oot o'.'

'Angus!' Mick was incredulous. 'Whit the hell are ye daein' that fur?'

'You lea'e the boay alane,' Tam said. 'He's developin' 'is brains.'

'Naw, but imagine daein' that efter a day's shift in the pit. Ye canny be richt, Angus.'

'Energy tae burn.' Angus struck a classical pose. 'How's that then? Greek God in a semmet an' drawers.'

Normal madness was quietly resumed for a time. Then Tam, angling his mirror expertly, caught a glimpse of Conn reflected in it.

'Hey, boay,' he said. 'Conn.'

'Whit?'

'When i' you gettin' a haircut? Ye're walkin' aboot there like a tree.'

'It's a' richt, Conn,' Mick said. 'He's oan the hair the nicht.'

'Aye.' Angus was timing his words to fit his exercises. 'Jist because you've decided tae wear yer noastrils shoart.'

'Naw. But that is bloody scandaleerious. Jenny. D'ye see this boay?'

'Aye. Ah see 'im. There's no' a thing wrang wi' 'im.'

'Oh, very good. Behin' every man there's a wumman richt enough. Layin' oan 'is heid wi' a backdoor brush. Ye're fine, son. Jist buy yerself a wee periscope the morra.'

Tam retired behind his nostrils. Conn suddenly stretched and stood up. He looked at his grandfather, Mick and his father and shook his head. He was bored. He watched Angus for a minute.

'A' right, then,' he said to Angus. 'Ah'll take ye oan.'

'Son,' Angus said, still watching the mirror, 'that's no' a challenge. It's a suicide threat.'

'Come oan then.'

'Ach, see, boay. Ah don't want tae brek yer mammy's hert.'

'All-in wrestlin'.'

Conn made a lunge and they closed. They scuffled about in the middle of the floor.

'Tam! Can ye no' stoap that?'

'It's these boays wi' long hair, Jenny. They've that much strength, ye see. They've goat tae get it oot.'

'Here!' Jenny said. 'Lizzie doonstairs'll think we're havin' a richt fight. Ye'll be doon oan tap o' 'er in a meenit.'

Conn and Angus tried to wrestle in whispers. Angus was forcing

Conn steadily back until Conn found himself nearly touching his father's chair.

'Christ, watch whit ye're daein' there. Ah don't want a paira shears up ma nose. Get back fae me.' Then, as they struggled away from him, 'An' watch yer gran'feyther there. If he swallies his teeth, ye'll hear a' aboot it.'

The knock at the door separated them at once. Jenny looked at the clock.

'Who could that be, Tam?'

'Ah don't ken, Jenny. But Ah ken a guid wey tae fin' oot. We'll open the door.' He was whispering. 'Come an' we wull?'

'Ach, you. Angus, you get yer shirt oan. Folk'll think it's wan o' thae nudist places. Hurry up. Wait a meenit, Conn. Get it oan! Oan ye go noo, Conn.'

Angus was still tucking in his shirt when Conn opened the door. Conn knew at once it was trouble. The man was wearing what you could tell were his good clothes. His bonnet was folded in his hand.

'Is yer feyther in, son?'

'Who is it, Conn?' Jenny was asking.

'Feyther. It's a man fur you.'

Tam blew the clipped hairs off the mirror and into the fire, rubbed his nose, and put mirror and scissors on the mantelpiece. He was whistling tunelessly below his breath as he crossed to the door.

'Yes, sur! Whit can Ah do fur ye?'

'It's ma lassie, sur. Eh. It's no' very haundy tae talk aboot it here.'

Tam's mouth came open and he stared into the man.

'Come in, sur.'

Conn shut the door. The room became very small. The man looked out of place in it. He was a tall, thin man, his face very strained and red with the cold night air. He didn't wear a coat and his suit didn't fit him well. The atmosphere of warmth and pleasantness was like an affront to him. He and the room didn't get on together and just by standing in it, he made the place seem colder. It was very quiet.

Old Conn gulped himself awake. Jenny put her hand on his knee to signal him that something was happening. Old Conn stared round at them.

'Well, sur,' Tam said. 'Whit's a' this aboot?'

'Ask yer boay there. He kens.'

He was looking at Angus. Just the two of them facing each other expressed an injustice, the man worn and worried, and Angus burnished with his exertions, looking callous with health. Like a confession, Angus looked down at his hands and rubbed them together.

'Whit does he mean, Angus?'

'He kens whit Ah mean. Don't bloody well worry aboot it. The bloody no-user.'

'Here, here, sur.' Tam's voice was quiet. 'Ye look like a worrit man. Ye've maybe guid reason. But don't get strong-airmed in ma hoose. Or ye'll be noddin' tae the pavement kinna quick. Ah'm askin' you, Angus. Whit's this aboot?'

'Ah'm no shair who the fella is,' Angus said.

'Naw, but ye were bloody shair who ma dochter wis. Ye kent her weel enough. Sarah Davidson. Too bloody weel.'

'Dae ye ken this lassie, Angus?'

'Aye, Ah dae.'

'She's in the family wey then,' the man said. 'She's greetin' 'er hert oot there in the hoose. An' her mither alang wi' 'er.'

'Oh my Goad,' Jenny said. It was a worry she had always dreaded with her own daughter and she understood what it meant.

'It's you that made 'er that wey.'

'Wis it?' Tam was asking.

'It coulda been.'

'Whit's that supposed tae mean?' The man took a step towards him.

Humility had never been a natural role for Angus and, seeing the man's threatening stance, his attitude of withdrawal fell off him like a cloak. He straightened up, his eyes widening as he watched the man.

'Ah've a dampt guid mind tae . . .' The man raised his arm, back-handed.

'Uh-huh,' Angus said. 'That wid be a guid wey tae hiv a daith in the family an' a'.'

'Hey, you.' Tam was pointing at Angus. 'Talk that wey tae this man an Ah'll pit yer heid oot through that fuckin' windy.'

'Fur Goad's sake!' Jenny stood up. 'There's a pair lassie expectin' in that hoose. She'll be near oot 'er wits. Noo wid ye stoap shapin' up like bantam coacks. Whit's tae be done?'

'Ye're richt, missus,' the man said. 'That's whit Ah want tae ken. That's a dacent lassie Ah've goat doon there. A' her days she's been dacent. She's no' some kinna tail, ye know.'

'Calm yerself, sur,' Tam said. 'There's only wan thing tae be done. He'll mairry 'er.'

The silence grew round Angus. Conn found it remarkable how Angus was able to withstand the pressure of that quietness without flinching. He gazed at the floor. It was a telling moment, one of those times when a privately shaped resolve first comes under the heat of other people's disapproval and either collapses in the glaze or survives to harden.

'Ye'll be mairryin' the wee lassie, Angus?' Jenny asked.

Angus was testing. When he was satisfied, he spoke. 'Naw,' he said simply. 'Ah'm no' exactly shair. But Ah don't think sae.'

He looked up at the man and it was the man who looked away, shaking his head.

'Oh Jesus Christ,' he said. 'Oh Jesus Christ.'

'Ah'll be peyin' fur it, of coorse,' Angus added.

'Peyin'! Whit? Coal an' a bob or two a week? Whit dae ye think ma lassie is? Some kinna credit hoor?'

'Well, that's the wey it is, Ah think,' Angus said. 'Ah can see Sarah aboot it again if ye want.'

'By Christ, ye'll no'. Ah widny pit 'er through that. Ah don't want 'er contaminatit. Ya bloody no-user!'

Tam stood wincing at a charge he couldn't refute.

'Sur,' he said. 'This thing isny feenished. If ye let me talk tae 'im.'

'Save yer braith, sur. Ah widny want that fur a son-in-law. We'll manage some wey.'

'Wait, Mr Davidson,' Jenny called, but he was already going out and she was left to say to the open door, 'My Goad, that pair wee lassie. Whit she must be goin' through this nicht.'

Tam crossed and closed the door. He came back slowly into the room. Angus hadn't moved, felt himself at bay against his father. He understood the wound constraint with which his father moved. What followed might very well be physical. He made a decision—he wasn't going to let his father strike him. There was no way he was going to take that without hitting back. He felt a tremor of almost elated nervousness. He couldn't believe that they could really come to blows and, in the instant of even thinking about it, he desperately didn't want it to happen. But in this mood it was his father who made the possibilities, and you couldn't calculate them. Angus had seen him demolish a man for much less than this.

'Tam!' Jenny said.

But the force Tam had generated made everybody else just an onlooker. Angus accurately read the pallor in his father's face. It was the containment of a mounting rage.

'Noo you explain this tae us,' Tam said quietly.

'Hoo dae ye mean?'

'Noo you explain this tae us,' Tam said quietly. 'Fur there must be somethin' here Ah don't unnerstaun'. Ye goat this lassie in the family wey. Is that correct?'

'Ah suppose Ah did.'

'Dear Goad,' Jenny sighed.

'Whit dae ye mean ye suppose?'

'She an' me. Ye ken whit Ah mean.'

'Oh aye. Ah ken whit ye mean.' Tam hesitated. 'Is it because ye think she micht no' hae been quite the thing? Wi' ither folk like.'

Tam was looking for a way out of his own anger. It took Angus a moment to understand what he meant. When he did, he was too honest to take that escape.

'Aw naw,' he said. 'Ah hivny seen 'er fur a while. An' it's poassible. But Ah don't believe it fur a second. She's no' like that.'

'Then why wid ye no' be goin' tae mairry 'er?'

'Feyther. Ah don't particularly want tae mairry 'er.'

'Too fuckin' late!' Tam bellowed. 'Too fuckin' late. Ye shoulda thocht o' that before ye did whit ye did.'

'We didny fill in forms, feyther.'

'Don't you be smert wi' me, boay. Fur Ah canny guarantee no' tae kick your ribs in.'

Angus breathed noisily.

'Naw, but Ah can maybe guarantee it fur ye,' he said.

Conn threw himself on to his father, catching him more or less round the shoulders. The force of his father's movement swung Conn off the floor so that his feet hit Angus about the waist, knocking him to the side.

'Don't dae it, feyther!' Conn was shouting. 'Don't dae it!'

'Fur Goad's sake, Tam! Whit's happenin' in this hoose?'

Conn realised it was his mother's voice, though it wasn't an easy thing to realise. It came to him always receding, like something heard from a train. He bucked on the baffled jerk of his father's rage. Angus was on one knee. He jumped to his feet. His eyes were flaring. Mick was instantly between them.

'Feyther!' he screamed, as if Tam was a long way away. 'Whit are ye daein'?'

Over Conn's shoulder Tam was pleading with them to release him from his anger, to *show* him how he couldn't kill his son. Angus was waiting, breathing as if his lungs were injured.

'Whit hiv we reared here, Jenny?' Tam was shouting. 'Whit hiv we reared in this hoose? Tell me that. He cares fur nothin'! A man comes in wi' his hert in his haun an' he disny bat an e'e. He sells his mates fur fuckin' pennies. An' he doesny care! Ye canny leeve an' no care. Ya bastard! Can ye no' see that? Whit dae ye think that lassie is? Your fuckin' toay? Ye're gonny lea'e her tae luk efter your wean the rest o' 'er life? Whit'll she dae? This isny fuckin' Mayfair, ye know. That's her fur the rest o' 'er days. Naw, naw. She cairries yer wean, ye mairry 'er. There's nothin' else. Who the hell dae ye think you are, no' tae respect ither folk? Ye care, boay, or ye're nothin'. You're deid, son. You're fuckin' deid. They've jist furgoatten tae bury ye.'

The following silence was broken only by Jenny's sighs. Conn felt his father subside.

'Lea'e me alane, son,' Tam said, pushing him away. He pointed at Angus. 'You've got a choice, son. You mairry that lassie or you can get oot this hoose. The fuckin' midden-men can collect ye.'

'Tam, Tam,' Jenny said. 'Ye canny say that.'

'Ah've jist said it, Jenny. An' Ah mean it.'

'Feyther,' Mick said. 'Ye're wrang. Ye're completely wrang.'

'He's richt, Ah suppose?'

'Maybe he's no'. But he's a wee bit less wrang than you are. Ye canny dae that. Whit dis that lassie want wi' a man that disny want her? Whit's the *sense* in whit ye're daein'.'

'Ah'll tell ye the sense,' Tam said. 'We walk a nerra line. Ah ken hoo nerra it is. Ah've walked it a' ma days. Us an' folk like us hiv goat the nearest thing tae nothin' in this world. A' that filters doon tae us is shite. We leeve in the sewers o' ither bastards' comfort. The only thing we've goat is wan anither. That's why ye never sell yer mates. Because there's nothin' left tae buy wi' whit ye get. That's why ye respect yer weemenkind. Because whit we make oorselves is whit we are. Because if ye don't, ye're provin' their case. Because the bastards don't believe we're folk! They think we're somethin' . . . less than that. Well, Ah ken whit Ah believe. It's only us that can show whit folk are. Whit dae they ken aboot it? Son, it's easy tae be guid oan a fu' belly. It's when a man's goat two bites an' wan o' them he'll share, ye ken whit he's made o'. Maist o' them were boarn blin'. Well, we areny, son. We canny afford tae be blin'. Listen. In ony country in the world, who are the only folk that ken whit it's like tae leeve in that country? The folk at the boattom. The rest can a' kid themselves oan. They can afford to hiv fancy ideas. We canny, son. We loass the wan idea o' who we are, we're deid. We're wan anither. Tae survive, we'll respect wan anither. When the time comes, we'll a' move forward thegither, or nut at all. That's whit Ah've goat against you, boay.' He pointed at Angus. 'You're a fuckin' deserter. Ah don't harbour deserters. Ye're wi' the rest o' us or ye go elsebit.'

Angus had put his jacket on.

'Ye'll no' hiv tae worry aboot it,' he said. 'Is it a' richt if Ah spend the wan mair nicht here, mither? Ah'll no' can get a place tae the morra.'

'Oh, Goad preserve us,' Jenny said. 'Whit a thing fur a boay tae ask his mither. Ye can stey the nicht an' every nicht, son.'

'Naw. Ah canny dae that. Ah jist want the wan nicht, if that's a' right.'

'Ye can stey the nicht,' Tam said. 'Ah wid dae as much fur a dug.'

Angus walked out. He walked in an utter numbness. His father had defined for him the loneliness he had long been moving towards, given it to him like a map. He paced it out. Later, he would have to work out what he felt about it.

# CHAPTER SIX

The voice came at Conn before he knew where it was coming
from.

'Hey, you! Whaur i' ye gaun?'

He had to look round for a moment before he located the wooden
hatch that had opened in the glass and the thin face that looked out
like a greyhound with malnutrition.

'Me? Ah'm jist gaun through here.'

'Come 'ere, you.'

Conn walked over.

'It coasts money tae get in here. Noo hoo long wull ye be wantin'
tae stey?'

'As shoart a bluidy time as poassible,' Conn said. 'Ah'm nearly
suffocatit already. If ye cut up the smell in here, ye could build hooses
wi' it.'

The instantaneousness of his own anger surprised Conn. He was
usually much more awkward at coping with strange situations. The
past few weeks must have aged him.

'A bloody smert boay, eh,' the man said. 'Well, ye canny go in.'

'Listen, eejit,' Conn said. 'Ma brither's in yer doss-hoose. Angus
Docherty.' He saw the name register. 'Ah'm goin' in tae see 'im. If
ye're gonny get the fire-brigade, get them noo.'

As he walked away, he heard the man say, 'Cheeky bugger,' and
slam the hatch shut.

The light in the dormitory was dull, a kind of second-hand daylight,
as if it tarnished by coming into touch with the furnishings. Conn
made out Angus at the far end of the right-hand row, lying on his bed
and smoking. Angus flexed open his right hand by way of greeting.

There was a man half-way down the row, kneeling between beds and polishing his boots. He had the rags spread on the floor around him and as Conn passed, his foot scuffed one of them.

'Watch whaur ye're walkin', hawkheid!' the man snarled.

Conn stopped. But before he could answer, Angus's voice was there.

'Hey, you. If ye don't want yer bits roon' yer neck fur a grauvit, watch whit ye're sayin'.'

'Ho-ho. It's a freen' o' yours, big Gus. Ah never kent, Gus. Ah never kent.' He winked elaborately at Conn. 'Pass, friend. Ha-ha!'

On the way towards Angus, Conn passed a man on the other side lying reading a comic. Otherwise, the place was empty.

'Home, sweet home,' Conn said and sat on Angus's bed.

'Ye get used tae it ance ye're deid,' Angus said. 'Want a fag?'

He threw him the packet. Conn took one out and lit it. Giving the packet back, he noticed how garishly out of place Angus was here. He was scrubbed to a shine and all his clothes were clean.

'Ah've goat ye the place then, Angus, if ye want it.'

'Wi' that Mrs Meldrum? Whit does it luk like?'

'Aw, it's nice. Ye'll hiv the wan room, like. An' she's goat a sink.'

'His she? Ye're shair she's a complete stranger?'

'Aye. Ah didny ken 'er fae Eve. She's a gey auld wumman. Jist leeves hersel'.'

'That'll be fair enough.'

'Christ, Angus, this is terrible in here. If ma mither kent ye were here, she'd go aff 'er heid.'

'Ye hivny tellt 'er, hiv ye?'

'Don't be daft.'

'Naw. Because Ah tellt 'er Ah wis in wi' Buzz Crawley's mither.'

'Why did ye no' go there?'

'Ah don't want ony favours. That's why Ah had tae go wi' somebody that's a stranger.'

Conn smoked, watching Angus sprawled there in utter ease. He was in complete contradiction to the place around him, seemed to have found himself where Conn couldn't believe there was anything to find. Conn couldn't understand it. He needed to probe.

'Christ, whit a place, Angus!' he started again. 'Ah mean, there's no' onythin left aboot even. Ken whit Ah mean. Belongin' tae onybody. It's as if naebody leeved here.'

'Ye daurny lea'e things aboot,' Angus said. 'They wid mooch them. Mooch everythin' here. Naw,' he added as Conn started to laugh. 'Richt enough. They've goat tae nail doon the coabwebs. There's a place whaur ye can get things loacked up. Though Ah don't trust the bugger that loacks them. Naw, naw. Ye canny sleep too heavy in here. They'd mooch yer belly-button.'

Feeling Angus opening out, Conn encouraged him further.

'Whit did ye come here fur, though? Wur ye jist hopin' ma feyther wid hear aboot it an' get annoyed?'

'That's the least o' ma worries. Naw. Ah wisny in ony hurry tae get oot o' here. Ah've been studyin' it. Sortin' maself oot. It's like Mick wi' his books. This has been ma book, Conn. These are the kinna folk ma feyther's aye oan aboot. The folk at the boattom. Well, this is the boattom. Tae get ony lower than this, ye'd hiv tae burrow. An' ye should see them. See that bloke wi' the coamic. Pathetic wee man. Dae onythin' fur a drink. Eat yer shite fur a drink, he wid. See that bugger polishin' the bits. A nothin'. Ye'd need a microscope tae fin' his hert. But gi'e 'im the chance an' he'd stamp ye intae the grund. The folk at the boattom are only there because they canny be onywhere else. Did ye see the yin at the wee hatch?'

'Aye,' Conn said. 'He wis nigglin' right away.'

'Of coorse, he wis. Hoo's that fur a welcome mat? Sets the tone o' the place right away. He's goat nothin' an' he's lookin' fur folk wi' less so that he can screw them tae it hurts. Ah've watched them in here, Conn. An' they're a' like that. Maybe ma feyther wis richt. Ye can see the truth at the boattom. Ah've seen it. Dug eat dug. They'd take the hairs oot yer erse if they thocht they could sell them fur brushes.'

Angus stubbed his cigarette out in a saucer.

'Ah don't ken,' Conn said. 'You seem tae be survivin' a' richt.'

'Aye, but Ah ken who Ah am. An' whit Ah've goat tae dae. They don't interfere wi' me. Ah'm a separate state. They'd get the hob-nailed bit in the teeth if they did. An' they ken it.'

Conn finished his cigarette and put it out in the saucer. Angus swung round off the bed. He stood up and stretched, pulled on his jacket.

'Come oan,' he said. 'Ah'll get up tae ma digs.'

'Ye want tae see whit they're like?'

'Naw. Ah'll jist get ma stuff the noo an' move in the day. Sunday's a guid day fur movin' intae a new place.'

'But ye better check it first.'

'Naw. Ah'm feenished wi' this place. Ah only steyed in it this long tae fix in ma mind whit it's like. In case Ah wis ever tempted tae get saft. But Ah'll no' forget it noo. An' Ah'll never be back.' He looked round it, smiling. 'Ah've passed ma exams.'

On the way out, Angus stopped beside the man with the boots. The man was giving them a final going-over with a duster. The way he was drawing it out gave the impression that this was his idea of passing a pleasant Sunday. He nodded brightly to Angus.

'Don't poalish too hard, noo,' Angus said. 'Ye micht see yer face in them.'

At the hatch Angus rattled the wood with his fingers. The head poked out of its kennel.

'Ah'm collectin' ma gear,' Angus said.

'Ye'll need tae pey fur the nicht then.'

'Why?'

''Cause yer bed's been booked. Ah thocht ye were steyin'. Ah coulda been turnin' awa' bookin's fur a' you ken.'

'Whit bookin's? Jesus Christ. Ye've goat tae Shanghai folk tae get them in here.'

'It disny maitter, Gus. The rules is the rules. We hiv tae be inform't before nine o'cloack. Or ye're due the money fur the next nicht.'

Angus paid him off. His stuff was in one suitcase and a sack. Angus checked the stuff in the sack and gave it to Conn. It felt as if it was mainly two pairs of boots. Angus put his hand in the hatch as the man tried to shut it.

'Jist wan thing,' he said. 'Ah hear when Aul' Fiddler left, his parcel wis wee'er than when he came in. Ah'll be checkin' this case et ma digs. Ah want you tae tell me aboot it the noo.'

'Nut a body's been near it, Gus. Untouched by human haun.'

'Pray tae be honest,' Gus said and slid the hatch.

He was laughing as they came out into the street. They were headed towards the Netherton.

'Ach, it doesny maitter too much whit this place is like onywey. Ah'll no' be in it that long.'

He was waiting for Conn to ask.

'Why will ye no'?'

'Because Ah'm gonny get mairrit.'

Conn looked at him. Angus was walking briskly, looking around him, his case tucked under his arm like a cardboard box.

'Ye didnt tell ony o' us that.'

'Naebody asked me, did they?'

'When is this?'

'Oh, a wee while yit. There's nae hurry. This time.' And he was laughing again.

'Who's the lassie?'

'Ah don' think ye ken 'er. Annie she's ca'ed. She comes fae Irvine. She's a' richt. She isny hauf. Ye'll see 'er at the waddin'. If no' before.'

Conn was still recovering when Angus stopped at the corner of the street.

'This is the street?'

'Aye,' Conn said vaguely.

'An' it's number seeventeen.'

'Aye.'

'Richt, Ah'll take that.'

He took the sack from Conn.

'Thanks fur yer help then, Conn. Ah'll be seein' ye efter.'

Conn started to wave and found he was waving at Angus's back. There was nothing else that Angus wanted to say.

# CHAPTER SEVEN

'Pathetic!' Jack said, throwing down the paper. 'That's the miners goin' back fur the same money they were gettin' before the lock-oot. Eleeven weeks they've been oot. Fur nothin'. They huvny as mony brains as gi'e them a sair heid, thae miners.'

He said it to the room, as if Kathleen were an eavesdropper. He rose and stretched.

'Whit will yer auld man say tae that then?'

Working with the iron, Kathleen didn't look up.

'The great Tam, eh. Eleeven weeks ago he wis sayin' they were gonny dae it this time.' He gave a grotesque parody of Tam's voice. 'We're gonny make it coont this time.' He laughed disproportionately. 'It's always the next time wi' him, intit? He's daft enough tae believe in Santa Claus. Ah wonder whit his excuse'll be this time. Ah'd like tae hear it.'

Kathleen knew she mustn't answer. If she answered, she would lose her temper, and if she lost her temper, he would strike her. She bore it, knowing he would be out of the house soon. He was putting on his shoes. She wondered if it was guilt that made him like to exit on a quarrel, to put himself in the role of a man righteously storming out of a house in which he could get no peace.

'He's supposed tae be a hard man, tae. He's jist a coomie. Like big Gus. Muscle fae the neck up.'

She considered what skill enabled him to choose the thing that most denied him and attack it. For in a way he was right to be against her father. It was a question of survival. If there had been no Tam

Docherties, Jack Daly would never have needed to face what he'd become. He went on and she gave him nothing but silence, letting his words drip on her thoughts like water torture.

'They divert me, these folk that are a' worrit aboot the workin' classes. Like yer feyther. Ah mean, whit guid his it done 'im? He's jist a wee nothin' like onybody else. Whit has he achieved wi' it a'? He's right back where he stertit. Runnin' oan the spot. That's whit he's been daein' a' his life. Pair wee bugger.'

He had his jacket on. He was waiting for her to respond. He grew tired of waiting.

'The next time ye're up at yer mammy's, ask 'im whit his excuse is this time. Will ye ask 'im? Will ye? Whit's his excuse?'

Her face clenched and her body buckled at the slamming of the door. She waited, opened her eyes. She had expected to weep but no tears came. There was nothing to cry about in what Jack had said. That was the saddest thing. She wondered if perhaps she had no tears left. People had to connect with you before they moved you. Their marriage was monologues set in silence.

She damped the collar of Alec's good shirt, sprinkling water from the bowl beside her, ironed the cloth meticulously. She buried her thoughts in the mound of washing beside her, pressing out seams, flattening cuffs. So she had no idea how long it was before the knock came at the door.

She was surprised. She crossed and opened the door and was more surprised. He never came. But he was there, looking almost apologetic and suddenly old.

'Feyther. Come in.'

'Hullo, hen.'

He took off his bonnet and walked into the room. Her first thought was that something had happened to her mother. But he crossed to the window and she knew at once that he didn't know why he was here either.

'Whaur i' the wee yins?' he asked.

'They're oot playin'.'

'Aye. So they should be. It's a guid nicht.'

He threw the bonnet on a chair, turning into the room.

'Hoo are ye, hen?'

'Ah'm fine, feyther, Ah'm fine.'

'Ken, Ah wis jist oot walkin'. There. An' Ah thocht. Oor Kathleen. Ah'll go up an' see her. An' Ah came up.'

'Ah'm gled ye did, feyther.'

She went back to her ironing.

'An' ye're a' richt, then?'

'Ah'm fine, feyther. Ah'm fine.'

She knew instinctively that she mustn't tell him the truth. She couldn't worry him. He looked so vulnerable, so lost, as if the world was a place he had never seen.

'Ah see ye're gaun back then,' she said.

He had lit a cigarette and turned towards the window again. He spoke with his back to her.

'Aye. We're gaun back.'

She understood from his voice that she had touched a wound.

'Funny thing. Ah've been in mair strikes than Ah can coont. Ah've argied an' focht wi' pit managers till Ah wis blue in the face. An' Ah think Ah'm worse aff than when Ah stertit.' He blew a jet of air down his nostrils, deprecating himself. 'This is the feenish.'

She watched his back, aware with sudden panic of what the failure of the lockout meant to him. He had no more hope.

'Ach, ye've aye managed before, feyther.'

'Before wis before, hen. Och, Ah'll manage. But it's no' goin' tae happen. Whit Ah thocht could happen. Funny thing. Ah'm fifty-three. An' Ah micht as weel be ninety. Fur Ah'm by.'

She remembered Jack's last question going out. That was its answer. Her father had no excuse. He accepted Jack's definition of himself. The unfairness of it hurt her terribly. She remembered what he had been like, how much he had meant to all of them, how long he had survived complete and unbreakable, it seemed. Standing etched against the window, he seemed to her simply a marvellous man, and no one had the right to make him believe in his failure. She wanted to tell him but there was nothing she could say.

She stood just loving him and understanding at last why he had come. He had always needed to let them see him as he was. He had come to tell her who he was now. And she didn't believe him. He was making a kind of apology and there was nothing he should apologise for.

'Ach well,' he said, turning from the window. 'Ah'll hiv a dram, Ah think.'

She watched him helplessly as he lifted his bonnet and felt with his left hand in his pocket.

'Here, hen,' he said, and put two shilling pieces on the mantelpiece. 'Get the weans something wi' that.'

'Naw. There's nae need fur that, feyther.'

'Take it. Ah'd jist drink it onywey.'

He touched her arm gently on the way out, smiling and saying, 'Ye're a guid lassie, Kathleen. Ah'm a wee bit kinna prood o' ma dochter.'

She lifted the two shilling pieces from the mantelpiece as if to put them away, but instead stood clutching them like a talisman.

It was then she cried.

# CHAPTER EIGHT

The wedding went well, it was generally agreed. At various points in the evening, the older women informed one another of the fact with some relief, like experienced nurses checking the temperature of a worrying patient. They knew the symptoms of deterioration to look for: the failure of the two sides to mix, withdrawal of the men to the bar, general paralysis round about half past nine. All crises were averted.

Conn took some of the credit. It was the first wedding he had been at since he started going to the dancing. He was old enough to participate fully and young enough to have everybody's indulgence. He drank beer. He talked with the men. He chatted up every partner, old and young. He abducted elderly women from their groups, among raucous comments of 'Watch that yin' and 'Ah'll tell yer man.' He suggested elopement to Mrs Daly. He elicited sixteen-year-old giggles from fifty-eight-year-old Mrs Andrews. He made a date with a girl he had never seen before, one of the other side, and wondered how he was supposed to travel fifteen miles to meet her.

It became like an unofficial coming-out party for him. He was celebrating being a man, and everybody was invited—even Angus, he realised with something like surprise when his brother came up to him at the end of a dance, holding two glasses of beer. Immediately, a lot of things he had noticed during the evening without being aware he was noticing them came together in Conn's head. The ambiguity of his mother's expression, as if only half of her was at the wedding and the other half was at a wake. Mick giving her much of his attention. A stranger, obviously a relative of Annie, saying, as Conn danced past, 'Is the feyther deid then?' Together, they forced Conn to face the aspect of the wedding from which he had been hiding in movement.

'Here,' Angus said. 'Anchor yerself tae that an' hiv a rest.'

Conn took the glass and sipped, fingering sweat from his eyebrows.

'Ye better come through here a meenit an' cool aff.'

They picked their way among the scatter of people beached haphazardly on their own exhaustion. Tendrils of conversation caught at them as they passed. 'There's that auld mairrit man.' 'Whit shift are ye oan the morra, Gus?' Angus led the way into the small room at the end of the hall. It wasn't lit but with the door open it turned down the volume of light in the dancehall to a pleasant gentleness. Coats and jackets hung round the walls. A table and some stacked chairs were the only furniture. Conn sat on the table, drinking. Seen from the outside, the hall became a fact.

'Hey,' Conn said. 'Ye're mairrit. Whit does it feel like?'

'Ah'll tell ye the morra.'

Conn watched another young man ask the girl he had dated to dance. He couldn't remember her name.

'Yer wee hoose is a' right, onywey,' he said. 'Ye're a' right there.'

'That's no' a',' Angus said. 'Look at this.'

He reached into his hip pocket and pulled out a bundle of notes, spreading them with his thumb, like a deck of cards. It was more money than Conn had ever seen. There must have been about twenty pounds, he thought.

'Where did ye get that?'

'Ah'm a workin' man.'

'Jesus. Ye must be mair than wan workin' man tae have that kinna money.'

The joke was automatic, grew out of the words, but having said it, Conn found that he had stumbled reluctantly on to a possibility. Angus's smile wasn't reassuring.

'Does a' yer squad make that kinna money?'

'They a' make whit they earn,' Angus said. 'An' there's plenty mair yet. Listen. If ye ever fancy makin' some real money, jist let me ken. A special openin' fur ye. Only brithers need apply.'

They looked across and each surprised the same thought in the other. Neither knew which of them it came from first, but the money took on the significance of a bribe, and Angus put it back in his pocket. Conn looked away. He saw Kathleen and Jack dancing the two-step. They looked happy.

'Whit dae ye make o' him then?' Angus said.

'Who?'

'Come oan. The place is hauf empty withoot 'im.'

Conn drank to avoid talking.

'It's no' believable, is it? Why did he no' come? Ah kept thinkin' he was bound tae show up. Whit dae ye think o' that?'

'Ye ken hoo he is.'

'Aye. Tadger came,' Angus said, watching him pilot the stately bulk of Mrs Daly round the floor. Angus suddenly laughed. 'Luk at 'im. He's like a bit that fell aff her. But ma feyther couldny come.'

'Don't let it worry ye, Angus.'

'Who's worried?' Angus said. 'RIP.'

Conn looked at him and saw that he meant it. It was then that Conn realised how short he himself still was of being a man. What he had been doing during the evening was just a boy's game. Being a man didn't mean drinking beer and sharing jokes and pattering girls. It meant being where Angus was. He sat beside Conn now on the table, taking a sip of beer, his eyes quietly reflecting on what was happening in the hall. His carefully laundered white shirt had wilted in the heat, fusing on to his skin, so that it was like a peeling disguise for the hardness of his body. Conn saw his preoccupation as more than temporary. It seemed to Conn he had always had that quality about him of moving along private corridors, an area whose counterpart Conn felt he hadn't yet discovered in himself. You could always shout but chances were he wouldn't hear you, whereas Conn heard every incidental noise and was distracted by it. Where Angus found the decision to quietly bury a living father baffled Conn and frightened him.

'He wid dae the same fur me,' Angus said. 'An' Ah'm gled. Ah'm daein' whit Ah hiv tae dae. Let him dae the same. Poor bugger. Maybe he's richt to haud it against me the wey he does. Ah used tae wonder whit the fuss wis aboot. Because Ah punched a few faces. An' lifted up a few skirts. An' made some extra bob. But he kent there wis mair tae it than that. Ah'll gi'e him that. He kent whit it wis daein' before Ah did. Ye ken whit bothered ma feyther? Ah wisny punchin' the right faces. Ah didny lift up skirts with proper respect. See, ye ken whit Ah've come tae think? Ma feyther still believes in some kinna holiness. At least he's tryin' tae. He's no' a Catholic, all richt. An' Christ knows whit he believes. But he believes it strong. An' whit Ah did wis Ah shat in his wee church. An' he's havin' tae live wi' the smell. Good luck tae 'im. Because Ah agree wi' him on wan thing. Ah'm no' playin' fur his team. An' whit he kens is his team's gonny lose. An' Ah'm gonny win. Ah've done no' bad already. Ah'm still comin' oan. Ah ken who's side Ah'm on. Whit aboot you?'

Conn didn't answer. Angus had been speaking compulsively but not because he needed reassurance, rather because he was so sure of himself that he needed to tell somebody else. He was like a pretender so certain of his own assumption of power that he checks his support not to see if he'll succeed but just to know who his friends are when he does. Having come back from some kind of exile of his own, he had learned that he could do without anybody except himself. Looking at him sitting easily there, Conn felt him dangerous, just because you didn't know which way he might move. Whatever he did would be according to his own promptings and not foreseeable. You couldn't make too many assumptions about Angus.

Conn remembered something that had happened when they were both boys. One of the houses on Wullie Mair's brae attracted a group of them once when they were going up the country, because the door of the back-garden had a sign saying 'Beware of the Dog'. They had knocked at the door of the house. Having made sure nobody was in, they climbed on to the wall of the garden and there it was, an Alsatian attached to its kennel by a chain. Two or three of them ventured into the garden and left again quickly. Angus stayed. Determining the length of the chain, he moved in and out of range, teasing and testing, for so long that the others got tired of watching and left, including Conn. When he rejoined them up the road, the sleeve of his jersey was torn but he seemed satisfied. Conn thought that in a way he hadn't changed. He was still looking for his limits.

Angus brought out a packet of cigarettes and they lit up. Smoking so soon after his exertion made Conn cough.

'Look at them,' Angus said.

In the hall they were doing the Gay Gordons. They were all ages, advancing and receding, polkaing past in frantic procession; middle-aged women moving their bosoms around like ponderous pieces of furniture; Tadger sweating harder than he did on a shift; somebody's children who hadn't yet fallen asleep hammily mocking the dance since they couldn't do it; an old couple making a minuet of it; a young boy and girl trying to copy the steps of those nearest them. The fiddlers sounded as if they were going mad. Most of the dancers' eyes had a look of glazed acquiescence.

'Ah mean Ah like them,' Angus went on. 'Hoo could ye no'? They're great, aren't they? But Christ. That's whit they've been daein' a' their lives. Dancin' tae whitever tune gets played. Whit's ma feyther waitin' fur? They're no' gonny chinge. They're a' too guid a' losers. That's whit they're best at. They've hud that much practice. Well, no' me. Ye ken a funny thing? There's no' wan body in that hall, or ootside it that Ah ken o', that Ah don't think Ah could cope wi'. Ah don't ken anything that'll stoap me fae daein' whit Ah'm gonny dae. Frem noo on, it's just Annie an' me. An' we're gonny make oot.'

'That's mair than a wee bit wild,' Conn said.

'Who's arguin'?'

Angus looked at him and smiled.

'Hard times, Conn,' he said. 'Harder times aheid. You stey among them, ye micht jist get buried in the boadies.'

As the dance came to an end in the hall, the small, half-darkened room he and Angus were in seemed to Conn like a threat the others were unaware of. He felt as if Angus had involved him in a conspiracy from which people like Tadger, mopping his face with a handkerchief and laughing, were excluded. They all looked somehow terribly vulnerable, the three young men pretending to hold one another up, the girl repinning a fallen strand of hair, Mrs Daly easing herself into a seat beside his mother and having a flushing, Mick reaching under his chair for his glass of beer. He thought of a phrase his mother used a lot: God save us. Who else? He sensed himself a part of their openness. For beside Angus, Conn seemed to himself to be vague and ineffectual, wanting to go in five different ways at once.

They announced the 'Drops O' Brandy.' A voice at the door of the small room said, 'There, he's there!' Buzz Crawley appeared in the doorway, pulling a partner. Rab Lawson and his girl-friend were there too.

'Come oan, come oan,' Buzz Crawley said. 'This is some time tae be gettin' fou. Whit are ye? Feart? Annie's oot here waitin' fur ye.'

'We're gonna hiv the best set in the hall,' Rab said.

Angus laughed, finished his beer, punched Conn's shoulder, and went out. As Conn followed them, he noticed that the girl whose hand Buzz was holding was the one he had dated. She gave him a look that said 'What could I do?' Conn winked and leaned against the doorway while Buzz and Rab pretended to be pulling Angus across the dance-floor. Buzz was singing, 'Here comes the groom.' Rab shouted, 'We found 'im, Annie. He wis hidin'.'

Conn stayed where he was when others signalled him to join their set. He raised his almost empty glass of beer as an excuse. The real reason was that, after talking to Angus, he felt as if he'd only just arrived at the wedding. When the music started up, he watched them dance. Angus and Annie were leading off in their set. People in the other sets were looking across at them, smiling and clapping in time to the music. Angus spun Annie in his own vortex, volleying laughter all around him. The quickening tempo drew Conn's mood after it. The music, the stamping feet, the whirling bodies, the clapping hands, the set, smiling faces of the ones sitting around oppressed him. He thought confusedly that what was happening wasn't what seemed to be happening.

# CHAPTER NINE

'Where is he the nicht then, mither?'

Conn slung his jacket over a chair, an echo of his father.

'Och, he jist went oot fur a daun'er, son,' his mother said, very casual, unconcerned.

'A mystery tour tae the nearest pub,' Mick added.

Conn sat down in his father's chair and lit a cigarette with a piece of paper at the fire. It was no use offering Mick a cigarette. He had given up smoking—one of those exercises he liked to subject his will-power to. What was he training for?

Conn looked at his mother. She was darning socks. She was darning bloody socks. It injured his eyes just to look at her. If it wasn't socks, it was washing. If it wasn't washing it was moleskins. If it wasn't moleskins it was making food. When she died, she shouldn't have a headstone. She should have a pyramid of washing two miles high. Let the bastards know what her life was like. And where was he? Out swallowing glasses of painkiller. He would come in numb.

'Where've ye been yersel', son?'

'Knockin' aboot. We saw the Charlie Chaplin. It wis great.'

'He's a funny wee man.'

'Aye.'

Mick hadn't once looked up from his book.

'Pit the soacks doon an' hiv a blether, mither,' Conn said.

'Ah can talk fine the wey Ah am, son. It's goat tae be done.'

Christ, lay them down. He could hardly remember her without something in her hands. Perhaps she was frightened to look at the world except round the edge of a chore.

'Whit's the book, then?'
'*The Ragged Trousered Philanthropists.*'
'The whit?'
Mick said nothing.
'Whit's it aboot?'
'Us.'

Conn wasn't in the mood for trying to crack the code Mick liked to talk in these days. He felt annoyed at his mother and Mick. His coming-in hadn't shifted them out of their positions for a second, as if they knew exactly who he was. Yesterday evening, he'd been with a girl who thought he was marvellous. Tonight, after the pictures, he'd had an argument with Mickey Ray that was coming to fists until Mickey had reneged. He felt important. It was a good feeling, as if wherever he threw his cap was where it would lie, and nobody dare shift it. He felt pity for his mother patching her life together day by day, Mick hiding in his books. Generously, he wanted to talk to them.

'See that picture the nicht? Charlie's in a ship, ken? An' he's supposed tae be makin' the grub . . .'

The footsteps on the stairs were his father's. Conn saw how the sound passed like a pain across his mother's face. Mick cracked the spine of his book against his leg.

'But the ship sterts rockin' . . .'

His father came in and Conn knew that nobody was listening. Half of his father was still too much to ignore. He was drunk and he had more beer in his pocket.

'Good evenin' to youse all,' Tam said archly. 'An' a Happy New Week.'

His eyes never quite rested on any of them, flickered like those of a man who was watching trains go by. He took his jacket off, covered Conn's with it, put the beer on the table.

'Ah could go a drap o' soup, hen,' he was saying. 'Is there some in the poat?'

'Aye, Tam. Ah'll just fetch it.'

'Naw, ye'll nut. Ye'll sit jist where ye are, lass. Tak' yer ease.'

The irony of his generosity embarrassed them all, as if having immured her alive he should give her an armchair. But Tam made a fuss of putting the pot on the fire, unaware that he was a stranger in the house. While he busied himself, he kept throwing words about like conversation.

'Ye're there, Conn, son. Ye're there.'

'Aye.'

'Hoo are ye comin'?'

'Ah'm a' richt.'

'Ye're mair than a' richt, son. Don't forget it. Mair than a' richt. Aye, Jenny. Ye made a joab o' them, hen.'

He glanced across at Mick but said nothing to him. With a plate, a spoon, some bits of bread and a cup of beer on the table, he stood rubbing his hands.

'Who's fur some?' he asked.

'No' me, feyther.' Conn's voice was kinder than he had intended it to be. For he shared against his will the luxury of what the moment meant to his father—some hot soup, some beer, the warmth of the fire, and what was left of his family round him. That much at least he had earned.

'Mick?'

'Mick an' me's no' long feenished, Tam,' Jenny said quickly.

'Aye. Weel.'

His pleasure was diminished to a solo performance. He crossed and crouched in front of the fire, stirred at the pot with the ladle, sniffed.

'Aw, Christ!' he said slowly. 'Like a poat o' bull's bluid. Tak' yer time noo. Ah can wait.'

He stayed crouched, his eyes watery in the firelight, staring blindly into the heat.

'Ye ken whit Ah've a hellu'a notion o' daein', Jen?'

'What's that Tam?'

'Gettin' a haud o' a wee plot o' grund. A gairden plot. An' growin' things.'

'Aye. Ye could dae waur than that.'

The serious consideration his mother was able to give the suggestion amazed Conn. His father had a new idea almost every night and not one of them went beyond his mouth. She was remarkable. Where did she find the strength and the patience to go on suckling this man's stillborn dreams?

'Jist fur wurselves, like. Nothin' big. But we wid always hiv wur wee bit extra there.'

'Aye, it wid be a help.'

Tam's face relaxed as if all the planting was already done.

Mick said over his book, 'Whit wid ye grow in it? Hops?'

Conn's body contracted slightly, waiting for the reaction. But his father's face merely went very still, and stared on into the fire, as if he hadn't heard. It was his mother who lowered her head slightly, seemed to draw the hurt away from his father.

'Aye,' Tam said and ladled himself out a plate of soup.

Eating, he went on talking—about gardens, about 'gettin' oorselves pu'ed thegither', about going to Cronberry in the summer, about getting a good greyhound. At some point on every tangent, a remark of Mick's intercepted him, and Tam went off in another direction. 'Things could be worse,' Tam said. And Mick said, 'They will be.' Tam said, 'Ah could buy a guid grew,' and Mick said, 'Or take up opium.' Tam said, 'Ah've seen better coal,' and Mick said, 'There's too mony banes in it.'

The baiting became so merciless that Conn wondered why his mother didn't speak. He saw she was troubled and thought she was silent because for her to speak would force Tam to admit what was happening, and perhaps he couldn't admit what was happening. Conn didn't say anything to stop it himself for, no matter how reduced his father might be, Conn couldn't patronise him. In a sense he had to let it go in order to see his father clearly as he was, because too much of himself was invested in Tam to let him hide from what his father had become.

When Tam started on the beer, his talk became even more emptily self-confident, as if to justify the indulgence his drinking represented. A fragmented theme emerged from his ravings: 'Aye, we've had no' a bad life through it a', Jen.' He developed it haphazardly, remembering unlikely idylls. Mick became more openly contemptuous as he went on. Apparently oblivious, still seated at the table, Tam continued on a collision course with Mick's rancour.

Both Jenny and Conn could see it coming, and Jenny was desperately trying to think of a diversion when Mick suddenly stood up.

'Christ, man!' he shouted, crossing towards his father. 'Yer brains are droonin'. There's piss comin' oot yer mooth. Hiv ye no' had enough?'

Before Tam knew what was happening, Mick had taken the cup with its dribble of beer out of his hand. But the next second, still sitting and with a reflex that came from twenty years ago, Tam had back-swept the cup out of Mick's one hand, shivered it against the wall. And as Mick jumped back, Tam stood and heaved the table over in one movement. As Jenny called, 'Oh my Goad!', the table crashed and juddered on the floor, the plate smashed, the spoon skittered across the waxcloth, and a bowl of sugar that had been in the centre of the table spilled itself. Beer bled down the wall.

The room was fused. Light raced, converging on one glowing filament of rage. The three of them hung petrified. They knew without the slightest doubt that anything could happen, absolutely anything, and there was nothing they could do about it.

Conn watched, mesmerised by an anger as awesome as a mystic's ecstasy. He saw the shoulders heave and they seemed to him like hills. He saw that terrible stare volleying past them, making its own horizons. In the instant, his flippant pity and the arrogant mood of an evening became trash, and he was again a believer, not just in what his father had been but in what he was, because he saw the frightening place where his father had learned to live. He knew how petty his and Mick's judgements of him were, because this man had long ago taught them the terms in which to judge him, and did they imagine that the man who had made the terms so harsh in the first place didn't now apply them with a rigour and a severity that made their strictures like a salve by comparison? Conn didn't even feel insolent to have thought of his father as he had. He just felt cheeky.

He thought he understood the paradox of his father standing there, having summoned an annihilating force into himself, yet motionless. He thought he understood why he accepted Mick's taunts, his family's secret pity. He took it because his quarrel wasn't with them. They were midges in the scale of his own rage against himself. He had fed his children to a system that gave them back as the bread he ate every day of his life. And it wasn't until he had eaten them that he discovered what he had done. Now that it was too late, he understood.

It was that he lived with. And who was there or what was there with which he could confront the force that his realisation had generated? Raging helplessly inside him, it eroded him.

Conn was very afraid. At the same time, having seen this, he couldn't imagine much else of which he would ever be afraid again. Tam slowly subsided. He walked round and lifted the table back on its legs. Nobody else had moved. Leaning as if suddenly exhausted on the table, his head lowered, Tam spoke.

'It's no' a wean ye're dealin' wi', son,' he said quietly. 'Ah'm no' in ma dotage yet.'

Without speaking, they all helped Jenny to clear up the mess. In the silence, Conn heard the scuffling of his grandfather's feet on the bare floor of the next room, and then the creaking of the bed. He must have been listening at the door.

Conn looked at his father. The belly sagged a bit, the shoulders were thickening. But what remained with Conn was the image he had seen—his father standing making everything afraid of him, because you realised that he had learned to live where you daren't, and in his utter defeat there was an absolute power.

For the rest of his life, from time to time, those eyes would flare, like meteors in his outer memory.

# CHAPTER TEN

Hammy Mathieson was the nearest thing to a witness and he hadn't seen it. He had heard and he had felt. Asked about it afterwards, as he so often was, he took refuge in the same repetitive statements, ritual responses to the awe he felt. Death had brushed his back and he hadn't known about it at the time. 'It happened that quick,' he said. And, 'Ah can still feel his hauns oan ma back. Ye've heard o' birth-marks. These is daith-marks.' And, 'That man did ma deein' fur me. Every bite Ah eat, he gave me.'

Hammy's awe was only increased by the fact that the most stunning event of his life had happened on such an ordinary morning. Messiahs are born in stables. Going back to that morning again and again, he constructed it like a church. Having made it the most important place in his memory, he regularly re-enacted there those brief, blinding movements.

'The auldest boay had a cauld, Ah mind, that mornin',' he told others.

Davey was in the set-in bed to get the good of the fire. He was talking about going to his work just the same. His mother was appealing to Hammy.

'Wid ye make that galoot see sense?'

'Mither, they're busy at the factory the noo. An' they'll dock ma wages.'

'Better that than you doon wi' pneumony,' Hammy said. 'We canny afford the funeral. Ma piece no' ready yit, Jinty?'

'Ah've only two hauns.'

'If Ah'd kent ye were deformt, Ah widny a mairrit ye.'

Dennis came through, shivering in the long shirt he used as a nightgown.

'Boay!' Jinty said. 'Whit are ye daein' up the noo? The schil's 'oors yit. Get back tae yer bed.'

'Ach, let 'im stey, Jinty,' Hammy said.

Dennis got himself in front of the fire and stood there, his eyes still splintered with sleep and gouged by the heat. Jinty laid out Hammy's piece and the cold tea. Davey subsided on the bed, his breath hirsling like leaves in a wind. Hammy gathered up the piece and the bottle.

'Daddy,' Dennis said, mesmerised by his own thoughts. 'Can Ah get buyin' squeebs?'

'We've a' got wur ain worries richt enough,' Hammy said. 'Staun' back a bit. If that fire catches yer shurt-tail, ye'll no need a squeeb. Ye'll be wan.'

Hammy hung over the fire for a time, his hand on the smokeboard, trying to take in enough heat to see him to the pit.

'It's nae use tryin' tae stoap me, Jinty,' he said. 'Ah'll have tae go. Greetin'll no' help ye.'

She humphed, and he went out.

Nothing had happened to warn him there—the first moment of the morning, familiar, like a step worn by his own feet, the first of several. Who could have guessed they were leading to a sheer drop?

Outside, a black wind was blowing. A skin of frost on the causeys and a face that felt like raw beef inside minutes. He caught up with big Dan Melville on the way to the pit. They walked stiffly through the cold, their bodies held like metal casts that have set.

'A widny mind a word wi' Goad,' Big Dan had said. 'He's no' provin' onythin' wi' this kinna wather.'

At the face Hammy had worked as usual along with Abe. It wasn't a bad morning. They shifted more coal than they expected. At the break, Abe went along first to where the pieces were. The men always sat down together and talked while they ate. Hammy was finishing off.

He could hear the noise of somebody else still working, then it stopped. Hammy packed up himself.

He came out of the working and started along the tunnel towards the men. Nothing was different. The water noises, the whisper of timbers, the voice of one of the men wandering at him through the tunnel, ghost of a friend. It was then it happened.

All Hammy's memory held of it was really one instant. Though so much must have happened, the speed of it had pelletised everything. He had found himself thrown on his face. It was only in retrospect he was able to analyse that capsule of sensation into what must have been its component parts. There had been sound, what seemed just an instantaneous and deafening roar. But he was sure later he could distinguish two parts to it—the scream of the cracking timber, the fall of the roof. There had been the blow, smashing into his back, blessedly low enough not to buckle him but to force his legs into motion, so that he staggered for yards before he pitched on his face. There had been the outraged grumble of the settling debris. There had been silence.

Into his petrified stillness, bringing the renewal of time, ran the men. Two helped him to his feet. Dazed, he looked at them, reaffirming his life in their known, ordinary faces, and followed their eyes past himself to where he had been. The fall was big but contained, a high, neat mound of rocks and wood and rubble. The dust still drifted, choking. Someone hoasted. Automatically, he made the gesture of dusting himself down, trying to be casual in shaking off the residue of his almost death. Instinctively, he stopped. He looked at the men. He looked back at the mound of debris and he knew. It was a burial mound.

'Feyther!'

The voice was Conn Docherty's. Some of the men tried to hold him.

'Son! It hisny settled yit,' Tadger shouted.

But he broke from them, snarling with grief. They watched, frozen by dread, while he dived, scrabbling the rubble. While Conn whimpered with effort, the realisation of it broke through Hammy. He knew himself walking in the tunnel with Tam Docherty behind him. He knew a man diving into his own death to push Hammy out of his. He saw the stunning speed with which Tam must have moved. He felt those last handprints burned into his back. He saw Jinty and Davey and Dennis given back to him. He felt the joy of Davey having a cold. He stood accepting the magnitude of an unasked for gift. The generosity of it made it hard to breathe. There passed through him like a lightning-bolt love for someone who had always been for him just a hard wee man.

Conn gasped and recoiled. They saw a hand projecting from the rubbish, fixed in its final reflex, Tam Docherty's hand. It was pulped by the weight of the fall. The hand was clenched.

# CHAPTER ELEVEN

Conn didn't know what had happened until he saw his mother. He had been weightless since he found his father's hand. While the men dug his father out, while they brought him up the pit, while they certified him dead, while they brought him home, while they carried him up the stairs of the entry, Conn was with them and was nowhere.

At the turning of the stairs Tadger gave over his share of the weight of Tam's body to his own son. He put his hand on Conn's shoulder.

'Ah'll tell yer mither, son,' he said. Then to the others, 'Come up ahint me.'

They followed him up and along to the door. He hesitated, then knocked. The door opened on to the first firmness Conn had been aware of since it happened. He saw her from a terrible distance. To him she seemed someone standing on a small solidity surrounded by endless space. She was wiping her hands on her pinny. Her face had that expression of polite inquiry she wore at such times.

It was already beginning to wilt into doubt by the time Tadger had taken her by the arm and turned her back into the room. She was instinctively pulling away from him as he spoke. His voice was weird, occurring at different pitches.

'Jenny, hen. Noo ye'll hiv tae prepare yersel'. Ah'm sorry, hen. Ah'm sorry. It's bad news. It's the worst news, Jenny. It's Tam.'

She was frozen, facing towards the window. She didn't look towards them.

She said, 'No', as if it was a conspiracy. 'No. No. No. Ye will not. You will not!'

The sound of his mother forbidding it to happen broke Conn's stillness. He said, 'Oh', and the small word was a physical release, was the shock that was dammed in him breaking. The enormity of it went through him. It wasn't possible.

Tadger said, 'Aw, Jenny. It's happened. It's happened, love. It's happened.'

'Naw,' she said. 'Ah'll no' hiv it. D'ye hear me? Ah'll no' hiv that.'

'There, Jenny, there. Goad bliss ye.'

The others still waited outside, and Conn, too, like a stranger. Jenny stood clenched on herself, her hands still wrung in her pinny, as if holding to her the last moment of normalcy. Tadger's arm rose towards the others and fell. They carried Tam in and laid him on the set-in bed that wasn't used. Coming to him, Jenny admitted his death into the room. It possessed her frighteningly.

'Aw,' she wailed. 'Naw, Tam, naw. Ah, the best. The best o' them. Why? Nae richt, nae richt. They couldny, they couldny.'

Her words weren't like words. They were like sounds a strong wind makes against any object that baulks it. Through her Conn sensed the force of what they were confronting, felt the waste it came from, gauged its mercilessness against her, and he couldn't stop his tears. His only answer was to wipe his hand across his face and shake his head. He felt the shapelessness of everything. He knew that there was nothing to be done.

But incredibly there was. For while Jenny moaned on, another voice began to happen in her weeping, as if she was two people. The sound of it shivered through Conn like madness. His mother's voice had begun to be a conversation. Within the incoherence of her keenings, a small voice was asserting itself like a descant.

'Ach, but we'll wash ye, Tam,' it was saying. 'We'll make ye clean. Ye canny be left like this. Ye canny be.'

It gathered strength until she was pulling at his shirt and saw his body battered with bruises.

'Oh my Goad. Oh my Goad. We'll wipe ye, Tam.'

'Ah'll help ye, mither,' Conn said.

'Naw, naw, son,' she said absently. 'It's no' fur you tae dae. Is it, Tam?'

Her movements were very gentle, as if she didn't want to hurt him.

'Conn,' Tadger said. 'You go an' tell Mick and Kathleen an' Gus's wife, son. They'll need tae ken. Harry,' he said to his own son. 'Go doon an' tell yer mither tae come up. Ah'll wait here till she comes.'

He signalled the others out and shut the door. Conn waited on aimlessly and then, on his mother's strength, he went out. It was that same strength that gave what followed shape.

The event was defined in Jenny. Since it happened most to her, the griefs of the others were contained in hers. She gathered the whole thing to her and withstood it. So Mick's bitterness that his father should die in an aimless accident was mollified into memory of his worth by the simplicity and intensity of his mother's feeling. When Kathleen came, she was already shattered and it took her mother to teach her how to meet what had happened. With Angus, it seemed to Conn, his grief was for his mother. Conn wondered if Angus would have been able to feel anything without her there.

The last of her gifts to Tam was the dignity with which she mourned for him. After the undertaker had laid out Tam in his coffin, people came endlessly, relatives and friends and neighbours. Through the next two days, Jenny sat in their midst, enduring her private grief in a public place. They too had their respects to pay to Tam and she accepted that. She made no plea to be left alone, because she was alone.

Within their muted talk, she communed with her own grief. Sitting beside the fire, she would say, 'Ach, Ah had the best o' them. There's naebody kens the guidness that wis in him as a young man. Ye couldny guess.' And she would cry again a little. From time to time she would refer to something that had happened in the past and that didn't mean anything to anybody else. She was making her death-mask of him.

Conn had never loved her more. He needed her certainty as a compass for his own feelings. For there were confusing cross-currents around him. Even in the mourning for him his father had managed to generate factions.

Old Conn with his rosary beads was one. He was saying prayers for a son at last safely Catholic. Conn could understand how his grandfather felt and wondered if perhaps he wasn't right enough.

But beyond the old man's innocence were the rest of his family, some of Conn's aunts and uncles, and for him their presence was almost sinister. They kept gently badgering his mother about when the priest would be coming. They didn't ask if Tam had expressed a desire at any time to have a priest.

The problem bothered Conn. He saw some kind of technical justification for their attitude, yet at the same time felt that it showed no respect for his father, only for their own ideas. It was in watching the unwavering concentration of his mother's grief that he knew quite suddenly that he was opposed to them. There were two groups here. There were those who were mourning the death of a man and those who were mourning the death of Tam Docherty. Conn knew which group he belonged to.

For Old Conn's family Tam Docherty had only become a habitable presence once he was dead. The demands he had put on his life had always been too much for them while he was alive. Now that he was reduced in death, they had come back to claim the body. The body wasn't for claiming. It belonged to those who had loved the man in it for what he was, not for what he was called. His life meant more than his baptism. He should be allowed to die in the terms he made for himself, not that others made for him. Conn decided that he would be. When the crisis came, he was ready for it.

'Jenny,' his Auntie Mary said. 'Ah ken ye canny think the noo, hen. Ye're a' at sixes an' seevens. But arrangements hiv tae be made. D'ye want me tae get the priest fur ye.'

'There'll no' be a priest,' Conn said.

There was an incredulous pause.

'Son,' his uncle Alec said. 'Ah hardly think it's your place tae settle a thing like that.'

'Who else's wid it be, like?' Mick was asking before his uncle had finished speaking. 'We're his faimly. An' whit Conn says is richt. There'll be nae priest.'

'Why no'?' Old Conn's voice was shaking.

'Gran'feyther.' Mick was patient. 'Ma feyther leeved withoot a priest. He deed withoot wan. A' ma life Ah never heard him wantin' wan. Noo ye've a' got your religion. That's your business . . . But ma feyther's no gonny be some kinna sop fur you. Tae make ye feel better. He wisny that guid at soothin' at the best o' times. He'll no be stertin' noo. He'll get buried the wey he leeved. Jist his raw sel'.'

'But the funeral!' Auntie Jean said. 'Ye canny ha'e a funeral like that.'

'We'll bury him oorsel's,' Mick said. 'Withoot the mumbo-jumbo.'

'Ah never came across the likes o' it.' Uncle Alec couldn't believe it.

'Ah never came across the likes o' ma feyther,' Conn replied.

'Jenny!' Auntie Mary was drawing the final line between them. 'Dae you hear this? Hiv ye got nothin' tae say? These boays o' yours is blasphemin'. This is ma brither they're talkin' aboot.'

Jenny looked at her.

'Naw. It's their feyther they're talkin' aboot. An ma man. An' a lot o' hurt you caused him, Mary, that you should never ha'e caused him. Fur a faimly tae him wis an awfu' important thing.'

'Jenny. Ah'm no' here tae argy wi' ye. Ah'm here tae demand a proper Christian burial fur ma brither. Ah'm waitin' fur you tae answer.'

Jenny spoke quietly but what she said wasn't to be disputed.

'If there's wan thing he loved it's his weans. His boays'll bury 'im. An' if Goad disny want 'im like that, Ah don't want Goad.'

Tam lay bland in his coffin, making a quarrel in nature even in death.

# CHAPTER TWELVE

In the house on the day the atmosphere was less that of a funeral than of a polling-booth. The poll was secret. People voted with their bodies, present or absent, but the exact significance of such declarations wasn't clear. Some stayed away because the whole proceedings were an affront to their sense of propriety, some because they wanted to avoid trouble. Some stayed away because others stayed away. Some came for the sake of Tam, some for the sake of appearances, and some because they wanted to show Jenny she was right. The divisiveness of the whole thing was revealed in the way that one brother-in-law had come but not one of the others, a husband had arrived without his wife, though both had been invited.

There was no service. There was Old Conn at his rosary, joined by some others. There was silence and consolation of Jenny and hobbled talk. There was the twenty-third psalm, which Tadger had asked Jenny if they could sing. They sang it for themselves rather than Tam, as a way of acknowledging the solemnity of what was happening. There was the undertaker, embarrassed by the amorphousness of it all, finally managing to organise them out.

The trip to the cemetery simplified things further. Old Conn had said he would go out later. There were others who, though they had gone to the house, felt they couldn't participate in what would happen at the graveyard. They peeled off outside the house. Only those were left who felt they could go the whole way with Tam.

At the cemetery gates a large group of men were waiting, and Conn understood why there had been so few men at the corner when they passed it. They were most of them here. He found that moving. The men stood with their bonnets off and followed the cortege into the cemetery.

At the grave the coffin was placed on the planks. The wind flapped at the motionless figures, ruffled their hair.

'This is where there would normally be a short service, sir,' the undertaker whispered to Mick.

Mick shifted his feet, looked up at the people round the grave and the other men clustered beyond them on the pathway. He looked back down at the coffin and made to speak. He had to stop and clear his throat. While he spoke, his eyes remained on the coffin.

'Ah jist want tae thank all of ye fur comin' here tae see ma feyther buried. There's nae service because we don't think he woulda wantit a service. Ah think he would've wantit it the way it is. Wi' jist his freen's tae see 'im aff. Ah think a' he believed in wis folk.'

Mick hesitated and fell silent. It was Tadger's voice that went on.

'Yese a' ken ma poseetion. Ah wis born in the Church an' brocht up in the Church an' Ah'll dee in the Church. But Ah never kent a man inside it or oot that Ah thocht mair o' than Tam Docherty. He wis a hard wee man. But a guid wee man. Ah thocht the world o' him. He wis baptised a Catholic but Ah respect his boays fur daein' whit they think is richt by him. An' it canny dae him ony herm. If there's a place efter this that he's no' allooed intae it canny be much o' a place. Whaurever he's gaun'll dae me fine. Ah widny want tae be whaur he wisny.'

Hammy Mathieson said, 'Ah'm no' wan fur the talkin'. But Ah jist want tae say Tam Docherty saved ma life. An' Ah'll no' forget it the longest day Ah leeve. In a kinna wey he gi'ed me the rest o' his life tae leeve fur 'im. That's a big responsibeelity. Ah don't think I'll be as big a man as that wee man wis a' his days. But, by the holy Christ, Ah'll be a better man than Ah wis.'

There were murmured voices. The business with the cords was slightly confused. It was only then Conn noticed that Angus wasn't here. He couldn't believe it. He looked at Mick and Mick's eyes showed he knew what Conn was thinking about. He made a resigned expression and Conn gave his cord.

The undertaker was muttering, 'Oh dear, oh dear!'

Because of the unwillingness of some people to go to the cemetery, only three of the cords were allocated to people actually related to Tam. These were Mick and Conn and their Uncle Harry, who, at the cost of a lot of rancour from his wife and Old Conn's family and a lot more to come, had said that he had respect for Tam and knew no other way to show it. The other cords were taken by Tadger and Andra Crawford and Hammy Mathieson and two men brought out of the group on the pathway.

When the coffin had been lowered, the undertaker dropped dirt on it and said the part about 'ashes to ashes, dust to dust'. The grave was covered and they all walked slowly away.

It was much later that Old Conn stood alone at the grave. In the gathering dusk he conducted his own small service, conjuring God to accept Tam as a Catholic.

# CHAPTER THIRTEEN

Although their lives seemed to close over the fact of Tam's death soon enough, with Conn continuing to work alongside Tadger and his sons in the pit, and his grandfather staying with them because there was nowhere else for him to go, and Jenny somehow managing with only the two wages coming in, Conn was a long time trying to come to terms with his father's death.

For some time afterwards people were making remarks to him about it. Somebody in the pit would mention Tam or someone at the corner or Andra Crawford would speak incidentally about him while Conn was in the house. They were all generous remarks, the kind people make about a dead man. Usually they would mention his concern for other people and his guts. Conn accepted them as Tam's due. They seemed to him to be true but they were not true enough. They were all right for other people but Conn had lived all his life in the almost overpowering proximity of his father's presence and with him gone, their house seemed at first emptier than any place as small as that had any right to be. Conn found himself wondering how exaggerated his sense of his father had been. He felt that it was very important to be honest in his response to what was happening to him. He trusted no one to tell him what he was experiencing.

It was an ambivalent time. It was then, Conn was later to feel, that for him things fell apart. The tightness of texture he had always known in his life loosened slowly. He saw things clearly that had only been hazy before. Kathleen's marriage was a pretence. Jack drank like a fish and she was suffering. He wondered why he had never been fully aware of that before. His father was the answer. He had left his father to notice things like that. He saw his father anew and that was a surprising realisation, to have lived in the same house for so long with a man and find a dimension of him you hadn't known.

He saw it now. His father was like one of those animals Conn had read about. When danger threatened, they attracted attention to themselves and drew it off. The danger was the realisation of what had happened. His father's passion for each of them was such that he couldn't admit their defeat, the loss of themselves. He accused himself of their failures, he took them upon him. That was his final drunkenness.

Conn saw it now—the ruins his father had finally lived among, the weakness he had to protect. He tried to absolve them of his demands by failing to meet those demands himself. The last gift of his fatherhood was that of giving them the chance to disown him. He took the blame for himself to himself. He offered them escape from the force of his need to connect with everyone, to be known to the uttermost for what he was.

Angus had accepted that escape. Angus must have welcomed the chance to move out of the house. It was the easiest thing he could do. He hadn't been to the grave because he couldn't acknowledge truly what his father had been without denying what he was himself. For his father was a dangerous man, even dead. Conn understood that now. He felt it in the way his own life had atomised into contradictory fragments—his recurrent sadness at his father's death, the sense of release he felt, an increasingly critical attitude towards High Street. There gathered in him a kind of rootless anger.

One night he went out, not knowing why. The mood stayed banked in him while he walked, while he stood in a pub and drank more than he had ever drunk before, and it wasn't till he was out in the street again and suddenly saw Angus that the feeling in him found a home.

Angus was turning away from talking to someone, his hand still raised in a flick of farewell. Conn crossed towards him, and was in front of him before Angus had noticed, and said, 'Ah want you.'

Angus's head jerked up and then was breaking into a laugh when Conn threw the punch. Angus swung clumsily away, just managing to deflect the blow with his wrist.

'Hey!' He stepped back. Incredulity baffled his anger. He looked down at his wrist, flapping his hand and drawing in his breath. It was the pain that told him what was happening. 'Whit's the gemme? Wee brither or no' wee brither Ah'll pit yer nose oot through the back o' yer heid if ye come that wi' me.'

'Ye better stert then,' and Conn made to throw another punch.

Angus jumped back, both hands held up, palms towards Conn. From behind his sign of truce, Angus stared, his mouth coming open.

'Whit's it fur Conn?'

'Fur whit ye did tae ma feyther.'

Angus's hands came down slowly. They stared at each other from three yards apart.

'Jesus Christ! You're drunk, son, aren't ye?'

'No' that drunk.'

Angus looked round to see if anybody was watching them. The street was quiet.

'Ye mean the funeral, daen't ye? Well, come oan hame an' we'll talk aboot it.'

'There's nothin' tae talk aboot.'

Conn took a step towards him.

Angus's right hand came up again, still palm towards him.

'Richt,' he snarled. 'Fuckin' richt. But we're no hivin' it here. Ah widny let them see ma brither gettin' murdert.' He pointed at Conn. 'Ah still think you're drunk, son. Ye're aboot fower pints awa' fae yer brains. The morra mornin'. You still feel like this, you come doon tae the house fur me first thing. We'll go up the road. The nicht, you jist go hame. An' get ma mither tae pit a poultice oan yer heid.'

Conn stood staring at him. Angus shook his head and went past him widely as if there was a fence round him. Conn was still standing there when Angus looked back.

# CHAPTER FOURTEEN

Annie shook Angus awake, saying, 'Angus. There's somebody et the door.'

'When? Who?'

He raised himself on one elbow. His eyes were open but blank as a statue's in the dimness.

'Lusten.'

There was a double knock at the door. In the stillness it sounded threatening, its purpose unimaginably secret. Angus lay with Annie's hand still on his shoulder, sighing himself awake. He swung out of bed, pulled on his trousers and, buttoning them, padded across to the sideboard. He lifted the clock and held it close to his face, waiting for his eyes to absorb the time.

'Hauf past six?'

'Who could it be?' Annie asked.

Angus stood gouging his eyes with the heels of his hands. He yawned and crossed and opened the door. It wouldn't have occurred to him to ask who was there. By the time he realised it was Conn, he understood what was happening. They looked at each other for some time as if to verify it.

'Come in,' Angus said.

'Ah'll wait here fur ye.'

'Christ. Come in. Ah canny come oot yet. Ye widny hit a man when he's sleepin'.'

Conn came in reluctantly. He had spent all night honing himself down to what he had to do. The edge of his anger depended on keeping Angus clear-cut in his mind, as an abstract of his faults. It didn't help his purpose to have to meet the monster's relatives and see him yawning and scratching his head and stubbing his big toe on the table.

'Oh, it's you, Conn,' Annie said. 'Is something wrong?'

Conn didn't know what to say and Angus saved him.

'Conn seems tae think there is. Stoap actin' it, Annie. Ah telt ye aboot it last night.'

Annie lay with the covers pulled up to her chin, trapped in bed. Conn stood undecided, embarrassed to be embarrassing her. While they neutralised each other, only Angus seemed himself. He brought himself out of his stupor without haste. He struck the coal in the fire, releasing flame. He crossed to the window and held back the curtain for a moment.

'Aye,' he said. 'It's mair or less daylight. Ye must've chapped the sun up this moarnin', Conn.'

He walked slowly back and forth, scratching his bare torso and shaking his head.

'No' bad, richt enough. Ye're only here.'

'Ah think it's the daftest thing Ah ever heard o',' Annie said.

'Don' blame me, missus,' Angus said. 'Ah've tae get banjoed whether Ah like it or no'.' He pursed his lips and his eyes suddenly filled with something like admiration. 'Christ. A gunfighter in the faimly.'

'Haun me ower that frock, Angus, please.'

'Aye. Make us somethin' tae eat, hen. Ah don't want tae dee oan an empty stomach.'

Angus gave over the dress and pulled the curtain of the set-in bed for her. He started to splash his face with cold water from the pail beside the hearth. Annie got out of bed and crossed to the cradle.

'Ah hope Ah didny waken the wean,' Conn said.

'No' him,' Annie said. 'He takes efter his feyther's side.' And then, as if she had just remembered why Conn was here, 'But Ah'm hopin' he'll hiv mair sense than his feyther's side.'

Towelling himself, Angus said, 'Sit doon, Conn. Sit doon. Rest yer footwork.'

For the next twenty minutes or so, Conn kept losing the reality of what was happening. He found himself thinking at one point that they were preparing to go poaching. Past times with Angus interrupted his thoughts, like mutual friends who didn't know that things had changed. Drinking a cup of tea while Angus ate, he couldn't believe that they were really going to fight. He looked round the house and admitted to himself his admiration for what Angus had done. The place impressed him. Angus had decorated it himself, some of the furniture was new.

But the most impressive thing about the place was the atmosphere:

Angus and Annie communicating in half-phrases, the warmth, the ease, the breathing of the baby gentle in the middle of it. It seemed an impregnable fortress with Angus as its central pillar. The feeling weakened Conn. He stood up, still finishing his tea.

'Thanks, Annie.'

Angus looked past him at the wall and nodded, tied up his laces, rose, pulled on a jacket over his collarless shirt.

'The condemned man ate a hearty breakfast,' he said.

'Wull the pair o' ye no' sit doon,' Annie said.

'Now, now.' Angus was smiling. 'We'll no' hiv a foreigner fae Irvine tae tell us hoo tae soart things oot.'

They walked up High Street towards the country. It was a fresh morning. Once Angus snittered and said, 'Ah thocht it wis the rent man.' Then, 'Maybe it is, eh?' But talk was something that was left behind, like the town. They passed places plaqued with private memories. From a tree a piece of frayed rope hung, reminding them of their own games. Past the swinging bridge, a man with a glass eye, out walking his dog, said, passing, 'A sherp moarnin', boays.' They both said, 'Aye'. About a hundred yards later, Angus said: 'Ma Uncle Wull. When he wis drunk wance. He put his gless e'e oan the mantelpiece an' says, "Ah'm fur a sleep. You keep yer e'e oan them."' Conn said nothing—inadmissible evidence.

It was hard enough to get where they had to go without taking any unnecessary luggage with them. By the time they had reached the bridge above Moses' Well, their road was beginning to turn back on itself. To go on would be to retreat from the edge they had created in themselves. Conn stepped through the gateway in the stone beside the bridge, ducked through a gap in the hedge and into the field above. Angus followed.

They stood in the uneven field, not looking at each other. Beyond the hedge, the trees were stirring slightly in the wind. Down the shelving slope where the occasional tree was rooted half in air, the river ran among its stones. If one of them had laughed, it would have been all right. Instead, Conn dropped his jacket on the grass and pulled off shirt and vest. Angus did the same.

Stripped, Angus looked bigger than he had done in his clothes, as if the jacket had been serving to disguise a quarry as a man. Conn looked lean beside him. Both their bodies shone pale in the growing sunshine, immersed as they had been in the pallor of the pits.

They squared up, circling, arms revolving, for an unconscionable time. Conn threw a punch like a signal and they found themselves released into making a series of embarrassed passes at each other until, Angus stumbling on a tuft of grass, Conn's left hand connected with his cheekbone. Meeting the pain, Angus suddenly came alive. He bull-rushed Conn and for seconds they threshed in a tangle of arms out of which Conn miraculously escaped, like a man passing through a mincing machine intact. They came slowly together again.

The fight had become real. The next couple of collisions tapped the anger in the two of them. Angus burst Conn's lip and left a red weal like a birth-mark under his heart. Long buried feelings re-emerged, grievances queued up for a go. Each found himself called to answer for the anguished frustrations and complex resentments that had massed up in the other.

The punches were fired from what both had at first believed were unassailable positions. Conn had begun believing that he was so right that he couldn't lose. He had felt the insuperable justice of his position. Angus had been convinced that his strength was annihilating.

Each proved the other wrong. Conn learned quickly that his assumption was as stupid as trying to stop a stampede by calling it names. Angus saw that Conn simply wouldn't annihilate. There was something extra there now. He would just have to be beaten.

They wove a crazy pattern in the sunlight. Anyone watching from the farm a mile above them on the hill would have seen them blunder like butterflies about the field, while the grass went black in the shadow of a cloud, greened again in the sun. What they wouldn't have seen was that the field was crowded. Its bigness, in which they seemed lost, was cluttered with the furniture of their past. They bumped into their father's failure, backed against countless incomprehensible memories, struck against their mother's pain. And in their rage they made a wreckage of it all and tried to heap it on each other's head.

Their breathing became their total context, contained them like a cloud that threatened suffocation—the grunts and gulps and barking exhalations all that was left of their father's talk, their mother's silence. They wrestled, their hands skidding on their bodies greased with sweat, and broke apart. Honking for air, they plunged back in. Conn, whimpering with anger, swung a right at Angus and buckled his fist on his shoulder. They closed again, Angus bear-hugging Conn until his spine bent like a bow, Conn writhing and butting and finally kicking himself away.

They moaned at each other, watching. Conn started to let Angus come to him, trying to withhold his punches till Angus was almost on him, his nerves taut with the fear of it. Angus tried to bury Conn under sheer weight of pressure, his assaults failing time after time, like powder refusing to fire, until he hit Conn with a punch that landed like a boulder on his ribs, lifted him and jarred him on to his back. Angus jumped in with one foot raised to kick. By witholding it, he made a counter-pressure in the fight, an eye of self-awareness that inhibited them. At once he was angry with himself. As Conn rose, Angus took a savage swing at him. Conn threw himself clear and Angus spun on his own momentum and sat down.

Instantly, both felt how tired they were. Angus sat heaving. Conn bent over, retching for air. They had to finish it soon. Looking up, Angus was enraged at the injustice of Conn standing. He got up and charged.

Conn came into his best phase of the fight. Faced with Angus's self-neutralising anger, he was given an extension of life. He backed and dodged, leading Angus on to his punches. But his temporary success was a guarantee of his ultimate failure. Time and again, he set up perfectly the mechanics of the kill and couldn't effect it. He was like a matador who had everything that was needed except a sword. And then, without preliminary, Angus hit him once above the temple and the inside of his head distended like a balloon. His feet went into a strange vaudeville routine and he travelled an astonishing distance, a drunk man going for a walk. But he wouldn't go down because if he did he could never get back up. He stood, shaking his head and peering patiently among the splinters of his vision, looking for Angus. When he finally saw him, Angus was waiting at the end of several badly lit corridors.

They started towards each other. It was a long journey. Both seemed caught in separate currents, so that they circled out of distance and started all over again. Conn was aware of a badge of blood fastening painfully to his upper lip. Angus's arms weighed on him like a couple of corpses. He felt as if he might need help to lift them. Finally, they were level but still some way apart. Heads drooping, they looked across at each other, like men on opposite sides of a street.

The sweat frosted on their bodies. Conn was prepared to go on but knew at the same time that it would only be a matter of going on. Angus sensed that he could stay with it forever but he would only be the servant to Conn's own exhaustion, and his victory would be like the action of a bystander. The fight was reducing them to ciphers, like swimmers caught in a storm. Whatever positions they were finally beached in would prove nothing about them. Nobody had won. But the fight had lost.

Their breathing gradually subsided, admitting the other sounds around them. A cow mooed. The river was still there. They turned together to pick up their clothes and in doing that they acknowledged more than the futility of one fight. Like the retiring champions of a way of life, they felt the pointlessness not just of their own actions but of their father's and their friends'. All they had achieved was to pay homage to a dead ethic. What they had done had courage and dignity and even a kind of grandeur but no relevance. In a last defiant gesture, Angus stopped and held Conn by the shoulder.

'Holy Christ!' he said. 'Ah'll say wan thing. Let them come a hundred-fuckin'-handed, an' we'll eat them. Bring ony ten men intae this park, an' you an' me wid punch them intae the grund. A' richt, then?'

They stood swaying slightly, drunk with exhaustion, as if waiting for an answer. Only the wind ruffling the grass around their feet. They went back to searching for shirts and jackets. As they stumbled around the field, astonished at how far from their clothes their crazy pilgrimage had taken them, the total oppressive failure of it gelled. Their white shivering bodies, mapped with a scuffle but enlisted in a war, hunted for covering. Holding their clothes at last, they looked vaguely round the field where they had buried some family ghosts.

They went down the banking and drank at Moses' Well. But the water only added to the pain of Conn's mouth. Angus scudded on down from the well to the river's edge and Conn went after.

'Ah'm fur a soom,' Angus said.

He stripped buff and hit the water like an avalanche. Watching him, Conn wanted the water round himself. As he took off the rest of his clothes, his body became a crowd of pains. He drowned them in the searing cold of the black water, where it ran deepest under a ledge of rock. They splashed and lolloped and lay, while the leaves made patterns on them.

They dried themselves with their vests, which they afterwards put in their pockets. Walking back down the road, they were very quiet, almost drugged with the day. Like Siamese twins who had wrenched themselves apart, they were each in pain, but at least the wounds of each were unmistakably his own.

In the town Angus wanted to buy cigarettes. Standing beside him in the shop, Conn watched him buy two copies of the *Sunday People*. He gave one to Conn.

They walked to the corner where they would separate. Conn watched the people passing in the street. The bells were ringing, inviting some of them to church. Conn looked at Angus.

'Well,' he said, 'Ah'll be seein' ye.'

Angus held up his palm in a salute. As they walked away, a few yards broke between them like an ocean. Each held the paper tucked under his arm, a flimsy rudder.

# CHAPTER FIFTEEN

Conn was alone with Mick in the house. Jenny and Kathleen had gone with the weans and Old Conn to the park. The book lay across Mick's knees as usual, his forefinger sifting through it. Empty of the others, the place seemed oppressively still to Conn, even the sun motes suspended. He felt that if he spoke, his voice would reverberate. He thought of going out but couldn't think of anywhere to go.

Instead, he crossed to the partly open window and looked down at the corner. A haphazard group of men stood and crouched there. The sun shone full on them and their postures—back-tilted head, splayed hand, minutely tapping foot, chin crutched on palm—were shadowless, like a mural. They seemed stunned by the sunlight.

Conn walked back and forth in the room. Everything oppressed him, looked ugly. He sat down beside the empty hearth, gnawing the back of his hand.

'Hoo did ye make oot against Angus?'

Mick's head was still lowered to his book. Conn wondered if Mick meant what he had thought he meant.

'Whit?'

'Aw, come oan,' Mick said. 'Ye can maybe kid ma mither oan aboot a gamey catchin' up wi' ye. But Ah ken ye had a go wi' Angus. Hoo did ye get oan?'

'Ach, it just kinna petered oot. A guid thing fur me.'

'Whit's the oadds, onywey?' Mick said. 'It wis a no-contest.'

'Hoo d'ye mean? Dae ye think he's that guid?'

'Conn, be yer age. That's no' whit Ah'm talkin' aboot. Ah mean who cares which wan o' you two can punch the ither yin's heid in. Whit did ye want tae fight wi' Angus fur onywey?'

'Whit fur? Because o' whit he did tae ma feyther.'

'Och, Conn. Dae ye no' unnerstaun' yit? Don't waste yer time worryin' aboot whit Angus does. He's gave up the joab a while ago. He disny ken whit it's a' aboot. He's like a man shapin' up tae his mirror.'

'Hoo can ye be so cauld?'

'We leeve in a cauld place. Maybe Ah've jist adaptit.'

'He's oor brither,' Conn said. 'Ken? The fella that used tae stey here.'

'Aye, he's ma brither,' Mick said. 'Ah like 'im fine. But don't ask me tae take 'im seriously.'

'Jesus Christ!' Conn stood up. 'Whit's happenin' here?'

He started to walk. Mick stayed still. Only his mouth had moved. Conn stopped again at the window, looking out. Mick was staring at the floor.

'Whit's happenin'?'

'Whit's happenin' is that folk don't ken whit's happenin'. They jist want wages an' they canny accept that they'll hiv tae tak' mair. Tae get whit ye want, ye've goat tae settle fur mair, that's a'.'

'But ma feyther,' Conn said. 'Is that him by, jist like that?'

'So whit? He did the joab the only wey he kent. He did a joab a' richt. Ye mind the fight wi' Angus because he went tae work in Number Eicht? He wis richt aboot that. Nae won'er he wis liked. Every time he went tae the pit-face he turned up as a man. Nothin' less.'

'That's great,' Conn said. 'So that's it feenished. Jist like that.'

'That's *him* feenished,' Mick said. '*We*'re no' feenished. This is jist a beginnin'. Folk like ma feyther wur oor Winter Palace.'

'Whit does that mean?'

'Ah'll tell ye sometime. Ye see, this wis us trying it wan wey. An' it didny work. We came an' stood in a line wi' oor bunnets oot. An' a' we goat wis a bunnetfu' o' air. Ah mean, we've been waitin' in a queue for hunners o' year. An' by the time we get tae the front, the shoap's shut. So whit dae ye dae?'

Conn said nothing, watching him.

'Ye hiv tae brek in. Because ye ken there's grub in there a' richt. They'll jist no' gi'e ye it. Whit we're daein' the noo is hingin' aboot ootside, tryin' tae make up oor minds. Because it's no' legal tae brek in. An' that worries folk. But whit's legal? Legal is whit they need tae keep whit they've goat. We hiv tae brek in. An' we hiv tae batter onybody that gets in oor road oot o' existence.'

Conn studied his brother. Watching him, he understood that out of all the talk that had raged for so long in this house Mick's voice had emerged as the strongest. It was a fact which surprised him. Conn remembered how he had almost patronised Mick as somebody on the edge of things, his presence frequently all but erased. But his silence had been a gathering of speech. His stillness had been making bombs. He was so sure. Conn was impressed.

Yet Conn was also disturbed and suspicious of him. What Mick said was too simple. What had been a dialogue had turned into a pronouncement. It was as if Mick hadn't heard a lot of what had happened, had just missed out so much that was important—their father's respect for people, no matter who they were, their mother's patient persistence, the fact that they had only been able to reach this place because they had all loved one another. But the only voice left that could thaw Mick's icy certainty back into argument was Conn's own. He couldn't find it.

'Naw,' he said. 'Naw. That's too easy.' He hesitated and said the only thing he could think of. 'That's only hauf an answer. Ye ken whit Ah think, Mick? Ah think maybe whit's happened tae you his made it easier. It maybe makes life easier only hivin' wan airm.'

'Maybe,' Mick said, and smiled. 'But no' as easy as it is bein' in twa minds. Like you, Conn. That wey ye never hiv tae make wan o' them up.'

'But maist folk mean weel.'

'Ah'm no' fussy whit they mean. Jist whit they dae. An' nae rulin' cless ever gave its power awa'. It has tae be ta'en. Always.'

'Naw. Ah don't want tae smash folk. Ah jist want them tae see hoo guid folk like ma feyther were. Tae gi'e us room tae leeve.'

'Ye use yer hert like a hearse, Conn. Fur collectin' the deid. As long as the wans that ruined them take aff their hats, ye're happy. Ye should be mountin' the pavement tae rin the bastards doon.'

Mick's stare was uncomfortable. It had the same fire as his father's look but under steady control. Conn turned towards the window. He spoke without looking round.

'Ah canny hate folk the wey you dae, Mick.'

'Well, ye'd better learn. Tae hate a certain type o' folk.'

'Onywey. Whit can you dae aboot it?'

'Ah've jined the Communist Party.'

'When?'

'A wee while ago.'

'But ye didny tell onybody?' Conn turned back towards him.

'Who wis there tae tell? Ma mither wid jist worry. She's hud enough worry. Whit's it tae Kathleen? She's goat the weans tae contend wi'. Angus widny ken the difference between the Communist party an' the Freemasons.'

'Why are ye tellin' me then?'

Conn knew the answer in just looking at Mick. He knew that this was what survived of his family—this new division, this argument between Mick and himself. It was the legacy they shared. He heard his brother confirm it.

'Because you an' me's whit's left o' ma feyther, Conn. It's between you an' me. Me wi' wan airm an' you in twa minds, eh?'

# CHAPTER SIXTEEN

It was more than a year after Tam Docherty's death that somebody said, 'Ah hear somebody doon the Foregate's been pestered wi' a Peepin' Tom.'

He was among the men at the corner. It was late at night, cold. Most had gone home. Only a few remained against the wall of the Scotia. Jacket collars were up, hands were in pockets.

'Lucky fur him Tam Docherty's deid,' Andra Crawford said.

They laughed, reflecting.

'Aye,' Tadger said, the fag bobbing in his mouth as he talked past it. 'Ye mind o' yon? Dear oh dear. Ah've seen angry men. But yon wis different.'

Slowly, as they stood shrugging off the night wind, they began to realise that they had a clear view of Tam. Their sense of him had hardened. They began to talk themselves towards it.

'Jesus Christ. A hellu' a man fur the size o' 'im.'

'Aye.'

'Aye.'

'Mind ye,' Dan Melville said. 'Ah don't think he wis as hard as they said he wis.'

'Aye, that'll be richt,' Tadger said. 'He wis harder.'

'Naw. Listen, Tadger . . .'

'Lusten nothin'. Talk comes easy. If the wee man walked doon that street the noo, you wid ken. The wee cauld bit in the pit o' yer stomach.'

'He wis a' hert.'

'Aye. Ask Hammy Mathieson.'

They began to go over stories about him. Tadger told about the hand-wrestling match with Angus. Dan Melville talked about the time Tam had come looking for him. 'No' again,' Dan said. 'No' if Ah'd had a gun.' Somebody told of money given to him by Tam to get a drink. Somebody mentioned how he had dealt with the priest. Tadger said how much Tam had loved weans. Andra Crawford related for the first time in his life what he had overheard on the stairs at Tam's mother's wake.

They were the right men to judge him—his peers. They knew the hardness of his experience, because it was theirs too. They could appreciate what he had contrived to make of it. With their words they sketched out some sense of a life built out of all those small moments. Only they could come near to appreciating the architecture of it, its monumental quality. They grew excessive.

'A hert like a bell.'

'Tae him his wife wis the only wumman in the world.'

'Ye had tae come tae the line wi' that wee man. Don't worry aboot it. Nae shite from naebudy. Nut accepted.'

'He died wi' his balls on.'

Their talk was as much a definition of themselves as it was of Tam. Normally taut with understatement, they loved to be given licence to be generous, to inhabit hyperbole. Tam had given them that chance. They felt the gratitude always owed to those who enlarge our sense of ourselves. When they contemplated Tam Docherty, he helped them to define themselves.

'An awesome wee man,' Andra Crawford said.

There were noddings. Tadger brooded, finding the exact words towards which the mood of their talking had inspired him. When he spoke, his voice was formal, almost polite, like an official statement.

'He wis only five foot fower. But when yer hert goes fae yer heid tae yer taes, that's a lot o' hert.'

One of them rubbed his hands together against the cold. Their silence was agreement, a vision achieved. They had found his epitaph.

# NOTES

## Introduction

The notes and texts that follow are intended to provide both additional background knowledge about the main aspects of the novel and to assist readers in appreciating the author's methods and purposes.

The use of texts from different sources does not imply a particular view of the novel. The aim is rather to try to examine areas of life and society as reflected in the novel which may be remote from many readers' own experience. Thus there is an emphasis on the local and historical dimension of the novel; on the social, political, religious and occupational frames of reference in the action; and on the literary and linguistic tradition from which, to some extent, *Docherty* derives.

After reading these notes, the reader will be able to form a fuller and more soundly based set of personal responses to a powerful and imaginative novel. The Bibliography on p. 317 will help the reader in following up the experience of reading *Docherty* in different ways—either by reading more of William McIlvanney's work, both prior and subsequent to *Docherty*; or reading other novels on similar or parallel themes; or investigating that real world of the Scottish working class of which *Docherty* is a fictional representation.

# The Local and Historical Background

## Ayrshire

William McIlvanney was born and brought up in Kilmarnock, an industrial town in north Ayrshire, to the south-west of the city of Glasgow. His Kilmarnock origin is of great importance in the detailed appreciation of the novel *Docherty*, as will be shown later. The Ayrshire connection is of wider, more general, but equally great significance. Ayrshire is a part of Scotland that has produced more than its expected share of literary figures over the last three hundred years, so much so that one might almost begin to start talking about the Ayrshire school of writers.

The writer most notably connected with Ayrshire is, of course, the poet Robert Burns. Yet Burns did not exist in a literary vacuum, one eloquent poet and song-writer in the middle of a desert. The circumstances of his education and the range of his correspondence and acquaintance with local poets and lovers of literature make it clear that Ayrshire in the eighteenth century was already a highly literate community, one in which a talented person could write on local themes and concerns and find an appreciative audience. Burns's satires, epistles and other poems have a local application as well as a universal relevance, made all the more telling by being written for the most part in the Ayrshire dialect of the Scots language. After the Union of Scotland with England, first in the Crowns and then in Parliament, Scots had wilted and faded as a literary medium, despite the strong medieval and Renaissance tradition of literature in all the genres. The example of Burns did much to make Scottish writers think again about the merits of their own language as an element in their creative processes.

Here, by way of illustration, is an extract from a poem by Robert Burns, 'Tam Samson's Elegy'. It clarifies a reference in *Docherty*, page 84 —'He (Conn) discovered who Tam Samson was.' A reading of these verses, in the traditional Scottish Standard Habbie form, will reveal how Burns uses both older Scots vocabulary and rhymes on characteristic Scots pronunciations. (The occasional use of apostrophes in words like a'/all, o'/of and wi'/with is an eighteenth-century printer's convention to aid the English reader with the regular forms of Scots words—in this case, aa, o and wi—not a suggestion that these words are slovenly or incomplete versions of English words.)

## TAM SAMSON'S* ELEGY

An honest man's the noblest work of God—

POPE.

* When this worthy old Sportsman went out last muir-fowl season, he supposed it was to be, in Ossian's phrase, 'the last of his fields;' and expressed an ardent wish to die and be buried in the muirs. On this hint the Author composed his Elegy and Epitaph.

Kilmarnock lang may grunt an' grane,
An' sigh an' sab, an' greet her lane,
An' cleed her bairns, man, wife, an' wean,
    In mourning weed;
To Death she's dearly pay'd the kane,
    Tam Samson's dead!

The Brethren o' the mystic *level*
May hing their head in wofu' bevel,
While by their nose the tears will revel,
    Like ony bead;
Death's gien the Lodge an unco devel,
    Tam Samson's dead!

When Winter muffles up his cloak,
And binds the mire like a rock;
When to the loughs the Curlers flock,
    Wi' gleesome speed,
Wha will they station at the *cock*,
    Tam Samson's dead?

He was the king of a' the Core,
To guard, or draw, or wick a bore,
Or up the rink like *Jehu* roar
    In time o' need;
But now he lags on Death's *hog-score*,
    Tam Samson's dead!

Now safe the stately Sawmont sail,
And Trouts bedropp'd wi' crimson hail,
And Eels weel kend for souple tail,
    And Geds for greed,
Since dark in Death's *fish-creel* we wail
    Tam Samson's dead!

Rejoice, ye birring Paitricks a';
Ye cootie Moorcocks, crousely craw;
Ye Maukins, cock your fud fu' braw,
    Withoutten dread;
Your mortal Fae is now awa',
    Tam Samson's dead!

[. . .]

Heav'n rest his saul, whare'er he be!
Is th' wish o' mony mae than me:
He had twa fauts, or may be three,
    Yet what remead?
Ae social, honest man want we:
    Tam Samson's dead!


THE EPITAPH
*Tam Samson*'s weel-worn clay here lies,
    Ye canting Zealots, spare him!
If Honest Worth in heaven rise,
    Ye'll mend or ye win near him.


PER CONTRA
Go, Fame, an' canter like a filly
Thro' a' the streets an' neuks o' *Killie*,
Tell ev'ry social, honest billie
    To cease his grievin,
For yet, unskaith'd by Death's gleg gullie,
    *Tam Samson's livin!*


ROBERT BURNS


In the earlier years of the nineteenth century, when Sir Walter Scott and James Hogg were adorning the literary life of Edinburgh and producing some of Scotland's major works of prose fiction, Ayrshire had its own novelist, regarded as of equivalent merit, even though he did a lot of his later writing in London and the South. John Galt made Ayrshire the subject of nearly all his best novels, and the way in which he used his home county has been an influence on later Ayrshire novelists like George Douglas Brown and William McIlvanney. Galt's 'theoretical histories', like *Annals of the Parish* and *The Provost*, present a picture of how the West of Scotland underwent great social changes during the reign of George III, affecting industry, town and rural life, as well as everyday habits.

Galt's technique was an interesting one, and very relevant when we begin looking at *Docherty*. The places in his novels are often thinly disguised versions of real communities. For instance, the Reverend Micah Balwhidder's parish of Dalmailing in *Annals of the Parish* is recognisable as the parish of Dreghorn on the outskirts of Kilmarnock, and Provost Pawkie's burgh of Gudetown in *The Provost* is clearly the seaside town of Irvine. In both these novels, the events and often the characters are closely based on reality, and the topography of the communities can be seen to be almost identical with the real places.

At the very end of the nineteenth century, another Ayrshire writer, George Douglas Brown, used the same technique in his bleak and pessimistic novel, *The House With The Green Shutters*. His little Ayrshire town of Barbie is closely modelled on the real village of Ochiltree, and it is surrounded by other real towns with fictional names; Kilmarnock is recognisable even when called

Fechars. In *The House With The Green Shutters*, we read about the coming of industry and improved communications to Ayrshire in the middle years of the century, the time when Brown's own parents would have been young. Among the new developments in Ayrshire described are the first coal mines and the railway. Fechars is particularly mentioned as having 'lots of mineral'. The most visible result of these changes is that there come to be two Ayrshires —the rural Ayrshire of the farms and the small burghs and villages, a beautiful green place where the traditions of the past are maintained and remembered, and an industrial Ayrshire of pits and factories, grimy and ugly, where a new way of life develops in an urban working class made up partly of transplanted local inhabitants and partly of incomers, notably Irish immigrants who have come to Scotland to escape the hunger and poverty of their own land.

It is the second Ayrshire that is the setting of *Docherty*, although the young Conn has contacts with the first Ayrshire as a boy exploring the Bringan, and Tam enters it to poach trout. It is also these two aspects of Ayrshire that William McIlvanney acknowledges as his roots. In the following early and untitled poem he describes what his boyhood environment means to him:

I had the run of the day in the cobbled town,
Was cock of the leafy walk and the drayman's yard,
While the steeples kept my green and casual time
And the lazy hours drifted like thistledown
Past the square and the pub and the darkened arch
Where the coopers hammered manhood into rhyme.

I was fish to the water and fowl to the banking air,
League-booted lord of a land where in castled mills
Men wove out the sullen patterns of their mood,
Was prince of the storied dust and the sun-laid streets
Where women impassive in massive womanhood
Were folded like Sphinxes on their windowsills.

[. . .]

And all of the brewing and baking and shoemaking town
With the evening shawled on its shoulders and wearing cloud
Was calling my truant manhood to come down
Where the pubs burst with laughter, windows were lit and loud

And the men had come home from the day with the wagging dogs
Bundles of barking chained to their iron heels.

[. . .]

WILLIAM McILVANNEY

(McIlvanney uses some of the images of this poem in *Docherty*, Book 1, Chapter 18.)

# Map of Kilmarnock, 1909

Longpark
Sanitary Pottery

Hillhead Fireclay
Works

TO GLASGOW

Kilmarnock
Forge

Townholm
Engine
Works

Bonnyton Colliery
Nº 8 Pit

Bonnyton
Colliery
Nº 6 Pit

G & S.W.
Railway Works

DEAN STREET

HIGH ST.

Kay Park

Lake

Station

BONNYTON ROAD

WEST LANGLANDS STREET

PORTLAND ST.

FORE ST.

SOULIS ST.

REGENT ST.

Grange
Iron Foundry

GLASGOW SOUTH WESTERN RAILWAY

IRVINE ROAD

FULLARTON STREET

NORTH HAMILTON STREET

WOODSTOCK STREET

THE
CROSS

KING STREET

STURROCK STREET

LONDON ROAD

PORTLAND ROAD

JOHN FINNIE STREET

DUKE STREET

ST. MARNOCK ST.

DICK ROAD

CANEHEAD ST.

OTTER ROAD

SOUTH HAMILTON STREET

DUNDONALD ROAD

WATERSIDE ST.

TITCHFIELD STREET

Football
Ground

Portland
Colliery
Nº 5

Howard Park

NEW MILL ROAD

IRVINE BANK

Rugby Park

River Irvine

W. NETHERTON
STREET

HIGH GLENCAIRN STREET

E NETHERTON
STREET

LAWSON ST.

FAIRY HILL RD.

SQUARE

WEST SHAW STREET

EAST SHAW ST.

LOW GLENCAIRN STREET

Glenfield
Hydraulic Works

River Irvine

Engineering
Works

BURNSIDE ST.

KIRKSTYLE ROAD

Gas Works

Station

G & SW RAILWAY    RICCARTON TO HURLFORD BRANCH

HURLFORD ROAD

FEET
1000    500    0    1000    2000 FEET

SCALE

## 'Graithnock'/Kilmarnock

The setting of *Docherty* is Graithnock, a mining town in Ayrshire, a place of industrial slums and poverty, but also a place of tradition and history, of green spaces and a rapid river, ringed with grand estates and idyllic rural retreats.

The name itself is interesting. The ending, '-nock' or '-ock', is a common one in Scottish placenames (Greenock, Cessnock, Kilmarnock, Cumnock, Gourock, etc.). The word, 'graith', however, is given a range of intriguing meanings in the *Concise Scots Dictionary*. For the purpose of understanding McIlvanney's choice of the name for his imaginary town, one or two seem especially relevant.

> **graith**: (n) 1. materials or equipment (for a particular purpose, job or trade); tools, implements, machinery.
>
> 2. accessory equipment, esp. of a mechanism, e.g., a mill, plough or loom [. . .]
>
> 10. possessions, wealth, money [. . .]
>
> 13. stale urine used in washing and dyeing [. . .]
>
> 14. a soapy lather; dirty, used soapsuds.
>
> 15. (contemptuous) people, riffraff.
>
> (CSD, p. 244)

There are three kinds of meaning here: first, a functional meaning that relates 'graith' to industrial processes, describing tools suitable for particular jobs; second, an evaluative meaning that relates 'graith' to items of value; and third, a derogatory or dismissive meaning that suggests 'graith' is of no value or consequence, even to the extent of being foul and dirty. If the 'graith' of Graithnock is its people, then, according to the definitions, they are simultaneously useful workers who are mere tools or hands in the greater industrial system, despised elements in society who are abhorred for their supposedly inferior qualities, and yet beings of great worth and merit in their own right. Merely by naming the town in which the lives of Tam Docherty and his family are to be the focus of our attention, a political arena has already been marked out.

Yet, look beyond the name, Graithnock, and the town turns out to be McIlvanney's own Kilmarnock. A study of the old town plan (see p. 286) reveals all the streets mentioned in the text of the novel; High Street, Soulis Street and Fore Street (or the Foregate) run to the Cross; King Street and Portland Street run roughly parallel; there are the river and the Kay Park, and the Crawfurdland Estate, Conn's childhood paradise in the Bringan, is reached along the Grassyards Road. Like Kilmarnock, Graithnock is built above the Barren Red Coal Measures and the pits used to ring the town within walking distance of Tam Docherty's High Street tenement.

Equally, the life of High Street, as McIlvanney describes it in Chapter 2 and elsewhere in *Docherty*, closely resembles the way it really was for the generations prior to the Second World War. McIlvanney has hinted at this in an autobiographical piece, 'Growing Up in the West':

> My town is Kilmarnock. The population is given as around 50,000, which surprises me, since I always felt I knew most of them. I don't know

what such guide-books as there may be of the town and district would say, but I'm fairly sure they wouldn't mention very many of the places that have mattered to me: The Twelve Steps, Nailer's Close, The Swinging Bridge, Moses' Well, Mason's Ragstore—names that make up a private mythology of childhood. [. . .] Built above the Barren Red Coal Measures, Kilmarnock is very much an industrial town, but one under siege from what Pound calls 'the green world'. The numerous parks and trees and green spaces are a strong fifth-column, and, no matter where you may stand in the town, it isn't far, as a boy runs, to the fields. For me as a boy, the country was an escape route, a place for divesting the identities the town imposed on me and going naked in my imagination. [. . .]

But the heart of any place is the relationships you have there. Geography is people. Where I come from is my family. And I'm not sure that my family is typical of anything so much as my family. By the time I was born we were living in a council house. We seemed comfortable enough; the amenities were fine; hardship I never knew about. [. . .]

Through it all I had a growing sense of how the stability and the comfort and the opportunities which I had taken for granted had been earned, and only with a lot of tenacity. I had a growing sense of the past. And that sense set up in me a series of dialogues which don't show much sign of abating. There were plenty of voices present to start it going. Apart from having a lot of relatives, my mother and father had lived most of their lives in High Street, one of the oldest streets of the town, in one of a long line of tenements. From there they brought with them a kind of kibbutz mentality. People helped one another with flittings, sat with one another in times of illness, sought one another's advice in anything from filling up a form to treating a sick dog, and visited without warning. You knew you were having people when they came in the door—endlessly, I sometimes felt. Friends they hadn't seen for years seemed to be dropping in every other month. Uncles came mellow from the pub, cousins callow with first boyfriends. And they talked. And then talked some more.

Especially with the older people, the anecdotes threaded each other subtly until some nights were a Bayeux tapestry of stories: characters caught in characteristic poses, events picked out in luminous colours. The stories were multiform: about the six-foot-or-so Peeping Tom, an Irish labourer from the nearby lodging-house, whom my father's five feet four, wrought by contempt into a lethal weapon, reduced to bloody unconsciousness in roughly 30 seconds; about the street-sweeper who was seen in the early hours of a wet morning, walking the deserted street, under his arm a basket from which he was sowing pieces of cut paper on the cobblestones that were due to be swept next day by a colleague; about the 'daddlum-drinker' who, sitting by the bed on which his brother's life was ebbing, was stealing mouthfuls of the meths used to rub the dying man's bedsores. They were funny, sad, gruesome, grotesque, and sometimes all of these at once. They were a history, a revelation, oral scriptures.

(from 'Growing Up in the West' in *Memoirs of a
Modern Scotland*, ed. Karl Miller)

So Graithnock's High Street is in one sense the fictional setting for *Docherty* and in another sense the real place of William McIlvanney's boyhood:

High Street was the capital of Conn's childhood and boyhood. The rest of Graithnock was just the provinces. High Street, both as a terrain and as a population, was special. Everyone whom circumstances had herded into its hundred-or-so yards had failed in the same way. It was a penal colony for those who had committed poverty, a vice which was usually hereditary.

High Street and its continuations of Soulis Street and Fore Street made a straight line to the Cross at the centre of town. Together, they had at one time been the main street of the town, a residential district for the rich. But when this predominance was taken over by the roughly parallel line of Portland Street and King Street, the older area, like a tract of land gone marshy, had been abandoned to the poor. (p. 18 of this edition)


## Graithnock in history

Graithnock, however, is not simply the setting for Tam Docherty's present life in the novel, based on the author's personal and family experience of Kilmarnock. It is a town with a history, an Ayrshire burgh with its roots in the history of Scotland, affected by the great concerns and the little by-products of that history. The lives of the Dochertys are played out on the same historical stage as the characters evoked for the young Conn by his maternal grandfather, Mairtin Wilson. When presenting the events and characters of Graithnock's past, McIlvanney is drawing, as with the streets and buildings, on the real town of Kilmarnock, using its recorded history to fuel the imagination of Conn Docherty.

To walk through Graithnock with Mairtin was to be ambushed at every corner by the past. From the pillar inset in the wall of the Old High Kirk 'To the memory of Lord Soulis AD 1444' (of whose murder Mairtin was able to give an eye-witness account) [. . .] (p. 84 of this edition)

Not long after this period, namely in 1444, a Lord Soulis, an English nobleman, was killed, it is said, in Kilmarnock, by one of the Boyds. Of the circumstances that led to this occurrence we find not the slightest trace in published records; but that such a deed was actually perpetrated would appear by the monument erected to his memory. It is probable that he was a descendant of the Lord Soulis to whom, according to Pont, the Dean Castle at one time belonged. The monument stands near the entrance to the High Church, at the head of Soulis Street, on the spot, it is believed, where he fell. Prior to 1825 it was a slender stone pillar, eight or nine feet high, but of very rude appearance, being entirely without architectural finish or ornament, except a small cross which was fixed upon its top. At that date it was tottering with age, and some of the more respectable inhabitants of the street in which it stood collected among themselves a sum of money for rebuilding it in a style more in harmony with modern taste. In the wall that encloses the burying ground of the church a niche was formed, fronting the street, and a fluted pillar, surmounted by an urn or vase placed within it. Over the whole is a handsome pediment, on which are the following words:

'To the memory of Lord Soulis, A.D. 1444.
Erected by Subscription, A.D. 1825.
"The days of old to mind I call."'

The old monument, or Soulis Cross, as it was called, appears to have existed as far back as 1609, when Pont wrote his work on Cunningham. When speaking of Dean Castle he observes: 'Near to it is ther a stone crosse called to this day Soulis Crosse, quher they affirme ye Lord Soulis wes killed.' [. . .]

(from *The History of Kilmarnock* by Archibald McKay)

[. . .] to the house of Alexander Smith in Douglas Street ('a genius wi' words' of whom Mairtin hadn't read a line) the town came alive with ghosts. (p. 84 of this edition)

ALEXANDER SMITH,

poet and essayist, is certainly the most considerable man of letters that Kilmarnock has produced, and deserves more than a passing notice. He was born at Kilmarnock on the 31st December, 1829, in a little thatched house, which has since been demolished, near the middle of Douglas Street, and on the site of which now stands a part of the factory of the Saxone Shoe Company, Ltd.

(from *The History of Kilmarnock*)

The best story of all was the one Mairtin told about the Foregate. When he was a boy, he said, there had been a two-storeyed thatched house there. When they were knocking it down, one of the workmen had found a leather pouch concealed under the thatch. As he lifted it out, it burst, and in seconds people were scrambling in the street for the hoard of silver coins that had scattered. The coins belonged to the reigns of Charles I and Charles II. How had they come there? 'Only the grave kens,' Mairtin would say. (p. 84 of this edition)

In June, 1863, another quantity of ancient coins was found at the taking down of an old house near the foot of Fore Street [. . .] They were all silver, and amounted in number to several hundreds. The most of them were about the size of our present crown pieces. Some bore the date 1553, and others belonged to the reigns of Charles the First and Charles the Second. The greater proportion of them were foreign pieces, and were comparatively beautiful specimens of ancient coinage. They were discovered in a leathern bag at the top of the wall immediately below the thatch, and were divided among the workmen employed in demolishing the building. The house, which was of two storeys, had been at one time an inn, and had a little court in front.

(from *The History of Kilmarnock*)

In these references, and in the others accompanying them on page 84 of this edition, McIlvanney draws freely on local historical sources (notably *The History of Kilmarnock* by Archibald McKay, revised by William Findlay, Kilmarnock, 1909), and on his own local knowledge, to create the sense of 'exotic past' being conjured out of 'mundane present' (p. 84) to play its part in shaping the character of young Conn. Conn is an inheritor of the past of his country and his town; yet his grasp of it is patchy and uncertain, as with so many Scots people in the face of their own history. McIlvanney comments on this in his later novel, *The Big Man*, set in the Graithnock area more than half a century later. Visiting Glasgow, his hero, Dan Scoular, meditates about Scottish history:

> There was an elusive but coherent unity he sensed behind the fragmentary impressions he took in, a feeling that identified Glasgow for him as distinct from other places he'd been in. To try to fix it for himself, he groped for a comparison. He knew Edinburgh slightly. He tried to lay his impression of one against the other, wondering where he felt the difference was. He had heard often enough of the supposed rivalries of the two places, familiar crutches for stand-up comedians, how Edinburgh was cold and Glasgow warmer, both in climate and people; how Edinburgh was snooty and Glasgow coarse. He didn't believe it. He had always liked both places and the people in them. But for him there was a difference, just as physical places, that had always made him feel more at home in Glasgow.
>
> Walking with Frankie, he worked out without saying it what he thought this was. It went back to something he had felt when they had taught him Scottish history at school. He had been aware of no continuity in it, just a series of jumps from one dramatic figure to another, until the figures became English. It had been as if nobody wanted to try to link the gaps or find out what they meant. It was almost as if Scotland didn't have any history or, if it did, not many people knew what it was. And he realised suddenly that was where he felt he was when he was walking through Glasgow, in the truth of Scottish history, the living reality of it. It seemed to him that of the few cities he had been in, it was the most serious one, the one that spoke to you most directly [. . .]
>
> That was the difference of the two cities for him. He liked being in Edinburgh but he could never take its beauty quite seriously. It was a monument to a false sense of Scotland. Glasgow bothered him in its own way, the way its handsomeness was pitted with harshness, but it seemed to say without pretence: this is where we've really been, this is where we are.

(from *The Big Man*)

In the same way that Edinburgh does for Dan Scoular, historical Graithnock presents Conn with a false sense of itself and gives him no real context for his own life or the lives of his family. The historians take no account of the lives of colliers, even in a mining town. It is very significant that the standard local history of Kilmarnock for Conn's generation does not mention the development of the coal mines in the area and carries no reference to the miners who lived and worked within its boundaries in sizeable numbers. Working people like the Dochertys have been ignored in the traditional histories of Scotland. For Conn, the realities are more truthfully held in the tension between the childhood dream-paradise of the Bringan and the adult world of High Street (Book 1, Chapter 18).

## Religious Division in the West of Scotland

It is possible to argue that the Docherty family in the novel is both an echo of McIlvanney's own family (father an ex-miner, earlier residence in High Street, three sons and one daughter) and a dynamic unit charged with many of the larger concerns of Scotland, particularly the urban West of Scotland. Issues of religion, class, education, political philosophy and psychological conflict are exemplified and developed within the family situation in such a way that we can see that they are not only real to that particular family but representative of larger divisions and tensions within Scotland as a whole.

In the earlier chapters of *Docherty*, one of the most obvious issues is that of religious division. Conn's first consciousness of this affecting his own life and his family is observed at the end of Book 1, Chapter 2.

> Then he had to go to school. It astonished him that the simple expression of his unwillingness to go didn't banish the necessity. Out of the rubble of his old security he picked some weird new perceptions: that Kathleen's chest was getting bumpy, that Mick could touch the top of the door if he jumped, that Angus could lift a full pail of water off the ground. His having to go to school was just part of the general strangeness.
>
> So he went. Very soon he accepted it. It didn't occur to him that Angus was the only other one of the family who attended the same school at the end of the street. It didn't occur to him that Mick and Kathleen were going somewhere else. (pp. 22–3 of this edition)

Conn and Angus are going to the High Street School, a non-denominational State primary school. Mick and Kathleen have been going to a local Catholic primary school. The divided nature of the family between devout Catholics (represented by Old Conn and Kathleen) and Protestants (represented by Jenny and her parents), with Tam himself as a lapsed Catholic agnostic in the middle, is fully worked out in incident and dialogue in Book 1, Chapters 3, 4, 6 and 7. In historical terms, the division is the larger one between Scotland's Calvinist Presbyterian tradition and the re-imported Catholic tradition brought by Irish immigrant workers into the West of Scotland in the nineteenth and early twentieth centuries.

Conn had been shown an example of the older Presbyterian tradition in his walks around Graithnock with Mairtin.

> He [Conn] memorised, like a mystic message of grandeur, the words: 'Here lies John Nisbet who was taken by Major Balfour's Party and suffered at Graithnock 14 April 1683 for adhering to the Word of God and our Covenant—Rev. XII and II. Renewed by public subscription AD 1823.' 'Who was taken . . . and suffered'—the words haunted him. (p. 84 of this edition)

In the spring of the same year, John Nisbet, younger, as he was called, to distinguish him from John Nisbet of Hardhill, was tried at Kilmarnock for having been engaged in the battle of Bothwell Bridge. [. . .] It does not appear, as we have already seen was unhappily too frequently the case in those distressful times when even the mere semblance of justice was the last thing to be expected, that any witnesses were examined at his trial; and the principal charges brought against him were his being at the rising at Bothwell, and owning its lawfulness—his refusing to tell what he knew regarding the place of concealment of John Nisbet of Hardhill—his acknowledging Jesus Christ to be the only Head of the Church, and Mr Donald Cargill, Mr John Kid, and Mr Richard Cameron to be faithful ministers of the Gospel. Kilmarnock, though familiar enough, in all conscience, with the cruel and exactious fines, imprisonments, and even barbarities of the persecutors, had as yet beheld no martyr executed within its boundaries; and it was therefore resolved by the enemies of the Covenant that Mr Nisbet should be hanged at the Cross, in order that the inhabitants and those in the neighbourhood might be awed into submission by the dreadful spectacle. No symptoms of fear were observable in his demeanour at the place of execution. He ascended the ladder with the greatest composure —prayed for some time—sung part of the 16th Psalm—and read the 8th chapter of the Epistle to the Romans. He prayed again, delivered his Bible to his uncle, and spoke for some time to the multitude, which tradition says was so great that many in order to hear and see him had placed themselves on the roofs of the houses. Every step of the ladder, he said, he reckoned a step nearer heaven; but when he came to expatiate on his previous sufferings and the injustice and mockery of his trial, a tumult was raised by the soldiers surrounding the scaffold, on observing which he at once drew the napkin over his face, and was launched into eternity when earnestly commending his soul to the care of his heavenly Father. The gallows stood at the south corner of the Cross. The spot is marked by a circular granite stone, on which are inscribed his name and the date of his execution as follows:

In the Low Church burying ground there is also a stone to his memory, on which is this inscription:

'Here lies John Nisbet, who was taken by Major Balfour's party, and suffered at Kilmarnock, 14th April, 1683, for adhering to the Word of God and our Covenants. Rev. xii. & ii.

(from the *History of Kilmarnock*)

The fanaticism and devotion of the seventeenth-century Covenanters to their extreme Protestant cause in the face of Government repression was a direct continuation of the aggressive intolerance shown by the original Scottish Reformers towards the Catholic Church and its Royal supporters in the previous century.

By the early nineteenth century, however, the Presbyterian cause was so predominant in the West of Scotland that it is treated as a matter of amusement by John Galt in *Annals of the Parish* when the Rev. Micah Balwhidder finds a Catholic priest active in his parish:

> But the story of the turtle is nothing to that of the Mass, which, with all its mummeries and abominations, was brought into Cayenneville by an Irish priest of the name of Father O'Grady, who was confessor to some of the poor deluded Irish labourers about the new houses and the cotton-mill. How he had the impudence to set up that memento of Satan, the crucifix, within my parish and jurisdiction, was what I never could get to the bottom of; but the soul was shaken within me, when, on the Monday after, one of the elders came to the Manse, and told me, that the old dragon of Popery, with its seven heads and ten horns, had been triumphing in Cayenneville on the foregoing Lord's day! I lost no time in convening the Session to see what was to be done; much, however, to my surprise, the elders recommended no step to be taken, but only a zealous endeavour to greater Christian excellence on our part, by which we should put the beast and his worshippers to shame and flight. I am free to confess, that, at the time, I did not think this the wisest counsel which they might have given; for, in the heat of my alarm, I was for attacking the enemy in his camp. But they prudently observed, that the days of religious persecution were past, and it was a comfort to see mankind cherishing any sense of religion at all, after the vehement infidelity that had been sent abroad by the French Republicans; and to this opinion, now that I have had years to sift its wisdom, I own myself a convert and proselyte.
>
> Fortunately, however, for my peace of mind, there proved to be but five Roman Catholics in Cayenneville; and Father O'Grady, not being able to make a living there, packed up his Virgin Marys, saints, and painted Agnuses in a portmanteau, and went off in the Ayr Fly one morning for Glasgow, where I hear he has since met with all the encouragement that might be expected from the ignorant and idolatrous inhabitants of that great city.
>
> (from *Annals of the Parish* by John Galt)

The religious division in the Docherty household rarely becomes a matter for argument, mainly because Tam is strongly protective of his father and his right to reminisce about Ireland and to express a Catholic viewpoint. In Book 1, Chapter 14, pp. 85–87, there is an episode which brings out the disrespectful attitude of Angus and Conn towards their grandfather's fixation on the old days in Ireland in conflict with Tam's fierce readiness to defend Old Conn from even the lightest teasing. Tam's touchiness on the subject is understandable, given the way in which people of Irish Catholic origin have felt themselves to be a minority, often discriminated against and likely to be the focus of violence in the community.

The extreme Presbyterian Covenanting tradition was particularly strong in the West of Scotland, but, as has been suggested, it moderated considerably in the nineteenth century. The Protestant faction that became the nucleus of opposition to the incoming Catholic workers also drew its strength from Ireland; it was the Ulster Protestant workers coming or, in a sense, returning to the Scotland of their ancestors and establishing their Orange Lodges in honour of William of Orange (King Billy) who saw themselves as the champions of Scottish Protestantism against an alien threat. At workplaces, in the streets and on the football terraces, religious division and bigotry have blighted life in Scotland, especially in the West. The Glasgow poet, Edwin Morgan, has expressed something of this violent spirit as exemplified by the heyday of the Glasgow gangs of the 1930s in his poem, 'King Billy'.

## KING BILLY

Grey over Riddrie the clouds piled up,
dragged their rain through the cemetery trees.
The gates shone cold. Wind rose
flaring the hissing leaves, the branches
swung, heavy, across the lamps.
Gravestones huddled in drizzling shadow,
flickering streetlight scanned the requiescats,
a name and an urn, a date, a dove
picked out, lost, half regained.
What is this dripping wreath, blown from its grave
red, white, blue, and gold
'To Our Leader of Thirty Years Ago'?

Bareheaded, in dark suits, with flutes
and drums, they brought him here, in procession
seriously, King Billy of Bridgeton, dead,
from Bridgeton Cross: a memory of violence,
brooding days of empty bellies,
billiard smoke and a sour pint,
boots or fists, famous sherrickings,
the word, the scuffle, the flash, the shout
bloody crumpling in the close,
bricks for papish windows, get
the Conks next time, the Conks ambush
the Billy Boys, the Billy Boys the Conks till
Sillitoe scuffs the razors down the stank—
No, but it isn't the violence they remember
but the legend of a violent man
born poor, gang-leader in the bad times

of idleness and boredom, lost in better days,
a bouncer in a betting club,
a quiet man at last, dying
alone in Bridgeton in a box bed.

So a thousand people stopped the traffic
for the hearse of a folk hero and the flutes
threw 'Onward Christian Soldiers' to the winds
from unironic lips, the mourners kept
in step, and there were some who wept.

Go from the grave. The shrill flutes
are silent, the march dispersed.
Deplore what is to be deplored,
and then find out the rest.

EDWIN MORGAN

## Language as a Social Issue in the West of Scotland

There has to be some kind of convincing solution to the problem of representing the speech of a particular area and social group on the printed page. Any Scottish writer trying to convey a variety of Scots dialect has to make choices in the ways that words and idioms belonging to a community are reproduced in order to be understood by a readership that is nowadays unlikely to be informed about the speech of any Scottish area. These choices are very likely to involve compromises between the authentic speech, which probably has no accepted spelling conventions, and an artificial 'literary' version, either based on an unsatisfactory set of conventions for spelling Scots dialect (deriving from the eighteenth century) or Anglicised to accord with the expectations of non-Scottish readers.

It is a problem that many Scottish writers have had to face over the centuries. John Knox, in his *History of the Reformation in Scotland*, was actually accused by some Scots of his day of writing in an Anglicised style. William McIlvanney, in representing the speech of Tam Docherty and his family and friends, has slightly modified the more usual Scots spellings of some words to convey the new West of Scotland speech that was developing in the industrial areas, influenced not only by the traditional Ayrshire or Lanarkshire dialects but by the speech habits of Irish and Highland immigrants. However, that is a literary problem for the writer. The big language issue in the West of Scotland, reflected in *Docherty*, and in other areas of Britain is the social attitude towards the use of local speech as opposed to the imported Standard English of education and social mobility.

A key chapter in the novel, where young Conn is faced with this conflict in a painful manner and consequently makes a significant choice affecting his whole future life, is in Book 1, Chapter 15. The belting with the tawse inflicted on him by Mr Pirrie for daring to say 'Ah fell an' bumped ma heid in the sheuch, sur' instead of 'I fell and bumped my head in the gutter, sir' causes

Conn to evaluate the relative merits of Scots and English words and expressions, and finally opt for family and community solidarity. Other Scottish writers have examined the same conflict between Scottish community spirit and Anglicised education.

The most eloquent view of this inner tension comes from Lewis Grassie Gibbon in his portrayal of a young girl growing up in North-East Scotland before the First World War:

> So that was Chris and her reading and schooling, two Chrisses there were that fought for her heart and tormented her. You hated the land and the coarse speak of the folk and learning was brave and fine one day and the next you'd waken with the peewits crying across the hills, deep and deep, crying in the heart of you and the smell of the earth in your face, almost you'd cry for that, the beauty of it and the sweetness of the Scottish land and skies. You saw their faces in firelight, father's and mother's and the neighbours', before the lamps lit up, tired and kind, faces dear and close to you, you wanted the words they'd known and used, forgotten in the far-off youngness of their lives, Scots words to tell to your heart, how they wrung it and held it, the toil of their days and unendingly their fight. And the next minute that passed from you, you were English, back to the English words so sharp and clean and true—for a while, for a while, till they slid so smooth from your throat you knew they could never say anything that was worth the saying at all.
>
> (from *Sunset Song* by Lewis Grassie Gibbon)

Conn was, therefore, in good company when he:

> . . . despaired of English. Suddenly, with the desperation of a man trying to amputate his own infected arm, he savagely scored out all the English equivalents.
>
> On his way out of school, he folded his grubby piece of paper very carefully and put it in his pocket. It was religiously preserved for weeks. By the time he lost it, he didn't need it. (p. 92 of this edition)

## Scottish Working-class Life and Attitudes

*Docherty* presents a vivid picture of how miners and their families in the Ayrshire coal towns and villages thought and felt in the years immediately preceding and following the First World War. However, McIlvanney does not labour the details of their everyday lives. The visible signs of poverty and hard labour are suggested or referred to in passing rather than carefully described. It is not the writer's purpose to provide a documentary picture of the working-class way of life at the time. What interests McIlvanney primarily is the ethos or spirit of the working class as represented by Tam Docherty and his immediate associates.

Early in the novel, in Book 1, Chapter 2, there is an examination of the ethics of the people of Graithnock High Street, and in succeeding chapters we see Tam Docherty's attitudes being rounded out and made specific in matters of family responsibility, sex, religion, poaching and acceptable social behaviour. The physical and sociological conditions of work and domestic life that would have strongly influenced these attitudes do not significantly intrude on the psychological exposition. For information about these physical and social conditions we need to go to other writers. Here are some extracts from an account of working-class life and working conditions in the later nineteenth century and the early years of this century.

[. . .]
People whose daily work was of such eroding length [8–12 hours a day] often lived amid insanitary and dangerous conditions. Miners, in particular, generally had no option but to live in company houses which were among the most inadequate and disgusting of all Scotland's miserable housing stock. For example, the Royal Commission on Labour heard in 1892 of the houses provided by William Dixon and Company at Auchenraith. There were 42 single-roomed and 41 double-roomed houses, containing 492 people: there were no wash-houses or coal cellars (coals were kept under the bed): there was an open sewer behind, with 12 doorless 'hen-roost privies' (so called because you could not sit down): there were 2 drinking fountains. When miners left these homes for work they were exposed to industrial disease—even at the end of the period, between 150 and 200 miners died annually from pneumoconiosis alone—and to accidents, which, though they killed far less than disease, were an omnipresent threat in the pit. Terrible incidents, like that at William Dixon's colliery at Blantyre in 1872 which claimed over 200 lives, evoked national sympathy, but it was the everyday tension at work that few outsiders appreciated. Kellog Durland spoke of the 'number of hairbreadth escapes that daily pass without comment; the acts of real heroism that are performed as a matter of course in the day's work . . . There are few old colliers who have not met with some accidents in their lives.' [. . .]
Under these circumstances, who did the workers learn to hate? Often, and very justifiably, they hated the boss: this did not preclude them, more immediately, from hating another worker, the next person above them in the hierarchy—the skilled plater who shouted at the young, unskilled plater's helper ('I resented this foul, violent language . . . it seemed so unfair and unnecessary seeing that we were all doing our best'), or the foreman who 'used to go round quietly on a Friday night to the men he was going to pay off'. The skilled workers and the foremen—the 'NCOs of industry' —in turn despised and kept in order those below them, a fact that combined with sectarianism to keep the workers even within one occupation from fully developing their sense of a common interest. [. . .]
There was undoubtedly a heightening of class consciousness and solidarity after the turn of the century, when the skilled workers found themselves pressed towards the kind of insecurities that had long been the lot of the unskilled, and this had important political consequences. [. . .]
There remained, however, many workers who were apathetic, or who believed the system to be unalterable at least in their factory, or who hated

Catholics more, or labourers more, or who thought that the boss was not a bad chap at heart. [. . .]

(from *A Century of the Scottish People—1830–1950* by T. C. Smout)

Such facts go far in explaining Tam Docherty's anger when he is faced with the apparent class treason and social irresponsibility of his problem son, Angus, in Book 3, Chapter 5. Tam's outburst, his last major statement of the novel, is an eloquent and forceful expression of the working-class ethic as he perceives it and as he has tried to live it all his life.

'Ah'll tell ye the sense,' Tam said. 'We walk a nerra line. Ah ken hoo nerra it is. Ah've walked it a' ma days. Us an' folk like us hiv goat the nearest thing tae nothin' in this world. A' that filters doon tae us is shite. We leeve in the sewers o' ither bastards' comfort. The only thing we've goat is wan anither. That's why ye never sell yer mates. Because there's nothin' left tae buy wi' whit ye get. That's why ye respect yer weemenkind. Because whit we make oorselves is whit we are. Because if ye don't, ye're provin' their case. Because the bastards don't believe we're folk! They think we're somethin' . . . less than that. Well, Ah ken whit Ah believe. It's only us that can show whit folk are. Whit dae they ken aboot it? Son, it's easy tae be guid oan a fu' belly. It's when a man's goat two bites an' wan o' them he'll share, ye ken whit he's made o'. Maist o' them were boarn blin'. Well, we areny, son. We canny afford tae be blin'. Listen. In ony country in the world, who are the only folk that ken whit it's like tae leeve in that country? The folk at the boattom. The rest can a' kid themselves oan. They can afford to hiv fancy ideas. We canny, son. We loass the wan idea o' who we are, we're deid. We're wan anither. Tae survive, we'll respect wan anither. When the time comes, we'll a' move forward thegither, or nut at all. That's whit Ah've goat against you, boay.' He pointed at Angus. 'You're a fuckin' deserter. Ah don't harbour deserters. Ye're wi' the rest o' us or ye go elsebit.' (p. 238 of this edition)

Young Conn's decision to turn away from education and follow his father down the pit at the earliest opportunity was a sign that he was strongly motivated to continue the family tradition. Both of his brothers later departed, for different reasons, from this tradition. Ironically, even though Conn was keen to go down the pit like his father, it had been Tam's fancy that Conn might have a different kind of life by staying on at school. Yet the family poverty had ruled that out.

He [Tam] regretted the two pressures that had made him agree to this: Conn's insistence and their poverty. He couldn't have felt worse if he had given Conn a suicide-kit for Christmas. But more hurtful than the immediate irony was seeing in front of him the incarnation of the inevitable. That he had refused to face the fact that it was inevitable until now made him more ashamed. He could never have afforded to keep Conn on at school. It had been a silly dream for a grown man to allow himself. Now Conn had made him admit the obvious. He had fathered four children and all he had ever been able to give them was their personal set of shackles. (pp. 191–2 of this edition)

To take a wider historical perspective, Tam's shame and sense of being imprisoned with his family in a jail of occupational poverty have been the lot of the Scottish miner through many centuries. From the beginning of coal-mining in Scotland in the Middle Ages, right down to the end of the eighteenth century, colliers and their families were legally slaves belonging to their mine-owning masters. Even after the Act of Parliament that technically freed them in 1775,* there were many restrictions on their real freedom, and it took another generation, until an Act of 1799,† before they had equal legal rights with other workers.

Yet throughout the nineteenth and earlier twentieth centuries there was a considerable amount of social and political prejudice against the coal-miners. Relations between 'polite' society and the coal-miners were marked by contempt and indifference to the hardships of the job on the part of the former, and by resentment and a determination to struggle for improvement on the part of the latter. Miners' wages were liable to fluctuate up or down depending on the economic situation, and strikes were common. One historian of the Scottish working classes has charted this troubled time in mining development.

At the beginning of the 'freedom' period the coalowners brought their labourers annually. The collier contracted to work for 12 months, to produce a fixed quantity of coal weekly for a fixed wage, but if the owner saw fit to lower his selling price, the collier must lower his wage in proportion; 'and if the whole of the coaliers shall at any time be idle without reasonable excuse' they must pay the owners' 'rent of the coal for such time, or if one, or whatever number less than the whole of them, shall be idle, they must pay their proportion of the rent for such time.' For giving 'insulting language' they were fined 5s. for each offence; every collier had to provide his own 'bearer'—usually wife or daughter—and if the collier was idle through the fault of the owner, he was given 1s. 8d. per day of 'play wages.' [. . .]

Trade Unions were formed and bitter strikes took place in the west country. At Bo'ness blacklegs were savagely maltreated. According to a Mr Taylor, a coalmaster, the Ayrshire miners were organised into a Union in 1817 by a weaver named Fallhouse Wilson; a strike ensued, but it was broken in a fortnight. In 1818 markets were high and wages low, and one coalmaster at least is said to have simultaneously taken 1s. off wages and raised prices by 2s. per wagon. At Govan, in 1821, a strike lasted for eleven weeks, but the men were beaten. In 1824 a strike lasted six months in the Edinburgh district, and blacklegs had their ears cut off. But in the same year a strong Union in Lanarkshire, Renfrewshire and Dumbartonshire raised wages from 3s. 6d. to 5s. per day. In 1825 colliers' wages are said to have averaged 4s. per day of 8 to 10 hours. During the strikes of that period we find the first references to the importation of 'strangers from

* Act for altering, explaining and amending several Acts of Parliament of Scotland, respecting colliers, coal-bearers and salters (1775)

† Act to explain and amend the laws relative to Colliers in that Part of Great Britain called Scotland (1799)

Ireland' as strike-breakers, a practice which seems to have been one of the contributory causes of that intense anti-Irish feeling which has scarcely yet died away in many districts. It is noticeable, too, that, down at least to a legal decision in 1817, no one, owner or collier, believed that the Combination Acts applied to Scotland. [. . .]

In April, 1876, the colliers wages were 4s. 6d. a day for 4 days a week, and the masters had intimated a reduction of 10 per cent., and the Attorney General had the impudence to declare in Parliament that 'they all knew mining was a dangerous employment and that it was well paid'; in December wages were 'falling.'

Sheer hunger abode with the Scots miners in 1877. Wages were 2s. 6d. to 3s. per day for two and three days a week, and the Fife and Clackmannan miners were locked-out altogether for six months rather than submit to a 10 per cent. reduction, the lock-out occurring in the midst of a great shipbuilding strike and damped down iron furnaces, which diminished the demand for coal and rendered the struggle easier for the masters. Finally the men compromised on a partial reduction with a sliding scale; sixpence per ton increase in the selling price of coal was to mean 4 per cent. increase on wages, sixpence decrease was to mean 4 per cent. reduction, and so on. But the trade depression continued, aggravated in 1878 by the City Bank failure, and wages fell to 2s. 6d. per day; in most districts the Union went to pieces [. . .]; occasionally there were riots, as at Slamannan, where the houses of owners and managers were wrecked. In December a miners' conference asked Parliament to make enquiry into the causes of the trade depression which was causing them so much misery.

(from *The History of the Working Classes in Scotland* by Tom Johnston)

The most graphic account of the arduous nature of the miner's life was written by George Orwell in the 1930s when he spent some time living in a mining community and describing the conditions there. In *The Road to Wigan Pier*, he feelingly describes conditions down a coal-pit. The observations he makes were based on diary entries he wrote of his visits to different pits:

*21 March*
This morning went down the Grimethorpe pit. Not exhausting this time, because in order not to clash with the visit of some students from the Technical College we went to the nearest working, only about ¼ mile and little bending. [. . .]

This time I saw the fillers actually working at the coal face, and now having seen the different operations of coal-getting, except blasting, in progress separately, I understand more or less how it is done. The coal-cutter travels along the face cutting into the bottom of the ledge of coal to the depth of 5 feet. Then the coal can be tumbled out in boulders with picks, or—as here, the Grimethorpe coal being very hard—is first loosened with blasting charges and then extracted. Then the fillers (who have also extracted it) load it on to the conveyor belt which runs behind them and carries it to a chute from which it runs into the tubs. As far as possible the three operations are done in three separate shifts. The coal cutter works on the afternoon shift, the blasting is done on the night shift (when the minimum number of people are in the pit), and the fillers extract the coal on the morning shift. [. . .]

The place where the fillers were working was fearful beyond description. The only thing one could say was that, as conditions underground go, it was not particularly hot. But as the seam of coal is only a yard high or a bit more, the men can only kneel or crawl to their work, never stand up. The effort of constantly shovelling coal over your left shoulder and flinging it a yard or two beyond, while in a kneeling position, must be very great even to men who are used to it. Added to this there are the clouds of coal dust which are flying down your throat all the time and which make it difficult to see any distance. The men were all naked except for trousers and knee-pads. It was difficult to get through the conveyor belt to the coal face. You had to pick your moment and wriggle through quickly when the belt stopped for a moment. Coming back we crawled on to the belt while it was moving; I had not been warned of the difficulty of doing this and immediately fell down and had to be hauled off before the belt dashed me against the props etc. which were littered about further down. Added to the other discomforts of the men working there, there is the fearful din of the belt which never stops for more than a minute or so. [. . .]

During this week G has had two narrow escapes from falls of stone, one of which actually grazed him on its way down. These men would not last long if it were not that they are used to the conditions and know when to stand from under. I am struck by the difference between the miners when you see them underground and when you see them in the street etc. Above ground, in their thick ill-fitting clothes, they are ordinary-looking men, usually small and not at all impressive and indeed not distinguishable from other people except by their distinctive walk (clumping tread, shoulders very square) and the blue scars on their noses. Below, when you see them stripped, all, old and young, have splendid bodies, with every muscle defined and wonderfully small waists. I saw some miners going into their baths. As I thought, they are quite black from head to foot. So the ordinary miner, who has not access to a bath, must be black from the waist down six days a week at least.

> (from *Collected Essays, Journalism and Letters Vol. 1,*
> *An Age Like This 1920–1940* by George Orwell)

The traumatic event for Tam Docherty in the third book of the novel is the lengthy struggle of the miners in 1921 against the policy of Lloyd George's Government to abandon the national control of the mines that had been operating during the First World War and to leave the way open for private mine-owners to reduce wages and conditions, and cut the numbers of employed in the face of a world economic recession. The miners' strike and the accompanying lock-out lasted for fourteen weeks, and ended with a return to work without significant concessions being achieved. During the stoppage, there were some violent incidents in the Scottish coalfields.

In the Fife coalfields there were some demonstrations and processions, and strikers succeeded, after some scuffling and fighting in putting out the boiler fires at a number of pits. Cowdenbeath saw some fighting between strikers and police, and a number of arrests were made.

But for a week all remained quiet in Cowdenbeath, including the pits where the furnaces had all been drawn. Then, without warning, the town suddenly suffered what amounted to an armed invasion. The *Dunfermline Press* says: 'On Wednesday, April 13, Cowdenbeath rate-payers woke up to find that the burgh had, overnight, been converted into what was virtually an armed camp'. In the early morning, motor-buses packed with soldiers and marines poured into the town and also into Lochgelly.

The officers commandeered for billets all the available hall accommo-dation, and at once posted guards in all the pits in the district. The soldiers are drafts of the Argyll and Sutherland and Seaforth Highlan-ders. Firing of the furnaces was begun at most of the collieries, the work being performed by managers and other officials. At each colliery where this work was begun, there was a mounted military guard, and wire rope barricading was erected all round each pithead.

In the small hours of the morning Fife County police swooped on Cowdenbeath, Lumphinnans and Lochgelly and arrested eight more men. The description of the arrests runs as follows:

Taking place, as they did, at a time when few persons were about and while the men sought for were asleep in their beds, the arrests were quietly effected. A motor char-a-banc in which a strong force of police was seated, conveyed the prisoners to Dunfermline, which was reached before day-break. In their passage through the streets of Dunfermline, the prisoners vociferously sang 'The Red Flag'. Pending their appearance at the Sheriff Court, the prisoners were incarcerated in the cells within the Court buildings. [. . .]

That spirited scene was taking place on the eve of 'Black Friday', when J. H. Thomas was to announce that the railwaymen and the transport workers, the allies of the miners in the Triple Alliance, were not to support them by strike action. The miners were isolated, and left to fight on alone. Negotiations with the owners were broken off. [. . .]

On July 1 the long drawn-out conflict ended with a decision to return to work.

The struggle was over. The deferred Annual Conference was held on Friday, August 12, 1921. Hugh Murnin, the President, was in the chair, and only necessary business was transacted. Robert Smillie, who was specially invited to attend, said:

The fight was not of the miners' choosing. It was forced upon us. Never in the history of industry and of Trades Unionism has a better army entered on a defensive fight. There was not a waverer in the million-odd miners from Campbeltown to Kent. Not only were the men and boys enthusiastic and determined, but their womenfolk were with them

(Applause). It was a glorious struggle, and I congratulate our people on the great fight which they made. But I would not have been able to congratulate them had they accepted the brutal, impertinent terms offered to them by the employers. [. . .]

(from *A History of the Scottish Miners* by R. Page-Arnot)

For a man like Tam Docherty, committed to the cause of workers' rights without being particularly militant or political, these events were demoralising and crucial in explaining his decline in the last book of the novel. Yet the struggle was not over and only a few years later the miners were again heavily involved in industrial action. During the General Strike of 1926, they resisted longer than other groups of workers and consequently suffered more. William McIlvanney's own father remembered this time for the rest of his life:

### 'INITIATION', V

My father's personal Midian was The Strike.
Say 'Nineteen twenty-six' and watch his eyes.
Bruise still with images of boot and pick.
Beyond the room's bright warmth he heard the cries
Of children starving and the feet of men
Subduing anguish to a measured walk.
You didn't interrupt his anger when
He brought up gouts of dead blood in his talk.

'Sam Harris hanged himself.' 'I've seen a wean
Whose staple diet was a dummy tit.'
'The batoned bastards beat up unarmed men.'
Not an economist's view. He didn't find
The key that locks pain safely in a law.
Raw facts still looted comfort from his mind,
Broke into his indifference. He saw
Only the cold blind heaving ranks who crushed
Into the closing justice of their time
Only to be rejected. Pictures strung
Out of his mind unbroken, newsreel rushed
Straight from the scene of an historic crime:
The pit-cage talk before fierce hopes were hung
On a slender thread of unity; the bands
That grouped lean jowls round any bone of news
To sharpen hope's teeth on it; big quiet men
Who rotted with their pockets round their hands;
The shame of looking at your children's shoes;
Soup-kitchens; five fags shared out among ten;
At countless corners the spontaneous wake
Held by silk-mufflered men for self-respect.
Hearing him talk you came to realize
That history is what time leaves in men's eyes,
The shapes their thinking takes. [. . .]

(from *The Longships in Harbour* by William McIlvanney)

## Democratic Socialism and the Celebration of the Common Man

In the poetic extract on p. 304, William McIlvanney was examining a crucial event in his father's life, an event that is paralleled in its effects by the 1921 lockout within the life of Tam Docherty. McIlvanney has written about the significance of the General Strike for his father and, by extension, for himself:

It was a happening he kept going back to. I think this was because it contained the baffling residue of all his experience, the small recalcitrant nugget which he couldn't break down into viable currency. Certainly, it wasn't until my own experience had enlarged a bit that I felt capable of setting my own against his, and came to the conclusion that they helped to interpret each other. What I think he felt was what I feel: simply that the most appalling thing in the world is not the vanity of human wishes, but the vanity of human suffering; that people can endure such things as should make the world stop turning and it may not even make their neighbours pay attention. I think it was my reaction to that realisation as much as anything which gave me such identity as I have, as a person and as a writer. I believe the only worthwhile thing that can be salvaged out of the frequently unnecessary suffering which people have gone through, and still go through, isn't glory or admiration, or even regret, but the bettering of the lives that come after them. And I believe that this is only achieved through honesty, this in turn bringing in two related skills which we don't seem too eager to practise: the ability to admit the depth of our involvement in the lives of others, and the ability at the same moment to allow them room to be themselves. I take social responsibility to mean, not the need to make sure that people keep their places, but the need to care that each one has the right to the conditions which will give him the chance to fulfil himself. This is to me not primarily a political need, but simply a human one. It is essentially a matter of the stance you adopt towards any other person. It is at its most fundamental merely a way of seeing other people.

(from 'Growing Up in the West' in *Memoirs of a Modern Scotland*, ed. Karl Miller)

One of the themes of *Docherty* is certainly the importance of people, particularly people whom the larger world has not really noticed because of their poverty or their lack of economic or social importance. Allied to this sense of the importance of the Common Man is an explicit rejection of the large ideologies, especially religion, which seem to ignore real humanity.

In a recent short story, McIlvanney expresses through the mouth of a talkative pub bore a more developed view of the claims of ordinary humanity against superstition than was expressed at Tam Docherty's funeral by his son, Mick, and his friends, Tadger and Hammy:

'Religion?' Gus McPhater was saying. He was always saying something. 'Don't waste ma time. The opium of the masses. It's done damage worse than a gross of atomic bombs. Chains for the brainbox, that's religion. Ministers? Press agents for the rulin' classes. Ye'll no' catch me in a church. If Ah could, Ah'd cancel ma christenin' retrospectively. Take yer stained-glass windaes. Whit's a windae for? To see through. Right? So what do they do? They cover it in pictures. So that when ye look at the light. The light, mind ye. That's how ye see, ye know. Light refractin' on yer pupils. When ye look for the light, it gets translated intae what they want ye tae see. How's that for slavery? An' whit d'ye see? A lot of holy mumbo-jumbo. People Ah don't know from Adam. What've a bunch of first-century Jewish fanatics got to do wi' me? Ah'll tell ye what. Know when Ah'll go intae a church? When it's man's house. When the stained-glass windaes are full of holy scenes of rivetters in bunnets and women goin' the messages wi' two weans hangin' on to their arse an' auld folk huddled in at one bar of an electric fire after fifty years o' slavin' their guts out for a society that doesny care if they live or die. Those would be windaes worth lookin' at. That's what art should be. Holy pictures of the people. Or a mosaic even. How about that? See when they made that daft town centre. The new precinct. The instant slum. See instead o' that fountain. Why not a big mosaic? Showin' the lives of the people here an' now. How about that? The Graithnock mosaic. Why no?'
(from 'Performance' in *Walking Wounded* by William McIlvanney)

As Mick says of his father, 'Ah think a' he believed in wis folk.' Mick himself takes a long step into another ideology by joining the Communist Party. Angus is anchored by self-interested chains of gold to his brand of enterprise capitalism. Only young Conn in an inarticulate way carries on along his father's path in life, in two minds about things.

Yet Conn was also disturbed and suspicious of him. What Mick said was too simple. What had been a dialogue had turned into a pronouncement. It was as if Mick hadn't heard a lot of what had happened, had just missed out so much that was important—their father's respect for people, no matter who they were, their mother's patient persistence, the fact that they had only been able to reach this place because they had all loved one another [. . .]
'Ah don't want tae smash folk. Ah jist want them tae see hoo guid folk like ma feyther were. Tae gi'e us room tae leeve.' (p. 277 of this edition)

In the writings of another Ayrshire man who has given himself for years to the twin causes of Socialism and Scotland, there is a full statement of this ideal of non-aggressive, humane Democratic Socialism.

Democratic socialism seeks to change some of the fundamentals in the character of the people. Specifically, those aspects of our nature which can so easily set person against person: greed, the desire to acquire power over others and a propensity to exploit human need for private gain. It is a creed that can only achieve its objective of a change in the character of humankind by an intellectual conversion which leads people to accept and support the higher morality inherent in the socialist ethic and do so voluntarily. [. . .]

The democratic way is a hard road. It calls for qualities of character, stamina, determination, tolerance, reason and audacity. But above all, it requires solid commitment to progress through persuasion and education so that new principles of individual and community conduct take root and grow to strengthen socialist action by making changes by consent of the people. What makes it a particularly hard road is that the democratic socialist is required to accept defeat, to see injustice and poverty stalk the land, and to witness the re-emergence of cruel disregard for the weak and vulnerable, which has been the chief characteristic of the Conservative government elected in 1979—all without falling into the temptation of seeking forcible change through violence. [. . .]

What has all this to do with Scotland? Ours is a country which is heavily influenced by the basic idea, and several schools, of socialism. That is one reason why Scotland, unlike England, has proved so resistant to the right-wing values which Mrs Thatcher has been so successful in propounding south of the border. Because of our social and economic history, in which socialism played such a key role, Scots still hold firmly to ideas about common care and concern for humanity and the need for a sense of community solidarity. There is, therefore, a gulf growing between Scotland and England. Fewer and fewer Scots are able to escape from the conclusion that if our values are to prevail in our civil government, we shall need to seek self-government. That immediately raises the question of what kind of Scotland such a self-governing entity would be and that question can only be answered by reference to major influences on attitudes and potential political development. Socialism is not the only influence at work of course. Calvinism and Scots Catholicism (quite different from its English counterpart) have a profound influence on matters other than the purely religious; so too do the values of those parts of Scotland where we find the small sturdy towns of the North East and the Borders, where divisions in class terms are less sharp and painful than in the industrial conurbations. But there is no dispute that socialism and its development are a major factor in how we think and act now and will continue to be of crucial importance. [. . .] Unlike large countries, where big populations of fifty million and above make it easy for pure theory and geographical division to work on raw feelings, with alienation increased through lack of all but minimal human social contact, Scotland is a small and remarkable homogeneous nation. [. . .]

Democratic socialism should have a special appeal to the people of Scotland, not because we are intrinsically kinder than others, but because our history, experience, size and homogeneity makes us more open to its salient features—responsibility and obligations to the community, the sense of solidarity it creates, the unremitting effort to harness economic forces to serve the people and its freedom from hatred. Democratic socialism applied in Scotland will shift the balance of wealth and power to working people and their families: it would fail if it failed to do that. It will cause those who hold disproportionate power to relinquish it for the common good. It will encourage the organisation of labour and will have a bias towards the rights of working people. And it will do all this in a sensitive and humane fashion, mindful that taking power from one group is not a licence to humiliate or wound people from that group. People, who are not socialists, are first and foremost our fellow citizens and their dignity and well-being must be taken into account in all that we do. Humanity and socialism are indivisible.

(from *Scotland—The Case for Optimism* by Jim Sillars)

It is this ideal that Tam Docherty, uncertainly and inarticulately (except on one or two occasions), expressed in his life and death through his dealings with family and friends and his attitudes to work and leisure.

## William McIlvanney as a Writer

Over the years, the reviews of William McIlvanney's novels have been rather mixed. Critics have often focused on matters of style—the love of metaphor and the striking phrase used sometimes at the expense of clarity and immediacy, the strong language, the idealisation of the urban proletariat in rather sentimental rhetoric (what has been dubbed 'The Urban Kailyard', after the nineteenth century Scottish literary taste for idealised pictures of rural life centred on the cabbage patch and the parish pump)—without seeing how cumulatively his work has been building up into a vivid and many-sided picture of working-class experience in the West of Scotland. All newspaper comment has been, in one way or another, lacking in a clear perspective of McIlvanney's work. The first reviewer quoted below has not been able to bring any significant knowledge of the social background and historical situation in *Docherty* to bear upon his comments, although he does make one or two perceptive observations; the second writer, with McIlvanney's own interview statements to assist him, sees that there is a pattern to McIlvanney's work so far, but does not analyse it very fully.

What might be called the Kelman Effect determines 'our' (i.e. effete and literary Southerners') response to recent Scottish writing. We grasp at words like 'tough' and 'gritty' and think we've got the hang of it. McIlvanney might almost typify what we're looking for. His working class is tougher and grittier than anything we'll find in a dozen Amises.

Even if there's some stage Scots, some workerism in McIlvanney, it would be unfair to dismiss him for stereotyping. His Laidlaw thrillers (*Laidlaw*, *The Papers of Tony Veitch*) brilliantly marry tension and acute observation with a style that would do justice to the best American urban tradition. They're his most successful books, but *Docherty* and *The Big Man* are no small achievements.

*Docherty* was first published in 1975. The location is Graithnock, a small town near Glasgow, the year 1903. The word 'heroism' occurs twice in the first three pages, and heroes are what McIlvanney's after. Tam Docherty is Graithnock's Big Bad John, a strong and occasionally violent man ground down, like everyone around him, by the iniquitous bastards who live off working people. There is in the town 'an ooze of hopelessness . . . None of them here had any chance.'

McIlvanney takes the Docherty family up to and beyond the Great War, his attention focused first on Tam and Conn, his youngest son. Men preoccupy him, women are resolute but victims of the male world.

We drive quickly through contemporary Graithnock at the beginning of *The Big Man*, arriving at Thornbank where the men, out of work, are trying to hold on to their lives—without much luck. Dan Scoular, almost Tam's twin, needs money to keep his family together. Foolishly he takes part in a bare knuckle prize-fight which will settle things between two thuggish businessmen. Continually confronting his maleness, Dan saves his self-respect, redeems the lives of everyone in Thornbank. The 'ooze of hopelessness' still threatens, and even 'God's a hard case' who'll nut you at the drop of a hat. Where there was something doomed about Tam's heroism, Dan is a 'rebel', battling his way out.

Both books are clogged with metaphors and similes, each illuminating in its own right but eventually submerging McIlvanney's perceptions: *this* world can only be explained in terms of *that*. Similarly, the bleakly laconic speech of his characters is undercut as McIlvanney explains the thinking behind the pith. Occasional poetspeak ('variousness' for 'variety') doesn't help.

But his people are powerful creations, his dialogue a crisp slap in the face of defeat. Laidlaw briefly appears in *The Big Man*. I hope this signals McIlvanney's intention to return to the thriller, a form custom-made to undercut his weaknesses, emphasise his strengths.

(review of *Docherty* and *The Big Man* by Nick Kimberley in *City Limits*, 30 August 1985)

Unlike his previous novels which had a strong narrative line, [*Walking Wounded*] is a collection of loosely related short stories which examine the different sensations of living in late twentieth century Scotland. Part observation, part confessional, the stories both celebrate the essential common decencies of ordinary people and mourn the erosion of those working class values which have guided McIlvanney through the better part of his life.

'The stories are about lives colliding,' he explains. 'And it struck me that if I wanted an undercurrent of communal life, besides the individual lives I was dealing with, the pub was a recurring motif.'

And so it became. In one of the collection's finest stories, 'Performance' [. . .] a small-time con-man returns to Graithnock—a thinly disguised version of McIlvanney's native Kilmarnock—and uses the local howff to promote his image. Sharply dressed, quick-witted, big-spending and out to impress, the character is brought vividly to life by McIlvanney's brutally honest, yet utterly human, observations.

Does this make him merely a recorder of social manners. 'No,' he insists. 'With fiction the creative element is brought into play. It's the imposition of the imaginative pattern on top of the experience. Anything I write is going to have an element of the autobiographical but that might just be something I've seen or heard or experienced myself. Hopefully you can't see the joins.' McIlvanney likens the process to the way in which an anecdote improves with the telling so that the original story is buried beneath layers of half-truths and fictional embellishments. By the same token some of the stated facts of his own life can become blurred at the edges with the fiction he has created. That problem, he concedes, is one for the critics!

William McIlvanney was born on November 25, 1936, in Kilmarnock, educated locally and then went to Glasgow University to study English. After graduating he became a school teacher at Irvine Royal Academy in 1960. To his surprise he found that he liked teaching but by then the compulsion of writing had gripped him too strongly to turn a personal inclination into a life-long career. Gradually he eased himself out of the classroom, becoming first a part-time teacher and then by way of university fellowships, two novels and a collection of verse he became a full-time writer in 1975.

That was the year of *Docherty* which many people still feel is his greatest achievement. Loosely based on Kilmarnock as it was in the first quarter of this century, McIlvanney's chosen instrument of interpretation is the young all-seeing boy Conn Docherty. Through his eyes we see the strengths and weaknesses of the small claustrophobic community he inhabits and become aware of its inner sense of rhythm. Striding through the novel like a colossus is the figure of Tam Docherty, Conn's father, a man possessed by an austere morality which brooks no opposition. Exalted to a kind of grandeur, Tam Docherty is one of the great figures of Scottish fiction.

Like a father who sees virtues in all his children, McIlvanney refuses to prefer one of his novels to another but one cannot avoid the feeling that *Docherty* occupies a special place in his affections. For a start, it grew straight out of his own roots. 'An old miner came up to me with tears in his eyes and shook me by the hand,' he remembers. 'He told me that *Docherty* was the story of his life—which it wasn't, but I admired the generosity of spirit.' McIlvanney calls incidents like that 'the sustaining moments when the audience turns up to help validate what I'm trying to do.'

The trouble was that, after *Docherty*, there was a large gap in his literary output which threatened to empty the full house. Partly the silence was caused by an adjustment to full-time writing: partly to blame was the break-up of his marriage but the most compelling reason is that McIlvanney refuses to write to order.

For his former agent, George Greenfield, who knows the literary jungle better than most people, the gaps came as a bitter disappointment. While admitting that McIlvanney is one of the most outstanding talents he has ever handled, Greenfield fears that the novelist might have been too sparing of his gifts. 'He never made the mark he should have done,' Greenfield claims. 'Novelists need to publish prolifically during their early years—every eighteen months or so to establish their reputations. Willie hasn't done that.'

It's a point taken up by John Bright-Holmes, the other half of the duo who have attempted to manage the course of McIlvanney's literary career. Bright-Holmes has edited most of the fiction since *Remedy is None* in 1966 and he, too, regrets that the output has been so small. 'The reviewers tended to forget him after *Docherty* was published and when *The Big Man* came along in 1985 it attracted only sparse attention.' With the gift for encouraging authors which has made Bright-Holmes a top editor, though, he finds the fallow years easy to forgive. 'You can't make Willie do the things that he doesn't want to do. He's far too committed to his craft. In fact he's about the only author I know who has to be begged for more product!'

McIlvanney goes along with that assessment of himself. After *Docherty* came *Laidlaw*, a Glasgow crime thriller in 1978, *The Papers of Tony Veitch* in 1983 and *The Big Man*, spiritual successor to *Docherty* in 1985. 'As soon as people know what you should be doing,' says McIlvanney, 'you should do something else. I've never believed in the sanctity of being an author—writing isn't wonderful unless it's good.'

While this might be a stock answer, a glib response to the knowing comment that he might have sold himself short, McIlvanney is far from touchy when the subject is brought up. 'When I get down to write, I would be disappointed if I sat for eight hours and got what I wanted. What's interesting about fiction are the ambushes you don't expect, when you discover what you really want to say.'

Fame, too, came as a surprise and some of his friends believe that McIlvanney found it difficult to cope with *Docherty*'s success—as well as being hailed by the critics it won the prestigious Whitbread Award. McIlvanney acknowledges the point but adds a rejoinder: 'Success, however comparative, is only a hotel. Nobody really lives there. You can't live in the past and go on writing. I always like to think that the next thing I'm doing will be the best.'

The thought is shared by George Greenfield and John Bright-Holmes. Both these custodians of McIlvanney's talent firmly believe that *Walking Wounded* is by far and away his tightest and most thoughtful piece of fiction. Gone is the artificial straining for the telling phrase which punctuated the earlier novels and in its place is a more straightforward and harder-edged realism. For Greenfield that inner strength seems to have ebbed into the writing from McIlvanney's deeply personal relationship to Scotland. 'Willie has the great Scottish strength of sticking to his roots,' he says, 'He never became a literary figure on the London scene—that might have given him a bigger reputation but he would have lost a lot. Scotland has given him great sustenance.'

The background to *Walking Wounded* is a Lowland Scotland which many readers will recognise, a scarred landscape which is redeemed only by the humanity of the people who inhabit its towns and cities. It's the world which McIlvanney himself has long lived in. 'I've retained a living daily contact with that background so that my sense of it abrades continually against the reality of it,' he says, not without a touch of pride. 'What I am trying to do is to see what is there, to construct a vision from fragments of reality, to make it all coherent. After all,'—he smiles at the notion—'I still go to the same pub where I had my first drink and I'm accepted there as part of the congregation of the pub and not as some sort of literary visitor.'

Fourteen years on from the first publication of *Docherty*, it's possible now to see a pattern emerging from McIlvanney's output. The hard core is provided by the fictional town of Graithnock and its near neighbour

Thornbank and by the people who live there—Tam Docherty, Dan Scoular, the 'Big Man' and the many characters from *Walking Wounded*. Their problems come not with the inevitable changes to their environment but with the gradual erosion of deeply felt social and political virtues.

McIlvanney's way of regarding their predicament is to see Tam Docherty as an expert in moral trench warfare while Dan Scoular fights his end in the uniform of a guerrilla, striving to find an acceptable form of socialism in order to survive. The characters he has created for *Walking Wounded*, though, have a different moral dilemma for their kind of Scotland is slowly changing in front of their astonished eyes. 'The society which is based on production can only be productive, not creative,' he claims, quoting Camus. 'To me, the fairly rough ideological socialism I grew up with mattered— and still matters today. You can be better off materially, sure, but still be lesser as a person.'

As he admits, there are no easy answers and McIlvanney the novelist shies away from the idea that writers can be seers. All they can do, he concedes, is offer the kind of platitudes demanded by the media or they can turn—as he has done—to the real texture of common humanity. 'My sense of place only goes out as far as the people who live in the place. I don't see myself ever writing about a depopulated highland valley because it's physically beautiful. All my fiction—and, I suppose, all my poetry—is essentially that which grew out of people. With Glasgow and the West of Scotland, for example, I have many images, but they're all populated.'

(from a review in *Scotland on Sunday* by Trevor Royle, 1 January 1989)

These reviews need to be supplemented with some specific comment on one or two aspects of *Docherty* that force themselves upon a thoughtful reader today. The image, or myth, of 'the hard man' as exemplified by Tam Docherty, the father-son relationships in the novel, and the implied attitudes to women in the narrative are all interconnected, but merit some separate treatment.

## The 'hard man' myth

It is only in the light cast back upon *Docherty* by the later novel, *The Big Man*, and the short stories in *Walking Wounded*, and to a lesser extent the detective novels about Laidlaw, that we can see how, within McIlvanney's work, *Docherty* describes the beginning of a twentieth century Scottish working-class myth. Over the compact and outwardly self-assured figure of Tam Docherty, his sons and fellow-miners erect an edifice of self-flattering delusion about the importance of the male spirit that can assert its freedom in everyday situations and personal relationships by aggressively physical means while still being held in social and economic chains. With the gangsters and detectives in the Laidlaw books, the self-doubting Dan Scoular the 'Big Man', and especially the social and psychological casualties of *Walking Wounded*, that myth of the hard man is subverted and shown to be hollow and inadequate. At his best, the hard man, like Tam Docherty, is sensitively self-aware and inwardly eloquent, transcending his 'persona'; at his worst he is an unsympathetic parody of himself. An interesting matter for analysis in

*Docherty* would be the degree to which Tam Docherty escapes being this stereotype in action and words, although he appears so frequently in aggressive postures.

## Father and son

Another aspect of the novel that merits some comment is the way in which it incorporates and gives prominence to a traditional recurring theme in Scottish fiction, the father-son relationship within a family. Often it has been used as a mainspring for psychological interest and plot tension. There are respectable antecedents for this in nineteenth and twentieth century Scottish writing, from Hogg's *Confessions of a Justified Sinner* and Stevenson's *Weir of Hermiston* through George Douglas Brown's *The House with the Green Shutters* to the present day. Perhaps the Calvinist ethos of Scottish society has had something to do with it: an authoritarian God controlling his wayward children through fear is a strong model for family life. In *Docherty*, however, McIlvanney avoids the obvious clichés of this situation. The fact that there are three sons and a daughter allows the writer to set up a variety of parent-child relationships. An interesting activity that will help to illuminate this aspect of the novel would be to identify and categorise chapters in which Tam is seen in interaction with Kathleen, Mick, Angus and Conn; the concentration on the sons will be immediately apparent, as well as the different kinds of relationship that he has with them. It is only with Angus that Tam appears to act as the heavy-handed father of the stereotype, and even there his reasons are clearly articulated within a working-class ethical code. As the novel proceeds, moreover, it is in his relationships with his children that Tam begins to appear at his most vulnerable: his final weakness is exposed by Mick in Book 3, Chapter 9. He gains a kind of posthumous success from the way in which his sons, in one way or another, carry on either his ideals or his physical power. So McIlvanney's working of this theme can be seen as not conforming to any stereotype, and enables him to elevate Tam beyond the macho images of his culture.

## Attitudes to women in the narrative

Both the 'hard man' myth and the father-son theme, as they are developed in the narrative of *Docherty*, serve to throw into strong relief to our feminism-conscious eyes the male-orientated nature of the novel and the community within it. To our age it probably comes across as a major weakness of the novel that it gives such little room on the main stage to the female characters. When Tam is at his most dominant, there is no room in the action for any women; they can only keep out of the way. We have probably seen that Kathleen occupies very little of the action compared with her brothers. Even Jenny Docherty has comparatively little to say or do; her consciousness is only an occasional variation from the male norm expressed mainly through the narrator or Tam or Conn. The same holds true for the other main female character, Miss Gilfillan the middle-class spinster; her objective perception of the life of High Street comes from her different class origins rather than from her gender. An activity that will serve to illuminate this aspect of *Docherty* is to look through the chapters to identify those in which a female consciousness plays a significant part in the narrative, e.g. the thoughts of Jenny or Kathleen or Miss Gilfillan. It will probably emerge quickly that the female viewpoint is marginalised throughout the book, making the narrative predominantly a male discourse.

This male orientation of the novel ignores what is seen in some other writings about Scottish working-class life as being almost a truism, that it was the women in the family and the community who tended to hold the social fabric together, giving it what precarious stability it had. As a result, it might be a reasonable criticism of *Docherty* to say that it only tells half the story of the Docherty family and the community of High Street. There is a submerged and unarticulated half that can only be guessed at. Thus in an age in which society as a whole, and many of its most eloquent writers, are moving away from macho images and male-orientated scenarios, McIlvanney's writing may have come to have a rather dated feel about it. This criticism is being made more and more about McIlvanney's writing, particularly by women critics and commentators, and McIlvanney has shown awareness of this and responded to it in his most recent newspaper articles. This is a healthy criticism and the most positive outcome from it would be if McIlvanney's future writing were to give greater weight to the female element; there are already indications of this in his most recent short stories in *Walking Wounded*.

## *Critical Comment on* Docherty

To conclude these notes, here is an extract from a critical essay on *Docherty*. The critics here have been looking at a number of major twentieth century Scottish novels and seeing how they often deal with similar or connected themes arising out of the nature of Scottish society and how it has developed over many generations. Such themes may be social or economic or emotional deprivation within a circumscribed or confined environment. Prior to this comment on *Docherty*, there has been consideration of another novel dealing with a boy growing up in the West of Scotland, *From Scenes Like These* by Gordon M. Williams. The boy, Dunky Logan, finds that his home environment, the town of Kilcaddie in the 1950s and the rural area around it, is both limiting and ultimately desensitising. From this springs a fruitful contrast with young Conn in McIlvanney's *Docherty*.

When the reader of *From Scenes Like These* turns to William McIlvanney's *Docherty*, he will find that the novels have a lot in common, in terms of the surroundings and social pressures which impinge on the characters. But the first sense is of contrast, not similarity. For while in *From Scenes Like These* harsh surroundings are generally echoed in the bleak, loveless consciousness of the characters, a major component of *Docherty* is its celebration of aspects of humanity. McIlvanney seems to indicate more belief in human beings than we find in the Williams novel: if the characters in both are caged, or everywhere in chains, it is possible for McIlvanney's characters to 'sing in (their) chains like the sea'. While dog ate dog—or man —consistently in *From Scenes Like These*, in *Docherty* there is insistence on love, on real relationships, the affirmation of a real community.

But McIlvanney is certainly no less critical of the social situation his characters are trapped in, and he sees the trap as just as effective. Is there a way out? In both novels, poor teachers have themselves seized on education as a way out: in both, education is seen as a possible escape for intelligent boys, lads o' pairts. Nicol cannot understand why education does not seem a sane option to Dunky: Tam Docherty is totally earnest in his desire to give Conn an education which the boy does not want. The analytical voice of the narrator explains how Conn sees school as a rejection of home and all it stands for—and also that Tam's wish was only ever a wistful dream: the Dochertys could never have afforded to keep Conn at school.

Other escapes tantalise: Dunky might have 'made it' at football. In *Docherty*, echoing Dunky's rabbits, we find a series of possible activities discussed to sweeten captivity—poaching, keeping dogs or pigeons. Although we are very much aware of the harshly matured Mick observing and making political points in the latter part of *Docherty*, in neither novel is any political solution seriously entertained or promulgated.

The books are also very differently written. Williams concentrates on his characters' thoughts, and limits himself to what they can verbalise, virtually enacting some of the constrictions of their lives by his narrative method. McIlvanney renders his characters' thoughts also, but outside direct dialogue we often find the unobtrusive intervention of a much more sophisticated, articulate authorial voice, analysing and interpreting the material—and doing so on occasion with hindsight. So for example in Book II chapter 17 we get an over-view of how Jenny retrospectively and over years came to know that Tam had faced defeat and secretly admitted it, something impossible to realise at the time, so imperceptible were the changes.

This indicates another difference: while Williams chooses a hero of his own generation, and presents just one year of his life in the span of the novel, McIlvanney is writing what amounts to a historical novel, beginning seventy-two years before the time of publication, and covering a quarter of a century. In some ways this undertaking could more appropriately be compared to Gibbon's *Quair*; and the unending debate between the non-aligned Conn and Communist Mick at the end of the novel arguably to some extent echoes the stances of Chris and Ewan at the end of *Grey Granite*.

*Docherty* is a strange and interesting book, not least because it is possible to read it with such different emphases: there are at least two views here of Tam Docherty. In what seems to be a characteristic first reading, the novel strikes the reader as warm, celebratory, witty and uniquely affirmative of the value of Tam Docherty and people like him. This is a fair reading, but can dissolve in memory into a suspicion of cosiness, softness, a touch of the kailyard. We would argue that these suspicions will hardly survive re-reading.

Indeed, re-reading may sooner or later precipitate the reader to a very different view of the novel, seeing it as essentially gloomy and pessimistic. In this view, the most the novel can possibly be said to 'celebrate' is a very brief momentary stay against confusion: fate or inevitability is briefly defied by the will of Tam Docherty, but his faith is always undermined, always seen by the reader to be precarious and doomed. Tam Docherty will be defeated; this is inevitable, and we know it from the start. [. . .]

A central theme of the novel, inseparable from the portrait of Tam himself, is his search for a faith, for an alternative to the religion that has failed to be relevant to his experience. Tam is in many ways a naturally religious man, and he is a man who lives by faith more markedly and more admirably than any of the Christian characters in the novel. Tam's finest years are sustained by faith, faith is an amalgam of the ideal of Keir Hardie and the community of his class, and above all in the ideal of family: he sees families in terms of little fortresses, held together by love and solidarity, in an essentially unjust if legal world of conflict. It is the most blatant demonstration that the family fortress is no protection, the mutilation of Mick in the Great War, that cracks open the creed that Tam has lived by. In a startling development of the recurring metaphor, McIlvanney describes Tam now:

> He was like a gunfighter, practised to perfection, unafraid, heroically hard, and pitted against germ warfare.

Tam can find no replacement for the faith, or illusion, that he has lost: he simply has to live with his failure. The crippling of Mick is for him only the underlining of his failure, his misguided faith. A few chapters earlier, Conn's start down the pit ends the futile dream of his escape by education: the family provision of all the appropriate gear is to Tam like giving him 'a suicide-kit for Christmas'. Now he has only to live out his natural span in the knowledge that his failure was inevitable and his faith always illusory. It is possible to consider Tam's heroic and self-sacrificial death as a happy release for him.

The search for faith is echoed in other members of the family. Jenny's faith in Tam and her family was always more practical and immediate and down to earth, less a matter of willed idealism than Tam's and so it survives time, if saddened. Andra Crawford finds in Tam's determination to give a home to old Conn in the face of the unwillingness of the 'religious' daughters, a triumph of humanity:

> Andra sensed quite simply that Tam was not defeated. And if Tam wasn't, neither was he.

Angus develops a faith based largely on his own physical strength and an embattled attitude towards the world as a whole: refusing to be bound by family or class loyalties or traditional moral ideas, he embraces an ethic of success: 'Frem noo on, it's just Annie an' me. An' we're gonny make oot'. Mick's wartime experience is devastating: all he is left with, at the Front, is the ordinariness of his fellows: 'They became what Mick had in place of a religion' (194). His postwar reflections and reading lead him to an act of faith when he joins the Communist Party, while young Conn has reached no conclusions as yet. All the sons find Tam's beliefs to some extent redundant to their present, but Conn resists the logical clarity of Mick's faith:

> Ah don't want tae smash folk. Ah jist want them tae see hoo guid men like ma feyther were. Tae gi'e us room tae leeve. . . . Ah canny hate folk the wey you dae, Mick.

It is significant and appropriate that Conn is left in two minds at the end. He has always been less than a fully formed or highly individualised character. McIlvanney uses him throughout as a sensitive human recording mechanism which is more involved in reacting to or simply registering things and people, and above all Tam, than in initiating ideas or opinions. This is the crucial aspect of Conn, from the first chapter of Book I. He is realistically presented, of course, and his development is fully credible, but often related on the side. Odd chapters fill in his adolescence, his secret happiness in the Bringan, his school experiences, his obsession with sex, but often these are only loosely connected to the main thrust of a book. In essential respects he is a responder, and almost a representative character, not a million miles away from Dunky Logan: what Dunky might have been, brought up in Docherty warmth instead of Kilcaddie bleakness?

(from *Ten Modern Scottish Novels* by Isobel Murray and Bob Tait)

## Bibliography

*Other works by William McIlvanney*

*Remedy is None* (1966) Eyre and Spottiswoode.
McIlvanney's first novel explores the complex feelings that a young university student has for his dead father and the disastrous action that he is led towards.
*A Gift from Nessus* (1968) Eyre and Spottiswoode.
In this novel a salesman faces a crisis in both his business and personal lives that threatens to destroy them both.
*Laidlaw* (1977) Hodder and Stoughton Ltd.
*The Papers of Tony Veitch* (1983) Hodder and Stoughton Ltd.
These two novels about a Glasgow police detective depict more of the reality of Glasgow life than many a supposedly more serious novel. Equally, they avoid the clichés fostered by the television imitation, *Taggart*.
*The Big Man* (1985) Hodder and Stoughton Ltd.
McIlvanney returns to the world of Docherty but two generations later in this story of a local fighting hero who is persuaded by a Glasgow gangster into a bare-knuckle fist-fight that will restore his financial security.
*Walking Wounded* (1989) Hodder and Stoughton Ltd.
A collection of Graithnock-set short stories that are reckoned by many to embody some of McIlvanney's finest writing.

*Poetry*

*The Longships in Harbour* (1970) Eyre and Spottiswoode.
*These Words: Weddings and After* (1983) Mainstream.

*Autobiographical essay*

'Growing Up in the West' in Karl Miller ed., *Memoirs of a Modern Scotland*·
(1970), Faber and Faber Ltd.

*Other novels of interest*

John Galt (1986) *Annals of the Parish*, Oxford World's Classics.
John Galt (1982) *The Provost*, Oxford World's Classics.
Two classic novels from the early nineteenth century which depict Ayrshire
life at a time of momentous social change and expansion.
George Douglas Brown (1983) *The House with the Green Shutters*, Penguin
Books. The definitive anti-Kailyard novel with its bleak pessimism about
Scottish small-town life and its powerful depiction of the decline and fall of
a local and family tyrant.
Lewis Grassie Gibbon (1988) *Sunset Song*, Canongate Press. The first part of
Gibbon's trilogy about life in the North-East of Scotland in the early twentieth
century, *A Scots Quair*. It deals with the adolescence and first marriage of
Chris Guthrie, one of the greatest of Scottish literary heroines.
Gordon M. Williams (1968) *From Scenes Like These*, Martin Secker and
Warburg. With its ironical title derived from Burns, this is a hard look at the
spiritual and psychological coldness of Scottish small-town and rural life in
the 1950s.

*Works of background interest*

Archibald McKay (1909) *The History of Kilmarnock*, 5th edn revised by
William Findlay, Kilmarnock.
Thomas Johnston (1946) *The History of the Working Classes in Scotland*,
4th edn, Unity Publishing Co. Ltd. The classic treatment of the subject
by one of Scotland's foremost Labour politicians of the post-war
period.
Robin Page-Arnot (1955) *A History of the Scottish Miners*, George Allen and
Unwin.
Geddes Thomson (1981) *Identities: an Anthology of West of Scotland Poetry,
Prose and Drama*, Heinemann Educational. For anyone wanting to experience
the flavour of Scottish urban writing of recent years, this is an indispensable
collection.
T. C. Smout (1986) *A Century of the Scottish People: 1830–1950*, Collins.
Along with Professor Smout's earlier work, *A History of the Scottish People:
1560–1830* (1985), this is a necessary introduction to the real history of
Scotland. It provides a healthy antidote to the Bonnie Prince Charlie syndrome.

George Orwell (1968) *Collected Essays, Journalism and Letters: Volume 1, An Age Like This 1920–1940*, Martin Secker and Warburg.
Jim Sillars (1986) *Scotland: The Case for Optimism*, Polygon. An eloquent examination of the current state of Scotland from a Socialist and Scottish Nationalist standpoint.

*Criticism*

Isobel Murray and Bob Tait (1984) *Ten Modern Scottish Novels*, Aberdeen University Press. A very useful critical introduction to some of Scotland's most significant novelists this century, with reference to one of the novels of each writer.

NOTES

NOTES

NOTES

NOTES

NOTES